For a few seconds, the thief fought like a tiger, clawing and scratching, and doing his best to squirm from beneath Devellyn.

"Why, you bloody, snot-nosed shite!" the marquess roared. He tried to grab the lad round the waist again. The boy twisted violently. Devellyn caught him. But not by the waist.

"Well, damn me for a fool!" Devellyn's hand was full of warm, plump breast.

The thief stopped twisting. He—no, *she*—lay splayed beneath Devellyn's body, panting for breath. Something about the sound made Devellyn freeze.

"What the bloody hell?"

"Look 'ere, gov'," whispered Ruby Black. "Let loose, awright? It ain't wot yer thinkin'."

Understanding slammed into him. In the pitch black, Ruby's lissome body was round and warm beneath his. Devellyn tore the hat from her head and slicked his hand over her hair, as if that might disprove what his aching, itching body already knew.

Ruby twisted impotently. "I didn't nick nothin'," she hissed. "Let me up, and I'll be on me way."

"Oh, no, Ruby." He fisted his hand in her hair and forced her face back into his. "Oh, no. You've the devil to pay this time, remember?"

LIZ CARLYLE

The Devil to Pay

POCKET STAR BOOKS

New York   London   Toronto   Sydney

To Sandy,
who has been my best pal
and emotional dumping ground
for, oh, about four decades . . . ?

Girlfriend, we are getting old!

An *Original* Publication of POCKET BOOKS

A Pocket Star Book published by
POCKET BOOKS, a division of Simon & Schuster, Inc.
1230 Avenue of the Americas, New York, NY 10020

ISBN: 0-7434-7004-4

First Pocket Books printing January 2005

10 9 8 7 6 5 4

POCKET STAR BOOKS and colophon are registered
trademarks of Simon & Schuster, Inc.

Front cover illustration by Alan Ayers
Front cover lettering by Iskra Design

For information regarding special discounts for bulk purchases,
please contact Simon & Schuster Special Sales at 1-800-456-6798
or business@simonandschuster.com

Manufactured in the United States of America

Chapter One

The strange Goings On in Bedford Place

He was not the sort of man she usually chose. Across the roulette table she studied him. He was young; yes, younger than she preferred. One wondered if he yet shaved. The pink blush of innocence still tinged the pretty Englishman's cheeks, and his bones were as delicately carved as her own.

But he was not innocent. And if he were delicate, well, *tant pis*.

The croupier leaned over the table. *"Mesdames and messieurs,"* he said in his bad French accent, *"faites vos jeux, s'il vous plait!"*

She waved away the smoke from a nearby cheroot and placed a corner bet, pushing three chips across the baize with a perfectly manicured fingertip. Just then, the gentleman between them rose, scraping up his winnings as he went. An exchange of backslapping and bonhomie followed. *Bien*. The young man was alone now. In the dim light, she partially lifted the black veil which obscured her eyes, and shot him a look of frank interest. He shoved a stack of chips onto black twenty-two, and returned the stare, one brow lightly lifting.

"No more bets," the croupier intoned. *"Les jeux sont faits!"* In one elegant motion, he spun the tray and flicked the ball. It leapt and clattered merrily, punctuating the drone of conversation. Then it went *crack! clickity-clack!* and bounced into black twenty-two.

The croupier pushed out his winnings before the wheel stopped. The Englishman collected them and moved to her end of the table.

"Bonsoir," she murmured throatily. "Black has been very good to you this night, *monsieur."*

His pale blue eyes ran down her black dress. "Dare I hope it is the beginning of a trend?"

She looked at him through the fine mesh and lowered her lashes. "One can always hope, sir."

The Englishman laughed, showing his tiny white teeth. "I don't think I know you, *mademoiselle,"* he said. "You are new to Lufton's?"

She lifted one shoulder. "One gaming salon is much like another, *n'est-ce pas?"*

His gaze heated. The fool thought she was a Cyprian. Understandable, since she sat alone and unescorted in a den of iniquity.

"Lord Francis Tenby," he said, extending his hand. "And you are . . . ?"

"Madame Noire," she answered, bending far forward to place her gloved fingers in his. "It must be fate, must it not?"

"Ha ha!" His gaze took in her daring décolletage.

"Madame Black, indeed! Tell me, my dear, have you a given name?"

"Those with whom I'm intimate call me Cerise," she said, the word husky and suggestive.

"Cerise," echoed the Englishman. "How exotic. What brings you to London, my dear?"

Again, the lifted shoulder. The coy, sidelong glance. "Such questions!" she said. "We are taking up space at the wheel, sir, and I am quite parched."

He jerked to his feet at once. "What may I fetch you, ma'am?" he asked. "And may I show you to a quiet corner?"

"Champagne," she murmured. Then she rose, inclined her head, and went to the table he'd indicated. A corner table. Very private. Very perfect.

He returned in a trice, a servant on his heels with a tray and two glasses.

"*Ma foi!*" she murmured, looking about as the servant departed. "I must have left my reticule at the roulette table. Would you be so kind, my lord?"

He turned away, and she snapped open her vial. Deftly, she passed it over his glass. The tiny crystals drifted down to greet the effervescing bubbles.

He returned just as she flicked a quick glance at the watch pinned to the lining of her shawl. Timing was essential. He smiled suggestively, and she lifted her glass to his. "To a new friendship," she murmured, so quietly he had to lean nearer.

"Indeed! A new friendship." He drank deeply of the champagne, and frowned.

But he was easily distracted. For the next ten minutes,

she laughed her light, tinkling laughter, and said very clever things to Lord Francis Tenby, who hadn't a brain in his beautiful head.

The usual questions followed. She told her well-practiced lies. The widowhood. The loneliness. The wealthy protector who had brought her here tonight, quarreled with her, then so cruelly abandoned her for another. But *c'est la vie,* she suggested with another shrug of her shoulders. There were other fish in the sea.

Of course, she proposed nothing. He did. They always did. And she accepted, flicking another glance at her watch. *Twenty minutes.* They stood. He lost a little of his color, shook it off, and offered his arm. Her hand on his coat sleeve, they walked out of the hell together, and into the damp, gaslit gloom of St. James. A passing hackney rolled to a stop as if it had been planned. It had.

Lord Francis gave the driver his address, almost tripping as he followed her in. By the weak light of the carriage lamp, she could see that perspiration already sheened his face. She bent forward, offering him a generous view of her cleavage. *"Mon coeur,"* she murmured, laying her hand on his pink cheek. "You look unwell."

"I'm fine," he answered, holding himself erect now with obvious effort. "Jush fine. But I want . . . I want to see . . ." He lost his train of thought entirely.

She slithered out of her silk shawl and leaned even closer. "What, *mon cher?*" she whispered. "What is it you wish to see?"

He shook his head as if willing away a fog. "Your . . . your *eyes,*" he finally said. "Want to shee your eyes. And face. Your ha—ha—*hat*. Veil. *Off.*"

"Ah, that I cannot do," she whispered across the carriage, beginning to peel down her left sleeve. "But I can show you something else, Lord Francis. Tell me, would you like to see my breast?"

"Breasht?" He leered drunkenly.

Another inch of fabric eased down. "A bit of it, yes," she answered. "Look this way, Lord Francis. Yes, that's it. Focus, love. Focus. Can you see this?"

He made the fatal mistake of leaning closer. "Tatt . . . tatt . . . *tattoo?*" he said, cocking his head to one side. "Back. No, *black* . . . angel?" Suddenly, Lord Francis's eyes rolled back in his head, his mouth dropped slack, and his head thudded against the carriage door, leaving him gaping up at her like a dead carp at Billingsgate.

For his safety, she lifted his chin and pushed him back against the banquette. He flopped limply against the leather as she rifled through his pockets. Purse. Key. Snuffbox—silver, not gold, blast it. Watch, chain, fob. A letter from his coat pocket. A lover? An enemy? Oh, Lud! She had no time for blackmail! She stuffed it back and plucked instead a sapphire pin from the snowy folds of his cravat.

Finished, she looked at him in satisfaction. "Oh, I do hope it was good for you, Lord Francis," she murmured. "It certainly was good for me."

Mouth still open, Lord Francis made a deep, snorking sound in the back of his throat.

"How gratifying to hear it," she answered. "And I daresay your pretty, pregnant, newly unemployed parlor maid shall soon be gratified, too."

With that, she dropped her loot into her reticule, thumped twice on the roof of the carriage, then pushed open the door. The cab slowed to take the curve at the corner of Brook Street. The Black Angel leapt out, and melted into the gray gloom of Mayfair. Lord Francis's head bobbled back and forth as the hackney rattled on into the night.

The Marquess of Devellyn was in a rare fine mood. So fine, he'd been singing "O God Our Help in Ages Past" all the way up Regent Street, despite not knowing the words. So fine, he had the sudden notion to have his coachman set him down near the corner of Golden Square so that he might stroll in the pleasant evening air. At his signal, the glossy black carriage rolled dutifully to a halt. The marquess leapt out, hardly staggering at all.

"But it's raining now, my lord," his coachman said, peering at him from atop the box.

The marquess looked down. Wet pavement glistened back. Well. Damned if the old boy wasn't right. "Was it raining, Wittle, when we left Crockford's?" he asked, slurring none of his words, though he was drunk as Davy's sow and wise enough to know it.

"No, sir," said Wittle. "Just a heavy mist."

"Hmph!" said Devellyn, tucking his hat brim a tad lower. "Well, fine evening for a walk anyway," he countered. "Sobers a chap up, fresh evening air."

Wittle leaned down a little farther. "B-But it's morning, my lord," he answered. "Almost six."

The marquess blinked up at him. "You don't say?" he answered. "Wasn't I to dine with Miss Lederly tonight?"

Wittle looked at him in some sympathy. "*Last* night, sir," he said. "And then, I believe, the theater? But you didn't—or the club didn't . . ."

Devellyn scrubbed one hand along his face, feeling a

day's worth of bristled beard. "Ah, I see," he finally answered. "Didn't come out when I ought, eh?"

Wittle shook his head. "No, my lord."

Devellyn lifted one brow. "Got to drinking, did I? And playing at hazard?"

The coachman's face remained impassive. "There was a lady involved, I believe, sir."

A lady? Oh, yes. He remembered now. A delicious, big-breasted blonde. And definitely *not* a lady. He wondered if she'd been any good. Hell, he wondered if *he'd* been any good. Probably not. And he didn't give a damn, really. But the theater? Christ, Camelia was going to kill him this time.

He rolled his big shoulders restlessly beneath his greatcoat and looked up at Wittle. "Well, I'm going to walk to Bedford Place," he repeated. "Don't need anyone else witnessing my humiliation when I get there, either. You go on back to Duke Street."

Wittle touched his hat brim. "Take your stick, my lord," he advised. "Soho's rife with footpads."

Devellyn grinned broadly up at him. "A mere footpad?" he chided. "Taking on the old Devil of Duke Street? Do you really think he'd dare?"

At that, Wittle smiled wryly. "Not once he'd seen your face, no, sir," he agreed. "Unfortunately, they do tend to strike from behind."

Devellyn laughed hugely and tipped his hat. "The bloody stick it is, then, you old hen," he agreed, reaching inside to grab it.

Wittle saluted again, then clicked to his horses. The carriage began to roll. Devellyn tossed his stick into the air with a spin, then gracefully caught it before it hit the ground. Not that drunk, then. The thought oddly cheered him. He set off along the pavement, picking up his hymn again as he hit his stride.

O God, our help in ages past,
Our hope for years to come!
Our shel-ter from the de-da-dum,
And our da-de-da-dum!

No footpad dared accost him on his short stroll through Soho and into Bloomsbury. Perhaps it was his abysmal singing. Or perhaps it was the fact that the marquess was tall and broad, and with his broken nose, not all that inviting. *Hulking,* he'd heard it said. He didn't give a damn what folks called him. At any rate, he had no need of his stick on his walk. But when he entered the portals of his very own house, still bellowing heartily, things changed.

A thou-sand ages in Thy sight
Are like an evening gone!
Short as the something something night!
Before the de-da-dum!

"*You bastard!*" The hurtling platter came out of nowhere. "By God, I'll give you an evening gone!"

The marquess ducked. Porcelain bounced off the lintel and rained down upon his head. "Cammie—?" he said, peering into the drawing room.

His mistress stepped from the shadows, brandishing a fire iron. "Don't *Cammie* me, you pig!" she growled. She picked up a Meissen figurine and hurled it at his head.

Devellyn ducked. "Put the fire iron down, Camelia," he said, holding his stick sideways as he walked, as if it might repel the next flying object. "Put it down, I say."

"Go frig yourself!" she screamed like the Spitalfields shrew she secretly was. "Go rot in hell, you hulking, oversized, ignorant bastard!"

The marquess made a *tsk tsk* sound. "Camelia, your limited vocabulary is showing again," he said. "You've bastardized me twice now. Pour us a tot of brandy, my love. We'll work it out."

"No, you work *this* out," she said, brandishing the fire iron. "Because I'm going to shove it sideways up your arse, Devellyn."

The marquess winced. "Cammie, whatever I've done, I'm sorry. Tomorrow, I'll go down to Garrard's and buy you a necklace, I swear it." He turned but an instant to put down his stick and hat. A very bad decision. She hurled the fire iron at his head, then came at him like a rabid rat terrier, eight stone of kicking, clawing female.

"Bastard!" she screamed, leaping on his back and pounding his head with one fist. "Pig! Pig! Stupid pig!"

Camelia was nothing if not theatrical. Servants were peering from the passageway now. Devellyn spun around, trying to get a grip on her; but Camelia had him round the neck, trying to throttle him with one arm, while pounding the living hell out of him with the other.

"Selfish, coldhearted son of a bitch," she cried, hitting him with every syllable. "You never think of me. You! You! Always you!"

And then he remembered—the blows having apparently beaten some sense into his head. "Oh, dash it!" he said. "Cleopatra!"

He finally grabbed her skirts and dragged her off. She landed on the floor on her rump and looked venomously up at him. "Yes, *my* Cleopatra!" she corrected. "My *debut!* My opening night! I was finally the star—and I brought down the house, you selfish dog! You promised, Devellyn! You promised to *be* there."

The marquess slid out of his coat, and his butler crept timidly forward to take it. "I swear I'm sorry, Cammie," he said. "Really, I am. I'll be there next time. I'll come—why I'll come tonight! Won't that do?"

Camelia rearranged her skirts and stood with as much grace as she could muster. "No, it won't *do,*" she said, turning and speaking theatrically over one shoulder. "Because I am leaving you, Devellyn."

"Leaving me?"

Camelia strolled to the mantel. "Yes, as in casting you off," she went on. "Throwing you over. Tossing you out of my life. Need I go on?"

"But Cammie, *why?*"

"Because Sir Edmund Sutters made me a very pretty offer tonight." Camelia looked down her nose at him, and the girl from Spitalfields vanished. "Whilst we were all drinking champagne backstage after the play."

"Backstage?"

"Where *you* should have been."

Camelia was caressing the matching Meissen figurine now, sliding her long, thin fingers over it in a way which he once would have thought erotic, but now looked faintly dangerous. "Of course," she went on, "had you been there, he would not have dared, would he? But you weren't. And so he did." Suddenly, she spun about. "And I accepted, Devellyn. Do you hear me? I *accepted.*"

She really meant it this time. What a bloody inconvenience. Oh, there were always other women. He should know. Well, he *did* know. He just didn't have the ambition to go looking for one. But he knew from past experience that once a woman got fed up with him, there was no stopping her from packing up and leaving.

Devellyn sighed and opened both his hands expressively. "Well, dash it, Cammie, I hate it's come to this."

She lifted her chin disdainfully. "I shall be moving out in the morning."

The marquess shrugged. "Well, there's no real rush," he said. "I mean, I'm in no hurry for the house, and I'll be a fortnight or better settling on someone else, so just take your ti—"

The last Meissen caught him square in the forehead. Shards flew. Devellyn staggered back, but she caught him before he hit the floor.

"Bastard! Pig!" The tiny fists flew again. "Pig! Bastard! I ought'er ring your neck like a scrawny Sunday chicken!"

"Oh, bugger all!" said Devellyn wearily. It was a good thing Camelia didn't write her own material.

"Bastard! Pig!"

Devellyn just collapsed onto the floor, Camelia still clinging to his neck.

Sidonie Saint-Godard was a woman of independent means, with far too much of the adjective, and just enough of the noun to pay the bills. At first, her independence had fit like a new shoe with a perilously high heel; something one teetered about awkwardly on, in the faint hope one would not trip and fall face-first into the carpet of polite society. Then she'd returned to London, her birthplace, and found that the shoe soon began to pinch. For unlike France, female independence in England came buckled and beribboned with a whole new set of *shoulds* and *oughts*.

It had taken her one full year of mourning before Sidonie had realized the solution was to kick off her shoes altogether and run barefoot through life. Now, at the great age of twenty-nine, she was sprinting for all she was worth. And when she died, she told her brother George, she wanted her gravestone inscribed with the epitaph A LIFE FULLY LIVED. It was what she planned to do, for life, she well knew, was uncertain, and despite old saws to the contrary, both the good and the bad often died young. Sidonie wasn't even sure which category she fell into. Good? Bad? A little of both?

Like many a wellborn French girl, Sidonie had gone from her mother's sheltering roof to the high, strong walls of the convent school. There, however, she'd suffered one of her more wicked moments. She'd run away with a handsome man who'd possessed neither roof nor walls—not in any conventional sense. Instead, Pierre Saint-Godard had possessed a fine new merchantman, fitted out with a two-room captain's suite and a bank of tidy windows from which one might view the world as it floated past.

But Sidonie had soon seen enough of the world. She had sold the ship, packed up her clothes and her cat, and moved to London. Now she lived in a tidy town house in Bedford Place, surrounded by the equally tidy homes of merchants, bankers, and almost-but-not-quite gentry. And at present, she was taking in the fine view from her upstairs window. One door down, on the opposite side of Bedford Place, a removal van had drawn up, and two men were loading trunks and crates into it with nervous alacrity.

"How many mistresses does that make now, Julia?" Sidonie asked, leaning over her companion's head and peering through the draperies.

Julia counted on her fingers. "The pale blonde in December made seven," she said. "So this would make eight."

"And this is but March!" Sidonie kept toweling the damp from her long black hair. "I should like to know who he is, to treat these poor women so cavalierly. It's as if he thinks they're old coats, to be thrown out when the elbows wear!"

Julia straightened up from the window. "No time for that now, dearie," she warned, pushing Sidonie toward the fire. "You'll be late as it is. Sit, and let me comb that mess of hair dry, else you'll catch your death going down to the Strand."

Dutifully, Sidonie pulled up a stool. Thomas, her cat, jumped at once into her lap. "But it really is vile behavior, Julia," she said, slicking one hand down the sleek black tabby. "You know it is. Perhaps the crossing sweep can tell us his name? I shall ask."

"Aye, perhaps," said Julia absently as she drew the brush down. "Do you know, my dear, you've hair just like your mother's?"

"Do you think so?" asked Sidonie a little hopefully. "Claire had such lovely hair."

"Left me green with envy," Julia confessed. "And to think, me on the stage with this mouse brown straw! If we were seen together—which we often were—she cast me in the shade."

"But you had a wonderful career, Julia! You were famous. The toast of Drury Lane, were you not?"

"Oh, for a time," she answered. "But that's long past."

Sidonie fell silent. She knew it had been years since Julia had played a significant role in the West End theaters. And far longer than that since the rich men who had once vied for her favors had moved on to younger women. Despite being several years younger, Julia had been a close friend of Sidonie's mother, for they had run with the same fast crowd; the demimonde, and all their hangers-on. And those hangers-on had always included a vast number of wealthy, upper-class rakes with a taste for women of less-than-blue blood.

But Claire Bauchet's blood had been blue. She had also been heartbreakingly beautiful. The first advantage had been cruelly and rapaciously stripped from her. The second she had cultivated like a hothouse orchid, for like Julia, Claire had made her living with her beauty. But while Julia had been a talented actress who had sometimes had the good fortune to be kept by a wealthy admirer, Claire had been, simply put, a courtesan. Her talent had been her grace and her charm, and very little else. Well, perhaps that was not quite fair. For much of her life, Claire had been kept by one man only.

When Sidonie had returned to London, her mother's old friend had been the first to ring her bell and welcome her home. And it had been painfully obvious to Sidonie that Julia was lonely. As it happened, Sidonie had been in dire need of a lady's maid. Not to mention a companion, a cook, and a confidante. Unfortunately, she had been unable to afford *all* of those things. The cook she had promptly hired. Julia, the consummate actress, had proven the perfect solution to all else. And although Sidonie had not asked, she suspected Julia had been living a little too close to the bone, as women who lived by their wits and their looks so often did.

"Missing her, are you?" Julia asked out of the blue.

Sidonie looked over her shoulder and considered it. Did she miss Claire? "Yes, a bit. She was always so full of life."

Just then, a horrible crash sounded. Thomas shot off her lap and under the bed. Julia and Sidonie rushed back to the window, boldly drawing wide the draperies. The remover's van was gone, and over the door of the opposite house, someone had thrown up a sash. A petite redhead was leaning halfway out the window, holding a chamber pot.

"Pig!" she cried, hurling it to the ground. "Bastard!"

"Lord God!" said Julia.

The next sash flew up. The redhead appeared again. Another pot. "Bastard! Pig!" Down it went, shards of white porcelain bouncing off the pavement.

Sidonie burst into peals of laughter.

Julia shrugged. "Well, whoever your mystery gent is," she murmured, "he won't have a pot to piss in when she's done with him."

Chapter Two

In which our Hero is beset by yet Another plague

"My lord?"

The voice was distant. Disembodied. And annoying as hell.

"Muuf!" said the Marquess of Devellyn, intent on sending it away again. *"Gumm smuzum!"*

"But really, my lord! I do think you must open your eyes!"

"Mmft umt," he countered.

"Yes, quite right, I'm sure, sir." The voice was growing distraught. "But I'm afraid you must get up now."

"I couldn't even get him out of his coat last night," came a second fretful voice from the fog. "Do you think it's ruined? I fear he's bled on it. I believe he's been boxing again. Does that not look like blood, Honeywell— just there, on the lapel?"

"Fenton, I am sure I neither know nor care." The first voice sounded peeved now. "My lord? Really, you must get up now. Brampton and his carpenters have gone, sir. I'm afraid we've bad news."

Bad news.

That cut through the haze and into his consciousness. Devellyn had more than a passing familiarity with the phrase. *"Buffum?"* he said, cracking one eye.

Four of the same stared down at him. Or was it six?

"He's coming round, Fenton." The voice sounded relieved. "Let's see if he can sit."

The marquess found himself unceremoniously hefted up. A pillow was stuffed hastily behind his back, and his booted feet flopped to either side, striking the floor. Well. He was up and awake despite his best efforts.

Fenton, his valet, frowned. "Really, sir, I do wish you'd rung for me when you came in," he said, wringing his hands. "You cannot have been comfortable sleeping on the divan. And now we have this terrible business about the floor."

"Wha—?" muttered Devellyn, blinking.

Honeywell, his butler, was dragging a small table across the room. Disembodied hands set a coffee tray atop it. "There!" said Honeywell. "Now, my lord, as I was saying, the carpenters have gone. I'm afraid the floor in the blue withdrawing room cannot be repaired after all."

Floor? What floor?

Fenton stirred something into his coffee, then passed him the cup with an unctuous smile.

"I fear, my lord, you're to be vastly inconvenienced," continued Honeywell in his voice of doom, a tone ordinarily reserved for thieving footmen and tarnished silver.

"Oh, I doubt that," said Devellyn, eyeing the coffee suspiciously. "Don't much fancy inconvenience. I always find it so dashed . . . inconvenient."

Honeywell folded his hands together like a pious country parson. "But my lord, I fear we have—" Here he paused for dramatic effect, "—the death-watch beetle!"

Devellyn swallowed too much coffee, and had to hack a little of it back up again. "The death-watch *who*—?"

"The death-watch beetle, my lord," he said. "That strange little *skritch-skritch-skritching* sound in the blue withdrawing room? I'm afraid they've eaten away half the flooring. And now they're in the staircases. *Both* of them, sir, spindles, newels, banisters, and all. Brampton says it is very dangerous, sir, and that we should account ourselves lucky we've not been killed."

"Killed by murderous beetles?" asked Devellyn.

"Lucky, sir, that the stairs haven't collapsed beneath us and sent us to an early death in the cellars."

They had cellars? Devellyn shook his head and drank more coffee. There was a fuzzy, dark brown taste in his mouth and a fierce pounding in his temples. "Well, what's to be done?" he finally said. "About these beetles, I mean?"

"The floors and stairs must come out, my lord."

Devellyn frowned. "Yes, and then there will be hammering, eh? Workmen thumping about in their boots? Dust! Racket! Dashed hard on a chap with my sort of social life, Honeywell."

"I fear it's rather more inconvenient even than that, sir." Honeywell clutched his hands a little tighter. "I'm afraid, my lord, that you must remove."

"*Remove?*" snapped Devellyn, shoving away the coffee. "Remove from Duke Street? And go where, old boy?"

Honeywell and Fenton exchanged glances. "Well, there is always Bedford Place," said the butler. "If Miss Lederly could . . . or would . . ."

"Oh, she *couldn't*, and she *wouldn't*," countered Devellyn. "But it little matters. She moved out yesterday."

The servants gave a collective sigh of relief. "Fenton can move your personal effects whilst I pack up the plate and such," said Honeywell.

The marquess looked back and forth between them, appalled. "And I'm to have no say in this, am I?" he asked. "The Devil of Duke Street is to become . . . what? The Hobgoblin of Bedford Place? Doesn't have much of a ring, now, does it?"

Sidonie was not late for her dinner engagement. Instead, she arrived early, which gave her time to stroll leisurely past the shops which lined the thoroughfare. The Strand possessed nothing like the quiet restraint of Oxford Street or Savile Row, places filled with elegant shops selling, as much as anything, rarefied ambiance and the smell of money. Instead, the Strand was a broad, busy place where buyers and sellers of every social stratum eventually crossed paths—if not in life, then in death, for the Strand boasted two undertakers and a coffin maker.

Ironmongers, booksellers, silk mercers, furriers, phrenologists, and fortune-tellers—all hung shingles in the Strand. Then there were the piemen, the orange girls, the news hawkers, the cutpurses, the pickpockets, and lastly, the prostitutes. Sidonie was not much bothered by rubbing elbows with what some would have called the dregs of society. She'd seen almost half the world's seaports, and the dregs didn't drop much deeper than that.

In that spirit, Sidonie bought six oranges she didn't want from a girl who quite obviously needed to sell them, and told her to keep the change. Her tour of the Strand complete, she paused to peer through the bow window of a very posh shop near the foot of the street. There was no shingle, no sign, nothing at all save a small brass plaque on the door, which was inscribed:

MR. GEORGE JACOB KEMBLE
PURVEYOR OF ELEGANT ODDITIES AND FINE FOLDEROL

Finding nothing of interest in the window display, Sidonie pushed through the door, and a little bell jingled merrily. A handsome young Frenchman came at once from behind the counter. *"Bonjour,* Madame Saint-Godard," he said, taking her hand and passionately kissing it. "I trust you are een good health?"

Sidonie smiled. "Quite well, Jean-Claude, thank you," she said, bending over a glass-encased collection of delicate dishes. "Oh, my! This faience *bonbonnière,* is it new?"

"We got et just thees week, *madame,*" he said, with a smile that showed all his teeth. "Your taste eez exquisite, as always. May I send eet to Bedford Place tomorrow? A gift, shall we say, from your devoted brother?"

Sidonie shook her head. She could not afford it. Certainly, she would not take it. "Here, Jean-Claude, have some oranges," she said, putting them down on the glass counter. "They keep away the scurvy."

Her brother's assistant smiled. *"Merci, madame,"* he

said. "You have found Marianne with the beeg eyes, *oui?*"

"Very beeg," Sidonie agreed. "And a very empty belly, I fear."

"*Que faire!*" he agreed. "They are starving, these poor urchins."

"Yes, what to do, indeed?" Sidonie muttered. Then abruptly, she changed the subject. "Jean-Claude, where is my brother? What is his mood today?"

The young man rolled his eyes heavenward. "Upstairs flaying the cook, may God help heem," he answered. "Heez mood eez very ill, like a vicious dog. A soufflé fell." Then he dropped both his voice and his eyes. "*Madame,*" he whispered, "have you sometheeng for me?"

Sidonie shook her head. "Not today, Jean-Claude," she answered. "I've just come down to dine with my brother and Monsieur Giroux."

"Ah, I delay you!" Jean-Claude stepped aside and waved her toward the green velvet curtains which led to the back of the shop. "*Bon appétit, madame!*"

Two hours later, Sidonie was finishing off a bottle of very excellent pinot noir in her brother's dining room above the shop. The food had been flawless, despite whatever crisis had occurred in the kitchen, and if George had killed off his cook, he'd wiped up all the blood. With great care, Sidonie slipped off her shoes, propped her feet in the seat opposite, and reclined against the back of her chair in contentment. Maurice Giroux, George's particular friend, was standing at the sideboard cutting thin slices of sponge cake while the maid carried in a carafe of port and two glasses.

"Eat this, Sid, whilst we drink our port," Maurice suggested, putting down a slice before her. "It is orange sponge, and particularly good since the oranges were fresh."

Sidonie looked across the table at her brother. "Let me guess," she said. "Marianne with the *beeg eyes?*"

George gave a Gallic shrug. "One must eat," he said. "So one might as well eat Marianne's oranges."

Maurice laughed, and poured two glasses of port. "George, she knows you too well."

"For God's sake, let us speak of something else besides my Christian charity." George took one of the glasses. "I have a reputation to keep up."

Maurice turned to Sidonie. "Tell us, my dear, have you many pupils this spring? And what, pray, are you teaching?"

Sidonie poked absently at the orange sponge, wishing she had instead a glass of port. "Well, I still have Miss Leslie and Miss Arbuckle for piano," she began. "And I have Miss Debnam and Miss Brewster for deportment. Then there is Miss Hannaday, who can neither dance, nor sing, nor play, and scarcely knows her fish fork from a canapé knife—and yet her father has arranged a match with the Marquess of Bodley."

"Good Lord!" said George. "That old roué? I'd heard he was nearly insolvent."

Sidonie nodded. "The poor child is terrified, and I have only until August, when the wedding has been scheduled, to get her over it."

"Ah," said Maurice. "You speak of the Hannaday who is in tea, do you not?"

Sidonie nodded. "The very same," she agreed. "He

has a monstrous house just below me in Southampton Street."

"Yes, and Bodley has a monstrous mortgage to go with it," George interjected. "In the last five years, his fortunes have been dropping faster than ladies' waistlines. His entire estate in Essex isn't worth what he owes his creditors."

Maurice nodded sagely. "And then, Sid, there is the matter of that ten thousand pounds he lost to Mr. Chartres in White's last week," he added. "The man is so deep in debt it will take two or three tea merchants' daughters to dig him out again."

"Yes, well, Miss Hannaday has a very sharp shovel," said Sidonie. "Three hundred thousand pounds."

"And Bodley has a very dull wit," snapped George, before sipping delicately from his port.

"What do you mean?" Sidonie asked.

"The man is a pompous blowhard and an inveterate pervert," said her brother, putting the glass back down again. "And let us hope Hannaday does not catch wind of Lord Bodley's latest penchant for enticing young naval officers into his bed. Some of them come very dear indeed. Particularly when one must buy their silence *après* the moment of passion."

"Oh, dear!" Sidonie pressed her fingertips to her chest. "That would explain his need for money. How ever does he find . . . find . . ."

"Find his partners?" Maurice supplied.

"Well, yes."

Maurice shrugged. "If they are willing—or in dire need of money—he finds them in St. James's Park, most probably."

"St. James's?" she echoed.

Maurice and George exchanged telling glances. "Sidonie, gentlemen who are interested in certain types of—well, *activities,* meet in a place which is generally known to them," said her brother. "Lately, St. James's Park has again been popular. So, one goes there for a stroll, and signals one's—er, interests—by tucking a handkerchief into the left pocket, or by hanging one's thumb in one's waistcoat."

"Just so," said Maurice. "But some of Bodley's victims haven't been so willing. For that, he retains a whoremaster. Their victims are young men who have played too deep or allowed themselves to be caught in compromising positions of some sort."

"And sometimes, their only sin is poverty," said George softly.

Maurice nodded. "Bodley occasionally prefers young girls, too," he supplied. "The bastard knows every bawd east of Regent Street."

Sidonie shivered. "Dear God, I begin to comprehend," she managed, pressing one hand to her chest. "Maurice, I believe I shall be unladylike and prevail upon you for a glass of that port. My poor Miss Hannaday! Now I almost wish she *would* elope with her shipping clerk."

"Her shipping clerk?" Maurice turned from the sideboard, holding a clean glass.

"She *has* a shipping clerk?" asked George.

Sidonie nodded, and looked back and forth between them. "Charles Greer," she said. "He works for her father, and they love one another madly. But it is thought a dreadful *mésalliance,* and Mr. Hannaday will not permit it."

George cupped a hand to his ear. "Oh, I hear Gretna Green calling!" he chortled. "And tell Mr. Greer to make haste, my dear, lest they move the date up."

"Elope?" said Sidonie. "George, you cannot be serious!"

Maurice handed her a glass of port. "I fear he might be, Sid," he said. "Some things are worse than a life of poverty."

"And Lord Bodley is amongst them," said George. "Besides, he must be at least twice her age."

Sidonie shifted her gaze from George to Maurice and back again. "But her father will cut her off if she elopes," she said. "And he'll discharge her clerk without a character."

George shrugged. "He'll likely come round when the first grandchild arrives."

"That's all very well, George, but what if he doesn't?" asked Maurice abruptly. "Is the clerk a decent sort?"

"Well . . . yes."

"You are sure?"

"I met him but once," Sidonie answered. "He's earnest and rather awkward, but there is no artifice in him, of that I am confident."

George lifted one shoulder. "Sid is no bad judge of character."

Maurice drained the rest of his wine. "Well, I shall give him a place, then."

Sidonie was shocked. "Will you, Maurice? But why?"

Maurice gave a wintry smile. "I feel sorry for anyone thwarted in love," he said. "Besides, old Hallings has asked to be pensioned come October. If the lad can inventory cloth and keep accounts, he can apprentice for a few months. It isn't much, my dear, but the chit shan't starve."

"Well!" said Sidonie, feeling as if she'd just been caught up in a whirlwind. "The two of you are frightfully helpful—not to mention a veritable spouting font of scandal and gossip."

Maurice patted her hand. "We work with the *haute monde,* dear girl," he said. "They have no secrets. Our business depends upon it."

Sidonie laughed. "I wonder if there is anything the two of you do not know—or cannot discover."

"I doubt it," said George.

"Oh, speaking of scandal, gossip, and discoveries!" Maurice leaned across the table, his eye twinkling. "I have something which meets all three criteria—and it's just too rich!"

"Go on," said George.

"Guess who the Black Angel's latest victim was!"

"I cannot," said Sidonie. "You must tell us, Maurice."

The haberdasher grinned. "That silly pup, Lord Francis Tenby."

George rolled his eyes. "Oh, it could not have happened to a more deserving fellow."

Maurice wrinkled his nose. "I myself think he has abysmal taste in waistcoats," he said. "But I have also heard he is spoiled and a little petulant, too. He is trying to hush up his little interlude with the Black Angel, of course, but servants will talk."

"Hmm," said George. "And what are they saying?"

Maurice leaned even nearer. "That the Black Angel pinched a sapphire pin worth a hundred pounds," he whispered. "And left him bound, gagged, and naked in a moving hackney."

"Bound, gagged, and naked?" murmured Sidonie. "How perfectly fascinating. Tell me, Maurice, what is being said of the Angel? Who do people believe she—or *he*—is?"

"A scorned mistress," he swiftly answered. "Perhaps even an actress. That is why she keeps changing her appearance and targets men of wealth and power. She is angry. Avenging. Not to mention hilariously entertaining."

Sidonie smiled. "Do the unfortunate victims know why they are singled out?"

Maurice and George exchanged glances. "I have heard it said," George began, "that the Angel fancies herself something of a Robin Hood."

Sidonie lifted her brows. "To whom, then, does she give?"

Something flickered in her brother's quick golden gaze. "I am not perfectly sure."

"But can you not find out, George?" she teased. "I thought you knew everything."

"I can *discover* anything," he corrected. "If it pleases me to do so. But I need not know the Angel's identity or whom she helps. Frankly, I wish her well."

Sidonie lifted her gaze to his and allowed a hint of a challenge to light her eyes. "Very well, then," she said. "I wish you to discover something else. Something of particular interest to me. It should not prove difficult for a man of your talents."

"By all means, dear girl," George agreed. "What is it you wish to know?"

"I wish to know who owns the house almost directly across the street from mine."

Her brother drew back and looked at her. "I keep up with gossip and crime, Sid, not the Bloomsbury real estate records."

"But this is all of a piece," she said. "A gentleman—a nobleman, I'm told—keeps the house for his mistresses."

"Ah!" said Maurice and George at once.

"The poor women come and go faster than the seasons," Sidonie complained. "And I should simply like to know his name, that is all."

"What is the number?" asked George.

"Seventeen."

Maurice frowned. "And the woman, is she a blonde? A brunette?"

Sidonie shook her head. "A redhead—and, according to the crossing sweep, an actress," she answered. "She moved out just this afternoon, obviously distraught. But there was a blonde this winter. Pale blond, with a mincing walk and a very sharp chin. And before that, an Italian dancer. Her name, I believe, was Maria. She left in tears. Indeed, I think he must be very cruel."

George looked suddenly ill at ease. "I believe the gentleman in question is Lord Devellyn," he said quietly.

He and Maurice exchanged odd glances. "Hmm," said Maurice. "Tell us, Sidonie, is he quite a large man?"

Sidonie shrugged. "I have never seen him," she said. "He comes and goes in a carriage or a hackney."

George swirled the port in his glass and stared at the ceiling. "A marked carriage?"

"Indeed."

"Describe his crest."

"Yes, of course." Sidonie closed her eyes and did so.

"It is he," said George again. "There is no doubt."

"None," agreed Maurice. "I fitted him for a pair of new waistcoats just last week. I saw the coach draw up."

Sidonie laid down her napkin. "Excellent!" she said. "Lord Devellyn. Do either of you know his club?"

George lifted one brow suspiciously. "The Beefsteak, the Yacht Club, and the MCC," he rattled off. "And White's, when they will let him in. Why do you ask?"

"Eating, sailing, and cricket!" she murmured, ignoring her brother's question. "Lord, what a well-rounded individual. I suppose he gambles, too?"

"Like there's no tomorrow," said Maurice. "At Crockford's, usually."

Sidonie's eyes widened. "A perilous place."

"And at any low tavern or squalid hell that will have him," George snipped. "Devellyn drinks like a parched pig, and has no standards whatsoever."

"That's not entirely true, George," said Maurice, pressing his fingertips to his chest. "He bought waistcoats from me."

"Well, you know what they say about swine," sniffed George. "Even a blind hog occasionally roots out a truffle. Besides, you told me his valet chose the fabrics."

"And where, pray tell, does this Renaissance man reside?" asked Sidonie.

"Oh, good Lord, Sidonie!" George was growing irritated. "He's the man they call the Devil of Duke Street. Figure it out. Now, may we please dispense with the topic of Devellyn? I find him tedious in the extreme."

Chapter Three

The Sublime Society of Beef Steaks

The Beefsteak Club was, simply put, a organization of unruly bacchanalians who liked to sing bawdy songs, gnaw slabs of bloody meat, and swill vast quantities of port before going on to their equally unruly gaming hells. The phrase *in the gout* did not exist in their vocabulary, because Beefsteakers were expected to turn up their toes in a far more dashing fashion long before that dread disease could set in.

The club convened on Saturdays, and Beefsteakers were few, as seating at the table was limited. Death, insanity, and insolvency were the prospective members' only hopes. There had been, regrettably, a few of each. Over its hundred-year history, the club had been moved from pillar to post, and was presently housed in a room at the Lyceum near Covent Garden.

The Black Angel had had no trouble at all finding the club's entrance. Now she waited deep in the shadows across the street as the nightlife of Covent Garden began to flood forth. The market gardeners and costermongers had long since found their beds, and the pavements were now crowded with pleasure seekers headed for the coffeehouses and theaters. A laughing couple dressed in worn brown coats passed by her hiding place, their steps light, their shoes scuffing softly on the pavement.

Just then, a brewer's dray came clattering up from the Strand, and for a moment, she could see nothing. Then the dray rattled on, and in the jovial crowd now spilling from the Lyceum, she saw him. She was certain. The man's height and breadth made him unmistakable. His hair was dark, chestnut, perhaps, and he appeared to be dressed in solid black.

After a few moments of repartee and laughter, he and two companions stepped from the throng and into a pool of gaslight. For an instant, her heart stopped, and she feared she'd lost her mind entirely. The Marquess of Devellyn towered over his friends, and beneath his sweeping greatcoat, his shoulders looked as wide, and almost as thick, as a beer keg.

But it wasn't that which made her heart lurch. It was his eyes. They were flat and cold, like gray slate. And horribly cynical, too, as if he knew more than he wished of the world and how it worked. For an instant, she felt an odd sort of kinship with him, then ruthlessly shut it away. But his laughter, still ringing down the street, seemed a sham to her now.

No crested carriage waited below the Lyceum. Instead, the three men set off, oddly enough, in the direction of Fleet Street. It was then that she began to worry just where her little lark might take her. But after a few minutes of brisk walking, the three men turned into the Cheshire

Cheese, a tavern favored by the literati. She slid into the
shadows of the alley for half an hour, then followed, but the
rabbit warren of rooms filled with tables and benches made
it impossible to see without being seen. No, this would not
do. She circled through the crowded taproom and back
into the street again, escaping with nothing worse than a
drunken leer and a grope on the arse.

An hour later, they came out again, their pace less
brisk but their steps still steady. All around them, a thick
evening fog was rolling up off the Thames, muting the
clopping hooves and creaking carriage wheels which
passed along the street, until they sounded distant and
disembodied. She could smell the river now, mixed with
the strange effluence which drifted up from the east. In
the gloom, the marquess's long, dark coat swirled eerily
around his boots. He moved with an easy grace as the
trio circled around St. Paul's and into Cheapside.

There, they went down a set of steep stairs beneath a
tobacconist's and into a pernicious, unmarked hell called
Gallard's. An unfortunate choice, for it was very private,
and she knew no way in. Two hours later, just as she was
longing for the warmth of her bed, her quarry came out
and staggered off toward the even more dangerous envi-
rons of the East End. Devellyn, she decided, was either
very bold or very stupid. She tucked her cloak close, felt
for her knife, and kept to the shadows.

At Queen Street, the men stopped to light cheroots,
then turned toward the river. They crossed the Southwark Bridge on foot, conversing in the bold, carrying
tones of men who'd had far too much to drink. She hung
back lest she be seen. But it little mattered. She'd already
guessed where they were headed.

The Anchor was an old riverside inn frequented by pirates, smugglers, thieves, and the occasional nob out on a lark. Opium, untaxed brandy, sex of any sort; all could be had at the Anchor. She knew the place, but not well. She watched them enter, waited ten minutes, then followed. The weary, unshaven innkeeper didn't blink an eye when she snapped a guinea against his counter and asked for a room upstairs—a room at the back, away from the river.

Upstairs, she pushed the window wide open and made a quick assessment of the inn's exterior. Dark. Deserted. A solid-looking drainpipe and a low garden wall. All perfectly acceptable. After hanging her cloak and opening her small valise, she rouged her lips and went down again. The taproom was dark, but she could see that Devellyn and his companions had joined three other, rougher-looking fellows in a card game near the door. She swished carefully past and allowed her fingertips to trail lightly across the shoulder of the man on Devellyn's left.

The marquess turned, and with heavy, hooded eyes, watched her hand slide away.

"How'll you have it?" asked the tapster when she approached.

The smell of cold ashes and sour ale assailed her nostrils. "Just a dram o' satin, lovey," she said, propping her elbow on the bar and turning to survey the room. Most of the tables were filled, and smoke hung low in the air.

The man put down her drink and leaned nearer. "I need to tell you, miss," he said quietly. "We'll be having no trouble in here."

She shot him a bemused smile over her shoulder. "Wot? Do I look like trouble ter yew?"

*   *   *

Devellyn noticed the fancy piece in the red velvet dress the moment she entered the room. One could scarcely miss the way her hand—a surprisingly clean, long-fingered hand—slid caressingly over Sir Alasdair MacLachlan's shoulder. Alasdair, of course, did not notice. He had fifty guineas on the table and was holding a fistful of cards which were quivering with excitement. Warming the sheets with some wench was the furthest thing from his mind.

It should have been far from Devellyn's. But he was losing, and looking for a little distraction. He was also foxed. He watched the tart lean against the bar and order a glass of gin. *Gin?* Good Lord. She certainly wasn't his type.

She was also tall and lush, with a bosom that was about to burst from her dress, which was cut right down to the nipples. Her hair was a garish shade of red which clashed so violently with her velvet dress the vision could have stopped a mail coach. She had one elbow propped on the bar and was boldly surveying the noisy room. In short, she looked like just what she was, a dockside dolly-mop with big breasts and abysmal taste.

But her eyes. Now there was something odd. She had quick, intelligent eyes. They did not seem to belong with the rest of her body. Devellyn kept glancing surreptitiously at them, wishing he could make out the color. Her cheeks were oddly high, giving her a bit of a tight, rabbity look about the face. The mouth, though, was not bad. She had a small mole just at one corner, and something about it tormented him. Yet the woman kept lowering her lashes and looking at Alasdair. That was beginning to annoy him.

Once, her tongue came out and teased lightly at the corner of her mouth, almost touching the mole. Devellyn ordered another bottle of brandy and hunkered down with his hand. Then again, a man who'd drunk as much as he had probably oughtn't be playing cards. But Alasdair had insisted. Well, of course he had. His luck was in tonight. Devellyn's, unfortunately, was not. He tossed down his hand and admitted it.

Again, the woman strolled through the room. Again, that hungry, sidelong look at Alasdair. Her hip brushed against his chair, but Alasdair held a handful of spades—enough to clear the table if he kept his wits, which he likely would. Alasdair was the consummate gambler. Devellyn pulled away from his friend's shoulder and began to debate with himself over what to do.

He wanted to tumble the tart in the red dress, dash it. He didn't know why. He just *did*. It was probably just the perversity of her behavior. She hadn't looked at him once all night, which was odd. Women always looked at him, if for no other reason than to take in his size. Perhaps she meant to tease him. Or perhaps he wasn't her type. On the other hand, perhaps he was? With a curt good night to his friends, he shoved back his chair, took what was left of his money, and ambled off to find out.

Apparently, he was her type.

"Wot, a big, strapping buck like you?" She grinned and dropped her eyes to his crotch. "Might ought'er charge you extra, I'm thinking."

Devellyn grabbed her by the arm and pulled her toward the stairs. "You might just find yourself so grateful you give my money back," he growled. Then halfway up, he stopped. He'd forgotten something, blister it. In the darkened stairwell, he pulled her around to face him. "What's your name, girl?"

She dropped her gaze suggestively. "Ruby." Despite her horrid cockney accent and oddly grating voice, the word came out silky, sending a chill down his spine. "Ruby Black."

He let his eyes drift down the tawdry red dress again. Ruby Black looked like she knew what she was doing. Devellyn was suddenly grateful. He was in no mood to tutor a virgin or anything remotely near it. And he was in no mood for a quick rutting, either. Camelia's leaving him had left him feeling bereft and severely sexually frustrated. He was in the mood for a woman that could take it hard and take it for a good long while. He stopped and jerked her around again.

"How much, Ruby, for the whole night?"

"Coo!" said Ruby. But she named her price. He gladly agreed.

Ruby tucked the money away, then looked up at him through her thick, dark lashes.

"I'm Devellyn," he grunted by way of introduction.

Her room was narrow and squalid, barely lit by one sputtering, stinking tallow candle. The furnishings were threadbare, the floor just rough planking, but the narrow oak poster bed looked as though it could bear his weight. What did he care for ambiance? He wanted sex.

Ruby ran her hands down his chest, then brushed one teasingly over his belly. "Oh, yer something, Mr. Devellyn, ain't you?" she said, her nostrils delicately flaring. She leaned into him, her thigh brushing his already jutting erection, and in the gloom, he saw her eyes widen. "Gawd," she whispered. "I'd hate ter see that one when you're stone-cold sober."

He was flattered. He shouldn't have been, and he

knew it. He was half cup-shot, and she was just bought accommodation, and it was all artifice and show. But there was something, he thought, in her face. A hunger. A yearning. Suddenly, he wished he could be certain. "Damn it," he said. "Why is it so infernal dark in here?"

Ruby looked suddenly injured. "I make me livin' on me back, gov'nor," she said. "And candles are a penny apiece at the Anchor."

He started to pull away, but she slid her hands between his legs, cupping his ballocks in her small, warm palm. "Oh, Gawd, don't go now," she whispered, sounding a little desperate. Desperate was good. Devellyn liked his women desperate.

Then he jerked himself up short. She wasn't *his* woman. She was a riverside strumpet, for pity's sake. But at the moment, he was having trouble remembering that. Lord, he'd best keep his wits about him. He snared her wrist and pulled her against him. "Look here, girl," he grumbled. "You'd best be clean."

Her eyes drifted insolently over him. "I ain't gonna tip you the token, me fine gent," she said. "If that's wot yer thinking."

"Good," he said, snarling a little. "The last bloody thing I need just now is a bad case of the clap."

She jerked her wrist away and stepped back. "Look 'ere, Mr. Devellyn," she said. "There's plenty o' warm coves'll pay ready money for wot I'm sellin'. If you don't want it, no 'ard feelings. Just move on, awright?"

Damn it all, he didn't want to move on. The woman—*Ruby*—seemed to possess something special. He didn't know what it was. Hell, he hadn't even gotten a good look at her yet. But he wanted her badly, and he couldn't say why. She seemed to ooze carnal hunger. He thought he could smell the lust on her skin. And she had a lot of skin.

Suddenly, he was eager to see more. His hand went to her breast, which was warm and heavy. He moved to tug the cheap velvet down so that he might fill his mouth with it, but she pulled his hand away and pushed it back.

"Wot's yer hurry, gov?"

"I'm paying you," he said. "What do you care?"

She pulled a little away. "You're a big man, Mr. Devellyn," she whispered. "P'raps I ought'er be afraid o' you?"

He tried to smile. "I think not."

She fluttered her lashes suggestively. "But I am a little," she confessed, her voice growing husky. "I think a great big buck like you needs ter be managed a bit."

"Managed?" he asked.

"Made ter go slow," she whispered. "Made ter take his time wiv 'is business."

He chuckled softly. "And how do you propose to do that?"

"Oh, I have me ways," said Ruby, her voice provocative. "Me specialty, you might say."

He couldn't help but be intrigued. "And just what sort of specialty would that be, my girl?"

She paused for a moment. "I can make you beg for it, Devellyn."

"I don't think so," he answered. "I'm a straightforward sort of fellow, Ruby. I don't fancy anything unusual. Just a good, hard ride will do."

In the dim light, he could see her mouth form an amazingly pretty pout. She was not really afraid of him, he didn't think—though he'd come across one or two women who were. But Ruby, he decided, just wanted to toy with him a bit. And what was the harm? He was tired of cards, tired of trawling from one hell to the next with his friends in search of something he hadn't already seen, had, or tasted. Tired of life, really.

Certainly he was too tired to go looking for a mistress to replace Camelia. Then he'd seen the redhead and realized he couldn't completely do without, either. But her lush bottom lip was quivering now, and she was looking disappointed. *That* seemed to be his specialty, disappointing women. Suddenly, and very foolishly, he decided not to disappoint this one.

He reached around and filled his hand with her arse. "All right, Ruby," he whispered, crudely lifting her pelvis against the erection straining at his trousers. "Have your way with me. I've got all bloody night to get what I want from you."

Ruby smiled and slid her hands up his chest beneath his coat, pushing it off his shoulders. Devellyn let go of his luscious handful and allowed the coat to slide onto the floor.

She made a sound of satisfaction in her throat. "Not an ounce o' padding on you, is there?" Her voice was thick as he urged his cock against her. "And that's a reg'lar tipstaff shoved down yer trousers."

He gave a wry smile, and watched her slender fingers brush his flesh through the wool. It felt wicked. Wonderful. He gave a little moan of pleasure. "Tell me something, gov'nor," she rasped, her hands going to his waistcoat. "You said yer wanted it slow. Do you?"

Devellyn watched the buttons slip free. "That depends," he said. "How do you like it, Ruby?"

She lowered her lashes and wouldn't look him in the eyes. "I likes it slow, Mr. Devellyn," she whispered. "Real slow. And I like my man to beg a little. Nothing gets a girl's blood up like a hot, sweating stallion of a man straining at the bit."

It sounded oddly tempting to him. She pushed his waistcoat off. Cool air breezed up the back of his shirt. "Perhaps you'd best tell me what your game is, Ruby," he murmured.

The pout reappeared. "No need ter play, Mr. Devellyn, if you've no interest."

He set his hands on her shoulders. "Just answer the damned question," he growled. "That tipstaff down my trousers is interest enough, isn't it?"

Ruby held his gaze for a moment. "It's just that you look ter me like a real fine gent, Mr. Devellyn," she answered. "You got any notion how many o' them we get over in Southwark?"

He snorted. "Not many."

"Not many is right," she agreed. "But I got me some aspirations."

"Aspirations?" He tried not to laugh.

She slowly nodded. "I'm good," she said. "Real good at what I do. And I'm tired o' working the South Bank. I want ter go uptown. Ter be kept in style a bit. I want me a proper place, somewhere snug and warm. And I want me some fine clothes."

He grabbed her hands and held them still a moment. "Sorry to dash your hopes, Ruby," he answered. "But I'm just here to rub a little rust off my pipe. I'm not looking for a permanent arrangement."

She fluttered her lashes at him. "Oh, I knows that,

gov'nor," she said. "But you knows other proper gents, don't you? Like them two chaps downstairs? P'raps you could pass me name around if I give satisfaction? That pretty bloke w'the yellow hair—I fancied the look o' him, I did."

Alasdair? The woman was still thinking of Alasdair? What a bloody damned insult!

Suddenly, something in him snapped. "To hell with this," he said. "You aren't getting paid to talk." He jerked her hard against him and crushed her mouth beneath his. He kissed her crudely, forcing her head back as he pushed her mouth wide and thrust his tongue deep. *Oh, Lord.* She tasted good. Like ripe fruit. Like cheap gin and red-hot sin, and something he craved but couldn't name.

She tried to pull away, but he wouldn't let her go. Instead, he kept kissing her, kept thrusting deep into her mouth with his tongue. Trapped against his body, Ruby began to struggle, shoving at his shoulders with her palms. Even then, he almost didn't stop. Lust and frustration surged through his body anew. He wanted to be inside her, wanted to keep kissing her so she wouldn't speak of things he didn't want to hear.

She was beating him with the heels of her hands now. *Good God, he had to get a grip on himself.* Gasping for breath, he tore his mouth away and stared down at her. Suddenly, despite the darkness, he thought he saw real fear sketch across her face.

"Oh, Lord," he gasped. "I'm sorry."

She was still shaking. He really had frightened her. Roughly, he dragged a hand through his hair. Perhaps Ruby did not have as much experience as he'd thought.

And whatever else she might be, she was a human being. He shut his eyes and felt the shame wash over him. "I'm sorry," he said again. "I just haven't . . . haven't had . . . oh, hell, I'm sorry."

She turned her face away and said nothing. But he could sense her fighting down fear.

He opened his eyes. "Look, let's just get this over with, Ruby," he said more gently. "Just take off your clothes and lie down on the bed, all right? Just let me have a quick pump and I'll be on my way. I didn't mean to frighten you."

"I am not frightened," she said, her voice so firm her cockney accent almost vanished. "I am not afraid of you, Devellyn."

He took her chin in his hand and turned her face into his, cursing the darkness that almost blinded him. But indeed, she did not look frightened. If she had been, she had reined it under control.

"I don't want to frighten you," he said, dropping his hands. He no longer touched her in any way. "I'm not that sort of man, Ruby. That's not how I take my pleasure."

"Awright," she said, her voice soft. Then she leaned into him and set her hands on his chest. "That's a posh-lookin' crumpler, gov." Her tone was light again. Stronger. "Let's 'ave it orf, *hmm*? P'raps we'll think of a better use for it."

He looked down to see her grinning unapologetically at him. Oh, what the hell? "Yes, perhaps we will," he agreed.

She untied the elaborate knot with no difficulty. She unwound half the cloth from his neck, circled it around her own, and drew their faces together. She kissed the corner of his mouth, then ran her tongue across his bottom lip.

"Umm," she moaned, then she drew the swell of his lip between her small teeth and bit, none too gently, either. A sudden, fierce craving shot through him, making his balls contract and his cock quiver. Inside, his stomach seemed to bottom out.

"Good Lord, girl," he whispered, as her mouth traveled down his throat. Her tongue traced a line of fire along his collar, and he realized she was already unbuttoning his trousers. He wasn't sure just what he was supposed to do, didn't want to bollix things up again, so he stood, still and stoic, as she touched him.

It seemed to be just what she wanted. She drew the cravat away and tossed it onto the bed pillow. Then, with another little sound of satisfaction, she went down on her knees to pull off his boots. That done, she tugged off his stockings with impatient little jerks, Devellyn clutching the bedpost for balance.

It was odd, but he couldn't recall ever having been undressed by a woman, other than the unfastening of a few token buttons or the untying of his cravat. He rather liked watching her do it.

He rather liked Ruby, too. He liked her lush figure and narrow shoulders. He liked her strange, raspy voice. And he especially liked how she looked on her knees. She was rough around the edges, and certainly not his type. But strangely, he found himself toying with doing just as she wanted. Letting her have her way with him. Letting her make him beg. Then keeping her someplace snug and warm and buying her some fancy clothes.

Good Lord, he'd be the laughingstock of all his

friends. But he didn't give a damn. Ruby started to stand, and abruptly, he set one hand on her shoulder and urged her back down again. "Wait," he said, the other hand fumbling at his trousers. He freed the last button and impatiently shoved the fabric down. His cock sprang free, so hot and hard he feared he might shoot wild before she got it in her mouth. He watched in satisfaction as Ruby's eyes widened.

"Take it," he rasped, touching himself. "Take it, Ruby. Please. *Please*. I'm begging you."

Devellyn had forgotten he was the one in control. He had forgotten he was paying her, and that the word *please* need not enter into the transaction. Ruby looked uncertain, but she slid a tentative hand back and forth along his length. Devellyn felt his whole body begin to shudder almost uncontrollably, as if he were a schoolboy again. His hand lashed out, grabbing for the bedpost.

Abruptly, Ruby released him and stood up slowly, letting her body rub over his as she rose. "Are you eager, Devellyn?" she whispered, leaning in so that her lips brushed his neck just below his ear. "*Are* you?"

He tried to nod. "Eager enou—"

He sucked in his breath on a gasp when her cool hands slid up his belly. He felt his muscles tighten and shiver beneath her touch. She pushed his shirt up as she went. Devellyn let go of the bedpost, and stripped it off over his head with one hand.

"Coo," murmured Ruby at the sight of his chest. "Built like a side o' lean beef, you are."

"What do you want, Ruby?" he asked through clenched teeth. "Whatever it is, for pity's sake, girl, get on with it before I explode."

Ruby leaned forward, and ran her tongue around one of his nipples, making his breath seize. "Not so fast, you fine, big buck," she whispered. As she licked him, her hands went to his waist, pushing down his drawers and trousers. They fell to his ankles, and he realized vaguely that he was bare-arsed naked, while she was still fully clothed.

His hands went to her bodice. "Take it off, Ruby," he whispered. "Now. Please?"

She made a purring sound in her throat, and pushed him toward the bed. "Lie down, Devellyn," she ordered, slipping off her shoes. "Lie down on the bed, love, and I swear, I'll give you just wot you deserve."

His every fiber alive with desire, he did as she asked. And he had to admit, his desire was heightening. She probably *would* have him begging before it was over with.

Ruby watched him, her eyes aflame as they ran down his naked body. Then she set one foot on the lumpy mattress, hiking up her skirts so high he could see her garter and then some. The woman had long, flawless calves, and thighs which looked slender and tight beneath her cotton drawers.

"Is this wot yer wantin', Devellyn?" she rasped, rolling her garter to her ankle. "Do you want this leg wrapped round yer waist?" With slow, erotic motions, she pulled the stocking off. "Or would you rather 'ave me ankle hooked round yer neck?"

He swallowed hard. "Both, please," he said, choking out the words.

"Please," she softly echoed. "Ooh, I do like the sound o' that. Now you just lie there real still, Devellyn. Let me

play me little game, lovey, and I promise you'll be screamin' afore I'm done wiv you."

"Christ Jesus," he whispered.

She tossed the stocking somewhere near his head, and proceeded to do the same with the opposite leg. Devellyn did as she asked. He lay still on the bed, simply watching her and wanting her, his cock twitching insistently.

"The dress now, Ruby," he pleaded, reaching out for her. "Take it off and let me see everything. Your breasts. Your belly. Everything. Oh, God, have mercy and hurry up."

Ruby smiled impishly, hiked up her skirts, and mounted him with her legs spread wide.

"Do you want me to beg, Ruby? Is that it? Please, then. *Please.* For pity's sake, take me."

He no longer cared about getting her clothes off. It seemed unimportant now. The scent of woman surrounded him, was drowning him. She smelled surprisingly clean and sweet. He groaned deep in his chest, dragging in air.

In response, Ruby leaned forward and kissed him, hot and openmouthed, and roughly, he shoved one hand between them, intent on finding the slit in her drawers, or just ripping them off altogether.

But Ruby, it seemed, had other ideas. Her slender fingers encircled his wrist and pushed his hand back over his head. "Go slow, lovey," she whispered against his mouth. "Let's go real slow, awright? I want ter tease you a bit. Get me mount in a real lather, so ter speak."

He realized what she meant when he felt her slip the stocking round his wrist. But Ruby was still straddling him, and kissing him again, thrusting inside his mouth now, and making sweet, urgent noises. He heard the rustle of fabric, felt the stocking go tight around his flesh, and felt a strange little thrill run through him.

He knew of men who were sexually excited by such things and worse. Apparently, he was one of them. Despite the vast quantity of alcohol he'd consumed tonight, his cock was hard as a door knocker, and throbbing with his every heartbeat. She shifted a little, and he almost lost control.

"Hurry," he whispered, as her lips slid over his.

Ruby let her teeth rake down his throat. The pain was sharp. Exquisite. "Hurry *up,*" he choked.

"Wot's the rush, lovey?" she asked, encircling his opposite wrist with his own cravat.

He turned his head, and tore his mouth from hers just as the second knot slipped tight. "Take me inside, Ruby," he begged. *"Now."*

"Ooo, Mr. Devellyn," she whispered. "I'm getting ready to give it to you real good."

"Ruby, you don't understand!" he rasped, squeezing his eyes shut and praying for control. "I'm going to—I just can't—can't wait—"

The knot jerked fast, drawing his wrist firmly against the wooden bedpost.

"'Fraid you'll have to, gov'nor," she said, her voice suddenly cool.

He felt her weight shift, and he opened his eyes "Ruby?" he said. "Wha—?"

She had the second stocking stuffed in his mouth so fast, he couldn't draw breath. For a moment, he was dazed. Confused. Then sudden knowledge slammed into him.

God damn her.

The bitch was on her feet, rummaging through his pockets like a squirrel. Purse. Watch. Keys. Loose coins. Everything he carried she took.

"Ah mm ghmm mmm!" he said.

"Oh, keep it stuffed, Devellyn," she said.

An open valise sat on the night table, and she unceremoniously dumped the contents of his pockets into it. Then she jerked out a length of rope, and snapped the valise shut. He twisted his torso and swung one leg off the bed, almost catching her round the waist, but the little jade danced away, the valise in hand.

"Oh, Devellyn, you bloody idiot," she said, swiftly tying the bag to her body with the rope. "I wish you could see yourself now."

She took the key from the door lock and pitched it out the window, then snatched a gray cloak from a peg on the wall and threw it over her shoulders. Her every movement was quick and efficient. By God, she'd done this before. For that, he was going to strangle her. Twice. He tried to tell her so.

"Amm ggnn kigg uggh!" he said, chewing furiously at the stocking.

Ruby just smiled and pushed open the casement window. "Ta, lovey."

"Gnnn unngh!"

"Lawks, yes, I almost forgot!" She stepped a little nearer the bed. "Promised you a peek at me dumplings, didn't I?"

The bitch. Rage ran bloodred through his brain. He shoved at the wad of stocking with his tongue, thrashing so hard the bed moved.

"Now, don't cut up so, Devellyn," said Ruby, as she worked down one side of her bodice. "Not unless yer wants an audience up here." She laughed as the creamy flesh spilled forth, not quite baring her nipple. And then he saw it. In the poor light, it was hard to make out, and she didn't dare come closer. But he could guess at what it was.

A black angel. She had a little black angel tattooed on the far side of her left breast.

Devellyn got his tongue wedged under the stocking and spat for all he was worth. The stocking burst from his mouth and rolled down his chest, as limp as his now-lifeless cock. "You bitch!" he roared. "You vile, sneaking, cheating little strumpet! You don't know what you've done, do you?"

She lifted one delicate eyebrow. "Coo! Don't I? P'raps you'd best explain it ter me."

"You've picked the wrong pocket this time, my angel!" he roared. "And this time, you'll have the devil to pay, do you hear?"

Ruby Black had one foot on the windowsill now, her hands braced wide on the iron frame. "Good night, my lord," she said sweetly. "Sorry about yer shriveled tipstaff."

"The devil to pay, bitch!" he bellowed. "I am coming after *you.*"

Then the Black Angel laughed and literally leapt into the gloom.

Chapter Four

In which we go Backstage with Julia

"Oooh, I don't like this, girl." Julia had Sidonie's head bent back over a chair and was scrubbing hard at the dark tint she'd helped Sidonie rub into her skin hours earlier. "No, not one bit, I don't. Jumping out windows! Ropes and such! And if something happens to you, it'll be blood on my hands, sure as I'd done the deed."

Sidonie tried to sit up straight. "I'm fine, Julia. Ow! Don't scrub so hard." She gentled her tone. "I'm home safe, aren't I? And none of this is your doing."

Julia dunked her sponge into the basin again. "But the Marquess of Devellyn!" She stared into the steaming water as if unwilling to hold Sidonie's gaze. "Lord help you, girl, what were you thinking!"

Sidonie laughed. "Julia, I'm hardly a girl. In fact, I'm on the downhill slide to thirty."

"Aye, and not like to see it, either, running wild about Southwark with a Satan's spawn like Devellyn."

"But, Julia," Sidonie whispered in a teasing voice, "I

got to see him naked. Stark staring, as a matter of fact."

Julia smacked her hand. "Stop it, Sidonie."

Sidonie laughed. "But you've heard the rumors, Julia!" she went on. "Don't you want to know what the Devil of Duke Street looks like out of his trousers?"

Julia wrestled with her conscience but an instant. "Yes," she hissed. "What?"

Sidonie closed her eyes. "Beautiful, damn him," she said. "Big and beautiful like nothing I've ever seen in my life—and not apt to see again. A body like Carrera marble, all smooth, firm planes. And hard, Julia. Hard all over."

"Got a good look, hmm?" A little too enthusiastically, Julia peeled off the strip of the gummed rubber which drew Sidonie's skin taut across her cheekbones.

"Ouch!" Sidonie yelped.

"Don't *ouch* at me," said Julia, flicking the gooey stuff into the dustbin. "Now good looks aside, Sidonie, I want you to stay away from Devellyn. He's dangerous, that one. And there's all manner of trouble he could start."

The thrill of the chase was still coursing through Sidonie's blood, and she was reluctant to have her spirits dampened. Devellyn had proven a most worthy adversary. "What sort of trouble could he cause?"

Julia cut a strange, sidelong glance at her. "Plenty of trouble," she said cryptically. "Serious trouble. And if your brother George catches wind of this, he's apt to take his hand to the back of your arse."

"George doesn't know."

"Yes, and you'd best quit before he finds out." The last strip of rubber came off a little more gently. Just then, Thomas leapt onto Sidonie's bed and pounced upon the red wig, which lay like a dead fox in the middle of her counterpane.

"Is that it? Am I done?" Sidonie rubbed beneath her ear, trying to ease the sting as she watched Thomas tussle and growl on the bed.

"Yes, you're done." Julia dropped the sponge into the water with a *plop!* and dried her hands off on her apron, then shooed the cat away from the wig.

Sidonie pulled the towel from around her neck and went to the demilune table by her bedroom window. The house across the street, she noticed, was steeped in darkness tonight. Now that she knew who owned it, and had exacted her insignificant pound of flesh, she was not at all sure she'd sleep any better. As it so often did, the rush of excitement would keep her awake for a while yet, leaving her to feel restless. Trapped. Indeed, she yearned to lose herself again in the dark danger of streets. But it would be a long time, she knew, before she met another adversary as worthy as Devellyn.

She poured two glasses of sherry and returned to press one into Julia's hand. "Here," she said softly. "We both need a drink."

"Do we now?" Julia glanced at her curiously.

Sidonie pressed her lips together. "All right, Julia," she finally answered. "I took a risk tonight. Devellyn's not the fool the others were."

Julia looked somewhat mollified, and by unspoken agreement, they settled into chairs by the hearth. Sidonie pulled up her knees and tucked her toes underneath her wrapper. It was an expensive, opulent garment in emerald green velvet, with collar and cuffs edged in a delicate gold braid. She wondered if her mother had bought it, or received it as a gift from one of her admirers.

She wondered, too, why she'd returned to London after her mother's death. Sidonie had told herself it was because George was here, and she had no one else. But after almost a year here, she was beginning to wonder. She felt as if she were seeking something; something frustratingly elusive. Closure, perhaps?

"You look like her in that robe," said Julia in a musing tone.

Just then, Thomas leapt into Sidonie's lap to purr. "Like Claire?" Sidonie dropped her gaze to the cat. "There, Julia, you are wrong. I am nothing like her."

Julia sipped at her wine. "No?" she asked softly. "She had a kind heart and a generous spirit. As do you, hmm?"

Sidonie was silent for a moment. "Some might say her spirit was rather too generous," she finally answered.

Julia looked suddenly angry. "She was no whore, Sidonie," she retorted. "Is that what you're thinking? Is it? Then don't say it in front of me, girl. Perhaps she wasn't perfect, but she was never a bad person."

"No, Julia." Sidonie shook her head. She wasn't saying that. But what was she saying? What had her mother been? Good Lord, *who* had her mother been? She did not know. Even after all these years, she did not know. And now Claire had taken her secrets to the grave.

"Perhaps she was just a foolish girl who let herself be taken advantage of," Sidonie finally whispered.

"Oh, to be sure." Julia leaned intently forward in her chair and shook her finger at Sidonie. "But only once,

Sidonie. Only once. After that, she did what she had to do. She got sharp. After all, she had your brother to think about, didn't she?"

"I don't know." Sidonie's voice was hollow. "Sometimes I think I never really knew her."

"Well, I did," Julia answered sharply. "And there she was, a babe in her belly, and no way to feed it. Who'll hire a French governess who's been diddled by her last employer? No one, that's who. And if you think for one minute her fine, fancy family would have taken her back in, you can think again. A daughter six months gone with child and no husband to show for it? Ha!"

Sidonie shrugged. "True enough," she agreed. "They didn't even want me, their own grandchild. They took me straight from the ferry to the convent door. I suppose I was . . . evidence. The proof incarnate of my mother's immoral life."

Julia sipped slowly at her glass. "Ah, Sidonie, life can be a bad business," she finally said. "Claire wasn't like me, you know. I was born sharp. But she was . . . victimized, I suppose. By Gravenel. He saw her, he wanted her, and he decided she was his for the taking."

Sidonie sipped pensively at her wine for many minutes. She had heard this story long ago—from George, as it happened. "Julia," she finally said. "What happened to him? Do you know?"

"What, to your father?" Julia looked surprised. "Gravenel died not long after your mother sent you away to France."

"I know that," said Sidonie. "But what *happened*? I was never told."

Julia just shrugged. "Well, they did say it was

apoplexy," she answered. "But I think the bitterness choked him. He died all alone in that great, empty country house of his. Stoneleigh, it was called. More like a stone tomb if you ask me."

"He . . . he had no one?"

Again, Julia lifted one shoulder. "Well, your mother had grown tired of him by then," she said. "Or tired of his excuses and lies. His new bride had run away with her Italian banker. Your mother had sent you off to France. And George—why, no one even knew what had become of George. He had just melted into the streets."

"And his . . . other daughter?" His legitimate daughter, she meant. But Sidonie could not bring herself to say it.

Julia looked deep into her wineglass. "Married and went off to India," she answered. "Then died there. But I don't think that troubled Gravenel. 'Twas a son he wanted."

"He had a son," Sidonie whispered. "He had George."

Julia lifted her gaze, her face softening. "I'm sorry, my dear," she said. "I meant he wanted . . . well, someone who could inherit the dukedom."

"Someone legitimate, you mean."

"Yes, someone legitimate," she agreed. "That, I daresay, is why he took the second wife."

Sidonie shook her head. "Mother said he'd promised to marry *her,*" she answered, ashamed of how soft and girlish her voice suddenly sounded. "I must have heard them quarrel about it a dozen times. Mother would cry and scream and throw things at Father. She kept saying he'd sworn that when his wife died, they would wed."

"And I believe her," agreed Julia. "But the duchess

clung to life. That one wasn't about to make things easy on Claire."

"But Father promised her," said Sidonie. "And he promised to make things right for George. Instead, he ruined his life."

Julia set her glass down and made a sound of sympathy in her throat. "There's no making things right here, Sidonie," she answered. "I don't care what manner of lies Gravenel told Claire. Illegitimate sons don't inherit dukedoms in England. It can't be done. And your mother knew why he wouldn't marry her."

"Because she was his mistress," Sidonie whispered. "He was ashamed of her. He was ashamed of *us*."

Julia leaned across the distance and took Sidonie's hand in hers. "In part, perhaps." she said softly. "English noblemen rarely marry their mistresses."

Sidonie looked at her. "Was there some other reason?"

Julia gave a wintry smile. "My dear, by the time the duchess finally died of her consumption, your mother was past thirty," she said. "She had given Gravenel her best years—a decade, give or take—yet at the time, she'd borne him but the one child."

"Julia, what are you saying?"

Julia hesitated, her expression pained. "Claire couldn't carry children well," she answered. "There were three between you and your brother, but they came to naught early. Some women are just cursed that way. It was a miracle George was born, let alone you."

Sidonie felt her face fall. "And by the time I came along, she and Father were falling apart."

Slowly, Julia lifted her shoulders. "Claire never got

over his taking a young debutante to wife," she admitted. "She had other wealthy admirers vying for her favors, and he dallied with other women frequently. But you knew that."

"I heard the quarrels, yes," said Sidonie.

"And eventually, it all fell apart, didn't it?" mused Julia. "Claire began to take younger lovers. It cheered her up, I think. Soon, Gravenel's new bride was in Italy, and the duke was left with nothing. No wife. No heir. No mistress. George had run away. You were little more than a babe. But I never felt sorry for him. He reaped what he sowed."

Sidonie stroked her hand down Thomas's length and exhaled deeply. The exhilaration she'd felt while fleecing Lord Devellyn was fast fading. Real life—her old life—was intruding again. She longed to return to the streets to lose herself in another quixotic quest for vengeance. But vengeance for whom? For what?

"Oh, Julia, it's all so sad," she said. "Sometimes I wonder why I came back. Perhaps I should have stayed in France."

"Eventually, Sidonie, we all yearn for home." Julia smiled, then slowly, she rose from her chair. Her eyes, Sidonie noticed, were beginning to tell her age. It was best, she supposed, that Claire had died young. She had been too vain to endure the indignities of old age with any measure of grace.

Julia rested a hand on Sidonie's shoulder. "You look lovely in that robe, my dear," she said again. "Claire had slippers to match, I recall. When we clean out the attic Wednesday, we'll poke about in her old trunks, eh? We will remember the good times."

"All right, Julia." Sidonie tried to feign enthusiasm. "That sounds pleasant."

But it didn't, really. Sidonie had no wish to think about her mother, her father, or even herself. Instead she found herself thinking about the Marquess of Devellyn. About the cold, flat look in his eyes, and the hard turn of his jaw. About the breadth of his shoulders and the size of his . . . of his ego. Then there was that smile; that half-crooked, totally self-effacing smile he flashed rarely, but which made him seem boyish and uncertain. Sidonie had only glimpsed it, but it had struck her as both incongruous and genuine. She didn't know what to make of it.

"Oh, before I go," murmured Julia absently. "Miss Leslie sent a note canceling piano tomorrow. She's taken that sore throat which is going round."

"How dreadful," she said. "Was there anything else?"

"Actually, there was." Julia fumbled in her pocket, and handed Sidonie a note. "The crossing sweep brought it."

Sidonie knew at once what it was. As usual, the envelope bore no name or direction, merely a seal. A griffin couchant, pressed into black wax. "Jean-Claude," she said quietly.

"I daresay," said Julia softly. "Good night, my dear." The door clicked softly shut.

As if it were a signal, Thomas bounded to the floor. Thus completely abandoned, Sidonie read her note and hurled it into the fire, destroying the evidence. Then she put out her candles and pulled a chair to the window. And there she remained, until dawn began to light the sky, simply staring through the gaslit gloom at the house across the street and, strangely, thinking about her mother.

The Marquess of Devellyn had been pelted with a great many slurs in his long and dissolute thirty-six years, and at least half of them were deserved. Inebriate, idiot, cad, coxcomb, rakehell, rounder, and rotter were amongst the ten most popular—the other three had momentarily escaped him thanks to a near-mortal morning-after headache—but no matter how drunk or dissipated he became, there were two invectives he always took pains to avoid: *cheat* and *coward*.

Today it was the latter which most concerned him. And so Devellyn put on his tall beaver hat, picked up his gold-knobbed stick, and forced himself to step out his front door and set off down Duke Street in the direction of Piccadilly just as a distant clock struck noon. There was no evading what he had to face now, so he might as well have done with it at the earliest possible opportunity.

It was a cool but bright morning in Mayfair; a little too bright, really, for the sunlight was making his pounding head worse. Fortunately, the walk was but a short one. Unfortunately, he had not even reached the steps of his club before the first round of applause broke out, sharp and clear in the crisp spring air. Devellyn looked up to see a trio of young bucks literally hanging out the bay window of White's, clapping and hooting like a cell full of bedlamites.

Wondering whether he ought to simply call one of them out and shoot him for sport, Devellyn cut the three a look of warning, a malicious black snarl which had left many a man shaking in his shoes. The hooting stopped.

Their color drained. The young men drew back through the window, their eyes averted, their voices lowered.

Devellyn soldiered on up the short flight of stairs, forced himself to push open the front door, then somehow managed a gracious smile for the porter who hastened to take his coat. Despite the hushed tones still ensuing from the morning room, the porter kept a straight face and bowed respectfully as Devellyn passed through to the drawing room.

Tales of the Black Angel's exploits had been providing grist for the *ton*'s gossip mill for months now. So it had been too much to hope, of course, that Sir Alasdair MacLachlan, raconteur extraordinaire, could have kept his mouth shut about last night. But Devellyn really had hoped he wouldn't draw quite so large a crowd. That hope was crushed the instant he stepped into the room. Alasdair already stood before the hearth, one boot set on the fender and one elbow propped on the mantelpiece, enthusiastically regaling what looked like half the membership.

"And by then, everyone in the taproom could hear Dev roaring!" Alasdair waved one hand theatrically. "Why, he was bellowing for the innkeeper, and demanding we break the blasted door down, and shouting some other wild nonsense about a red-haired doxy with a tattoo on her breast."

Mortification swept over Devellyn again. Damn it, he should have sworn Alasdair to silence. Then and there, the marquess renewed tenfold his vow to find the Black Angel and make her life a living hell. Assuredly, he was living one.

Alasdair—who now had tears running down his

face—was gesticulating wildly as he recounted the rest of the misadventure. "Finally, Quin Hewitt and I knocked the door off its hinges, and I swear on my life, gentleman, that the old boy was buck-arsed naked with one wrist still tied to the bed when we burst in," he recounted as the crowd roared. "And bellowing like a bull with his horns hung in a hedgerow. I tell you, it was a frightful vision indeed."

"Tell 'em about the window, MacLachlan!" shouted a young blade near the front.

Half-hidden behind a column, Devellyn watched Alasdair clutch his belly and laugh. "Well, he'd already ripped one wrist loose, and wh-when Quin f-f-finally got the other, he went—he went—oh, Lord!—he went straight for the bloody windowsill!" Alasdair was fighting off spurts of laughter now. "Crawled half out the window wearing nary a stitch. Took two of us to drag him out again! And Dev was kicking us, and throwing punches, and hollering that he meant to follow her out and throttle her! And I said to him, 'Dev, Dev, old chap! That's a fifteen-foot drop!'"

"And then *he* said—" interjected Devellyn loudly as he strode into the room, "'—stand back, Alasdair, you fool, or I'll throttle you, too.' And I shall yet do it, old boy, if you don't sit down and shut the hell up."

Alasdair's mouth fell open. His audience turned to gape. Then, like a flock of startled crows, the gentlemen burst into flight, most of them scurrying from the room. A few coughed, rattled their newspapers, and looked away. Alasdair and a couple of braver souls approached Devellyn to pound him heartily on the back and offer varying degrees of sympathy.

It was all Devellyn could do not to wince when Lord Francis Tenby tried to drape one arm over his shoulder. But Tenby was a full foot shorter, and Devellyn had no interest in empathy, camaraderie, or anything else from a spoilt, overbred fop, so he stepped away.

Tenby didn't take the hint. "Dashed sorry, Dev, that you got rooked by that bitch," he said. "That makes almost a dozen of us she's humiliated, and for my part, I mean to make her pay."

The crowd was falling away now. Devellyn stared down his crooked nose at Tenby. "Oh?" he said. "And just how do you mean to do that?"

Tenby's mouth turned up into a sour smile. "Some of us have got together and set a Runner on our Black Angel," he answered. "And when he catches her, he's bringing her to *us.*"

Devellyn grunted in disdain. "He'll have to beat me to her."

Tenby's smile tightened. "Nonetheless, old chap, send me a description of what was stolen," he suggested. "Our man has connections—pawnbrokers, fences, and such. One never knows what he'll turn up."

Devellyn considered it. "Perhaps I shall," he said.

Alasdair elbowed Tenby out of his way. "Brave of you, Dev, to turn up so soon," he remarked, setting a hand on his shoulder. "Never knew you to crawl out of bed at such an hour."

Devellyn glowered at him. "By God, I'll not be called a coward, Alasdair," he snapped. "And I've not yet seen my bed. I'm too bloody infuriated to sleep."

Alasdair dragged him toward the coffee room. "Come along, Dev," he said. "What you need now is a cup of bilgewater down the gullet. And after you've had it, you can call me out if you're still of a mind to shoot me."

"Believe it or not, Alasdair, you are the very least of my plagues just now," Devellyn answered.

They sat down in the nearly empty coffee room, and Alasdair sent a waiter scurrying off. "All right, Dev," he said, turning back to his friend. "What's wrong?"

Devellyn looked at him in mute amazement. "Wrong?" he finally muttered. "You dare ask?"

Alasdair narrowed his eyes. "Well, you looked merely infuriated last night when we untied you," he said. "But now you look . . . I don't know."

"Dyspeptic?" supplied Devellyn. "That's because I am. But I'm sober, right enough."

"And?"

Impatiently, Devellyn began to tap one finger on the table. "And now I realize what's been lost," he finally said. "Moreover, it is *not* a matter for public discussion, Alasdair, or I swear to God, I'll gut you from neck to knackers with a rusty letter opener."

Alasdair nodded effusively. "Wouldn't dare mention it, old boy."

Devellyn kept tapping his finger, faster now. "The Black Angel took my watch, my snuffbox, and every sou in my pocket," he said grimly. "But she took something far more valuable than that, Alasdair. Something irreplaceable."

Alasdair's eyes widened. "Good Lord, what?"

Devellyn felt like a fool. "A miniature of Gregory," he finally admitted. "And . . . well, and a lock of his hair. I carry it, you see, in my pocket sometimes."

Sometimes! he thought. *All the time. Every bloody second of my life. Just like I carry the guilt that goes with it.*

Alasdair was looking at him strangely. "Why, Dev?"

Devellyn was immediately on the defensive. "Damn it, I don't know why. I just do sometimes, that's all."

Alasdair shrugged. "Well," he said pragmatically. "A chap doesn't need a reason. Perfectly natural thing, your dead brother and all."

"It was the only likeness I had of him," growled Devellyn at the tablecloth. "And now that bitch the Black Angel has it. And for what, I ask you? For *what?* Why ever would she want such a thing? Of what use can it possibly be to her?"

Alasdair shrugged. The coffee came. "Dashed sorry, Dev," he said again as he slid one cup in Devellyn's direction. "But she's been at it for months, and no one knows who or what she is. No one can catch her."

The marquess eyed his friend over his steaming coffee cup. "Oh, you think not, eh?"

Two days after her rash encounter with the Marquess of Devellyn, Jean-Claude met with Sidonie. This was always done by prior arrangement, and they varied the time and the location. Often, Sidonie concealed her appearance, but today they were meeting at the British Museum, but a few blocks from her home. It was an innocent enough place for either of them to be seen, and not apt to be frequented by the sort of gentlemen the Black Angel targeted.

They had taken a table by a window in a little-used corner of the reading room and piled both sides with books they'd no intention of opening. While Sidonie kept one eye on the passageway between the shelves to ensure that no one approached, her brother's assistant slipped a jeweler's loupe into his right eye and began an assiduous study of Lord Francis's sapphire pin.

"Ah, Madame Saint-Godard!" whispered Jean-Claude. "Thees eez a very fine piece, indeed. Better, even, than the diamond pin you bring last month! In Paris, thees will fetch a fat price on the—the—how you say *au marché noir?*"

"On the black market."

Jean-Claude smiled. *"Oui,* the black market," he echoed. "The watch, I will also take. And the snuffbox! Eet eez very excellent indeed."

Sidonie looked across the table at Lord Francis's snuffbox. "I'm afraid, Jean-Claude, that it is only silver," she answered.

He gave a Gallic shrug. *"Oui,* but chased inside with gold," he said. "And the engraving! *Très élégant.*"

"Yes, well, get what you can for it," Sidonie instructed. "Lord Francis's parlor maid needs money desperately."

"I will do my best for *madame,*" he assured her. "There eez a shipment en route through Calais in two days' time."

Sidonie felt panic surge. "Jean-Claude, remember you mustn't involve George," she insisted, not for the first time. "If we get caught fencing this, his name cannot be mentioned."

Jean-Claude lost a little of his color. *"Mais non, madame!"* he said, slipping the glass from his eye. "Monsieur Kemble, he would cut off my—my *testicules,* no? Then choke me on them."

Sidonie winced at the vivid, but not inaccurate, suggestion.

"Now, what else have you there, eh?" He looked across the table a little greedily.

Sidonie thought of the solid gold snuffbox in her reticule and decided against it. She looked at Jean-Claude and shook her head. "No, the rest of it I shan't give you," she answered. "It is too risky."

The young man's expression was wounded. "What eez thees?" he asked. "*Madame* does not trust Jean-Claude? We have done beezness together for all of one year, and now you say——"

She cut him off by laying her hand over his. "I trust you, Jean-Claude," she said. "But I've also grown fond of you. These other things, they are simply too dangerous to sell, even in Paris. They are very fine, yes. But too easily identified. And they belong to a dangerous man. Should you be caught, you would almost certainly be hanged, and for that I would never forgive myself."

He wrestled with himself for a moment. "*Très bien,*" he finally said. "But just give Jean-Claude a leetle peek, *oui?* I wish to see theez so very fine things I cannot have."

Sidonie cast a judicious gaze about the empty room, then pulled the first from her reticule, enfolded in a plain white handkerchief. Jean-Claude unwrapped the snuffbox first, glanced at the lid, and blanched. "*Oui, madame,* thees one I think you may keep," he murmured, swiftly rewrapping it. "I recognize too well the leetle alphabeets—not to mention the crest."

The "alphabeets" were the letters *A—E—C—H* etched deep into the gold in a small, old-fashioned script. Sidonie wondered what they stood for, and opened her mouth to ask Jean-Claude. Then on her next breath, she chastised herself for caring and shoved the box back into her reticule. *Devellyn* was all she needed to know. His Christian name needn't concern her.

"What else have you there?" asked Jean-Claude.

Sidonie shrugged. "Another gold watch," she said, then hesitated. But curiosity got the best of her and she dug into her bag again, instead pulling out a smaller bundle. "And this," she said, passing it across the table.

Jean-Claude lifted one brow. *"Qu'est-ce que c'est?"*

"I haven't a clue," she admitted. "It is like a very thin pillbox, or some sort of square locket. I see a tiny hinge, but I cannot open it."

"Very interesting," said Jean-Claude, unfolding the fabric. "Ah! Thees eez a very rare thing, *madame.*"

"Is it?" Sidonie asked.

"Watch, and I show." Jean-Claude pulled a tiny tool from his coat pocket and worked it very gently between the lips of the mysterious trinket. It popped apart like a little gold book. "The latch, eet was stuck," he murmured, turning it so that she might look at it. "A petite treasure, *n'est-ce pas?*"

Stunned, Sidonie nodded. The thing really was something like a large locket. On one side was a gilt-framed miniature of a young man in the high collar and elaborate cravat of the Regency period. On the opposite side, under a tiny pane of glass, was a curl of dark hair.

Ma foi!" whispered Jean-Claude, obviously intrigued. "Exquisite! This comes from the Devil of Duke Street?"

Sidonie was still trying to make sense of it all. "Yes," she finally said. "From Devellyn." She peered more closely at the handsome young man. "What do you make of this fellow?"

Jean-Claude made a very French face and opened his empty hand expressively. "Eet eez his lover," he said. "What else?"

Given her recent experience with Devellyn, Sidonie had trouble believing that. "Or his father, perhaps?" she ventured.

But she knew at once she was wrong. The portrait was too recent. Jean-Claude gave a dismissive toss of his hand. "The Devil, he eez estrange from all his family," he said airily. "Everyone says that eez true. So the pretty boy, he must be a lover, no?"

"No." Sidonie frowned. "No, I don't think so."

Jean-Claude shrugged and snapped the miniature shut. "I can melt it down," he suggested, carefully rewrapping it in the cloth. "Only the gold has value, for the leetle portrait, it is too easily identified and cannot come out without making ruin."

Sidonie took back the bundle. "No, I cannot do that."

Jean-Claude shot her a look of warning. "Eet eez very dangerous, *madame,* to keep such a thing."

Sidonie tried to smile. "I know," she said. "Let me think on it. I shall be careful."

Their business concluded, Sidonie stood. "Go now, before George begins to wonder what's become of you. I'll have more trinkets in a fortnight or so."

Jean-Claude's eyes widened. "Ah, I almost forget, no?" he said, digging into his pocket. "For last month's shipment." He pressed a roll of banknotes into her hand.

"Oh, thank you, Jean-Claude." Sidonie squeezed the money gratefully.

He watched her in faint amusement. "What good deeds will your friend *l'ange* do weeth that, I wonder?"

Sidonie smiled and tucked the banknotes into her reticule with Lord Devellyn's baubles. "She will advance a generous sum to Lord Francis's parlor maid," she answered. "Whatever is left, the Angel will most likely deliver to Lady Kirton at the Nazareth Society."

Jean-Claude extended his hand. "Then I wish her well," he said, pretending he did not know perfectly well who was perpetrating the thefts.

Sidonie took his hand and squeezed it. "She sends you her gratitude."

Jean-Claude tightened his grip on her fingers and leaned very near. "*Merci, madame,* but also, I pass a leetle word of warning to her?" he whispered, his voice suddenly grave. "Her works are good, but the Marquess of Devellyn, he eez not one to be trifled with. You will tell her this, *oui?* She must choose her victims with more care."

Sidonie swallowed hard, and looked Jean-Claude straight in the eyes. "She made a mistake, perhaps," she admitted. "I shall warn her."

"*Oui, madame,* you do that."

Sidonie smiled wryly. "Trust me, Jean-Claude, she will take care never to see Lord Devellyn again."

Then, with a wintry smile and an elegant bow, the young man kissed her knuckles and took his leave.

Sidonie watched Jean-Claude go, a faint frisson of anxiety chasing up her spine. She forced herself to wait ten minutes, then gathered her wits and hastened out after him. Thank heaven she lived but a block away, for in ten minutes' time, Miss Hannaday would arrive in Bedford Place for her lesson.

Today she and Miss Hannaday were to review the order of precedence for nobility, then learn how to prepare a seating plan for a formal dinner. Such lessons were a good arrangement for both of them, since Sidonie needed the money, and poor Miss Hannaday needed to grasp all of society's nuances if she meant to marry Lord Bodley.

To Sidonie, such social skills had come almost as second nature. Her mother had been that most rare of creatures; a beautiful, well-bred courtesan with an impeccable lineage and a natural grace. Sidonie's grandparents had been minor nobility cast on hard times after the French Revolution. They had raised their only daughter in genteel poverty, educated her in the convent school, and shipped her across the Channel in the hope that her charm and beauty would catch the eye of some wealthy Englishman.

The plan had worked, so far as it went. Claire Bauchet caught the eye of the paunchy, middle-aged Duke of Gravenel, whose daughter she was tutoring in French. But Gravenel was no Prince Charming, and their relationship was no fairy tale. He impregnated his young French teacher, then stood idly by as his wife tossed her into the street. Then, and only then, did Gravenel make Claire an offer. She could be his mistress. Or she could starve. The choice was entirely hers.

Claire was not the sort of woman who starved.

As mistress to the wealthy Gravenel, Claire Bauchet eventually became famous for her lavish entertainments and elegant dinner parties. She began to enjoy her power and turn the heads of men younger and more powerful than her protector. Many of England's most influential noblemen dined at Madame Bauchet's table, including the Prince Regent himself. But England's noble*women,* that was another thing altogether. Ladies of the *ton* did not "know" women like Claire, despite the fact that she and her two children lived in Mayfair's exclusive Clarges Street, not a stone's throw from the Duke of Clarence's mistress and their vast brood.

Sidonie and George hardly constituted a brood, but they had still garnered plenty of stares and whispers. She had been little more than a toddler when George had finally taken her aside and explained to her how the world worked, and why their father did not live with them. For Sidonie, it had been a true loss of innocence.

She surely did not wish a loss of innocence on Miss Hannaday, but with a fiend like Bodley, that was just what the poor child was apt to get. Perhaps something ought to be done? Something more drastic than simply finding Miss Hannaday's beloved clerk a job? Lost in such musings, Sidonie hastened round the corner into Bedford Place, barely watching where she was going. As usual, two or three carriages were parked along the street. Foolishly, she did not pay attention to them, not even the nearest one, which sat almost opposite her house. Indeed, she was almost at a run when she passed by it.

Suddenly, something dark and hard slammed into her forehead. Sidonie hit the pavement like a sack of mortar, literally seeing stars. Next she knew, someone was kneeling beside her and trying to help her to her feet. "Good God, I did not see you!" the man exclaimed, sliding a hand beneath her shoulders. "Are you hurt? Can you stand?"

The stars finally winked themselves away, and gingerly, Sidonie sat up, touched her forehead, and groaned. She was slowly becoming aware of the pavement, cool and faintly damp beneath her hips, and the warm smell of cologne from above. "Wha—What happened?" she managed as the man lifted her to her feet almost effortlessly.

"I am so sorry," said the man. "I believe I hit you in the head with my carriage door."

Sidonie tried to focus on his face. "You *hit* me?"

"Miss, I did not see you," he protested. "You darted out of nowhere. Did you not see my carriage was pulling to the curb?"

"No, I—I didn't realize . . ."

Behind her, Sidonie heard his coachman leap down. "Is the lady all right, my lord?"

"Just a nasty bump, Wittle," the man reassured him. "Go tell Fenton to wrap up some ice. I shall carry the lady inside."

Still dazed, Sidonie let the man get his arm almost beneath her knees before pushing him away. "I am fine, sir," she said, one hand still pressed to her throbbing lump. "Really, I am."

"Really, you are?" he echoed skeptically. "Then tell me, miss, how many fingers am I holding up?"

Out of sheer stubbornness, Sidonie forced her eyes to focus, and she had to look up—far, far up—to do so. And then it was certainly not his fingers which caught her eye. Instead, it felt as if something slammed unexpectedly into the backs of her knees, and she'd sagged halfway to the pavement again when Lord Devellyn caught her.

This time, he scooped her up effortlessly and headed for his front door. "I thought as much," he murmured, swishing her skirts gracefully through the entryway. "Honeywell, shut the door and draw the drapes. I believe she's got a mild concussion."

Sidonie was settled onto a velvet divan in a dark, richly colored drawing room and tried at once to sit up. She really did not want Lord Devellyn touching her. But the man set a strong, warm hand on her shoulder. "Really, miss, I must insist," he said, kneeling as if to better examine her. "Fenton!" he shouted over his shoulder. "Fenton! Is there a physician in this part of town?"

She realized vaguely that the house was in some sort of uproar, with servants hastening to and fro carrying all manner of crates and boxes. Each of them paused to stare at her. Sidonie pushed his warm, heavy hand from her shoulder. "Thank you," she said. "I must go. Across the . . . the street."

"Across the street?"

"My house. I have an appointment."

Sidonie was growing desperate. In her weakened, woozy state, she was about to drown in the warm, all-too-familiar scent of the marquess's cologne. She had already spent far too much time in Devellyn's company. Worse, she was now laid across his divan, her reticule stuffed nigh to bursting with his personal effects. Thank God she'd not been knocked cold, else he'd likely be searching through it for some sort of identification.

Devellyn was still casting his eyes over her face, as if searching for something. A moment of panic struck. Good God, surely he couldn't recognize her? "Is there someone we should send for, miss?" he finally asked. "Your . . . husband? Your father?"

Her father? The notion almost made Sidonie laugh.

"I am widowed," she said as tartly as she could. "And now, if you will permit me, I wish to get up."

Suddenly, a dark-sleeved arm thrust over her. "Ice, my lord," said a servant. "Is some hartshorn in order? Or perhaps the lady has a vinaigrette in her reticule?"

"No!" Sidonie clutched her bag to her chest, pushed Devellyn away, and jerked to her feet. "I mean, I really am quite well. Thank you. I wish to go now."

The marquess had indeed stepped back this time. "Very well," he said calmly. "I will see you safely across the street."

"I can cross the street by myself, thank you."

His voice took on an ominous chill. "By all means, then," he said. "But allow me to introduce myself before you go. I am—"

"I know who you are," snapped Sidonie. "Thank you. I must go."

Devellyn shifted his weight, very subtly blocking her path. Good Lord, he was big. Bigger, even, than she remembered, and, damn it all, devilishly—no, *rakishly*—handsome. His jaw might have been chiseled from stone, his mouth was sinfully lush, and his slightly crooked nose merely served to make him look dashingly dangerous. Good God, life was not fair!

The sinfully lush lips had drawn taut now. "And am I to have your name, ma'am?" Lord Devellyn asked, his voice excruciatingly polite. "I should like the pleasure of knowing to whom I should address my letter of apology."

"You have already apologized, my lord," said Sidonie. "I am Madame Saint-Godard. Number Fourteen. No letter is necessary."

"You are French." It was not a question. "But you've little accent."

"Yes," she said tightly. "Now I bid you good day."

Somehow, Sidonie managed to stiffen her spine and escape. Outside, the light was indeed too bright. She squinted her eyes against the sun and immediately felt someone catch her elbow. She spun about, intent on slapping Lord Devellyn through the face for his persistence, but her hand stilled at once.

"Madame Saint-Godard?" Miss Hannaday's gaze searched her face. "Are you perfectly all right? This is not, you know, your side of the street."

Sidonie felt a strange sense of disappointment. "Indeed, it is not," she answered, taking the girl's arm to steady herself. "Will you help me across, Miss Hannaday? I fear I've had a slight accident."

Miss Hannaday's maid followed. Julia met them at the door, her face going pale at once. "Oh, Lord, what's happened now?" she squawked. "The two of you look like you've been in a street brawl."

It was only then that Sidonie truly looked at Miss Hannaday. In profile, it had not been noticeable, but now she saw that the girl's face was faintly bruised below her left temple. Unbidden, she reached up to touch it, and the girl shrank back. "A door," she said. "I—I walked into a door."

Sidonie knew it at once for a lie. "What a strange coincidence," she murmured. "So did I."

Devellyn watched through the drawing room window as his lovely new neighbor gingerly crossed the street. She now seemed perfectly willing—no, eager—to lean upon her young friend's arm. Almost as eager as she had been in rejecting Devellyn's.

She knew who he was.

But her every gesture had made it plain she'd no wish to know *him*. Devellyn watched her now, swishing the skirts of her dark amethyst gown over her front doorstep. He was not at all sure what to make of her. Certainly she was lovely, with her warm olive skin and remarkable eyes; warm, wide eyes the color of expensive cognac. Her hair looked long and heavy, and, like his soul, just a shade away from pitch-black.

Madame Saint-Godard exuded Continental sophistication and, despite her injury, moved with regal grace. She was also one of those rare women who gave the appearance of being tall, when she was really nothing of the sort. Her average stature became apparent in relation to her own front door—and to her companion, a short, pleasantly plump lady who had flung open the door to greet *madame* and her friend. But suddenly, the front door shut, and the women disappeared from his view.

Well, that was that, wasn't it? In all probability, they would never see one another again. His temporary residence aside, he and his new neighbors moved in vastly different social circles. Moreover, his wicked reputation had almost certainly preceded him. He'd kept better than a dozen mistresses in this house since buying it, most of them leaving in tears, a hail of china, or a drunken brawl. Camelia had more or less managed all three. No, it was not likely the good citizens of Bedford Place, with their bourgeois sensibilities, would be leaving a great many cards for the notorious Devil of Duke Street. And thank God for it.

Regrettably, however, that did make it almost certain Madame Saint-Godard would not be warming his sheets anywhere this side of hell—not that he'd suffered much doubt on that score. Still, he would have liked very much to bed her, he realized. Something in her flashing eyes stirred his blood. But bedding a woman like that would have required an awful lot of effort. It would have required him to make himself pleasant and presentable. Perhaps, even, to *court* her. Devellyn did not court women. He paid them.

"My lord?" Honeywell's voice cut into his consciousness, and Devellyn realized he was still staring at Madame Saint-Godard's door. "My lord, will you be going out for the evening? Wittle wishes to know what to do with the carriage."

Devellyn felt oddly embarrassed, like a schoolboy caught groping one of the chambermaids. "Just tell him to take it round to the mews," he said gruffly. "If I go out, I shall walk."

In Number Fourteen Bedford Place, Julia was smiling brightly at Miss Hannaday's maid and obviously wondering what in God's name had happened to Sidonie's head. "Mrs. Tuttle is taking a tart from the oven," she said. "You would be welcome to go downstairs and have a slice."

The maid shot an expectant look at her mistress, and Miss Hannaday nodded. The maid was gone in a flash. Julia urged them both into the parlor. "You'll be wanting some ice, Sidonie," she said in her no-nonsense voice. "And tea for Miss Hannaday."

"Thank you, yes," Sidonie agreed.

Julia shot Sidonie a veiled look and left, closing the door behind. Sidonie took Miss Hannaday's arm, and led her toward the table beneath the front window. "My dear girl," she said when they were seated. "Let me be blunt. I do not for one moment believe you were struck by a door."

Miss Hannaday made a sound; a short, strangled sob. Sidonie stared out the window and down the street at Lord Devellyn's carriage, which was rolling away. "Was it your father, Amy?" she asked. "Did you quarrel with him again?"

"No!" Miss Hannaday shook her head, sending her golden ringlets bouncing. "Oh, no, indeed, ma'am! You mustn't think it!"

Sidonie turned to look at her. "No woman inflicted that blow, I'll warrant."

Miss Hannaday looked away.

Sidonie laid her hand on the girl's arm. "Was it Lord Bodley, Amy?" she asked. "Was it? I want you to tell me."

Miss Hannaday bit her lip. "We quarreled," she finally answered. "He is always out of sorts with me of late. I grew tired of it, and said to him that if he would speak to Papa first, that I would be glad to cry off the engagement and relieve him of his obligation."

Sidonie's mouth fell open. "And for that, he hit you?"

The sob came again. "I think he imagined I was finding fault with him," she whispered. "So I told him . . . I told him that in truth, I had feelings for another, and that indeed, I should prefer to marry elsewhere. And that is when . . . is when . . ." A tear leaked from one corner of the girl's eye. "He needs Papa's money, you know," she resumed, her voice cold and flat. "He no longer even pretends to feel affection for me."

Sidonie stroked the back of her hand over Miss Hannaday's cheek. "What did your father say? Did he not hear the quarrel?"

"Bodley told Papa that I was impudent," she answered, tears falling freely now. "And at first, the bruise was not apparent. B-B-But Papa wants a title for the family so desperately, I don't think he will care when he *does* see it. After all, he knows I love Charles, but is perfectly willing to have me suffer a broken heart. What is a bruise to that, Madame Saint-Godard?"

"Very little," said Sidonie. Her head ached, and she hoped she was thinking clearly. She grasped Miss Hannaday's hand. "Amy, do you still wish to marry Charles Greer? Even if it means being poor?"

The girl stared at their joined hands. "I *was* poor not so very long ago," she answered sorrowfully. "Now, because of Papa's tea business, we are richer, yes. But we are none of us happier. Still, Charles says Papa will dismiss him without a character, and he won't be able to support me as he should wish."

On impulse, Sidonie seized her reticule, and drew out the wad of banknotes Jean-Claude had given her. She peeled off fifty pounds and pressed it into the girl's hand. "It is a loan," she instructed, squeezing the girl's fingers around the money. "Take it, Amy. *Hide* it. Now, can you get a message to Charles?"

Miss Hannaday nodded, her eyes wide and tearful.

"Good," said Sidonie. "Tell him to meet me tonight in Russell Square. I wish to speak with him. Does he know the statue of Lord Bedford which stands there?"

"Yes," whispered the girl. "Yes, he must."

"Tell him to wait there at midnight, or perhaps half past," said Sidonie. "I must escort Miss Arbuckle to a musicale, but I will be there as soon as possible. Tell him that, all right?"

She nodded with alacrity. "Yes, I shall tell him."

Sidonie looked her in the eyes. "And Amy, if you have any jewelry you're willing to sell for ready money, bring it to me. I can get you a good price, and you and Charles will need every penny."

Hope was beginning to light Miss Hannaday's face. Just then, Julia returned, followed by their only house-maid, Meg, who carried the tea tray.

"Julia, I am afraid my head hurts rather more than I should wish," said Sidonie, rising from the table. "I've asked Miss Hannaday to excuse me from our lessons and return tomorrow."

Miss Hannaday was already gathering her things. Julia handed Sidonie a cloth filled with ice, then saw their guest out. She returned quickly, the suspicious look still on her face. "All right, out with it," she ordered. "And put that ice where it belongs, if you please."

Sidonie lay back on the sofa and set the ice to her forehead. "Oh, Julia, I've had the most damnable luck," she said weakly. "I walked straight into Lord Devellyn's carriage door."

"Oh, dear God." Julia sat down abruptly. "He recognized you?"

Sidonie turned her head. "Don't be silly. It was almost dark in the Anchor, and I was painted and padded to within an inch of my life."

But Julia looked shaken. "There'll be no avoiding him now, Sidonie."

"It is odd he's visiting in broad daylight," she admitted. "But surely it won't become habit?"

Julia shook her head. "Oh, he isn't visiting, my dear," she answered. "He's moving *in*. I sent Meg over to make cow-eyes at one of the footmen when I saw all the commotion. It seems his house in Duke Street is being repaired, and he's to be here a month or more."

"*A month or more?*"

Sidonie felt a strange, sudden rush of emotion. It should have been panic. Fear. A little dread, at the very least. But it wasn't, heaven help her. Instead, it was the thrill of the chase coming back to her again. That vibrant, exhilarating sense of walking along the edge of disaster. And something else, too. Anticipation? But what had she to anticipate from the Marquess of Devellyn?

"Sidonie!" said Julia in a warning tone. "Sidonie, whatever it is you're thinking, girl, stop it this instant!"

Chapter Five

Madame Saint-Godard and the Secret Assignation

As it happened, Lord Devellyn did not go out that evening. Instead, mired in some sort of dull lassitude, he took the almost unheard-of step of hanging about the house and hinting that he might take his dinner in. It made little sense to remain, he mused, drifting through his dark, overdecorated drawing room; a room which always put him in mind of an expensive brothel. He had no special attachment to this place, nor did he find it particularly soothing. He associated it instead with sex, revelry, and bacchanalia. All very fine indulgences, to be sure, but not what a man yearned for when he sought the comfort of his own home.

A part of him realized that this strange mood—this restless pacing and pondering which had so thoroughly consumed him of late—had little to do with his usual blue devils, though they visited him often enough. And it had even less to do with this house, or with Camelia's having left him. No, it had begun instead with that woman at the inn. The Black Angel, damn her eyes.

It was said the Black Angel was some sort of avenging Robin Hood. But whom—other than perhaps himself and Greg—had he ever wounded unjustly? Devellyn did not call men out for trifling offenses, or bankrupt young bucks for sport. Well, not unless they begged for it, which the bolder ones were wont to do. And as black as his reputation was, he'd ruined but one innocent—and in hindsight, he was not perfectly sure just how innocent she'd been. So far as experienced women went, he'd created some scandals, certainly. But he'd never known a woman worth fighting over, a lesson he'd learnt young.

But the Black Angel had targeted him nonetheless. And now, it was not so much the fact he'd been made a fool of. No, what really fed his fury was how quickly and how profoundly he'd succumbed to the charms of a slick, twopenny whore like Ruby Black. But she hadn't been a whore, had she? And she wasn't Ruby Black either, he'd wager.

Ruby. Damn her. How could a man both hate and hunger for such a creature—and on the same breath? Devellyn closed his eyes and drew the scent of brandy deep into his lungs, pondering it. Good God, he felt . . . he felt *cheated*.

That was it, wasn't it? He still felt cheated, deeply so, but not of his personal possessions. Save for Greg's portrait, he didn't give a damn. No, he felt cheated of what her mouth and her eyes had promised him. Her body. The taste of her lips on his. The warmth of her beneath him. The way it would feel to bury his body deep inside hers. Yes, even now, those thoughts stirred him, and left him aching. Which made him angry all the more.

While he brooded on it, Devellyn poured himself another brandy. Then, inexplicably, he carried the glass to the window and pulled back the drapes. He stood looking out into the night; looking, really, across the street at Number Fourteen. Just then a stylish carriage spun round from Great Russell Street, halting near Madame Saint-Godard's front door. The lady herself stepped out onto the gaslit pavement, wearing a feathered hat set rakishly to one side, and a dark, sweeping cloak over a gown which looked very elegant. She was assisted into the carriage by an equally elegant brace of footmen.

So *madame* was going out for the evening. He wondered who owned the carriage. Perhaps it was hers, but he doubted it. Few in Bedford Place could afford such a fine equipage. A relative, perhaps? But Madame Saint-Godard was French. A lover? Yes, more likely. She might be a widow, but she was not the sort of woman who would be left to languish. And that insight stirred another question. Just what was it about her that kept drawing him to the window, anyway? Something nagged at him. But what? *What?*

Suddenly, it struck him. *She reminded him of Ruby Black.* He let the drapery fall and considered it a moment. No, they were nothing at all alike. The hair, the voice, the shape of her face; nothing was the same. Ruby had been taller, loose-limbed, more voluptuous. Madame Saint-Godard was slight and elegant. But both women exuded a sort of innate sensuality—the kind that would drive a man mad if he wasn't careful.

Devellyn, however, had learnt long ago never to let lust overcome logic; never to want a woman badly enough to do something stupid. And yet Ruby Black had made him do both, hadn't she? And with damned little effort. No wonder he'd so little enthusiasm for another night of carousing.

Abruptly, he went to the bell and rang for the butler.

"What is the name, Honeywell, of our new footman?" he asked when the servant appeared. "The one who was supervising the unloading of the van this morning?"

"Polk, sir. Henry Polk."

"Well, Henry Polk has rather an eye for the ladies, I noticed," said Devellyn. "Fetch him up here, will you, after the plate is washed from dinner?"

Honeywell gave a slight bow. "Certainly, my lord," he murmured. "Do you still intend to dine in?"

Devellyn rolled his shoulders restlessly beneath his coat. "I believe I will, yes."

It was a choice, however, he was soon to regret. An hour later, he was but halfway through a prime cut of beef and a good bottle of Bordeaux when Honeywell came into the dining room, appearing rather more nervous than one might wish one's butler to look.

"Yes?" said Devellyn, setting his glass down with a sharp clink.

"My lord, a most unusual thing . . ."

"Yes?" Devellyn repeated, folding his napkin and setting it aside.

The butler made a wincing face. "I fear it is . . . well, *Her Grace,*" he whispered. "Were you expecting her?"

A difficult question. God only knew what assignation he might have agreed to, then promptly forgot. A short list of *her graces* was already running through his head. He didn't know many. There was the Duchess of Esteridge, but she had thrown him out of her bed twice already. Then there was Keeling's luscious wife, but she'd slapped his face last time he propositioned her. Perhaps it was that black-haired cousin of Alasdair's—her name escaped him, but her very fine bosom was forever fixed in his memory.

Really, a chap could hardly go wrong. A woman who came calling alone at night wanted only one thing. Already, Devellyn's cock was half-hard and twitching with expectation. Strategically, he repositioned the napkin. "Memory fails me, Honeywell," he admitted. "Which—"

But it was too late. Her Grace had not waited.

"Good evening, Aleric!" said his mother, striding purposefully into the room. "Don't even think of turning me away. Now, what, pray, is this nonsense about beetles having eaten your staircases?"

Devellyn's erection withered at once, a circumstance he appreciated, since courtesy required him to stand. "Good evening, Mother," he said, eyeing her suspiciously even as he kissed her hand. "What a pleasant surprise."

His mother was already surveying the room. "Oh, I daresay it is mostly the latter," she said airily.

"Frankly, I'm shocked you'd call on me here."

She shrugged her deceptively delicate shoulders. "What choice had I?" she answered. "I've this instant come from Duke Street, and was quite put out to find the place shut up. Oh—do carry on with your dinner, dear." Her gaze dropped to the table. "Lud, have they served everything at once? They seem to think they're feeding the threshing hands."

"I'm not a formal sort of fellow, Mother," he said, as

Honeywell seated her. "I did not know you were in town. Have you dined?"

His mother waved at the butler dismissively. "At Great-aunt Admeta's, yes," she said. "I came up from Stoneleigh just yesterday. Cousin Richard has died."

Devellyn returned to hacking at his beef. "Didn't know we had a Cousin Richard," he said. "Cut down in his prime, was he?"

His mother's gaze turned on him, incredulous. "Lord, Aleric, he was ninety-two!" she said. "Which you would know if you did your family duty." Then she paused to purse her lips. "I don't suppose you would attend the funeral tomorrow?"

Devellyn chewed slowly, buying time. She was a wily one, his mother. "Are you alone?"

His mother clasped her hands and stared at the candelabrum in the center of the table. "I am not," she finally said.

Devellyn resumed his hacking, a little violently now. "No. I cannot. You know I cannot."

His mother made a hissing sound. "I don't see why!" she retorted. "Cousin Richard is—or was—*my* relation, Aleric, not your father's."

"A technicality," said Devellyn. "And you know it."

For a long moment, the silence was broken by nothing but the sound of Devellyn's knife at work. "Aleric," she finally whispered. "He misses you."

Devellyn dropped his knife. "No, he doesn't," he answered. "And I should think that after the first decade passed, Mother, you'd have grasped that fact."

His mother's eyes were wide now, and shimmering

with what he hoped was candlelight. Suddenly, she was on her feet again, roaming restlessly through the dining room, pausing here and there to pick up bric-a-brac or candlesticks. God, she was a tough old bird.

"Checking the hallmarks?" he asked, forcing the humor back into his voice.

His mother shot him a dark look, then ran a judicious fingertip down the wall covering. "Really, Aleric!" she said, obviously herself again. "Purple flock-paper in one's dining room? Have you any idea how vulgar that is?"

He didn't, really. Camelia, or perhaps her predecessor, had chosen it. "I'm hopelessly unaware, ma'am," he said, forking up a succulent black truffle. "But if you find that vulgar, go up and have a gander at my pink-and-red bed-hangings."

His mother groaned. "Oh, Aleric! I've already seen your drawing room, and it looks like a cheap bordello."

He grinned across his plate at her. "Mother, my mistresses hold orgies here, not literary salons."

"Aleric!" The flock-paper and bed-hangings forgotten, she marched down the length of the table toward him. "You live to shock, do you not?"

"A man's got to work with whatever talent God gave him." Devellyn was picking through a mixed salad now, and wondering if there were any radishes in it. He liked bright, spicy things. Like Ruby Black.

His mother set her hands on her hips. "Could you stop poking at that pile of greenery for just one moment, Aleric, and try to carry on an intelligent conversation?"

Devellyn looked up from his salad. "Certainly." He set his fork down. "But not two minutes past, you told me to carry on with my dinner."

"Yes, well, that was before you refused to go to the funeral."

"Planning to starve me out, eh?" he said, winking. "It won't work, Mother."

She set both hands flat on the table, and leaned into him. "Aleric, stop it," she said. "Stop joking and eating and drinking and talking about your whores, and just listen! It is time you and your father reconciled. He is very sorry, you know. He always had been. He never meant—well, all those things he said. That's why I've come. I *need* you to reconcile. Please."

Aleric gave her a sidling glance. "After you rag me about Father, is this going to turn into one of those lectures about finding a wife and doing my duty, isn't it?"

His mother threw her hands up in exasperation. "Heavens, no!" she answered. "As much as I love you, I wouldn't wish you on any female I know. Besides, I have not the heart to part you from your opera dancers and your actresses. I daresay you've one—perhaps one of each—upstairs lounging in your bathtub, even as we speak."

"There is no woman in this house."

His mother's eyes narrowed knowingly. "Ah," she said. "Left you again, has she?"

Aleric scowled. "Yes. Again. Try to contain your delight."

His mother sighed, long and deep. "Aleric, my dear," she began. "Find another. Find two or three. I no longer care. But you've stewed in your grief and anger long enough. We cannot all go on as we are. I need you and your father to at least try to get along. Please. I'm begging."

Devellyn was quiet for a long moment. He had no

wish to see his mother unhappy. It wasn't as if he chose to torment her. "Why must we do this again, Mother?"

He noticed this time that her hand trembled a little as she finally sat back down. She let her head fall forward onto the heels of her hands, and when she spoke, she addressed the tablecloth. "Aleric," she said quietly. "Aleric, it is his heart."

Suddenly, the room felt unsteady beneath Devellyn's chair. "His . . . heart?"

His mother looked at him with simple sorrow in her eyes. "Oh, Aleric," she whispered. "He has not long."

"How long?"

She shrugged lamely. "A few months?" she suggested. "A year, or perhaps two *if* he rests. *If* he suffers no stress. *If*—"

"*If* I swallow my pride and beg forgiveness?" Devellyn interjected. "Is that it? Well, it won't work, Mother. I did that for all of six months. It did not help. His *only son* is dead, remember? We are beyond this now."

His mother's face was one of anguish. "You are going to be the next duke, my dear," she whispered. Think how it looks."

It was Aleric's turn to shove back his chair and rise. "Good God, Mother!" He threw his hands in the air. "Do you imagine for one instant I care *how things look?* I've hardly lived a life of respectability and circumspection, now, have I?"

"Indeed not," she agreed. "And I wonder whom you most wish to punish by it, yourself, or your father."

His expression bitter, Devellyn shook his head. "Don't be melodramatic," he said. "I was never a saint, and neither was Greg."

His mother leapt from her chair again and crossed the room to lay her hand on his arm. "Listen to me, Aleric," she said. "All young men sow wild oats. And then, why, they turn their lives around! You and Gregory were just mischievous."

"You have been reading too many novels, Mother," he said quietly. "And I am no longer a young man. Does Father know you're here?"

Her expression softened. "A good marriage has no secrets, Aleric."

"What did he say?"

She swallowed hard and shook her head. "Nothing. But he did not forbid me."

Aleric gave her a sour grin. "No, no, he would not dare!"

Somewhere in the house, a clock struck the hour. His mother rose onto her tiptoes and kissed his cheek. "I should go," she said. "I'll be at Aunt Admeta's until Wednesday, all right?"

"Don't expect me," warned Devellyn. "Is Admeta still talking to that Norwich terrier? The one she thinks is her dead husband?"

"Well, what's the harm, dear?" she asked. "Horatio is, admittedly, a very fine-looking dog."

"God knows he's got more hair than Uncle Horatio ever did."

His mother grew suddenly impatient. "Oh, Aleric, let's stop talking about that silly dog," she said, the hand returning to his arm. "I have something important to say."

"I was afraid of that." And he already knew he wasn't going to like it.

"Next month, Aleric, will be your father's seventieth birthday, so I mean to open up the house on Grosvenor Square." Her hand tightened on his arm. "I am giving a ball, Aleric. The first we've had since—well, since Greg died. Please, will you just think on it? This may be his last."

Her fingers still digging into his arm, he somehow managed to nod. "Don't get your hopes up, Mother, all right?" he finally answered. "Just promise you won't get your hopes up."

His appetite finally ruined, Lord Devellyn saw his mother to the door, then promptly returned to the drawing room to resume his drinking and his pacing.

Miss Jennifer Arbuckle was almost asleep by the time her father's carriage returned from Mayfair to Bedford Place. Sidonie was tired, too, having suffered a tedious evening of smiling and applauding as one debutante after another took the stage at Lady Kirton's musicale. For Miss Arbuckle, the invitation to such a posh event had been a great honor. The Arbuckles were merchants, whilst Lady Kirton was a wellborn widow, known throughout the *ton* for her philanthropy and her volunteer work at the Nazareth Society.

Mrs. Arbuckle, however, was a frail, nervous woman who was uncomfortable with her new role in life. The invitations which her husband's wealth now brought their way almost always provoked in her a case of the megrims. And so it was that Sidonie had come into Miss Arbuckle's life, to teach and to do what Mrs. Arbuckle could not.

As with the Hannadays, Sidonie had been referred to the Arbuckles by a satisfied client. And as usual, they had been told Sidonie was a genteel widow recently arrived from France and the descendant of minor French nobility, all of which was true. Other than to remark upon her faint accent, no one ever asked about her parents, or why she'd come to England. Sidonie certainly did not enlighten them.

As the daughter of a duke—even an illegitimate daughter—Sidonie could have entered polite society if she'd had someone of good standing to make the necessary introductions. But polite society held little attraction for her. Teaching the social graces did, because the income left her nest egg intact. More importantly, it permitted her to move on the fringes of society, which in turn helped her learn all manner of interesting things about the gentlemen of the *ton*.

Tonight, however, had not been interesting. Stifling a yawn, Sidonie realized that tonight could certainly have been worse. Miss Arbuckle had accounted herself well at the pianoforte. Sidonie had played the duenna, and despite Lady Kirton's efforts to draw her out, had hovered in the background as she was being paid to do. Lady Kirton gave the impression of being a charming henwit, but Sidonie had sensed a keen intelligence in the woman's eyes. A heavy veil and an Italian accent would not fool her again, Sidonie feared. From now on, she would have to find another way to deliver money to the Nazareth Society.

Just then, the carriage began to slow. Sidonie reached for her reticule, and the movement roused Miss Arbuckle. Sidonie placed her hand lightly over the girl's. "You played beautifully tonight, my dear," she said, giving her a little pat. "Quite as well as any lady present."

Miss Arbuckle smiled dreamily. "It was a splendid affair, wasn't it?" she said. "And did you not think her ladyship exceedingly gracious? I think I shall tell Papa to give that Nazareth Club of hers a huge contribution."

"I believe it is called the Nazareth Society," said Sidonie innocently. "And a donation, I am sure, would be most welcome. The society houses fallen women, you know, and sets them on the path to a better life."

By the flickering light of the carriage lantern, she saw the girl blush. "Thank you, Madame Saint-Godard, for going with me tonight," she said. "Mother always remarks how much my piano has improved since you took me on."

Mr. Arbuckle's footman had put down the steps and opened the door. The pavement glistened with recent rain. Sidonie stepped down, then made a pretense of waving them off as she searched for her key. The horses' hooves rang sharply on the cobblestones as the carriage clattered down the street and around the corner. Sidonie closed her reticule, pulled her cloak a little closer, and set off down Bedford Place in the opposite direction.

Russell Square lay at the north end of Sidonie's well-lit street, and the walk was but a short one. Lifting her skirts to avoid the damp grass, she circled the statue of Lord Bedford, saw no sign of Charles Greer, then slid into the shadows to wait. Inside the square, little light fell, but the gloom had to be braved. Servants, even good ones, had wagging tongues. It would do her career precious little good if her prospective clients should hear rumors she'd helped one of her students elope.

Sidonie drew her cloak snugger still and paced through the darkness. It must be past midnight already.

It was quite possible, she considered, that Mr. Greer would not come at all. Perhaps he had not been sincere in his affections for Miss Hannaday. Or perhaps he was truly terrified of her father. Even if he came, perhaps he wouldn't find Maurice's offer of a position tempting. She paused and listened for a moment. There was nothing save for the faint sound of the traffic in High Holborn. In Russell Square, no living thing stirred. She would have sworn it.

Just then, she turned around, and walked straight into an immense, immutable wall. The wall grabbed her. Sidonie screamed.

"Good evening, Madame Saint-Godard." Lord Devellyn's voice rumbled deep in his chest. "A fine evening for a walk, is it not?"

Her heart was in her throat, and strong, solid hands were gripping her arms. "Devellyn!" she answered. "Dear God! Must you go skulking about in the dark, creeping up on people?"

The marquess chuckled. "I've been accused of many things, my dear, but being light on my feet is not one of them."

"Your feet are not my concern," she said. "But your hands *are*. Take them off me, if you please."

In the dark, she could feel his eyes search her face. "Whatever virtue you possess, *madame,* is safe with me."

"*Whatever* virtue—?" Sidonie considered kneeing him in the testicles. "What do you mean to suggest?"

In the gloom, it felt as though he leaned nearer, for she could feel the heat his big body radiated. "Well, oddly enough, I meant to suggest you kiss me," he responded. "But I believe you'd slap my face."

"And quite soundly, too."

"Ah, always unlucky in love!" he said lightly. "No wonder I drink so much."

Yes, he probably was drunk, thought Sidonie. He smelled of spicy soap and tobacco smoke and something which might have been brandy. Again, she tried to pull away. This time, he let her go, but very slowly, his heavy, warm hands sliding inch by inch down her forearms, his fingertips fleetingly catching hers. And then the touch was severed altogether, leaving Sidonie to feel inexplicably cold.

The marquess stepped back and lifted his gaze heavenward. He carried something—a black umbrella, she thought—hooked carelessly over his wrist. "I'm exceedingly fond of a late-night stroll myself," he went on, as if their strange interchange had not just occurred. "I find the night air a remarkable restorative."

"I suspect you've much to restore, my lord," she said tartly. "I believe, in fact, you are quite inebriated."

He laughed, but with neither humor nor cynicism. "Let's just say it took a vast quantity of cognac to wash my dinner down," he agreed. "Parts of it were hard to digest."

"I beg your pardon?"

"But enough about me," he continued. "I should much prefer to talk about you."

"I should rather not, thank you."

Devellyn went on as if she'd not spoken. "This fine air aside, ma'am, I cannot think it quite the thing for you to be out here alone," he said. "I think I should see you safely home. And then, perhaps, out of gratitude, you might invite me in for a rum toddy?"

"I think you should mind your own business, my lord," she retorted, pointing at the long, lamplit street beyond the statue. "And you should do it in your own house. That would be Number Seventeen, in case you do not recall. You will find it just there, on your left."

"But I should much rather go elsewhere," he said. "After all, I am reliably informed I have vulgar purple flock-paper in my dining room, and that my drawing room looks like a cheap brothel. What does your house look like, *madame*? Perhaps I should find it more inviting?"

"I beg your pardon?"

This time, Devellyn chuckled. "You seem to keep saying that to me, Madame Saint-Godard," he said. "Do you always require so much pardoning? You must be very wicked."

Sidonie laid her gloved hand on his coat sleeve and leaned nearer. "Let me rephrase that, my lord," she returned, enunciating every word. "It will be a cold day in hell when I invite you into my home."

"What ill luck," said the marquess evenly. "I daresay it's full of pretty chintz and homey needlecraft, and probably smells of fresh bread or beeswax or—" Here, he leaned forward to sniff her. "Or *that*—rosewater, isn't it?"

"Gardenia." She jerked sharply back. "Why do you care?"

"Well, you saw *my* drawing room," he said, missing her point. "Appalling, was it not?"

"You'd just conked me on the sconce with a carriage door, my lord," she answered. "Frankly, I did not spare your drawing room a thought."

"That's just as well," he answered. "It is truly hideous."

"Well, how very dreadful that you've been reduced to living here in Bedford Place with us lesser mortals," she retorted. "I am sure it is not at all the rarefied existence to which you are accustomed."

Devellyn roared with laughter. "Oh, Madame Saint-Godard, you have no idea how low my standards can go," he answered. "I meant only that the house is rather . . . uninviting. And empty."

"The latter, I collect, is your own fault."

"Yes," he said dryly. "I hear that a lot."

At that, Sidonie was compelled to choke back a burst of laughter. What on earth was she was doing, standing there in the dark parrying words with a scoundrel? "Really, Lord Devellyn, you must go home now." She spoke firmly, as if to a child, and gave him a little push.

"I cannot," he said. "It would be ungentlemanly to leave a lady alone in the dark."

"I came here alone in the dark," she said. "Go *away*. Please. I have . . . I have an appointment."

He grew very still for a moment. "Ah," he finally said. "I have interrupted an assignation."

"I beg your pardon?"

The marquess laughed hollowly. "My dear, one has appointments in the daylight hours," he said. "And engagements in the evening. But anything after the stroke of midnight, oh, that is most definitely an assignation."

"Well, who would have guessed the Devil of Duke Street was such an astute arbiter of social standards!" said Sidonie tightly. "Perhaps the patronesses down at Almack's should hang up their tiaras and leave you to it?"

"You have a sharp tongue, *madame*."

"And you seem remarkably willing to tolerate it."

Despite the darkness, Sidonie had the unsettling sensation the marquess was staring deep into her eyes. "Can I not pique your interest, then, in even the smallest of ways, *madame?*" he asked, sounding remarkably sober. "Do you find me so very unattractive?"

Sidonie's eyes narrowed. "You are strikingly handsome, and, I daresay, all too aware of it," she managed. "But I am meeting someone, and I wish for privacy. Do you mind terribly?"

The marquess hesitated, and for a moment, she almost believed his concern for her safety was real. "Very well, then," he finally said. "I shall go, but under two conditions."

"I rarely bargain, my lord."

"Yes, I thought as much," he agreed. "But they are very small conditions."

"Small," she echoed. "The first, then?"

He took the umbrella from his wrist, and handed it to her. "I wish you to take this."

"It is not necessary."

"That is why it is called a condition," he returned. "The rain, I fear, is not over."

"I thank you, then." Sidonie folded her hand around the crook, which was still warm from his wrist. "What is your second?"

"I wish . . ." He broke off, and his voice suddenly gentled. "I wish, Madame Saint-Godard, to know your given name."

She watched him quietly for a moment. "Sidonie."

"*Sidney,*" he repeated. "How . . . lovely. But is that not—well, is it not normally a man's name?"

"*Si-doh-NEE,*" she corrected, trying not to laugh. "Please say it properly if you must say it at all."

"Oh, I mean to say it," he agreed. "Even if only to whisper it to myself when I am alone in the dark. But for now, I think I shall presume upon our newfound friendship and just call you Sid instead."

That took her aback. "I am sorry," she said stiffly. "Only my family does so."

"Your family? I thought you had none."

She looked at him incredulously. "How would you know?"

Devellyn laughed again. "My dear Sid!" he chided. "A man of my reputation can hardly afford to employ total lackwits. Did you imagine you could keep sending your Miss Meg across the street to flutter her eyelashes at my poor footman and have him come away knowing nothing in return?"

Sidonie drew back. "Why—how dare you! I did no such thing!"

But she had, indirectly, had she not? Julia had told Meg to go see what she could find out about the marquess. But Julia had not, apparently, told the girl to keep her mouth shut.

Devellyn sensed her uncertainty. "Ah, she is caught out!" he murmured. "Madame Sidonie Saint-Godard, a lovely French widow of somewhat mysterious origin, who has lived in London all of eleven months, eight of them in Bedford Place, and who has no family—or at least none her servants know of. Your husband was a sea captain. He died of a tropical disease in the West Indies. Soon thereafter, your mother also died, leaving you a small inheritance."

"Really, Lord Devellyn!"

But the marquess had paused only for breath. "Your favorite color is dark blue," he rapidly recited. "You have a fondness for feathered hats. You adore sponge cake. You've not yet seen thirty, but you're getting perilously close. You like your tea very sweet. You have but two servants. Your companion's name is Mrs. Crosby. Julia Crosby. And you have a black-and-brown tabby cat named Thomas, renowned as Bloomsbury's fiercest mouser. There, how did I do?"

Sidonie was stunned. Abruptly, he seized her hand and kissed it. "Ah, I have left you speechless!" he said. "That would be my cue to exit."

And he promptly did so, walking briskly around the stone edifice of Lord Bedford and dashing across the street with a grace which seemed remarkable for so large a man—especially one she'd assumed was staggering drunk.

Chapter Six

In which Sir Alasdair rides to the Rescue

The afternoon sun cut through the tiny windows of Sidonie's attic, casting a sudden brilliance to the dancing dust motes. The room, she mused, reminded her of the *Merry Maiden,* Pierre's merchantman. It was probably the low, sharply pitched ceilings, and Thomas skulking round the rafters in search of mice.

Under normal circumstances, the cat thought it a great adventure to be permitted into the attic, with all its nooks and crannies. But today he was going about his work with something less than his usual zeal, probably because Sidonie had spent much of the night tossing and thrashing—and thereby forcing poor Thomas to periodically seize hold of the coverlet as if he were riding the seven seas again.

But Thomas would sleep away the afternoon and recover. Sidonie was less sure of herself. During the night, she'd begun to realize just how badly she'd misjudged the Marquess of Devellyn. Her haughty reserve had not put him off in the least, and for whatever reason—ennui, or sheer perversity—the marquess now seemed intrigued by her.

She must take care to change that. She must not pique his curiosity. Otherwise, Devellyn might start making inquiries elsewhere. Already he'd quizzed his footman. Men, silly, predictable creatures that they were, always found inaccessible women captivating, and intelligent women challenging. Sidonie must neither captivate nor challenge Lord Devellyn. Instead, she must bore him to tears.

It shouldn't be hard. Given what she'd seen, she doubted he was gifted with an overlong attention span. This afternoon, Sidonie decided, she would return the borrowed umbrella wearing a dowdy dress and her dullest expression. She would be amicable, polite, but exceedingly tedious. The marquess would almost certainly lose whatever interest he had in her. Indeed, by the time she was done prattling, Devellyn would be glad to see her go.

She'd been still puzzling over the details of her plan when Julia had sailed into her room with coffee and the announcement that today was the day they were going to sort out the attic. Sidonie had sold Claire's elegant Mayfair house months earlier and had her personal effects hauled to Bedford Place, an address more in keeping with Sidonie's station. Claire's trunks had been stored in the attic, where they now lay in wait, like haunting apparitions from the past.

Behind her, Julia was unpacking the last of an old trunk. Thomas had lost interest in the rafters and was twirling round Sidonie's ankles. She picked him up, then drifted to the window to look blindly through the glass. Thomas began to rumble, and pressed his forehead against her cheek, but even his best efforts could not always help her find peace.

She had never known quite what to make of her mother. Oh, Claire had loved her children, but as one loves pretty porcelain things—mostly from afar. She and George had been raised by servants and trotted out only to entertain their father, or to pacify their mother on those occasions when no admirers called. Eventually, Claire had come to treat George as . . . well, almost as an equal. She had doted on him, leaned on him, and promised him a grand future.

But Sidonie was much younger. She had been Claire's doll; her pretty plaything to dress up and show off. By the age of twelve, Sidonie had learned to play and sing with poise, to recite pages of clever poetry, and to speak three languages, all to the delight of her mother's friends. Sometimes she and her mother had even dressed alike. Sidonie remembered one summer day when they'd gone strolling around the Serpentine, wearing matching yellow frocks and hats, while merrily spinning their yellow parasols. It had been impossible to miss the many admiring gazes which came their way. Claire had thought it all perfectly delightful. For a while.

When she no longer found it perfectly delightful—or more specifically, when her newer, younger lovers began to spare Sidonie more than a passing glance—Claire had sent Sidonie home to France. Sidonie, she had decided, was wayward and in need of discipline. Only a bad girl would attract such attention; that had been the implicit message. Claire's parents, however, had declined the honor of raising their bastard granddaughter and taken her instead to the convent school. Sidonie had been but fifteen and not nearly as sophisticated as she'd seemed.

After two miserable years of exile, Sidonie decided she might as well *be* a bad girl, since she was already being punished for it. And so she did it in a big way, and ran away with Pierre Saint-Godard, a dashing adventurer ten years her senior. Pierre had thoroughly seduced her first, of course. He almost certainly had not meant to marry her. But marry her he did—claiming, strangely, that he'd fallen hopelessly in love. And he had loved her, Sidonie supposed, as much as a swashbuckling rogue could love anything besides high adventure and tavern wenches. Moreover, Sidonie could not particularly say that she had ever regretted what she'd done.

Behind her, something heavy scraped the floor. She turned around to see Julia pushing the trunk they'd just emptied into a corner.

"Oh!" Sidonie hastened to her side. "Let me help."

The job done, Julia straightened up. "Now, where's your mind gone off to, dearie?" she teased. "You've been far away all morning."

Sidonie let her gaze drift through the room. "I was just thinking of Claire," she admitted. "And strangely, of Pierre."

Julia turned her attention to some small bandboxes, which she hastily moved aside. "Nothing strange about a young widow grieving for her husband," she said.

Sidonie ran her hands down her skirts almost nervously. "But that's the thing, Julia," she said. "I don't precisely grieve. But I do miss him at times. Or perhaps I just miss the bustle of our old life, when I had no time to think or brood."

Julia looked at her a little oddly. "Did you love him, Sidonie?" she asked quietly.

Sidonie nodded. "I did, yes. But our marriage was really just . . . just one big adventure, I suppose. We married on impulse and lived life one day at a time. I don't know why, but I never saw us growing old together. I never saw us settling down in a little house by the sea."

"Or having children?" Julia interjected.

Sidonie shook her head. "It would have been unwise," she said. "Pierre would not give up the sea, and I did not wish to live alone. A ship was no place to raise a child."

"Ah, then you made the right choice, aye?" said Julia consolingly. "I'm sorry you lost him so young. Now, let's empty out just one more, then we'll call it a day."

Together, they pushed another trunk from the eaves into the center of the room. "This one I've not seen before," said Julia, studying it. "'Twas already in storage when Claire died, so likely it's full of junk."

Sidonie unbuckled the leather straps and threw them back. Julia lifted the lid on squealing hinges. "More old clothes," murmured Sidonie. "I vow, I never knew one person could own so many."

Julia shrugged. "Your mother was a beautiful woman," she answered. "People liked to lavish beautiful things on her."

Sidonie sat back down on one of the three-legged stools they'd carried upstairs and flipped through the first few garments. And then she saw it. She was sure. The yellow dress. *The Hyde Park dress.* The coincidence unnerved her. Suddenly, she couldn't get her breath. She shoved the garments away.

"Take this, Julia," she managed. "Take it away. I don't want it."

Julia sat down and patted her knee. "Well, we'll just give this lot to charity, along with that pile we already sorted," she said, then rummaged deeper. "But let's go through it first, just to be sure." She lifted out a stack of clothes, Claire's yellow dress amongst them, and set it aside to reveal a small box of carved ivory nestled in one corner of the trunk.

"How unusual!" said Julia, taking out the box. She lifted the little lid to reveal a mirror, and beneath it, several small compartments.

The yellow dress gone, Sidonie felt herself again. "What is it, Julia?"

Julia laughed. "Why, it's a patch box!" she said. "I saw such things in the theater many a time, but why would Claire have had one?"

Sidonie took the ivory box and stared into it until memory stirred. "Costume balls," she finally answered. "Dig deeper, and I daresay you'll find her old Marie Antoinette wig."

But Julia had licked one of the patches—a small black diamond—and stuck it on her cheek. "Do I look like a Georgian lady?" she asked, fluttering her lashes.

Somehow, Sidonie managed to laugh. Just then, the patch fell off, and disappeared into the folds of Julia's skirt. Sidonie took one, and affixed it at the corner of her mouth, where Ruby Black's mole had been cleverly drawn not so many days earlier.

"It's rather like a tattoo, isn't it?" said Julia, studying her. "Not permanent, I mean. But it has a way of . . . I don't know, enticing the eye to linger on a certain spot?"

Sidonie laughed again, and the patch fell off. "Are you suggesting I am trying to attract attention to my breasts?"

Julia immediately colored. "Oh, no, not you, dearie!" Then she hesitated. "But, well, I have often wondered . . ."

"Oh, go on, Julia! Ask."

"Well, why ever did you get that tattoo?" she finally said. "And in such a strange place!"

Sidonie lifted her gaze from the box of patches and considered it for a moment. "I did it because Pierre forbade it," she admitted. "I was a very wayward bride, you know."

"And a wayward daughter, too," Julia murmured. "Your poor mother had a fainting fit when the nuns wrote to say you'd run away with a sailor."

Sidonie scowled. "He was a sea captain, not a sailor."

"Yes, and you were what? Seventeen?"

Sidonie looked away. "Yes, just," she answered. "Anyway, Julia, you asked about the tattoo, not my reasons for marrying."

"Yes, go on," she answered. "Tell me about the tattoo."

Sidonie tried to picture life as it had been. "It was our first run to Martinique," she murmured. "We were to take on a cargo of sugar and rum. When we disembarked at Fort-de-France, we saw a strange old woman along the dockside, drawing a tattoo—with a needle, you know. That's how it is done."

"Oh!" Julia shrank back. "I did not know."

"It does not hurt," said Sidonie swiftly. "Not very much. Of course, I'd never seen such a thing. The old woman was drawing a sea serpent on a sailor's arm. She spoke little French, but the sailor said she was from . . . some island in the Pacific. I decided I wanted one of these strange, exotic things, so I sat down and made a few silly gestures. The woman touched my black hair, then all over my face. Finally, she took up her pencil and sketched this little angel on a scrap of paper. I don't know why. It wasn't what I'd asked for. Then Pierre turned round, saw what I was doing, and had a fit. He said no wife of his would have a tattoo for all the world to see."

"And quite right he was, too."

Sidonie looked at the floor. "I am afraid I did not take it well," she admitted. "I got it in my head I would have it anyway. The next day, when Pierre went off to see about the ship's reprovisioning, I went down to the docks and asked for the woman. She was not there, but I found her house in an alley not far away. She seemed to have been expecting me. She pulled me inside, and showed me the angel again. She had saved it. And so I had her draw it—but in a private place, you see? A place only Pierre would see, so he could not say I had disobeyed him."

"Oh, Sidonie!"

Sidonie gave her a sly smile. "Oh, don't feel sorry for Pierre," she answered. "Once his temper cooled, he decided he rather liked it."

Julia had turned to the next trunk. "Was he a good husband, Sidonie?" she asked, dusting off the cover of a book she'd extracted.

Sidonie turned on her stool to help her. "He tried," she answered, lifting out several more books. "But he was a restless spirit. And far too charming. Still, he was never harsh."

"Then you were fortunate in your marriage, my dear." Julia blew a puff of dust off another book. "What on earth are these? This trunk seems quite full of them."

Sidonie was still lifting out the books, her movements

mechanical, her mind still turned to Pierre. "These are Claire's diaries," she said absently.

But Julia was distracted by a small box. "Ah, here they are!" she said triumphantly. "The green velvet slippers."

Just then, someone dropped the knocker, and its sound carried all the way to the attic. Sidonie looked at the watch pinned to her bodice, then leapt from her stool. "Oh, gracious! That will be Miss Hannaday!" she said, shaking the dust from her skirts. "Am I presentable?"

"You're fine, dear," said Julia, reaching up to brush a little dust from her cheek. "But poor Miss Hannaday! I did not like that bruise she was sporting yesterday."

"Nor did I," admitted Sidonie. "But she needn't worry about Lord Bodley much longer."

Julia was closing up the trunk. "Why? What has happened?"

Sidonie caught Julia by the hands. "I met with Charles Greer in Russell Square last night," she whispered. "Maurice has offered him a position at Giroux & Chenault, and he is going to accept!"

Julia's mouth fell open. "Then he and Miss Hannaday will marry after all?"

Sidonie smiled. "Good news, is it not?"

Suddenly, Meg called up from the bottom of the attic stairs. Sidonie hastened away, and was halfway down when Julia spoke again. "Shall I put the slippers in your room, dear?"

"Yes, thank you, Julia."

"And what of these diaries? Shall you keep them? Shall I send them to George? Or just throw them out?"

Sidonie considered it for a moment. George would hurl them straight into the fire. She certainly did not want them. But nor could she bear to throw them out—which, when one thought on it, more or less summed up the whole of how she felt about her memories of her mother.

"I shall keep them," she finally said. "Oh, and Julia—?"

Julia peered over the balustrade. "Yes, dear?"

Sidonie went back up the stairs, out of Meg's earshot. "How hard, Julia, would it be for you to lay hands on a midshipman's uniform? Or perhaps a second lieutenant's?"

Julia looked at her incredulously. *"Naval uniforms?"* she echoed. "For what, pray?"

Sidonie smiled. "Well, I am, after all, an experienced sailor," she murmured. "And frankly, I think I'll cut a dashing figure in officer's togs."

"God help us!" Julia shut her eyes. "Say no more, I beg you!"

Be amicable, polite, and exceedingly dull, Sidonie reminded herself later that afternoon when she lifted the big brass door knocker at Number Seventeen. Miss Hannaday had been dealt with. Now it was the Devil's turn. *Insipid. Humdrum. Tedious.* That was how she must appear to him. Like an actress preparing to sweep onto center stage, Sidonie recited the words again, sent up a little prayer, and dropped the knocker.

Her nervousness ratcheted up at once. Despite her dowdy attire and good intentions, it felt more than a little risqué to call upon a man like Devellyn alone. But it had seemed silly to ask Julia to accompany her on an errand across the street. And Sidonie was, after all, a widow. That gave her a measure of freedom. More determined, she knocked again.

At last, a man she vaguely recognized as the butler opened the door. "Ah, Madame Saint-Godard!" he said as if he knew her well. "I trust you are fully recovered from the accident?"

"Quite, thank you," she managed, handing him the umbrella. "His lordship loaned this to me, and I should like to thank him. Is he in?"

The butler held open the door. "I shall inquire."

Sidonie handed him her card. The butler dropped it onto a silver salver near the door and whisked both away. Moments later, she was being shown, not into the garish drawing room, but into a cluttered, wood-paneled study overlooking the back gardens. It was very definitely a man's room, and the marquess filled it with his presence.

He sat sprawled in a massive leather chair by the hearth, wearing a dark jacquard dressing gown over his untidy attire. In one hand, he held a pipe; in the other, Sidonie's card, deftly flipping it back and forth through his fingers like some indolent gamester. He appeared to be sporting three days' worth of black stubble, and from the look of his hair, to have slept through all three whilst standing on his head. At his elbow sat a big earthenware mug which appeared to be brimming with cold coffee, and an ashtray which was brimming with twisted brown butts. Below, his slippers swam in a sea of newspapers he'd apparently tossed to the floor as he'd read them. Sidonie only prayed the twain never met, or the marquess would almost certainly go up in flames.

He rose languidly and laid aside the pipe. "Morning, Sid," he said with his unabashed grin. "To what do I owe such an unhoped-for pleasure?"

Resisting the urge to point out that morning was long gone for most folk, Sidonie tried instead to look insipid. "I came, my lord, to return your umbrella," she said. "Thank you so much. It did rain again, and but for your kindness, I'm quite sure I should be feverish now." She paused to cough delicately into her gloved hand. "My lungs are not what they used to be."

"No?" He let his eyes run over her. "They look dashed healthy from here."

Sidonie pretended to miss the double entendre. "I also came, my lord, to offer an apology." She folded her hands demurely. "I was rude last night. I hope you'll forgive me. In my defense I can only say that . . . well, I had not slept well the night before."

The marquess looked vaguely confused. "I'm sorry to hear it," he answered. "Please, sit down."

"Oh, thank you, my lord," she murmured, folding her skirts very properly. "It's a poor excuse, I know, but I do suffer terribly, you see, from the, er—" Suddenly, a vision of Mrs. Arbuckle stretched limply across her divan sprang to mind. "From the megrims," she finished. "It is my nerves, you see. And my—my widowhood. Life's many cruel disappointments. That sort of thing."

"Good Lord!" said the marquess, sitting back down abruptly. "I really expected better of *you,* my dear."

Sidonie batted her lashes. "I beg your pardon?"

Mischief glinted in his eye. "If you suffer from overset nerves, Sid, I'm the Queen of Sweden." He took up his pipe again and whacked a shower of red sparks into the ashtray. "Now, I know it's uncouth as hell, but do you mind if I relight this?"

Sidonie smiled tightly and waved her hand by way of permission.

"If it would help your nerves, Sid," he said with mock solicitude, "Honeywell might find us an extra pipe?"

"No, thank you," she retorted. "I prefer to swallow my poison."

"Ah!" he said. "That's more the sauce I expect from you." He shook open a leather pouch and artfully thumbed the bowl full of tobacco. "Help yourself, by the way. Brandy's on the side table."

"How kind you are, my lord." Sidonie resumed her prim expression. "But I never indulge in spirits before dusk."

The marquess shrugged. "Suit yourself," he said, then stretched back in his chair. "Now, admit it, Sid. You're working dashed hard not to like me—and now, for reasons I've not yet fathomed, I suspect you're trying to make *me* dislike *you.*"

Sidonie dropped her eyes demurely. "I'm sure, my lord, that in your own backhanded way, you are trying to comfort me," she murmured. "But I can't think what you mean."

He laughed around his pipe stem. "Oh, you can't, eh?" he answered, his eyes warming as they swept over her. "I think you can. And if I were trying to comfort you, my dear, conversation likely wouldn't enter into the process."

Sidonie drew herself up stiffly. "Really, Lord Devellyn!"

But Devellyn, apparently, was incapable of being

chastised. "By the way, my dear, I liked that snug amethyst-colored silk a lot better than this baggy mouse-colored thing you're wearing today. It does not show your—ah, your feminine assets to nearly so fine an effect."

Sidonie's palm itched to slap him, but somehow, she restrained it. *Be exceedingly dull,* she reminded herself. "Thank you, my lord," she managed. "But that was one of Julia's old gowns which I'd altered. I rarely wear bright colors."

The marquess lifted one of his satanic-looking eyebrows. "A hand-me-down?" he said doubtfully. "From a companion? And one who, even I have noticed, is a full foot shorter than you?"

Sidonie widened her eyes ingenuously. "I let the hem out," she said, hoping he knew nothing of hems. "I'm quite clever with a needle, my lord. Indeed, I love nothing so much as to spend my spare time sewing."

"*Sewing—?*"

"Yes. For the poor."

"Ah, the poor!" he echoed. "And what, pray, do you sew for them?"

Sidonie struggled to think of something. "Well, for the poor, actually, I mostly knit," she amended. "Mittens. Mufflers. That sort of thing. Sometimes Julia and I spend days at a time, just sewing and knitting. It is so deeply gratifying, you know, to help those less fortunate than ourselves."

"Hmm, I daresay," murmured the marquess, his gaze hooded.

"But I can see, my lord, that I've begun to bore you," she went on, "when my intentions were quite the opposite. I've come, actually, to issue a social invitation by way of apology. I do hope you won't think it forward—"

"No, not at all!" His expression brightened.

"You greatly relieve my mind, sir," said Sidonie. "You see, tomorrow, Mrs. Crosby and I are having the vicar for tea. We attend St. George's Bloomsbury, of course, and—"

"St. George's?" he interposed. "You are French, but not Catholic?"

Sidonie was surprised he cared. "My mother converted," she murmured, giving no further explanation. "As I was saying, since the vicar is coming, we should like another gentleman to even our number. And if you don't mind a little excitement, we thought we'd perhaps play a few hands of whist."

He clamped his smoldering pipe in one jaw and grinned. "A tad chilly in hell today, is it, my dear?"

Sidonie stiffened. "I do beg your pardon." But suddenly, she remembered what she'd said the previous evening. "Dear me, I am going to have to eat my words, aren't I?" she murmured. "Please, my lord, let me make amends for my snide remark. Do join us tomorrow."

The marquess shifted his weight in the armchair. "Just tea and cards with the vicar, eh?" he said, still without removing the pipe. "No blue ruin? No dicing? No naked dancing girls?"

Sidonie tried to look disapproving.

The marquess grunted dismissively. "No opium-eating, either, I suppose!" he muttered. "Well, sorry to crush your hopes, Sid, but I reckon I'll come anyway. Now, let that be a lesson to you."

Sidonie barely suppressed her gasp. *He was going to*

come? "Well, what can I say, my lord?" she managed. "I am honored."

"No you aren't," he answered. "You're appalled. Never try to bluff a hardened gamester. I may not know your game, Sid, but I know you are out of your league."

Just then, Honeywell burst into the room, leaving the door swinging wide. "My lord! My lord!" he said frantically. "Oh, sir! I'm afraid it is Miss Leder—"

But it was too late. An agitated woman with flame-colored hair had burst into the room behind him. Sidonie recognized her at once.

"Awright, what's this?" she squawked, pointing squarely at Sidonie without really looking at her.

The butler fled. The marquess sat up straighter in his chair. "Hello, Camelia," he said. "What an unexpected pleasure."

"Oh, I'll just bet it is," she said, stalking closer. *"Two weeks,* you said, you lying pig! *Ooh, dear Cammie, take as long as you want,* you said!"

Devellyn's eyes flicked toward Sidonie. "Camelia, what's this about?"

Sidonie jerked to her feet. "Perhaps I should go?"

Ignoring her, the woman leaned over the marquess, and jabbed the pointing finger in his face. "This is about you treating me square, Devellyn! Why, *I am in no hurry,* says you! And now I come home to this? You liar!" Her glower turned to Sidonie. "And 'oo the hell's this dish o' boiled custard anyways?"

Devellyn looked amazingly unperturbed. "Madame Saint-Godard, may I present Miss Camelia Lederly, the almost-famous actress?" he said. "Camelia, Madame Saint-Godard."

Sidonie tried to nod at the woman.

"And by the by, Camelia, you quite mistake the situation," the marquess went on. "Madame Saint-Godard is just a kindhearted, Christian-minded neighbor who has come to invite me to tea with her vicar, no doubt in some misguided attempt to save my stained and mortal soul."

"Oh, she is, eh?" The redhead eyed Sidonie nastily. "Well, in all the months *I* lived 'ere I never seen 'er at *my* door worrying about *my* soul!"

"That, my dear," he said around his pipe stem, "is probably because she heard you hadn't got one."

The redhead flew at him then, a screeching, clawing, flailing ball of fire. "Pig!" she screamed. "You selfish bastard pig!" She seized the overflowing ashtray, and knocked him over the head with it, sending ash and butts flying.

Sidonie sat back down, fascinated. Wedged awkwardly into the chair, the marquess was trying to get his arms round Camelia's waist and her hands behind her back. The redhead got one hand loose and cracked him soundly across the face with it. The marquess kept wrestling.

"Camelia, don't do this," he was saying. "Calm down. Just calm down. You need the house? Is that it? Is it?"

"Ooh, you lied to me!" she wailed, fists swinging.

"Then take—*ouch!*—" Camelia caught him in the temple with an elbow. "Just take the house," he went on. "I'll just go elsewh—*aaggggk!*"

She was trying to throttle him with his own cravat. "*A fortnight,* you said!" she gritted. "*Take your time, Camelia,* you said!"

Having shown a remarkable amount of restraint thus far, the marquess finally just wrapped his arms around her waist and stood. She clung to him like some sort of lunatic, alternately pulling his hair and pounding on him with her free hand, but Devellyn just kept walking.

"Camelia, I'm taking you to the chaise now," he said calmly. "And I want you to sit there and be quiet until we can work this—"

"Go bugger yourself, Devellyn!" Camelia grabbed a passing candlestick and began whacking him with it. *"Work it out! Work it out!* God, I hate when you say that!"

The candle tumbled out, and he trod upon it, snapping it in two. The marquess just kept going, then dropped her unceremoniously onto a brocade chaise. Camelia bounced once, showing a pair of fine ankles, and kept a firm grip on her candlestick.

"Camelia, my dear," said Devellyn, slightly winded. "Aren't you being a bit of a dog in the manger?"

"A *dog*? How dare you!"

Devellyn urged her down again. "Listen, Camelia, *you left me,*" he said, his voice finally cold. "As in you cast me off. Threw me over. Tossed me out of your life. Sound familiar?"

"Aye, and now I wants to move back!" she interjected, her accent getting worse. "I want me bleedin' fortnight! But you and Madame Custard here have already gone and set up—"

Suddenly, Sidonie became aware of a sharp, acrid scent in the air. She cut her eyes toward the empty armchair and gasped. "Fire!" she screamed, bolting for the smoldering newspapers. "Fire!"

"Let it burn!" hissed Camelia, seizing Devellyn's cravat again. "When it catches good, I'll throw him in!"

With Devellyn ensnared, Sidonie panicked. She snatched up his coffee and hastily dumped it. The smoking newspaper became a stewing, sodden mess. Somehow, the marquess extracted himself and bellowed for the butler, but a pale-faced Honeywell was already coming through the door. He saw the steaming debris, screamed, and seized a vase of lilies. He upended it, dousing the last of it with water and flowers.

"Oh, I say!" murmured a voice from the door.

Still shaking, Sidonie turned around to see the handsome man from the Anchor standing in the doorway, his golden hair gleaming in a shaft of sun.

Camelia let go of the cravat. "Hello, Al," she said. "Come to sober Dev up again, have you?"

Devellyn had crossed the room to stare down at his ruined rug. "Good afternoon, Alasdair," he said calmly. "You've caught us at an awkward moment."

"Oh, I say!" said the man again, stepping into the fray. "Cammie—? I thought you were—or had decided to—to—"

Devellyn lifted his gaze, and for the first time, looked at the red-haired woman with hurt in his eyes. "You thought she'd decided to leave me for Sir Edmund Sutters," he said. "And so she did."

At that, the fight seemingly went out of Camelia, and she fell back onto the chaise. "Aye, well, that's all well and good," she whimpered, her face suddenly crumpling. "But I can't 'ave 'im now, can I?"

Devellyn was silent for a moment. "Why not?"

At that, she broke down utterly and dropped her candlestick to the floor. "E's in the sponging house!" she wailed. "The bloody Peelers come got 'im last night."

Alasdair nodded. "I'm afraid it's true," he said. "Sutters is expected to be in insolvent debtor's court before the month is out. It was all the talk at White's last night."

"Ruined! Ooh, 'e's proper ruined!" Sobs wracked Camelia now. "'E's got debts up to his pretty blue eyes, and owes the moneylenders everything 'e's like to get 'is mitts on in this life, and probably the next."

"Oh, Camelia." Devellyn's voice was suddenly soft. "I am sorry."

Camelia exploded again. "Don't you dare feel sorry for me!" she screamed, lunging at him again. He caught her against him, but Camelia kept pummeling him with her fists.

"Now, now, Camelia!" Alasdair crossed the room, and gently peeled her off Devellyn, his voice soothing. "This is not necessary, my dear. You're far too lovely to be wasted on an insensitive lout like Dev. Besides, he neglected you dreadfully. You must on no account excuse him for it."

Camelia stepped back, sniffed, and began to pat at her hair. "Oh, 'e pretty much ignored me, right enough," she agreed. "Unless he wanted a little bounce on my bel—"

"Yes, yes, understood!" said Alasdair swiftly, shooting an uncertain glance at Sidonie. "Now, I collect you need a place to live, my dear, until you can chose from what will doubtless be a score of new suitors vying for your charms?"

Camelia looked at him hopefully. "It's a long, lonely wait, too."

Alasdair blanched. "Yes, well, you'll soon make some chap frightfully happy, I'm sure," he said hastily. "Now, if we turn our minds to it, surely we can think of some suitable accommodation for you?"

Camelia's face fell. "I've turned my mind far enough," she said insistently. "Devellyn promised me a fortnight, and a fortnight is what I ought'er have, after all I put up with."

The marquess cursed softly under his breath. Camelia shot him a venomous look, then turned her glare on Sidonie. Clearly, matters were sliding downhill again.

"Julia and I have an extra bedchamber," blurted Sidonie, feeling sorry for the woman. "Miss Lederly, you would be welcome to it until you've made other arrangements."

"I don't think so," she said, running an eye down Sidonie's attire. "Desperate, I'm not."

"By George, I've got it!" said Alasdair, going to the desk and whipping out a sheet of foolscap. "Camelia, you can use my brother Merrick's flat. He's gone off to Milan until Michaelmas."

"Well, I don't know . . ." said Camelia. "Is it some-place posh?"

"Quite," said Alasdair, scribbling. "The Albany."

"Ooh, the Albany!" said Camelia. "Lots of rich blokes live there!"

"Place is infested with 'em," agreed Alasdair, folding the note and thrusting it at her. "Just give this to the porter, and ask for the key to Mr. Merrick MacLachlan's flat."

Camelia's shrewd eyes narrowed. "What about me things?" she said. "I've got lots. Will he carry them up?"

Alasdair patted her on the shoulder as he urged her toward the door. "My dear, he will even cart them over for you," he reassured her. "But hurry along now. The night porter comes on at six, and he suffers terribly from the lumbago."

Together, they vanished down the corridor. Sidonie could only hold Devellyn's gaze and fight down a burst of laughter. The marquess groaned softly and covered his face with his hand. "God, I cannot believe this just happened," he said.

A moment later, the front door thumped shut. Alasdair rushed back into the room, slammed the study door, and fell back against it as if fearing she might return.

Devellyn swore beneath his breath again. "Alasdair, you've lost your mind," he said, kicking a wet lily from his path. "Camelia cannot go to the Albany! They won't permit a woman to live there!"

"Well, Merrick hasn't gone to Milan, either," his friend retorted. "Until Michaelmas or otherwise. But she doesn't know any of that, does she? And by the time she trots all the way down to Piccadilly and comes back again, I should hope you'll have put some proper bars on the bloody doors and windows. Good God, Dev! The woman's a menace to society!"

The marquess had hurled himself back into his chair and was staring morosely at the sodden mess of newspapers. "I like my women with a little fire in them," he said defensively.

"Yes, well, that one blows like a bloody Sheffield forge," Alasdair answered. "Melts my silver just to look at her. What were you thinking to let her back in?"

Suddenly, all of the marquess's restraint seemed to leave him. "Well, I didn't expect her back, now, did I?" he snapped, jerking back onto his feet. "I've never had one of them *come* back once they'd cast me off, have I?—and I've even begged a couple!—so, Alasdair, I guess you could say this took me by surprise! And thanks for rubbing it in."

"Well, you don't have to shout," said Alasdair peevishly. Then he turned to Sidonie and extended his hand. "Allow me to fall at your feet, ma'am," he said smoothly. "I am Sir Alasdair MacLachlan, your newest and most ardent admirer."

Still trying not to laugh, Sidonie took the proffered hand. "I am Madame Saint-Godard," she answered. "I live across the street. I was inviting his lordship to tea with my vicar."

"Oh." Alasdair's face fell.

But Devellyn's thoughts seemed elsewhere. "Honeywell!" he roared. "Honeywell, get back in here, you fainthearted hen!"

The butler dashed back into the room, looking at his wit's end. "Yes, my lord?"

Devellyn shot another nasty look at Alasdair. "Take a hundred pounds out of the cash box," he said. "Then go down to the Albany and fetch Miss Lederly."

Honeywell paled. "Oh, sir, must I?" he whimpered. "She really does not care for me. Can't you make Fenton go?"

"Both of you go," roared the marquess.

Honeywell made a pitiful mewling sound.

"Well, you know what my Granny MacGregor always says," murmured Alasdair. "Better a coward than a corpse."

"You!" said Devellyn, turning on him. "Stop spewing that Scottish drivel! And you, Honeywell, take a whip and a chair if it'll make you feel better. And for pity's sake, don't bring her back here. Rent her a flat—a nice one. In St. James. Or—hell, take two hundred and make it Mayfair."

"Cut your losses, Dev!" warned Alasdair. "You are well rid of that spiteful cat."

The marquess eyed him angrily. "She cannot very well live on the streets, Alasdair," he said. "I owe her, at the very least, a roof over her head."

Honeywell eyed his master suspiciously. "Well, with two hundred pounds, surely she can rent her own roof."

A vein popped out on the marquess's forehead. "Lord, Honeywell, don't *give* her the cash!" he returned. "She'll only lose it at Lufton's. You do it. Lease it for a year, and take that new footman—what the devil's his name?"

"Polk, sir," sniffed Honeywell. "Henry Polk."

"Yes, well, Polk can move her things," he said. "A strained back might keep him away from that house-maid across the street, mightn't it, Madame Saint-Godard? Now, Godspeed, Honeywell!"

The butler fled. Alasdair looked at him incredulously. "*Godspeed?*" he echoed. "What are you now, some sort of Puritan?"

The marquess clasped his hands rigidly behind his back. "Alasdair," he said very quietly. "Why are you here?"

Alasdair looked irritated. "You told me to be here before three," he snapped. "And it is now a quarter 'til. Need I remind you we've an appointment?"

Sudden understanding swept over Devellyn's features. "Ah, quite right!" he murmured. "And we shall keep it, too. Please be so kind, old friend, as to go up-stairs and wait for me."

Alasdair shot Devellyn an exasperated look and left. The marquess still appeared vaguely embarrassed. "You enjoyed that vastly, did you not?" he said, as soon as the door closed. His eyes were no longer flat and cold, but rather, filled with a hint of wry humor.

For an instant, all barriers were down between them. "I can honestly say it was like nothing I've ever wit-nessed before," she answered. "And I've hardly lived what one would call a sheltered life."

"Well, you shouldn't have witnessed it at all, Sidonie," he said, pronouncing her name flawlessly. "My apologies for allowing you to be dragged into such a mess."

"You did not drag me," she said. "I knocked on your door and came in of my own accord."

"Ah, Sidonie!" he said, looking past her and into the gardens beyond the window. "Tell me, my dear girl. There is no vicar coming to dinner tomorrow, is there?"

"Tea," she corrected. "It was tea." She dropped her gaze. "And no, there is not."

He gave a dry chuckle. "Oh, you really do owe me an apology now!" he said. "I shall be there at six."

"For . . . for what?"

"Dinner." He turned from the window and looked down at her, eyes twinkling. "And I shan't be fobbed off with tea, either. Now, why the open mouth, Sid? You and Mrs. Crosby do dine, do you not? Or do you sustain yourselves on something more ephemeral? Champagne and sugar-water, perhaps?"

He smiled, and for an instant, Sidonie felt the floor shift beneath her feet. "We . . . oh, yes, we dine."

"Capital," he said. "I shall bring Alasdair. He is, as you see, quite charming. And I find him rather more tolerant of my wicked ways than a vicar might be."

"I see." There seemed to be no arguing with him, and strangely, Sidonie was not at all sure she wished to. "Well, you like beef, I daresay?" she ventured. "Mrs. Tuttle does a lovely joint."

"Perfect," he said, the smile deepening. "And a sponge cake, perhaps? I am inordinately fond of it, too, Sidonie."

Oh, God. She liked the way her name sounded on his lips. That could not possibly be a good thing. "Yes, orange sponge, perhaps," she managed to murmur. "We've been rather flush with oranges lately."

Suddenly, Devellyn had her hand again and was carrying it to his lips, but unlike the previous evening, this time, he lingered. When he lifted his head, his eyes were filled with some sort of intense emotion. "Sidonie," he said, his voice strangely hoarse. "You are the most—I mean, you are so . . . I find you . . . ah, devil take it! Never mind!"

"I beg your pardon?"

"Nothing," he growled. "I misspoke. What did you say about oranges?"

But Sidonie had forgotten all about that. She withdrew her hand, and shook her head as if it might clear her vision. "My lord—" she began uncertainly. "My lord, forgive me, I cannot help but ask—did Miss Lederly really cast you off?"

He looked at her strangely. "You think it unlikely?" he asked. "If so, rest assured that Camelia is not particularly discriminating. It happens to me with a startling regularity."

"I see," said Sidonie. But she didn't. In fact, she was beginning to feel as if she understood nothing at all—particularly where Lord Devellyn was concerned. And she was beginning to feel dreadfully guilty, too.

The marquess shrugged, as if his failings did not matter, and drifted closer to the window, where he stood looking out at the fading sunlight. "The truth is, Sidonie, I don't fare well with women." He spoke coolly, and without looking at her. "It is my own fault, of course. I . . . I neglect them. I forget where I'm supposed to be, and when I'm supposed to be there. I'm irresponsible. I drink to excess, gamble to excess, and sometimes I brawl. I never remember special occasions. And I very often go to sleep before they've . . . well, never mind that." Devellyn fell silent for a moment. "And I cheat on them," he quietly added. "Dreadfully. Did I mention that?"

"You did not," she answered. "But a full disclosure of one's fidelity, or even one's skill in the bedroom, is not, strictly speaking, necessary before having dinner with someone."

Devellyn smiled down at her a little wearily. "Ah, Sid, I have no charm at all, have I?" he said almost regretfully.

"Very little," she agreed. "But I think charm can be a vastly overrated virtue."

He lifted his sharply arched brows. "Do you now?"

Sidonie smiled and laid her hand lightly on his arm. "I have had a great deal of experience with charming men, my lord," she said. "They do not always wear well."

Devellyn smiled. "I see."

"As do I," said Sidonie. "Indeed, my lord, I see a great deal more than you might guess."

He looked at her curiously. "How so?"

She gave a faint smile. "Well, for example, last night I saw the man who waited for me in the shadows along Bedford Place."

Strangely, the marquess turned back to the window and would not look at her.

"Indeed," she went on, "I saw him linger—very near your door, in fact—until it was quite obvious I had returned home safe and sound."

"Did you indeed?" murmured Devellyn.

"I did." She deepened her smile and cut a sidelong glance at him. "And he did not, in that moment, strike me as especially irresponsible. Moreover, I begin to suspect he was not that drunk."

"Be careful, my dear," said the marquess softly. "Don't imagine in him any virtues he does not, and will never, possess."

"Oh, I shan't," she said. "I am slowly learning to measure a man's character with the greatest care and patience."

And then, without another word, Sidonie slipped from Devellyn's study and made her way home.

Chapter Seven

In which Sergeant Sisk pays a social Call

"I owe you, Alasdair," Devellyn said awhile later as their carriage went rumbling over the Southwark Bridge.

"Oh, I've no doubt," his friend agreed. "But for what?"

Devellyn lifted his shoulders and rolled them restlessly backward. "Oh, for smoothing things out with Camelia," he finally said. "What a bloody awful mess."

Alasdair reached across the space between them and thumped him on the shoulder. "Well, you cannot keep two birds in the same cage, old chap," he answered. "And the French girl was too fine to let go."

"You much mistake the situation, Alasdair." Devellyn stared down the river at a barge drifting out to catch the tide. "Madame Saint-Godard is a neighbor. That is all."

"You aren't pursuing the lady, Dev?"

"I am not."

"Oh, I see," said Alasdair pensively. "Then you wouldn't mind if I did?"

Devellyn shot his best friend a long, dark look. "I did not say that, did I?" he answered. "I know you, Alasdair, and your intentions would not be honorable."

"I resent that, old chap," said Alasdair. "I thought her every inch a lady—and lovely inches they were, too, even in that dreadful dress. No, were I to approach such a woman, it would be with the best of intentions."

Devellyn withdrew his shiny new pocket watch, a replacement for the one the Black Angel had stolen. "Well, Alasdair, you have almost twenty-seven hours in which to ponder those intentions," he said grimly. "We dine with her tomorrow at six."

In the gloom of the carriage, he saw Alasdair's eyes widen. "Do we?" he murmured. "That should prove fascinating. I take it the lady is a widow of some means?"

"Of modest means, I collect."

Alasdair leaned nearer. "What else do you know of her?"

Devellyn was silent for a moment. "She is French, of course," he finally answered. "From a poor but noble family, or so it's said. She teaches deportment to the daughters of various cits around town."

"That sounds like a miserable job," answered Alasdair. "The lady obviously needs a pair of comforting arms."

Devellyn gave a snort of disgust. "Are you offering?"

"Lord, no," said Alasdair. "I cower from the competition."

Devellyn felt a moment of panic. "What competition?"

Alasdair had the audacity to grin. "It looked to me as if Madame Saint-Godard had eyes for only one man."

The marquess fell silent for a long moment, then said, "If you can do nothing but babble nonsense, Alasdair, kindly stop talking altogether."

And so Alasdair did. Instead of talking, he relaxed against his banquette, propped up his boots on the seat beside Devellyn, and grinned at him like a lunatic all the way down to the Anchor.

Devellyn should have been relieved when the carriage drew up at the door to the taproom, but he was not. Just seeing the old tavern again set his every nerve on edge. All thought of Sidonie Saint-Godard fled his mind, and he could think only of her. *Of the Black Angel.* Of how desperately he wanted to get his hands round that slender stalk of her neck, and force her to—to—well, he was not perfectly sure what he would force her to do. What he had paid her to do, most probably. He still wanted it, and badly.

Good Lord! Devellyn closed his eyes and tried not to think of what a fool he was. Instead, he tried to think only of what she had stolen—Greg's portrait—and not about the strange fantasies that lately haunted his sleep.

Once inside, they had no trouble finding the young man who had been working the taproom on the night of the Black Angel's trickery. He seemed cooperative enough, so Devellyn bought three pints of porter and pulled the lad aside to an empty table. But it soon proved impossible to get much information out of him, for he denied knowing anything of the woman Devellyn had met that night.

"She was pretending to be a doxy working the South Bank," Devellyn growled. "I'l wager she's tried her tricks in here before."

"No, s-s-sir."

Devellyn slammed his open hand on the table surface. "Bloody hell, man, I saw you talking to her! It was dark in here, but not that dark."

"No disrespect m-meant, your lordship, but I never laid eyes on the woman afore that night, I s-s-swear it," he stuttered. "That's *why* you saw me talking to her."

"What the devil does that mean?"

The young man looked at him earnestly. "We always warns 'em, the new ones what comes in. We tell 'em straight out that we'll brook no trouble at the Anchor. They can stay and ply their trade, long as they're quiet about it."

Irritated, Devellyn fished in his coat pocket, then slapped a gold guinea on the table.

For a moment, the young man just blinked at it. "I'm sorry, sir," he finally said. "You can lay out ten of 'em, but I won't be taking your money, for I've naught to tell."

Devellyn meant to drag the fellow over the table by his shirt collar, but Alasdair interceded, thrusting an arm between them. "Calm down, old chap," he said. "This place is affecting your judgment."

"No, *Ruby Black* is affecting my judgment," snarled Devellyn. "I want that woman under my thumb, Alasdair, and I don't care what it takes."

Alasdair looked at him strangely for a moment, then turned to the tapster in some sympathy. "Surely, if you search your memory, my good man, you can think of something which might be of help to us?" he said sweetly. "My friend, a regular patron of your fine establishment, was robbed of his most prized possession—a family heirloom, no less—by this Ruby Black person. He wants to find her. You can understand that, can you not?"

The young man blinked again, and laid both hands flat on the table. "Well, I know nothing more," he said. "But Gibbs was working out front that night, totting up the accounts for the week."

"Yes?" said Alasdair eagerly. "Can we see him?"

The man shook his head. "Gone down to Reigate to see his sister," he said. "But he did remark as how he'd seen her come in that night. Said she paid with one of them." He gestured at the gold guinea. "Thought it was a bit queer, he did, for her sort. And then, when he gave her the change, he saw her hands were fair and smooth. A proper lady's hands, he said."

Devellyn narrowed one eye and considered it. He'd noticed that, too, hadn't he? Ruby Black's hands—those delicate, long-fingered hands which had so cleverly undressed and caressed him—had scarce washed so much as a dirty dish, he'd wager. In the dark, they had felt like satin skimming over his heated flesh.

"So that's all we know, sir," the young man finished. "Now, I'll give you the key to the room, and gladly, if you think another look about would be of help?"

Devellyn shook his head. He hoped never to enter that room again. The memory of his night with Ruby Black was cut deep into his brain, and already, the rage and humiliation and raw sexual frustration were flooding back again.

Alasdair must have sensed something was wrong. He jerked abruptly to his feet. "Let's go have dinner at White's, Dev, and see if we can find Tenby," he suggested.

Devellyn pushed the memory of Ruby Black away,

pushed it deep into the cellar of his mind, and ruthlessly slammed the door. "Dinner, yes," he managed to say. "But that pup Tenby? Hell, no."

Alasdair stood, and the young man scurried back to his post. "Well, at the very least, I hope you sent him a list of what was stolen?"

"I did," Devellyn admitted. "But I hold little hope his Runner will find anything."

Indeed, he had sent it, but he had hated having to do so; had hated having to admit he still carried Greg's portrait out of guilt and sentiment, which was the conclusion everyone would draw when Tenby started gossiping. It had felt as though he was revealing a painful little piece of himself to the public, and he resented it. It had been a measure of his desperation that he'd done it anyway.

"What they've actually hired is one of those new policemen," Alasdair corrected, as they strode through the tavern and back into the cobbled yard. "A nasty, brutal-looking chap by the name of Sisk. But he is to work the case off duty, on a private basis."

Devellyn's breathing had calmed now. "Is that still allowed?"

Alasdair shrugged. "Probably not," he answered. "Still, having seen the fellow, I pity the Black Angel if he gets hold of her."

Something in his words sent a chill down Devellyn's spine. Oh, he wanted the Angel punished, all right. But he wanted the doing of it left to *him*. "Find out what they are paying this policeman, Alasdair," he said. "I shall offer to double his sum if he brings the woman to me first."

"Easily done, old chap," his friend agreed. "Money greases everyone's wheels."

"Truer words were never spoken." Suddenly, Devellyn reached up and banged on the carriage roof. At once, Wittle began to slow.

"What now, Dev?" asked Alasdair.

"Gracechurch Street," Devellyn bellowed through the window. His gaze returned to Alasdair. "I've a sudden notion to visit my solicitors. You will not, I hope, object to a brief detour?"

"Certainly not," he answered. "But why?"

"Because, Alasdair, as you say, money greases everyone's wheels. Perhaps it's time to throw a little in Ruby Black's direction."

In the Strand, the business day was fast drawing to an end, and Jean-Claude was in the process of hanging out the shop's CLOSED sign, and bolting the front door for the evening. Beyond the matching bow windows, the flow of clerks and shopgirls heading home to dinner had turned into a roiling river of gray wool which bobbed with floating black hats.

Such a pity, thought Jean-Claude. The English always dressed with a total lack of panache.

But just then, he spotted what looked like a salmon swimming upstream. A man wearing a bright pink waistcoat was fighting his way up from the direction of St. Martin's. Soon, his meaty red face was visible. Too visible. Unfortunately, Jean-Claude was too slow. The man placed his hand firmly on the door a mere instant before Jean-Claude shot the bolt.

"Not so fast, me pretty boy!" he said, giving it a hearty push. "I've business 'ere."

Jean-Claude backed away as he entered. *"Oui, oui, monsieur,"* he answered, recognizing the man well. *"Mais je ne parle pas anglais!"*

"Friggin' frogs!" said the man, obviously frustrated. "Where's Kem, eh? I knows 'e's in 'ere someplace, so go and tell 'im to get 'is scrawny arse down 'ere, awright?"

Jean-Claude widened his eyes and shook his head. *"Oui, monsieur, mais je ne comprends pas!"* he said. *"No anglais! No anglais!"*

The man raised both hands in the air and shook them. *"Où est* yer boss, eh? *Où est* Monsoor Kemble?" he bellowed. "I wants him right away, *capitare?"*

Suddenly, the back draperies flew open with a violent jangling of curtain rings. *"Capitare* is an Italian word, you dolt," said George Kemble. "And the wrong one, at that. Lock us up, Jean-Claude. I'll throw him out through the alley."

Jean-Claude wrinkled his nose, reached past the man, and shot the bolt tight.

Kemble turned his attention to their caller. "Good afternoon, Constable Sisk," he said. "To what do we owe the displeasure?"

"That's *Sergeant* Sisk now, I'll thank you," he said. "In the back, Kem. This is a social call, and I wants to talk private-like."

Kemble lifted his sharp black brows. "A capital notion, dear boy," he answered. "It does my sort of business no good to have the police seen hanging about, does it?"

Jean-Claude followed them through the green velvet draperies and began to polish a silver bowl from a baize table littered with similar pieces. Kemble pulled out the chair at his rolltop desk, and motioned Sisk to take a seat nearby.

Sisk eyed Jean-Claude across the room. "What about 'im?" he asked suspiciously. "I don't need an audience for this."

Kem shrugged. "Doesn't speak a word of English, old chap." Then he threw up the rolltop, and drew out a silver flask and two small crystal tumblers. "Armagnac?"

Sisk turned his suspicious gaze on the flask. "I don't drink noffink I can't pronounce," he said.

"Jean-Claude!" called Kemble over his shoulder. "Bring Sergeant Sisk a bottle of the cheap stuff."

Jean-Claude rummaged around in a nearby cupboard and produced a bottle of gin.

Sisk's expression shifted to one of outrage. "Thought he didn't speak *no anglais!*"

"He's psychic," said Kemble, as Jean-Claude skulked away. "Now, do you want a tot of the pale or not?"

Scowling, Sisk filled his glass. Kemble lifted his and lightly touched Sisk's rim. "Well, to the good old days, then," he said.

"What was so bloody good about 'em?"

"No organized police force?" Kemble ventured. "A fair-minded fence could do an honest day's work back then. Now thanks to Peel and our friend Max, this town is crawling with brass-buttoned blues. Speaking of which, old chap, where is yours?"

Sisk patted his pink waistcoat—and the ample belly beneath—with both hands. "Told you this was a social call," he said. "Not the sort of thing I wants to be doing in uniform."

Kemble let his gaze drift over the man's attire. "Sisk, you have a gift," he declared. "Only a rare sartorial talent would pair that shade of pink with a green coat and mustard trousers."

Sisk's brow furrowed. "Poking fun at me again, eh?"

Kemble splayed his fingertips over his heart. *"Moi?"* he said. "Never. Now, what can I do you out of?"

Sisk finished his gin, dragged the back of his hand over his mouth, then rummaged inside his coat. "Have a gander," he said, extracting a list. "Stolen property. And I wants to retrieve it bad, Kem. A private matter."

Kemble unfolded the grimy sheet of foolscap and let his eyes run down it. "I don't often deal in this sort of thing," he said quite honestly. "Pocket watches? Snuffboxes? It's trivial, Sisk."

Jean-Claude had drifted toward the desk and held out his hand. *"Donnez-le moi."*

"Mais naturellement," said Kemble, passing it to him.

Together, they read it again. Sisk's beefy finger wedged between them. "I want this piece in partic'lar, and I wants it bad," he said, tapping on one item.

"A sapphire cravat pin?" asked Kem incredulously.

"A *half-carat* sapphire cravat pin," Sisk clarified. "Mounted in gold with four prongs."

"Good Lord, Sisk. I've probably got a half dozen lying about this instant." Kem jerked open one of the desk cubbies, poked about, and extracted something. "Here, have this one." He dropped a large faceted sapphire into the sergeant's hand.

Sisk scowled again. "Awright," he said, stabbing with

the beefy finger again. "What about this one, eh? A solid gold pocket case. Handmade in France, glass on one side, and latch that sticks. *With* a miniature in it— which, by the way, was painted by that famous miniature fellow. Not, mind you, that the chap was miniature. He was a reg'lar-sized bloke, but he—"

Kem waved his hand. "I comprehend. You mean Richard Cosway, perhaps?"

Sisk settled back into his chair. "Aye, him," he agreed. "So? Unusual, ain't it?"

"A framed Cosway miniature?" Kem's voice was respectful. "Now, that, old boy, is something worth looking for. To whom did it belong?"

"To that chap what blowed off Lord Scrandle's left pinkie-finger at Chalk Farm last spring." Here, Sisk scratched his head. "'Twas some dustup over a pack of marked cards. Damn me, what was that name?"

Kemble settled back into his chair. "Devellyn," he said quietly. "The Marquess of Devellyn. How very odd."

"Odd how?"

"Never mind," Kemble murmured. "In any case, I shouldn't have thought Devellyn the sentimental type. I can't even think of anyone whose portrait he would care enough to carry."

Sisk stuck a finger in the air. "Now that I knows," he said. "'Twas his brother, or so they tol' me."

Kemble's brows shot up. "His brother?" he said sharply. "The one he killed?"

"Aye, he did, didn't he?" Sisk answered. "I'd forgot that old scandal."

"You may well have forgotten it," Kemble returned.

"But you can rest assured that his family has not. He is now heir to the dukedom."

Sisk shrugged. "Well, that'd be none o' my business, would it?" he said. "But what about the miniature? Seen anything like it?"

Kem shook his head and looked up at Jean-Claude.

The clerk lifted his hands in a bored, Gallic gesture. "*Non, pas moi,*" he said, and drifted back toward the baize table.

"Some help he is," grunted Sisk.

"You don't understand, dear boy," said Kem wearily. "Jean-Claude is a specialist in Ming Dynasty fahua— vases and bowls to you. He couldn't give two shites about this sort of thing. But obviously, you do. And you've taken the case on privately, hmm?"

Sisk drew himself up proudly. "A bunch o' nobs got diddled by some fancy piece," he said. "She's been collecting their pretties as she goes along. They wants to keep it quiet."

"Ah, the Black Angel!" Kemble mused. "Give up, Sisk. You'll never catch that one. She's a professional."

Sisk looked injured. "Aye, and what am I, eel bait?"

Kemble considered it. "Well, honestly, if anyone can bring her to heel, Sisk, you're just the fellow," he finally answered. "But I shan't help you do it. Sorry, old chap. I think your nobs are getting just about what they deserve." Then Kemble gave a humorless smile, and pulled out the flask again. "What say we drink to Peel's health before I toss you out in the alley?"

As the glasses clinked again, Jean-Claude slipped down the passageway and dragged on his coat. "I am going out for a walk," he said to Kemble in rapid French. "I will see you tomorrow."

But Kemble and Sisk were bent over their drinks and their memories again, and they seemed not to hear him go.

The next evening, Lord Devellyn dressed for dinner in a very foul mood. Nothing, it seemed, suited him. First, Fenton got his bloody cravat too tight. Then too loose. Then he tied it in a knot which the marquess took a sudden disliking to, despite the fact that he'd worn the style at least a thousand times in the last six years. Today it was all wrong. On a curse, he stripped it off, and hurled it violently to the floor.

"Another!" he barked.

But Fenton had already scurried off to fetch it. After another ten minutes had passed, the cravat was tied, and the process begun all over again, this time with waistcoats. "God, not brocade!" he snapped, when Fenton held out the first. "Do you want me to match her damned draperies? No, not gray! It's gloomy. The yellow one? Absolutely not."

"My lord, it is new," Fenton protested. "And very elegant."

Devellyn snorted. "It's the color of horse piss!"

"It is called champagne gold," sniffed his valet. "I chose the fabric myself."

But on and on it went. Too bright. Too dull. Too tight. Too . . . *gauche. Stupid. Uncouth. Insensitive.* Yes, that's what this was really about, wasn't it? Stupid he might be, but he was not a fool. Fools were ignorant of their failings. Fools strolled through life blithely happy. He wished to hell he was one.

"My lord," Fenton finally said, his tone one of exasperation. "You are out of waistcoats. You must take one of these, or go without."

"Horse piss, then," he growled, snapping his fingers at it.

With a deep sigh, Fenton shook it out and slid it over his shoulders.

The problem, Devellyn finally admitted, was not with Fenton. Nor did it have anything to do with his wardrobe. The problem was with him. *With what he had done.* Why in God's name had he pressed that poor woman into this dinner invitation? What did he hope to gain? Oh, he had enjoyed teasing her. Flirting with her. And she had, to some extent, let him get away with it. But Devellyn did not need another romantic liaison. He would only bugger it up.

Besides, Sidonie Saint-Godard wouldn't have him, no matter his wealth and title. She had too much taste. Too much class. She wasn't even his usual sort of woman—in other words, she didn't have a price tag hanging off her arse. She was the very thing he was not—*respectable*. If he pursued the woman—and to what end, anyway?— she would only be tainted by their association.

Devellyn lifted his gaze to his gilt-framed cheval glass. A man he barely knew stared back. He realized with a start that he had long ago ceased to look—*truly* look—at himself. The changes were stark. Lean, lithe grace had been replaced by brawn and obstinacy. The boyish lines of his face were a decade gone. An elegant, aristocratic nose had gone askew with his principles, and a jaw which would once have been called well-turned had been chiseled into severity.

Oh, he remembered too well the promise of youth—the invincibility he'd felt in those early years. They had been society's golden boys, he and Greg. Even then, the *ton* had assumed the dukedom would wind its way down the branches of the family tree and settle its mantle over their father's shoulders. Greg, handsome and charming, had been groomed to be next. Aleric had been less malleable. At the time, it had not mattered.

So who was he now, that man in his mirror with the cold, flat eyes and hard mouth? What did he want of life? Anything? *Nothing?* Devellyn shook his head. Who would know if he did not?

"I got me some aspirations," Ruby Black had said so proudly. But Devellyn had none. He had lived his life without purpose. Without ambition. And now, what little enthusiasm he'd had—his taste for revenge—was somehow lessening.

Yesterday he had jotted down the names of the Black Angel's victims—he thought he had remembered them all—and taken as a whole, the list did not particularly trouble him. For the most part, they were gentlemen like Lord Francis Tenby, men he did not particularly like. No doubt more than a few deserved what they had suffered at her hands. Perhaps he had deserved it, too? Many people surely thought so. He could not say they were wrong.

Oh, to hell with the embarrassment and the money, he decided, as Fenton helped him into his coat. Let the greedy witch keep it. But Greg's miniature—that he must reclaim, even if it meant capturing the Angel and turning her over to the likes of Tenby and his angry mob.

Fenton had stepped around and was looking at him warily now.

"Sorry, old chap," said the marquess, forcing his usual grin. "I think I've got it out of my system now."

"Got what out?" said a voice from the door. "Feel free to tell him to sod off, Fenton, if he's behaving badly again. I need a good valet."

Devellyn turned to see Alasdair standing on his threshold. "You're late," he said.

Alasdair opened his hands expansively. "And you are not ready. Besides, I've been serving a noble cause."

The marquess looked at him suspiciously. "What sort of noble cause?"

Alasdair gave a faint smile. "I spent the afternoon with Tenby and his cohorts," he answered. "You are in my debt—again—old friend."

Impatiently, Devellyn waved him down the stairs. Alasdair followed him into the study, where the marquess picked up a decanter of brandy. "Frog water?"

Alasdair grinned. "Nervous?"

Devellyn sloshed out two glasses. "Let be, Alasdair," he warned. "What of this business with Tenby?"

Alasdair went to the hearth, and propped one elbow on the mantel. His grin was gone. "I can't say as I much care for his new friends," he finally answered. "But they are a determined lot."

Devellyn paused with the glass halfway to his lips. "How so?"

Alasdair shrugged. "Their bulldog policeman has put together quite a lot of information on the Black Angel," he finally said. "Dates. Locations. Exact times. And a list of her aliases—which are inventive, to say the least."

Devellyn grunted and tossed back his drink. "I suspect no one else got stripped bare-arsed naked by one Ruby Black."

Alasdair's grin deepened. "No, I think Ruby was saving all her love for you, Dev. But Tenby got himself bloody near poisoned by a French high-flyer calling herself Madame Noire."

"*Noire?* That means . . . why, that means *black*, doesn't it?"

Alasdair nodded. "And get this: her Christian name, she claimed, was *Cerise.*"

"Cerise Noire!" Devellyn laughed so suddenly, he almost blew brandy out his nose. "Damned if the woman doesn't have a sense of humor."

"Oh, it gets better," said Alasdair. "Last month Lord Scrandle picked up a pretty Sicilian soprano backstage at the Haymarket. One Signorina Rosetta Nero, by name. Care to take a stab at the translation?"

Devellyn grinned and picked up the decanter again. "Rose Black?"

"Close enough," said Alasdair. "And then there was poor Will Arnsted, who fancied the chambermaid who came in to build up his fire one evening over at Mivart's Hotel. She managed to lock him in his private parlor, then leapt out the window with everything but his shirt and drawers."

"Let me guess," said Devellyn. "Crimson? Pinkie? Poppy? Or—ha, here you go, Alasdair!—*Scarlet Raven!* After all, she flies out windows!"

Alasdair laughed. "Not bad, old chap!" he said. "But no. It was *Cherry.* With a surname which Armsted took to be C-o-l-e."

"Well, I'm damned!" said Devellyn. "I've a hunch sweet Cherry would have spelt it differently."

"C-o-a-l," said Alasdair. "Depend upon it."

"Good Lord!" said the marquess. "Are we all that stupid? She's been laughing at us all the way to the bank, or wherever it is common pickpockets and sneak thieves keep their loot."

Alasdair shook his head. "Oh, this woman is no common thief," he said. "You may depend upon *that,* too."

"And what of this policeman?" said Devellyn. "What manner of man is he?"

Alasdair leaned over and slapped him on the shoulder. "You may see for yourself, my friend," he said cheerfully. "We're to meet him tonight after eleven at the Oak Tree Inn."

The marquess grunted. "The Oak Tree? Good God, Alasdair! That's on the other side of Stepney!"

Alasdair lifted his shoulders lazily. "Well, that's where he lives," he said. "And if you mean to bribe him behind Tenby's back, it must be discreetly done."

Just then, Fenton darted into the room. "My lord," he said a little frantically. "Honeywell says Mrs. Crosby keeps peeking out her parlor curtains and peering across the street! She's done it above three times now! Really, sir, I think you're going to have to get on with it."

Despite her years spent in retirement, Julia Crosby was still the consummate actress. That evening, Sidonie found herself greatly looking forward to watching Julia play the grand, gracious lady with people she'd not wanted to entertain.

Initially, Julia had laughed at Sidonie's assertion that

the Marquess of Devellyn had invited himself to dinner and that Sidonie had been able to think of no polite way around it. "What rubbish!" she'd snapped. "And you've no business at all associating with the Marquess of Devellyn. You must think of George and all that he is burdened with."

"What has George to do with any of this?" Sidonie had asked, suspicious.

But Julia had grown reticent. "It is just that you put me in a difficult position, Sidonie," she had said. "First you think Devellyn despicable, and wish to go after him on principle, which is dangerous enough. And now you apparently want to befriend the man, which is more dangerous still. George will blame me if anything goes awry."

"What do you wish me to do, Julia?"

"I wish you would stay away from him altogether."

Julia's brow had been furrowed with uncharacteristic worry. And there really was no reason, Sidonie considered, not to do just as Julia asked. She understood that she could not very well maintain a friendship with Devellyn, even if she wished to. Society did not work that way, and Devellyn was not that sort of man. In fact, she still did not know *what* sort of man he was.

And so Sidonie told herself that she would spend just this one evening in his company in order to judge his character fairly. After that, well, she might have a couple of wrongs to make right. But that, she swore to Julia, would be the end of her association with Lord Devellyn. Julia seemed much relieved. And at last, the appointed hour arrived.

And then it went.

For half an hour, Julia paced the floor, pausing only to peek out the window. Eventually, Lord Devellyn's butler began to peek back. It was a little embarrassing, really. Finally, the two gentlemen appeared, apologizing for their tardiness. Lord Devellyn behaved as if he were paying a neighborly visit and nothing more. Sir Alasdair MacLachlan, however, acted the dashing bon vivant, quickly charming Julia.

Throughout dinner, the two of them carried the conversation, Julia regaling Sir Alasdair with tales of her career treading the boards. When anyone tried to turn the discussion toward Sidonie's past, Julia turned it away at once. Sidonie was not precisely ashamed of her family or her background. Still, she had no wish to explain either to near strangers. She was a little surprised, however, at Julia's assiduousness.

Fortunately, Sir Alasdair was quite the theater aficionado. He and Julia were soon in the midst of a lively argument about the greatest actors of the previous decade. "And did you ever meet the wonderful Mrs. Siddons, Mrs. Crosby?" he asked as the last course was cleared. "I saw her in Home's *Douglas,* you know, just before she retired."

"A triumph, was it not?" Julia said.

"I thought her brilliant," agreed Sir Alasdair. "Do you, by chance, know Miss Ellen Tree?"

"Know her?" echoed Julia, pressing a hand to her heart. "Why, I played Maria to her Olivia in *Twelfth Night*. It was her London debut."

"I remember that!" exclaimed Sir Alasdair. "I attended opening night at Covent Garden. You were brilliant, Mrs. Crosby. Do you no longer act?"

Julia smiled tightly. "I am retired," she murmured. "But I believe, Sir Alasdair, that I still have my marked-up script for *Twelfth Night* and some other mementos of the play. I'm something of a collector, you see."

"So am I!" said Sir Alasdair. "But I'm a numismatist—a collector of rare coins. An obsession, collecting, is it not?"

"Indeed." Julia was enjoying herself. "Would you care to see my memorabilia? I have old scripts, playbills, even a few pieces of costuming. The duller bits are packed in the attic, but the interesting parts are in a box which Meg can fetch."

"What excellent after-dinner entertainment!" said Alasdair, just as the port was brought in.

Julia smiled. "Before or after cards?"

"After, by all means!" said Sir Alasdair. "I'll need an excuse to beg off if my luck runs ill. Dev, let's take our port in the drawing room with the ladies."

Lord Devellyn offered Sidonie his arm as they withdrew. It was a solid, well-muscled arm, and she could feel the taut strength beneath the fabric as they started up the stairs. It felt strange being with him like this, calmly, in her own home, as if they were the closest of acquaintances.

She wondered what he would say if he knew the truth; if he somehow discovered she was the woman who had so boldly undressed and caressed him that night at the Anchor. And he had been every inch a man, too. She had to admit a certain fascination still gripped her. Suddenly, a vision of Devellyn naked—the recollection of his impossibly broad shoulders and hard, insistent erection—flashed through her mind. Sidonie tripped on the last step, almost falling flat on her face. Unthinkingly, she clutched hard at Devellyn's arm. In an instant, he righted her, the motion so smooth no one would have noticed.

"Sidonie," he murmured. "You are all right?"

She nodded, flushed with heat, and caught his eyes. *Why, oh why, did he have to be so devilishly handsome?* She shut away that thought and hastened after Julia into the drawing room, dragging Devellyn along with her.

For a few moments, he roamed through the chamber as if taking it all in, Sidonie still on his arm. This room was large, well lit, and stylishly appointed. Despite the fact that most of the furnishings had been Claire's, Sidonie found that tonight she was proud of the impression of restrained opulence it gave. At the far end, four long windows draped in olive velvet overlooked Bedford Place, while at the other end, a gold brocade settee and two matching chairs bracketed the hearth.

The walls were hung with cream-colored silk thinly striped with gold, and an Oriental carpet in shades of emerald and chartreuse covered the whole of the floor. Little groupings of tables and chairs were tucked here and there throughout, including an inlaid mahogany card table, where Julia and Sir Alasdair were chattering as they set up the game.

"I was right," murmured Devellyn.

She looked at him curiously. "About what?"

"Your home is far more welcoming than mine," he said, casting his eye up the creamy marble chimneypiece. "But you haven't an inch of chintz anywhere, have you?"

"I am not a great admirer of it," she admitted. "Do you like it so very much?"

"Not really, it just sounded . . . well, homey. Whatever that is." The marquess covered her hand with his where it lay upon his arm. "By the way, my dear," he went on. "Are you a devotee of the theater? Shall we participate in Alasdair's little stroll down memory lane?"

"I know almost nothing of it," Sidonie answered honestly. "One sees little theater on board a ship."

The marquess's dark brows went up. "Did you spend much time at sea?"

"Most of my marriage."

"How remarkable," he murmured. "Of course, deeply devoted wives do sometimes accompany their husbands to sea." He turned to look at her from beneath a sweep of dark, almost feminine lashes. "Tell me, Sidonie," he said, his voice husky. "Were you a deeply devoted wife?"

She cut her gaze away. "I daresay," she finally answered. "My husband had no love of *terra firma*. And if I wished to see him with any frequency . . . well, what choice did I have?"

"To stay at home alone?" he suggested, resuming their stroll. "It does not sound ideal, does it?"

She still could not look at him. "Pierre was not the sort of man one left alone for long."

"Ah!" he said. "And what sort was that?"

"The charming sort," she said dryly. "I told you I had vast experience in the subject."

He jerked to a halt again. "My apologies," he interjected. "I have brought up a painful topic."

"Not at all." Swiftly, she turned the subject. "Tell me, my lord, why have you never married?"

He laughed, the sound rumbling deep in his broad chest. "Do I look like the marrying kind to you?"

"I hardly know," she admitted. "Pierre was not the marrying kind—and yet he married me. Why, I still do not know."

His answer was swift. "Because he yearned to possess you," he answered. "Is that not obvious?"

She looked up at him with astonishment, and he shocked her by sliding a finger beneath her chin. "A devoted wife," he whispered. "Tell me, my dear, were you a forgiving one as well?"

Somehow, she kept her words cool, and her lashes half-lowered. "I was, at the very least, a practical one."

His face seemed to hover over hers, his hard, disdainful mouth now somehow warm and inviting. For an instant, the room spun away, and they were alone. Would his mouth feel hard and crushing, as it had that night at the Anchor? Or would it soften and mold delicately over her own? She had only to rise onto her toes and bring her lips to his to find out.

In the distance, Julia laughed at something Alasdair had said. The sound jerked Sidonie back into the present. Her face flooded with heat.

Devellyn was still staring down at her through his heavy, hooded eyes. "Forgiving and practical," he echoed, his voice thicker than usual. "A woman like you should be neither, Sidonie. A woman like you should never compromise. Don't waste yourself again on a man like that."

For an instant, she found herself drowning in a pair of dark, silvery eyes filled with more questions than answers. Fortunately, Meg chose that moment to carry in a decanter of sherry for the ladies. Devellyn stepped away. Meg set the sherry down with the port by the bank of windows, then trotted off to fetch the box of theater souvenirs.

The marquess took the glass of wine Sidonie offered calmly, as if nothing had happened between them. *Had* anything happened? Sidonie was not perfectly sure. Lord Devellyn kept her constantly off-balance. Where was the irreverent, lighthearted rogue tonight? Did he even exist?

As she poured wine for Sir Alasdair and Julia, she observed Devellyn withdrawing to a distant corner. His keen, dark gaze began to drift languidly over the room again, as if he were not a participant, but an outsider, merely observing of what went on around him. Sidonie was left with the strangest impression he lived much of life in just that way. She took the opportunity to study his face. It was a strong face, with lean, hard bones, and what some might call the signs of dissipation etched about his eyes. She did not think it was that, but rather, a sort of world-weariness.

His gaze was hooded, but perceptive; as though he knew or saw some truth which others did not. And there was an almost disdainful curl to his lips, as if he found life perpetually disappointing. On the whole, he possessed a face of great character, though he implied he had none. He had the habit of rolling his huge shoulders beneath his jacket. The gesture should have made him look ill at ease, but instead, he looked like a caged beast.

Mechanically, she carried wine to the others. Devellyn strolled back toward the fireplace. Why, she wondered, had he wished to come here tonight? Surely there were a hundred other women he might more easily, and more rewardingly, tempt? And she *was* tempted. The realization shocked her.

Several hours after her strange visit to Devellyn's study yesterday, the crossing sweep had delivered a terse, urgent note from Jean-Claude summoning her to a corner near Bloomsbury Square. Dusk had been long gone, and the gaslights were flickering eerily when Jean-Claude seized her arm and pulled her into a nearby alley.

He had been shaken. *"Mon Dieu,* it is *la police, madame,"* he had whispered. "They come in the Strand tonight with *la—la—*what you say? *La* leest?"

"The list?" she had replied. "The list of what?"

"Of the missing theengs *l'ange noire* stole," he whispered. "All of them. And he wishes especially the leetle gold case of the Marquess *de* Devellyn. In it is heez dead brother whom he killed and which he wishes back very much."

Sidonie had laid a hand on his shoulder. "This is no time to practice your English, Jean-Claude," she said. "Now, who has come? And who is dead?"

But even in his native tongue, Jean-Claude still babbled. "His name is Sisk, *madame,"* he answered. "I know him well. A cunning man. No one is dead. Not today, yes? But this brother of Lord Devellyn, he was killed. Long ago, I believe. Lord Devellyn, he killed him. I think, *madame,* he, too, is very dangerous."

But even then Sidonie had known Devellyn was incapable of such a thing. Why she should believe this of someone she barely knew, and believe it so unreservedly, quite escaped her.

Lost in such thoughts, she was pouring herself a glass of sherry when she felt a warmth at her elbow. "My dear?" Devellyn's low, rumbling voice jerked Sidonie back to the present. "Am I boring you?"

"Oh!" Sidonie looked about, embarrassed. "I did not see you there."

"I am crushed," he said. "I have been here some time."

Sidonie realized she was being a poor hostess. "Shall we play at cards now, my lord?"

He shrugged. "Yes, why not?"

Sidonie lightly touched his hand. He seemed to start at the mere brush of her fingers. "You must find this evening very dull," she said. "I fear you are accustomed to a grander sort of society than Julia and I can provide."

He looked at her oddly. "Why do you say that?" he asked. "Because I am titled? Because I'll likely be a duke someday? I've done nothing to earn either, I assure you."

She looked at him in some surprise. "*Are* you to be a duke? I was not aware."

Devellyn lifted one brow. "If someone doesn't blow my brains to Kingdom Come in a dawn appointment, or knife me in the heart over a bad hand of cards, yes, it does seem inevitable."

"I did not realize," she murmured.

"Did you not?" he said. "Then there is a vast deal, my dear, you do not know about me. I am not much seen in polite society. Indeed, it is you who have no business entertaining me."

"I cannot think why."

The cynical smile curled his mouth again. "Can you not, Sidonie?" he answered. "How charitable of you. But have a care, my dear, for your reputation."

She laughed richly. "I prefer to live life to the fullest, my lord," she answered. "I am not worried for my reputation."

"You should be," he answered. "Associating with me shan't enhance it, I assure you." Then he lifted his chin and looked toward the card table. "Alasdair!" he called. "Alasdair, old boy, are you ready to take a proper thrashing?"

Alasdair's head jerked up from the large box Meg had just set on the table. "By all means, Dev, if you're man enough."

Julia laughed and rapped Alasdair on the arm with her fan. "But we have not drawn for partners, sir," she said. "You and Lord Devellyn might play together."

The gentlemen exchanged glances as Sir Alasdair moved the box. Clearly, they had not considered this a serious game. Devellyn shrugged. "Very well," he said, drawing up a chair. He fanned the fresh pack of cards across the table with a sweep of his hand. "Highest plays lowest. Ladies?"

Julia leaned over the card table. She drew first, turning the ten of clubs.

"Excellent." Lord Devellyn gave a half bow in Sidonie's direction. "Madame Saint-Godard?"

Sidonie ran her fingertip back and forth along the fan, her eyes closed.

"Oh ho!" said Alasdair. "We've a serious gamester here, Dev."

"Anything worth doing, Sir Alasdair, is worth doing seriously," Sidonie answered. With a sudden flick of her fingertip, she turned the queen of spades.

"Well, I'm damned," said Devellyn.

"So they say," answered Alasdair. He turned over the

three of diamonds, and sighed deeply. "Get on with it, Dev."

Devellyn drew, glanced, then flung down the two of clubs. "Kiss me, Al," he said dryly. "We're partners for the evening."

"Well!" said Julia briskly. "This should be fun. Gentlemen, what stakes?"

"A guinea a point," suggested Devellyn.

Julia made a pout with her lips. "That is hardly worth the effort, my lord."

"It *isn't* worth the effort," Alasdair complained. "I should rather see Mrs. Crosby's memorabilia."

"Shut up and play, Alasdair," said the marquess.

For half an hour, they tossed down their cards amidst generally witty conversation, with Sidonie determined to win. On the *Merry Maiden,* she'd learned all there was to know about cards, and Julia was a ruthless whist player. Unfortunately, things did not begin promisingly.

In the third game, their luck turned. When the deal passed to Sidonie, she dealt herself a handful of red, then turned up a trump that made Sir Alasdair chuckle. He snapped his cards together, and tapped the trump with the corner of his pack. "I have the feeling you're done for this time, old friend."

Devellyn eyed the trump card for a moment. "The queen of hearts," he murmured. "You think it a bad omen, Alasdair?"

It was. The ladies surged ahead, taking eight tricks in the first hand. The second and third went almost as well. With the gentlemen squarely at zero and the ladies on the verge of going out, Sir Alasdair began to make jokes about being trounced by Amazons.

Julia and Alasdair paused to refill their wineglasses. The deal passed to Lord Devellyn, who turned up diamonds for trumps.

"Oh, drat!" said Julia, surveying her hand. "Misfortune is mine tonight!"

Sir Alasdair laughed. "Might I remind you, ma'am, that you're leading four to naught?"

"Yes," said the marquess dryly. "If your luck is out, it is only for the nonce, I'm quite sure."

"Indeed, how would you like to be old Dev here?" added Alasdair. "Misfortune has followed him about for a sen'night like some sort of stray dog."

Julia looked up from her hand. "How perfectly dreadful," she murmured. "Ill luck at the tables, my lord?"

"Not exactly," muttered the marquess. "Lead on, ma'am."

Julia tossed down a black two, but Alasdair had seemingly lost interest in the game. "Had you not heard the story, Mrs. Crosby?" he asked, his voice a wicked whisper.

"Oh, for pity's sake, Alasdair!" said Devellyn. "Play the bloody game!"

Alasdair tossed down a worthless eight of clubs, and rattled on. "It started, you know, with Miss Lederly hurling all his chamber pots out the window," he went on. "Then there was the death-watch beetle in his staircases. And following that, his cousin Richard unexpectedly dropped dead—"

"A third cousin," grumbled the marquess. "And how unexpected could it have been, Alasdair? The man was ninety-two."

"Still, your luck has gone downhill from there, old boy," Alasdair continued. "I cannot believe, Mrs. Crosby, that you'd not heard the whole of it."

Julia had lost some of her color. She obviously sensed what Alasdair was leading up to. "Our condolences, my lord," she managed to murmur.

Sidonie forced herself to smile. "Gracious, Devellyn!" she said, tossing down another black. "Alasdair has quite forgotten your accident yesterday."

Julia looked even more confused. "An accident?"

"Yes, Miss Lederly set his carpet afire," Alasdair cheerfully interjected.

Julia looked aghast. "Why?"

Devellyn shot Julia a wry look. "Let us just say that I've had a run of devilish bad luck, ma'am," he said, trumping the trick and sweeping it up. "But it seems to be turning. Alasdair, perhaps you ought to attend the game instead of the gossip?"

Alasdair tossed his hand down with a grin. "Now I must tell all, Dev!" he said. "Ladies, my friend here is also the latest victim of the Black Angel. I would regale you with the sordid details, but they are not for ladies' ears."

"Do hush, Alasdair," said the marquess.

Julia tossed back the rest of her sherry.

"A black angel?" said Sidonie innocently. "I'm afraid I do not follow."

"No, *the* Black Angel," Sir Alasdair repeated, as if to jog her memory. "The female Robin Hood who preys upon gentlemen of the *ton*?"

Sidonie widened her eyes. "Really, Sir Alasdair! Surely there is no such creature?"

"Do you mean to say you've not heard of the Angel's exploits, ma'am?"

Sidonie shook her head. "I'm afraid we are not much in society."

Deep in the house, a clock could be heard striking ten. Julia cleared her throat. "I believe I shall have another sherry," she said. "I get the distinct impression this game just ended."

"Yes, I'd much rather pilfer through your memorabilia box," agreed Alasdair.

"Only a milksop quits when he's being thrashed, Alasdair." Devellyn looked at Sidonie. "Piquet, my dear?"

Julia and Sir Alasdair moved to the table by the windows. The marquess began to methodically sort the pack of cards, tossing the small ones aside.

Sidonie looked at him. "My lord, you don't really wish to play piquet, do you?"

"I quite loathe it," he admitted, deftly shuffling what was left of the pack. "But it is an excuse to sit quietly with you and avoid Alasdair altogether."

She stilled his hand, lightly touching his coat sleeve. For an instant, their gazes met. "You need no excuse," she said quietly. "This is my home, my lord. And Julia is my friend, not a chaperone."

He crooked one brow sharply. "You are very young, my dear."

"Not so far from thirty," she murmured. "As you recently reminded me."

"Badly done of me, I admit," he said. "Especially since you don't look it. How long, my dear, were you married?"

Sidonie's smile faltered. "Ten years."

He reshuffled the cards without looking at them. Instead, his gaze held hers, intense and steady. "A child bride," he said.

"Hardly. I was seventeen."

"Did you know what you were doing at seventeen? Assuredly, I did not."

"Many girls are married at that age."

Devellyn made a vague gesture with his hand. "Arranged marriages, yes," he said. "But you, Sidonie? Your marriage was not arranged, I'll warrant."

"Why do you say that?"

"I think you would marry only if you thought yourself in love."

"You know me that well, my lord, on such short acquaintance?"

"Yes," he answered. "Am I wrong?"

Across the room, Alasdair and Julia burst into peals of laughter. Alasdair turned in his chair and lifted something from the box, as if he wished Devellyn to look at it. It was an old-fashioned corset.

"What in God's name are they about?" muttered Devellyn. "No, never mind. They are a bad influence on one another. Now, answer my question."

Sidonie bit her lip. "No, you are not wrong," she admitted. "I eloped with Pierre—ran away from school, no less—because I thought myself in love."

"*Were* you in love?"

Sidonie hesitated. "I was . . . lonely," she answered. "But yes, I felt all those things one reads about in love poems, silly though they now seem."

"Are they silly?" he asked.

"Very silly."

"My dear, you disappoint me," he murmured. "I was hoping the poets were correct on the whole, and that the love of a good woman might someday redeem even me."

"I think you tease me, my lord."

He tilted his head to one side. "Do I? I am not sure."

"What sort of redemption do you seek, then? If you wish only the forgiveness of society, my lord, much can be forgiven for a title." She hesitated for a moment. "And for a dukedom, nearly anything."

Devellyn laughed so loud, Julia and Alasdair turned in their chairs. This time, Alasdair held a pair of red silk harem boots with curling toes.

Sidonie chose that moment to venture into more dangerous waters. When Devellyn's gaze recaptured hers, she drew a deep breath. "My lord, I collect you have family," she said casually. "Are you close?"

The marquess lifted one shoulder. "Not really," he said. "My mother disapproves of how I live my life, and my father and I are politely estranged."

"Oh," she said softly. "That often happens, does it not?"

"Family estrangement?" He looked at her warily. "You sound as if you speak from experience."

Sidonie hesitated. "My father died while I was away at school," she answered. "And my mother had her own life. We were not, perhaps, estranged. But we were none of us close."

"I'm sorry," he said.

She lifted one brow and shook her head. "There are worse things, I daresay," she answered. "What of you? Have you no other family? No brothers or sisters?"

The marquess's gaze turned inward. "I had a brother," he said, his hand dipping into his coat pocket. "Until he died, we were insepara—" His hand froze.

Sidonie felt suddenly ill. "What is wrong?"

Devellyn withdrew the hand, and smiled tightly. "I once carried his miniature," he answered. "But I was careless with it. Still, after so many years of having it with me, I cannot quite get used to this empty pocket."

Sidonie could feel the blood draining from her face. "I am so sorry."

He shrugged. "Ah, well, I merely wished to show you to see his likeness," he said. "Greg was very handsome, with a look of kindness about his eyes which I, alas, do not possess."

"I'm not sure that is true," said Sidonie awkwardly.

"An admirable lie," he answered. "What of you, my dear? Who is it that calls you *Sid* when I cannot?"

But Sidonie was still thinking of the young man in the miniature. "I've a brother, George," she answered dully. "He is much older, and something of a—" She stopped, unable to form the right words.

"Something of a what?"

Sidonie shook her head. "My relationship with George is hard to explain," she said. "He is more than a brother, but less than a parent."

"I think I see."

Sidonie smiled wanly. "I'm not sure you do."

"You could . . . tell me more?"

She opened and closed her mouth soundlessly. "George ran away from home when he was very young," she finally said. "He fell in with a bad, danger- ous crowd—I don't mean rakes, rogues, or spoilt rich boys. I mean *dangerous*. And after that, we were . . . estranged, too, I suppose. But not by choice, if you see the difference?"

"I think so," he said. "And I see you are very fond of him, too."

She managed to nod. "After George ran away, I did not see him for a long time. Mother sent me away to school. I thought never to see him again, but not long after my marriage, he found me. I was very glad."

"And now he is a changed man, I suppose," said Devellyn.

Sidonie stared at the table. "That would depend upon one's definition."

Devellyn lifted one brow again. "This brother of yours sounds like a man of mystery."

Slowly, she lifted her gaze to his. "It has always been just George and me," she said quietly. "George is . . . strong. A little ruthless, really. But when I was small, it felt as though he was the only person I could count on. Papa was rarely around, and Mother was forever quarreling with the nannies and governesses, so they did not stay long." She paused and covered her lips with her fingertips. "Oh, my God! Why am I telling you this?"

"My compassionate, caring face?" he ventured.

Sidonie looked at him skeptically. "No, definitely not."

The marquess grinned. "Just go on."

And strangely, she did, with no clear notion of why. "George was Papa's only son," she continued. "But our parents were . . . were not married. We were just Papa's second-best family."

"Ah, I do see."

"Yes, well, it is rather a long and miserable story," she said. "I shan't bore you with any more of it."

The marquess laid aside his pack of cards. "There is much in my life I'd rather not discuss," he admitted. "I think I understand."

Suddenly, Sir Alasdair stood. "Good Lord, Dev!" he said. "It's half past ten."

Devellyn withdrew his watch. "So it is," he agreed, standing. "Ladies, I am sure we have overstayed our welcome."

"Oh, no!" said Julia. "Must you go?"

Sir Alasdair looked a little embarrassed. "I'm afraid we have business in Stepney," he answered. "Unfortunately, it cannot wait."

"Stepney!" said Julia. "You must mean to be out half the night!"

Sir Alasdair laughed. "We usually are, ma'am," he said. "Thank you for the good company. We'll not find it so pleasurable where we mean to go, I fear."

After that, Lord Devellyn, too, thanked them, and all the proper bows were made. Then together, Sidonie and Julia showed their guests back down the stairs and restored to them their sticks, cloaks, and hats.

A little sorrowfully, Julia watched them cross the threshold, then shut the door with a sigh. "What thoroughly charming gentlemen!" she said, as if forgetting her earlier reluctance. "I've not had so much fun in many a day."

Chapter Eight

In which Ilsa and Inga are left Deeply disappointed

"We'd best go down to Great Russell Street for a hackney." Alasdair's voice was pensive. "It won't do to have Tenby hear that your carriage was seen anywhere near Sisk's house."

Lord Devellyn lifted his gaze from the piece of pavement he'd been assiduously studying. "I beg your pardon, Alasdair?" he said. "I was not attending."

Alasdair stopped walking. "The meeting with Sergeant Sisk," he pressed. "Christ Jesus, you're thinking about that woman, aren't you?"

Devellyn shook his head. *Women* was the word Alasdair should have used, since there were two of them plaguing him. Devellyn kept obsessing over them in turn—sometimes even in the same moment. But why now? And why *two*? Good Lord, could two females have been more different?

"Come on," said Alasdair. "Step lively, Dev."

Devellyn considered it but a moment. "I think not tonight, Alasdair," he finally answered. "I'm tired."

"Good Lord, do you want the Black Angel or not?" Alasdair sounded annoyed. "The sergeant is expecting us. We can bribe him out from under Tenby if you wish, but time is wasting."

The marquess set a hand on Alasdair's shoulder, then let it slip away. "No doubt, old chap," he answered. "But not tonight. I'll send a messenger to recompense the fellow for his wasted time. Will that do?"

Alasdair shrugged. "Well, it's your miniature she stole, Dev," he said, starting down the pavement. "Suit yourself. For my part, I think the night's young. I believe I'll go down to Mother Lucy's to see if Ilsa and Inga are engaged."

The marquess lifted one brow. "Ah, yes," he said. "The pretty Swedish sisters everyone is talking about."

Alasdair's expression heated. "Twins, Dev!" he corrected. "Limber, long-legged blondes with breasts like a Rubens painting, and cornsilk hair that hangs all the way to the cracks of their luscious little bums."

"That good, eh?"

Alasdair lifted one brow. "Quin Hewitt swears Ilsa can cross her ankles behind her head, and Inga can suck the brass off a ten-inch candlestick."

"Hmm," said Devellyn. "That's descriptive."

Alasdair slapped him encouragingly across the back. "And if Inga can suck the brass off a candlestick, she'll find it no challenge to suck all those troubles out your pikestaff, eh? Then Ilsa can use those clever little hands of hers to rub all the tension out of your shoulders. Metaphorically, I mean. Or even literally, if you prefer."

"My troubles, Alasdair, are in my head," said the marquess. "The one which sits on my tense shoulders.

And no amount of sucking or rubbing will fix it tonight."

Alasdair cocked one eyebrow. "Everything flows downhill, old boy," he retorted. "Metaphorically. *And* literally. Now, come on, be a sporting chap. Tell you what—I'll even sing hymns with you if you like. All the way down to Lucy's."

"Good Lord," said Devellyn. "We're neither of us drunk enough for that, Alasdair. Besides, I've every confidence you can keep both Ilsa and Inga productively engaged without me."

"But Dev, what you really need is—"

"A good night's rest," he interjected.

"But twins, old boy!" he persisted. "It would be better, even, than those three French *filles de joie* we hired in the rue Richer last spring! Remember the one who kept screaming 'Harder! Harder!' 'til you knocked yourself out cold on the headboard?"

Finally, Devellyn laughed. "Must you remind me?"

Alasdair grinned. "So come on, Dev. It will do you a world of good."

"Another time, Alasdair," he said firmly. "Pray make my apologies to Ilsa and Inga."

"Lately, old boy, I worry what's got into you," said Alasdair, turning to go. "Time was, you'd have buggered a knothole in a rotting fence. Now you're passing up Swedish twins."

"A grievous error, I've no doubt," he murmured, setting a heavy hand back on Alasdair's shoulder. "Hold up a moment, can you?"

"That's more like it," said his friend magnanimously. "And you can have Ilsa first, if you prefer."

Devellyn shook his head again. "No," he said quietly. "No, I'm not going. But tell me, Alasdair—what did you think of our evening? Or rather, what did you think of Madame Saint-Godard?"

Alasdair was silent for a long moment. "I think," he finally said, "that you are in shite up to your boot tops, Dev."

Below the street level of Bedford Place, in the scullery of Number Fourteen, Sidonie and Julia were helping Mrs. Tuttle and Meg carry down the plate, china, and linen so that all could be properly washed up. Theirs was a small, informal house. A dinner party, even a small one, taxed the staff.

After what felt like ten trips down to the kitchen, Sidonie at last dragged herself up the three flights of stairs to her bedchamber. Exhausted, she stripped off her clothing, dropped it into an untidy pile, then flung herself naked across the bed with a volume of poetry. But the book could not long hold her attention, and halfway through Shelley's "Indian Serenade," she rolled onto her back, and stared up at the plasterwork ceiling, the words running wild in her head.

> *I arise from dreams of thee*
> *And a spirit in my feet*
> *Hath led me—who knows how?*
> *To thy chamber window, Sweet.*

But she'd already been to *her* chamber window—and indeed, when no one else was looking, to every window which gave onto Bedford Place. And she knew that in the house across the street, the lamps had gone out long ago. Devellyn's chamber window, whichever it happened to be, was probably three floors up and steeped in darkness. No light burned in the front of his house—nor in the rest of it, either, she'd wager.

Sidonie sighed aloud, frustrated by something she could not name. Why did it feel so hot and muggy in London tonight? The clock downstairs was striking midnight. Sidonie rolled over again, then grabbed a pillow and punched it into a semisatisfactory shape. Perhaps it felt hot and muggy because, ever since she'd tripped going up the stairs on Devellyn's arm, she'd been thinking of him. Specifically, of her vision of him naked. And sprawled across his bed. Or *her* bed. Or—*oh, God!* She was losing her mind.

She couldn't think *why* she was obsessed with thoughts of the man. He was, by his own admission, a lout. He was not romantic. He was not lithe, not graceful, not even handsome in any conventional sense. He dressed decently, but there was no elegance in him. He was a man's man, open and brash. He was also a scoundrel—albeit a little more pure of heart than she'd first thought.

But why think of him at all? And in particular, why keep wallowing in lurid imaginings about him naked, whether he be saint or sinner?

Perhaps it was because Devellyn constituted a challenge. Admittedly, she wanted him—and in a deeply sexual way. It surprised her that she should be drawn to raw, brute strength. There was no charisma. Just pure visceral energy. Devellyn would simply take what he wanted without troubling himself to pretty up the process with words or tricks.

She thought of him that night in the Anchor. "*I want*

you," he had said to Ruby Black. *"Name your price."*

Those words—so blunt, so raw, and so honest—made her shiver now. But there had been tenderness in him, too. He had touched her gently for the most part, and apologized when he did not. In the lamplight, Sidonie eased her hand down the counterpane, closed her eyes, and touched herself. Oh, yes. That was her shameful secret. She wanted it, too. She had had a taste of him. And now, what he was did not matter.

It was, on one level, a relief to feel physical lust again. At least her ability to desire a man was not dead, as she had once feared. Sidonie had always enjoyed sex—until she'd discovered Pierre having it with someone else. Then it had lost its charm.

There it was again. *Charm.* That wretched word she'd come to hate. Lord Devellyn was not charming. He was a beast. And she knew beyond a doubt that he'd say *yes.* If she asked him. She'd seen that much in his eyes. She tipped her head back and stroked herself lightly. God, what a wicked woman she was.

For an instant, Sidonie toyed with the insane notion of just going across the street and asking Devellyn to take her to bed. The prospect was breathtaking to consider, and it had been a long time since anything had left Sidonie breathless. Even her midnight escapades of flirting, deceiving, and thieving no longer did so.

Could she do it? Could she just ask him, point-blank? No. Too bold, even for her. And then there was the matter of that damned tattoo . . . Besides, she consoled herself, Devellyn was out for the evening. He had gone off on some sort of caper with Sir Alasdair. One could only imagine what.

Just then, Thomas leapt onto the bed, severing the strange mood. And suddenly, Sidonie realized what she had to do. Or perhaps it was more a case of what she *wished* to do. Ignoring that small truth, she got up. Ever the opportunist, Thomas stretched languidly across the warm spot she'd left and watched her move through the room as she gathered her things. His face wore the dispassionate expression of a wiser, more superior being. He thought her an idiot, most likely.

"Curiosity killed the cat, eh, Tommy?"

The cat blinked his gold eyes, stretched out a hind leg, and began to nibble at his toes.

Thomas was right. She was about to do something inexplicably stupid. Yet she could not seem to stop herself. But it was the right thing to do. Wasn't it?

After washing off her perfume with plain, strong soap, Sidonie dressed quickly in nothing but soft-soled boots, a woolen shirt, and a pair of loose trousers. Then she braided her hair, coiled it high and tight, and pulled on a brimmed leather hat. That done, she wrapped Devellyn's possessions, including the gold miniature case, in plain handkerchiefs, tucked them into a small silk sack, and dropped Devellyn's money on top. She could not keep such ill-got gains. Whatever Devellyn's sins—and undoubtedly, they were legion—they weren't the ones she'd assumed him guilty of. He had not thrown Miss Lederly, or any of his other mistresses, into the street. Quite the opposite. And now she knew that the man in the miniature was his beloved dead brother. Sidonie felt ashamed of having jumped to conclusions.

The house had fallen silent. Swiftly, she tied the bag to her with a cotton cord and dropped into her pocket the cracksman's calling card—a slender, silver starring-hammer. Just in case. Then she wrapped her waist with a thin, strong rope attached to a small grappling hook, a trinket she'd salvaged from her seafaring days. She shoved her shirttails in to cover it all. Absent any braces, the trousers rode a bit low. Still, they would make her climb much safer.

With Julia abed and Meg still belowstairs, it was easy to slip out through the mews and into the fringes of Great Russell Street. When certain she could move un-seen, she slipped through the intersection like a shadow. Still, she knew that what she was doing was incredibly dangerous. Indeed, *everything* the Black Angel did was dangerous. And foolish. Not to mention futile, in all likelihood.

So why, she asked herself for the hundredth time, did she keep doing it? No matter how many exploited women she helped, no matter how many self-indulgent noblemen she punished, she would never have the re-venge she truly sought. Sadder still, her actions were but a finger in the dike of human misery. She would help but one or two, perhaps—out of one or two hundred. So why did she go on?

A death wish, Julia had once called it. Initially, Julia had rejected out of hand Sidonie's pleas to teach her about costuming and acting. But Sidonie had worn her down, and proven herself to be a natural mimic. Besides, it wasn't a death wish. It was . . . about giving people choices.

She herself had had very few of those. Her mother, almost none, once her virtue was gone. And all of it was the fault of her father, a powerful man who saw what he wanted, took it, and damned the consequences. She and George. They *were* the damned consequences; the living, breathing results of unchecked selfishness.

But she must not think of that. Not now. Thinking of it was a good way to slip up. To misjudge oneself—or one's quarry—when the error of a mere second might be critical. Only by focusing on the small things—a footfall, a whisper, an intuitive, well-timed glance in the right direction—would greater things be done. As if to remind her, something squeaked in the darkness. She froze. A weight, something almost buoyant, skittered ephemerally over her boot toe.

Just a mouse. She steadied her breathing and gathered her wits. It was dark as pitch in the mews behind Devellyn's house, and the gate, of course, was locked. She clambered up his garden fence and peeked over. No gaslight permeated here. One moved by feel and instinct. Sidonie threw her last leg over the top, balanced her weight for an instant on her hands, then dropped like a cat into the gloom.

She landed neatly, her soft boots crunching into the graveled yard. She hunkered down to listen. Silent as the grave. And twice as dark. The back of the house was unlit save for a narrow belowground casement beneath the study window. The servants' hall, most likely. Best to avoid that.

On the opposite side of the garden, she could see the faint silhouette of a row of outbuildings which abutted the house at one end. The privy. The boothy. Perhaps a shed where ashes were stored. She kept to the shadows as she approached, scuttling along with her back to the wall. A large dustbin sat at the end farthest from the house. It was an easy task to climb onto it, then up to the low roof of the privy. She made her way across the roofline to the house, then studied the dark windows above.

Now the hard part. She looked far up—two floors up—where the master's rooms would most likely be. Would Devellyn's bedchamber be to the left or to the right? In the end, it did not matter. A stout drainpipe ran up the right. She would go in the right-hand window and make her way from there. Perhaps she would get lucky and find herself in Devellyn's room. Perhaps she would be unlucky, and find the window locked. In that case, she would be wise to star the glass, hurl the sack inside, and bolt. But somehow, she knew she would not stop at that. Oh, how foolish she was.

Her eyes had adjusted fully to the gloom. Still, it took four tries before she was able to secure her rope to the drainpipe. That done, she shinnied slowly up, quietly hoisting herself along the side of the house. To Sidonie, the climb was no more difficult than working with sails, which she'd done on more than one occasion. Illness and desertion could take a toll on a crew, always inopportunely. Then "all hands on deck" would suddenly hold new meaning. Pierre had been open-minded, and glad for the help in a pinch. Sidonie had soon found herself familiar with calluses and trousers.

She peered up in the gloom and kept moving. The window was deep and of good size, thank God. And well used, too. It slid silently up with little effort. She threw one leg over the sill, and at once, the scent inside the room struck her. Tobacco and lime and the woodsy smell of soap. And underlying it all was the warm, earthy scent of male. *Of Devellyn.* She would have known it anywhere.

The thought disconcerted her, and her leg caught on the sill, jangling the bag round her waist. She paused just inside. It did not appear to be a large room. Sidonie tried to make out the sturdy, square pieces of furniture. On the opposite wall, a tall armoire. Beside it, some sort of chest or cabinet. Or was it a chair? No, too large. To her left, the vague outline of a bed draped in shadowy fabric. Then, opposite the foot of the bed, she saw it. A dressing table.

She went to it, hiked up her shirt, and swiftly untied the bag. She laid out the banknotes first. Then, one by one, she began to unwrap the other things and place them on the table.

Devellyn came suddenly awake to a sound he did not recognize. Someone was rummaging about in his room. Honeywell? Fenton? But he saw no candle. Even the one he'd been reading by had guttered. He lifted his head from the back of the chair, where he'd foolishly drifted off, and laid aside his magazine. *He was not alone.* Cool night air swirled through the room. The window. It should not have been open.

Silently, he eased his bare feet off the ottoman and leaned forward. At the foot of his bed, a slight figure loomed. Metal jangled softly on his dressing table. *A bloody thief?* Yes, and a young one, too, by the look of him.

By God, not again! Noiselessly, he rose to his feet. He wished to the devil he wasn't wearing a white nightshirt. In the gloom, he could barely make out the slender figure pilfering his things. *A mere boy.* He'd likely break both his arms before the rascal realized what had got hold of him.

Devellyn was unsympathetic. He lunged, taking the lad down in the narrow space between the bed and dressing table. Something metallic clattered across the floor. The boy grunted when the marquess landed, but strangely, he made no other sound. Still, he was quick. And deadly silent. He kicked and flailed viciously, then gave Devellyn a good elbow to the ribs in a blind, backward shot.

"Umph!" grunted Devellyn. "Hold still, you thieving bastard!"

For an instant, they rolled and tumbled across the rug, arms and legs entwined, elbows flying. Devellyn slammed the lad's head into the bed's footboard. But the lad was tough. He cursed softly, and caught Devellyn this time with an elbow to the throat. Devellyn choked. The lad tried to drag himself across the carpet toward the open window, and bloody near made it.

Devellyn scrabbled after him, snatching one ankle. "By God, I'll see you hanged!"

Another grunt, and the lad almost squirmed away, clawing his way along the carpet between the footboard and dressing table. Devellyn grabbed him round the ankle, then the knee, hauling him ruthlessly back inch by inch. When he had him, he rolled him over and slung a leg over the lad's body, weighing him down.

For a few seconds, the thief fought like a tiger, clawing and scratching, and doing his best to squirm from beneath Devellyn. It was then he made a near-fatal mistake. He tried to knee Devellyn in the knackers.

"Why, you bloody, snot-nosed shite!" the marquess roared. He tried to grab the lad around the waist again, but the boy was onto that trick. He twisted violently, but he wasn't fast enough. Devellyn caught him. But not by the waist.

"Well, damn me for a fool!" he said, his hand full of warm, plump breast.

The thief stopped wiggling and twisting. He—no, *she*—lay splayed beneath Devellyn's body, panting for breath. Devellyn wasn't even winded. He opened his mouth to bellow for Honeywell to bring a lamp when the thief cursed again. This time, something about the sound made Devellyn freeze.

"What the bloody hell?"

"Look 'ere, gov'," whispered Ruby Black. "Let loose, awright? It ain't wot yer thinkin'."

Understanding slammed into him. For an instant, Devellyn couldn't think straight. Ruby's lissome body was round and warm beneath his own. He didn't know what the hell was happening, but he had no intention of letting her go. Especially not her breast. He squeezed it roughly.

In the darkness, she gasped. "Now, it ain't wot you think," she whispered again. "Let me up, awright?"

Devellyn snapped. "Why, you bald-faced, light-fingered little bitch!" he spat. "Of all the unmitigated gall—"

Ruby twisted impotently. "I didn't nick nothin'," she hissed. "Let me up, and I'll be on me way."

Devellyn tore the hat from her head, and slicked his hand over her hair, as if that might disprove what his aching, itching body already knew. It did not help. It was Ruby, right enough. But this time, her hair was drawn back tight, coiled up high like some prim, proper governess. Suddenly, he wished he could see its vivid sheen. But that thought merely served to heighten his anger. He fisted his hand in the coil of hair and forced her face into his.

"Let me go," she whispered. "Please."

"Oh, no, Ruby," he answered. "You've the devil to pay this time, remember?"

"I brought yer goods back, gov. Let me go."

But Devellyn had ceased, really, to hear her. His brain had seemingly disengaged. He heard only her breath panting in the darkness. Felt only the warm, full curves of her body. And there was the rage; that simmering anger and frustration which had boiled down to a sort of nasty black pitch in the bottom of his soul.

Suddenly, she tried to jerk free.

"Oh, no you don't, darling," he hissed, pressing his lips to her ear. "We've unfinished business, you and I."

With all of his seventeen stone bearing down on her, Devellyn thrust one hand beneath her arse and lifted her hips against his cock. She squirmed desperately, a foolish thing to do. Devellyn felt the anger and lust course through him. He wanted a lamp. A candle. *Anything*. But he knew better. She was too fast. Too smart. So instead, he tightened his fingers in her hair, tilted back her head, and raked his teeth down her throat.

Ruby gasped, and writhed beneath him. But Devellyn's nightshirt was already twisted around his waist from their wrestling match. Her desperation merely served to rub the fall of her trousers back and forth against his hardening cock.

Roughly, he massaged her breast, rolling it back and forth in his hand, then plucking at her nipple. She wore nothing beneath her coarse frieze shirt. He was sure of it. He wanted more. Wanted to touch her. Impatiently, he moved to jerk her shirt free, only to find it already loose.

"Don't," she whispered. "Oh, don't. Let me go."

"Oh, no," he hissed, skating one hand underneath the shirt, up her bare, shivering flesh. "I mean to take what I paid for, you hot-blooded little bitch."

She trembled when he settled his bare hand over her breast. "I brought yer money back," she insisted. "On that table. *Look.*"

"And leave you to dive out the window again?" he whispered. "Not bloody likely."

She whimpered beneath him as he inched his hand up her body, but her breath seized, and her nipple peaked hard as soon as his bare palm brushed it.

"You like that?" he rasped.

"No."

"Liar," said Devellyn.

"Please. I'm begging you."

He chuckled, and lowered his mouth to hers. "Oh, Ruby, I do love to hear you beg," he said. Then he kissed her roughly, opening his mouth wide over hers and thrusting deep on the first stroke.

He felt her exhale, felt her warm breath on his cheek, and then he felt her hips rise. Lust surged through him, stronger than ever. He drew his tongue from her mouth, and thrust again, shoving her head back against the floor.

Ruby squirmed, heightening his desire. Devellyn felt

like he was going to explode. His hand went to the fall of her trousers, and roughly jerked. A button gave, flew off, and landed softly on the carpet. He kept kissing her, kissing her hard, and began pushing clumsily and urgently at her trousers. He had to have her. Had to be inside. He forced away the fear that she was not willing. The fact that they were on the floor, wedged between the table and bed. And, most importantly, that he had no clue who the hell she really was. He wasn't about to slow down and ask.

Her baggy trousers gave way easily. Too easily. He set his hand flat on her belly, and felt her warm skin quiver as he skimmed down. Suddenly, he halted. "Good God Almighty," he choked.

Nothing but her bare flesh lay beneath, soft and inviting. Devellyn tore his mouth from hers. "You don't have a stitch on under here."

Ruby twisted her face away. "Didn't plan on 'aving me trousers off, did I?"

But Devellyn was in no mood to talk. Instead, he jerked her shirt higher, baring both her breasts. He set his hands on her shoulders and held her down. His mouth nuzzled the sweet, hard tip of her nipple. Ruby's warm scent enveloped him. He inhaled it deeply, then sucked her areola into his mouth and bit.

Ruby gasped, and her hips came up to meet him again in a sweet, involuntary motion. Oh, yes. Her body wanted him, even if her mind did not. For long moments he sucked and nipped at her as she struggled beneath his weight. His teeth were more rough than gentle. His harsh beard abraded her tender flesh, he knew. But Devellyn seemed unable to gentle his motions. He was half-afraid if he slowed down, he'd think better of what he was doing.

But Ruby no longer felt so reluctant. Her hips kept rising to meet his. Her breath was coming in fast, desperate pants. Still suckling her, he shoved her pants down with one hand. It was a bad, awkward job, but he had to be inside. His cock was as hot and hard as an anvil. His head was swimming in the scent of her. He eased his hand down her belly, and didn't stop. Her heated flesh left him aching. He slid one finger into her curls, then deeper, plunging it into the warm, damp heat.

Ruby called out, a soft, thready cry. She was wet. Beyond wet. She was begging. Hot and inviting, her taut sheath pulling at his finger. Devellyn was shocked. He eased his finger back and forth, and Ruby groaned, her head going back as if in invitation. "Oh, God," she moaned.

He turned his face into her neck, and bit lightly at the soft flesh beneath her ear. "You want me," he growled. "Say it, Ruby."

"No."

"Tell me you want it, Ruby."

In the darkness she laughed, soft and bitter. "My *body* wants you," she whispered, suddenly sounding unlike herself. "Go on, then. Do it, Devellyn. Get it over with."

Devellyn shook off a sudden flash of uncertainty. "That's good enough for me."

Roughly then, he pushed her legs wide with his knee. He shoved his cock between her legs so that he could ease it back and forth through the slick, wet warmth. Beneath him, Ruby began to shake. Her breath began to ratchet up. Good Lord, she was as hungry for it as he was.

Devellyn couldn't wait. He held her down by both shoulders, and somehow managed to shove deep on one thrust.

Beneath him, Ruby screamed, but it was a short, soft sound. A sound of shock, he thought. But not pain. Still clutching at her, he drew out, and drove in again. For long moments, he pumped himself rhythmically inside her, with little thought to her comfort or need. It did not matter. *This* was what he had wanted. What he had dreamt of. What he burned for. The world spun away. He gave himself up to the hunger and let Ruby draw him down and down, into some sort of sensual abyss.

He set his face to the turn of her neck and drew in her clean, plain scent again. "Ruby, Ruby, Ruby."

The hoarse whispers were his, he realized. She was warm, almost perspiring beneath him now, and her hips kept rising to take him. For a moment, his mind cleared, and he thought of stopping. This was wrong. Wasn't it?

He must have hesitated in midthrust. Ruby's leg came round his waist, dragging him back down. "Don't stop," she choked. "Not—not *now*."

At some point, he must have released her hands. They were all over him, warm and urgent, stroking his body through the nightshirt. Then they found his buttocks, bare beneath his shirt, and urged him to go harder. Faster. Desire blinded him. They became like animals, frantic and hungry, clawing at one another, desperately seeking release.

"*Yes,*" she groaned, as if the word was torn from her chest. Then she drew his face to hers, bit his lip until he tasted blood, then forced her tongue inside his mouth, urging him on. Something inside him flew to her, melded to her, as beneath him, she kept rising to take his thrusts.

Devellyn closed his eyes, and prayed never to lose her again. He didn't mean to let her out of this room, ever. He'd never had sex like this in his life; never known a woman who could match him, but good God, this one did. Stroke for stroke, she met him. He pushed her hands high over her head, holding her down to take his thrusting hips. He drove and drove, so hard he could feel his knees burning from the carpet. Her soft, sharp sighs came faster. Her fingers dug into his flesh. God, she was close. Devellyn let go of one hand, and cupped the side of her face in his palm.

"Come for me, love," he crooned, then he kissed her, slow and deep, gentler now.

She was crying, he thought. He tasted salt and tears. Her sharp sighs had become little cries of pleasure.

"That's it, love, that's it," he answered. "Let yourself come to me."

Another cry, and her breath was sawing back and forth in her chest. "Oh, yes," she pleaded. "Yes, oh, like that . . . like that . . ."

Her words called to him, impelled him, in a voice so different now, and yet so familiar. Like some erotic dream he'd had again and again. He kept working her, driving so deep and so hard he could feel them inching up the carpet with his every stroke. His knees burnt as if raw. His lungs ached like bellows. And then he felt her explode, and fall inward, taking her down with him. He drove hard and furious for those last, mindless strokes.

Felt her inching up the carpet from their efforts. Then the white, explosive light took him, too. Again and again, he pumped his seed deep inside Ruby. Her legs and arms were wrapped tight round him as he finished on one last, glorious thrust.

And then something slammed into the top of his head. A blinding pain that seemed to cleave through his skull. It was his last coherent thought.

Sidonie heard the ghastly crack of bone, and snapped back to the real world. Atop her, Devellyn gave one last groan, then collapsed like a deadweight. Sidonie panicked. "Devellyn?"

Frantically, she shoved at him. *"Devellyn?"* she cried. "Good God! Are you all right?"

He didn't so much as twitch.

Urgently, Sidonie felt above their heads. *The footboard.* Its lower edge felt like a two-inch slab of oak. She had scooted almost beneath the bloody thing. But Devellyn was a very large, very tall man. Even lying prone. Oh, God! Had they worked that far up the carpet? Then suddenly, and very absurdly, it struck her that Lord Devellyn was going to die of a skull fracture, and she did not even know his Christian name. Indeed, he did not even know who she was. Sidonie's tears burst into a torrent.

Somehow, she managed to squirm her way from beneath him, still whispering his name. Devellyn weighed half a ton, all of it solid rock. She tried not to cry, tried to think straight. Once free, she stood on tremulous legs, hiked up her trousers, and dashed to the front windows. Light. She needed light. She threw open the heavy draperies, then hastened back to his side.

A hint of gaslight trickled up from Bedford Place. Enough, perhaps. Sidonie fell to her knees beside him. It was obvious now. Devellyn had struck his head on the massive wooden footboard, a victim of his own unflagging enthusiasm. Urgently, she felt for blood. *None.* Thank God. A pulse? Yes, strong and steady. Sidonie sagged with relief.

"Oh, Devellyn, you big ox!" she cried, stroking her hand down the back of his head. "You could have *killed* yourself!"

Just then, the marquess emitted a deep, inhuman groan. Sidonie leapt to her feet and looked about desperately. What now? Wait? Confess? Flee? Certainly, she could not leave him lying injured. Where on earth were his servants? Surely they'd heard *something*?

But his servants, she'd already noticed, were a tad craven. They were likely two floors down, cowering—if they'd heard anything at all.

The marquess groaned again. He would live, she thought. But he needed ice for his head. Perhaps even a doctor. Urgency cleared her brain. Swiftly, she jerked his nightshirt down. Then she fastened what was left of her trouser buttons, grabbed her hat, stuffed in her shirttails, and felt about for her hammer. Gone. As she should be.

Giving up on finding her bag and hammer in the gloom, Sidonie felt across the wall near the bed until she touched a bellpull. Then she yanked it hard—three times—and headed for the window. Once outside and balanced on her rope, she drew the window shut, shinnied down two feet, and waited until lamplight spilt over the windowsill. She breathed a sigh of relief. Someone had come. Devellyn would be cared for.

And in the morning, when he awoke to daylight, he would see the miniature lying on his dressing table. And perhaps he would remember their strange interlude with . . . what? Fondness? Frustration? Sidonie did not even know what *she* felt.

But she knew that something in her life had suddenly, inexorably shifted. Something unnerving was stealing over her. Lord, it was time to make her escape. Slowly, and with the utmost care and silence, she eased back down the rope. She wanted to go home. Wanted to be alone with her thoughts. And wanted to remember, just for a little while, what it had felt like to lie with the wicked Marquess of Devellyn.

Chapter Nine

A Judas Kiss

By eleven the next morning, Lord Devellyn was drunk. Not, mind you, totally tangle-footed or thoroughly tosticated. Just a trifle concerned. He was slouched in his leather armchair by the study hearth, sipping slowly at a tumbler of Scotch whisky—always his choice for medicinal purposes—and waiting for his teeth to float away when Sir Alasdair MacLachlan came into the room in something of a flurry, without waiting to be announced.

"What the devil's happened?" his friend demanded. "Honeywell says you've had an accident."

Devellyn studied the shimmering gold splinters in his glass. "So I have," he finally replied, enunciating every word. "An *accident*. Named *Ruby Black*."

"Ruby Black—?" Alasdair was standing over him now and peering at his head. "Lord, Dev, what a goose-egg!" he said. "And it's red, too."

"Yes, well, you ought to see my knees," muttered Devellyn.

Alasdair poked gingerly at the knot. "Does it hurt?"

"Not"— Devellyn paused to rip off a hearty belch— "anymore."

Alasdair narrowed one eye at the tumbler. "What's in the glass, old boy?"

Devellyn started to laugh, but it hurt too much. "What is that old Scots saying of your granny's, Alasdair?" he muttered. "Whisky won't cure a cold—?"

"Aye, but it fails more agreeably than most things," finished Alasdair.

"Yes, that one." Devellyn nodded, noting with vague indifference that the collection of hunting scenes on his walls were beginning to go in and out of focus. He wasn't sure if it was the alcohol or a concussion.

Alasdair drew up a chair, and sat down near his friend. "Honeywell says you tripped and hit your head," he said quietly. "Is it true?"

Devellyn laughed. "Not precisely," he answered. "I was paid a visit last night, Alasdair. From the Black Angel. And that lump, I reckon, could be a little love tap."

Alasdair drew back. "Dev, you really are concussed," he answered. "You're saying the Angel rang your bell and just waltzed in, pretty as you please? Then conked you over the sconce and bolted? What did she steal this time?"

My soul, he thought. But he said, "Nothing, Alasdair. And it was my bedchamber. I awoke to find the woman standing by my dressing table."

"She broke in?" said Alasdair. "Lord, she's a bold piece!"

"That's an understatement." Devellyn was beginning to feel a tad sober, a miracle he resisted.

"God, Dev! What did you do when you caught her?"

The marquess stared at the floor. "Ah, Alasdair, you don't want to know," he murmured, thrusting out his glass. "Here, refresh this for me, will you? And have one if you think it not too early."

"It is too early, by God," he said, going to the decanter on the table. "Even for me."

"Then your head does not ache like you've got a shiv in your skull," said the marquess. "Else you'd be grateful for anything that killed the pain."

"Just tell me what happened," ordered Alasdair, pouring.

With great care, Devellyn let his head fall back against the chair. "I am not perfectly sure," he said waiting for the room to stop spinning. "I think . . . I *think,* honestly, that I slammed my skull into the footboard of the bed."

Alasdair pressed the drink into his hand, and looked at him incredulously. "The footboard?" he echoed. "Good Lord, Dev! Doing what?"

Devellyn looked up at him sourly. "Remember those French girls in the rue Richer?"

His friend's eyes rounded. "Oh, God!" he groaned, the last syllable dropping like a stone. "Dev, you didn't! And she . . . she *let* you?"

He tore his gaze from Alasdair's. "There wasn't a vast deal of negotiation."

"Christ Jesus."

The marquess shrugged, picked up the silk bag beside his ashtray, and extracted a small silver hammer. "The other possibility," he said, turning it about as he studied its oddly pointed head, "is that she bashed me with this. That's Fenton's theory."

Alasdair took the hammer. "You told him it was the Black Angel?"

Devellyn shook his head. "I saw no need to enlighten anyone," he said. "I just told him it was a thief. He found the bag and the hammer—some sort of burglar's tool, I'm told—lying on my carpet. But no, I don't believe she hit me. Not with this, at any rate." The marquess was swinging the hammer back and forth rather daringly by the tip of its handle.

Alasdair snatched it in midswing, and slipped it back into the silk bag. "Dev," he said pensively, "perhaps I ought to go find Sisk?"

The marquess sipped at his whisky. "Don't trouble yourself," he answered. "No need of him now. Ruby brought everything back."

"You're hallucinating," said Alasdair. "And her name isn't even *Ruby*. I think we'd best call a physician to see to that lump."

"As I live and breathe, Alasdair," said the marquess, fumbling in the pocket of his dressing gown. "I woke up this morning to see the lot of it piled on my dressing table." Deftly, he snapped open Greg's miniature.

Alasdair gaped. "Well, damn me!" he said, already half out of his chair. "Tenby's got to hear this."

Devellyn reached across the distance, grabbed Alasdair by the coat collar, and pushed him down again. "Not a bloody word," he said, his voice lethal. "Not a hint. Not a peep, cheep, chirp, or chortle, Alasdair! Not if you value your life."

Alasdair shoved his hand away. "Good try, Dev," he said. "But I know you always shoot to wound."

"This time, I'll make an exception."

"Why? What does Tenby matter?"

Devellyn relaxed gingerly into his chair. "It's personal."

"As our dinner last night was *personal?*" Alasdair challenged. "Lord, Dev! I can't tell who you're more obsessed with, Madame Saint-Godard or Ruby Black."

Even drunk, something about that statement struck him strangely. Devellyn almost could not bear to hear them spoken of in the same breath. Ruby was darkness. But Sidonie, oh, she was light. She was cool elegance and refined beauty. Ruby was none of that. Ruby saw the blackness that lay inside a man. Like a wild animal scented fear, she could scent the hunger and desperation in him. And Devellyn only prayed that now he'd finally had the woman, he could forget about her once and for all.

But he would not, would he? Devellyn knew it—*feared* it—already. It was not a physical pain he sought to numb with alcohol. It was a gnawing hunger. Already he burned for her again. And somehow he knew that he might take Ruby Black a thousand times, but the darkness in her would still call to him.

Alasdair cleared his throat. Devellyn's head jerked up from his empty glass. It was then that he realized Alasdair had brought an envelope with him into the study. A perfect diversion. He was finished discussing women with Alasdair.

"What have you there, old man?" he said to his guest.

It was Alasdair's turn to look chagrined. "Well, this, actually, was my reason for calling on you at such an abysmally early hour," he said. "I found it lying on my desk last night."

Devellyn suffered one of life's more apprehensive moments. "What is it?"

Alasdair hesitated, then unfolded it. "A letter," he admitted. "From your mother."

"*My* mother?"

Alasdair looked suddenly guilty. "Do you remember, Dev, that Roman denarius her father had? The silver one, with the head of Vespasian on it?"

Devellyn was confused. "What? In that old coin collection of Grandfather's? That's all junk, isn't it?"

There was a fervency kindling in Alasdair's eyes now. "Dev, I swear, you never listen," he answered. "It might have been thought junk eighty years ago when he traveled the Continent collecting it. But by accident or design, he had some fine pieces. And the Vespasian denarius is, unfortunately, the finest."

Devellyn was suddenly suspicious. "How *unfortunately*?"

Alasdair winced. "Only three are known to exist."

The marquess studied him for a moment. "Alasdair, why do I feel as though I'm about to be kissed by Judas?" he asked. "After all, it is but one piece of silver we're talking about here."

"Comparing yourself to Jesus, Dev, is a remarkable stretch."

"A stretch!" Devellyn pushed his glass away in disgust. "I ought to stretch you, Alasdair—on a bloody rack! Go on, then. What has Mother promised you?"

Alasdair hung his head. "Dev, she's planning to open up the house on Grosvenor Square," he said. "And she is giving a gala ball."

"Yes? What of it?"

"And . . . well, it is in honor of the duke's seventieth birthday."

"Oh, good Lord, Alasdair. I know that!"

"And it comes at a time when the duchess is feeling inclined, she says, toward disposing of the coin collection."

"And?"

"And if I will come to the ball, she promises to give me first nod."

"*And—?*" The kept word growing louder.

"And if I can convince you to come along as well, her Grace wishes me to have the Vespasian," said Alasdair. "As a token of her esteem for—"

"—for your mercenary little heart," Devellyn finished.

"Dev, you don't understand!" Alasdair complained. "I'd sell my soul for that coin!"

"Yes, and mine, too, I gather."

"Dev, it's not like that! Besides, what will it hurt us to go over and do the pretty to your mother's friends for one evening? What is your father going to do, toss us out on our ears?"

At that, Devellyn hurled his whisky glass at the fireplace. He hit it, too. Shattering glass and golden droplets rained down upon the hearth.

Alasdair was already on his feet. "Well!" he said, hastily stuffing the letter into his pocket. "I collect I'd best be off then."

"Yes," said Lord Devellyn. "I collect you'd best."

The next day, Sidonie slept late, dawdled in her room for an hour, then busied herself with lessons and chores well into the afternoon, all while trying to avoid Julia. She was stiff and sore, and half-afraid that last night's misbehavior might show in her eyes. At eleven, she had Miss Leslie for deportment, and, immediately following, Miss Brewster arrived to prepare for her first formal dinner. By the end of it, Sidonie was drained. She did not see her friend at all until the afternoon, when she entered the parlor just as Julia was having tea.

"Sidonie!" Julia seemed grateful for the distraction. "Join me." She was already pouring another cup.

Sidonie had little choice. Besides, she could not go on avoiding the world, could she? And apparently the word *idiot* was not etched on her forehead, since Julia was behaving as if nothing was amiss.

"Thank you. A cup of tea would be welcome." Sidonie took her usual seat at the table by the window and dumped three heaps of sugar into her cup without a qualm. Today, she needed it.

"I'm sorry I slept so late."

Julia looked at her appraisingly. "A remarkable evening, was it not?"

You don't know the half, thought Sidonie, extracting her spoon from the sludge. She'd had to spend an extra half hour soaking in hot bathwater just to soothe all the sore spots.

"Lord Devellyn was rather more of a gentleman than I'd been led to believe," Julia went on. "And he obviously hadn't a clue who you were."

"No," said Sidonie. "And I mean to keep it that way."

"A most excellent notion." Julia set aside her teacup and snapped open the newspaper. "Oh, look! *Hamlet* opens tomorrow at the Haymarket!"

"Ugh," said Sidonie. "What a depressing play."

"I shall ask Henrietta Wheeler to go," she said with a sniff. "Her brother Edward has a box, you know."

"I hope you will enjoy it."

But to her regret, Julia returned to their original conversation. "Now, honestly, Sidonie, I had my doubts you'd fool anyone when you started this Angel business," she went on. "But you've taken Devellyn in quite thoroughly."

Yes, but how much longer could she get away with it? Sidonie was afraid—and the fear of being found out was but half of it now. *That* fear she was accustomed to. Indeed, she almost relished the rush of it. But her confused emotions were a stark, new torment.

How much longer? Oh, not long. Even she understood there were certain things the best mimic on earth couldn't hide. Height. Scent. The sound of a sigh. Instinct was a powerful thing. Already Sidonie knew enough, she thought, to pick Devellyn from a crowd in a pitch-dark room. Her skin knew the heat of his touch, her ears, the rough, rumbling gravel of his voice. And she'd long ago memorized his harsh, handsome face.

Sidonie set away the teacup and shut her eyes. Dear God, what had she done? What had she started? Why couldn't she get him out of her mind?

She was saved by another spate of self-flagellation by a rapid knock at the door. *Devellyn?* Oh, God! Her heart in her throat, she flew to the window, only to see Miss Hannaday and her maid on the doorstep.

"Goodness, Sidonie," said Julia, calmly rising. "You're jumpy as poor Thomas."

Soon Miss Hannaday was having tea urged upon her.

The girl wore a bonnet of sunny yellow and a blue-and-yellow-striped walking dress which was youthfully becoming. Her eyes were round and shining.

"I really cannot stay," she said on a breathless rush. "I'm so sorry to call when I've no lesson scheduled, but I just wanted to say—well, to tell you that—oh, dear, I sound such a gudgeon!"

"But you look to be a happy gudgeon," Julia soothed, passing a plate of biscuits. "Dear Miss Hannaday, do tell us your news."

She looked back and forth between Sidonie and Julia for a moment. "Tomorrow is the day," she finally blurted. "Can you believe it? Charles has arranged everything. But I have you to thank, Madame Saint-Godard." Miss Hannaday's youthful face was flushed with color and excitement.

"Tomorrow is the day?" echoed Julia.

"We elope at midnight," the girl whispered. "Mr. Giroux has loaned us his carriage, and we are going straight to Gretna Green. Oh, does it not sound exciting?"

Sidonie felt an instant of anxiety. "Charles has accepted Mr. Giroux's position then? You will have enough to live on?"

"Oh, Mr. Giroux has been the kindest soul imaginable," said Miss Hannaday. "Charles tried to do it all properly, you know. He asked for my hand, and braved Papa's temper. Of course, Papa refused him. Then Charles begged for time to prove himself worthy, and begged Papa not to marry me off to a degenerate like Bodley, and Papa promptly sacked him for his impudence."

"Oh, dear," murmured Julia.

"But it is all for the best," Miss Hannaday insisted. "Charles has been at Giroux & Chenault for all of three days now. Mr. Giroux says Charles is a genius with the accounts—which, of course, he is," the blushing bride proudly added.

Julia smiled like a cat in the cream-pot. "I vow, I should like to see your papa's face when he realizes you've gone."

"And I should like to see Bodley's," muttered Sidonie grimly.

"I should rather see neither anytime soon," said Miss Hannaday a little sorrowfully. But she brightened at once. "I feel the luckiest girl in the world, Madame Saint-Godard, and I owe it all to you."

"You are very kind, my dear."

Miss Hannaday scooted away her teacup. "Well, I mustn't make Papa suspicious," she said. "I'd best go home. I have the oddest premonition that I'm going to be struck with dyspepsia at half past six and go straight up to bed. But I've ever so much packing to finish first." She smiled and winked at the ladies, looking, for the first time, as a young woman on the verge of marriage should look.

The ladies laughed. Their conversation at an end, Sidonie rang for Miss Hannaday's maid and escorted the girl to the door.

With one last wave at Miss Hannaday, Sidonie half turned to reenter the house. It was at that precise moment, however, that the Marquess of Devellyn's elegant coach-and-four turned the corner and came rattling up the street. Apparently anticipating its arrival, the marquess stepped out his front door. Upon seeing Sidonie, he lifted his hat, smiled almost uncertainly, and started toward her.

Sidonie pretended not to see. She stepped back in and gently closed the door.

Once inside, she leaned against it, palms flat against the cool, smooth wood. It was time, she told herself firmly, to get back to business. She had Lord Bodley to deal with as soon as Amy Hannaday was safely en route to Scotland. And it was definitely time to forget the Marquess of Devellyn. To attempt to maintain any sort of friendship with him now was not just folly, it was dangerous. The man might be a scoundrel, but he was by no means as stupid as she had first assumed. Indeed, Sidonie was willing to wager that underneath all his self-deprecating humor and ramshackle ways, the man was as keen as a newly stropped razor.

It took Sidonie three days to make certain just who the Marquess of Bodley was, for this time, she was very careful in her planning. She had no intention of failing to thoroughly research another of her nightly adventures. Bodley's town residence, she discovered, was near the corner of Charles Street, just a few yards from St. James's Square.

Every evening after darkness fell, Sidonie slipped over the square's fence and hid in the shrubbery with a pair of opera glasses. From that vantage point, she had an unobscured view of his lordship's well-lit doorstep. Bodley, as it happened, was older than she had expected. He was a tall, lean man with a narrow, slightly hooked nose, a thin, cruel mouth, and hair which hung dark and heavy about his face. He lifted his nose at a very odd angle as he walked, and had the old-fashioned habit of carrying a quizzing glass limply between his fingers.

The image of his thin, clawlike hands on Miss Hannaday was enough to make Sidonie retch. And according to George, the appalling truth was that Bodley preferred his female bedmates significantly younger than his former fiancée. He had doubtless made an exception for her advanced years—she was all of seventeen, if Sidonie recalled—based on his expectation of her father's generous marriage settlement. Sidonie let that thought eat like acid into her heart so that she could feel not one trace of pity for Bodley, not one modicum of regret over what she was about to do to him.

Now certain she had the Black Angel's next victim clearly in her sights, Sidonie began to shadow Bodley, learning his haunts and habits. On Tuesday evening, he strolled over to White's Club, where he spent the entire evening. Sidonie gave up at two in the morning, and walked back to Bloomsbury deep in thought. When she arrived home, it was to find that Lord Devellyn had called earlier in the evening. Julia had been out, dining with old theater friends. Devellyn had left a card, but no message.

On Wednesday evening, Bodley took his carriage to a ball in Portland Place where, again, he remained well into the night. Sidonie arrived home to find Julia waiting up for her. It seemed Devellyn had once more called in Sidonie's absence, ostensibly to bring Julia a gift. It was a bottle of Bordeaux from his cellar, a vintage for which Julia had expressed a particular fondness during their dinner party. But Julia was not fooled. She teased Sidonie unmercifully.

For her part, Sidonie felt a little shaft of envy that it was Julia who had enjoyed a glass of Madeira by the fire with Lord Devellyn, while she'd been stuck skulking about in the damp alleys of Marylebone. Then, on Thursday, Sidonie had a stroke of luck. Following a late evening at the Oriental Club, Bodley dismissed his carriage and staff save for one footman and set off in the direction of St. James's Park.

It was an unhoped-for opportunity. Sidonie followed, keeping to the shadows and shrubs along the mall as best she could. Her male garb—she was dressed as a newsboy carrying an empty sack—kept her from being too boldly accosted.

Soon Bodley motioned for his footman to stop. They were deep in the park, and Sidonie was growing uneasy. Bodley slowed his stride and made his way past a milling crowd of dandies who were passing a flask and smoking thin cheroots. Once beyond them, he turned in the direction of the armory, toward a darker, less public side of the park. Sidonie decided it would be imprudent to follow.

In less than ten minutes, Bodley returned, motioned for his servant, then went straight to the Golden Cross Inn at the foot of the Strand. His servant waited outside. Sidonie was wondering whether to follow Bodley in when a handsome young lad in a second lieutenant's uniform strolled up the street. He greeted the footman by name, and the servant passed something—money, or a slip of paper—to him.

The young man looked at it almost disgustedly, muttered something, then pushed through the door. The implication was clear. A rendezvous had been arranged, and the young man looked less than enthusiastic about it. Alas, there was nothing she could do for him just now. Sidonie melted into the stream of late-night pedestrians and vanished.

It was just as George had said. Bodley was buying, or coercing, his lovers—and doubtless being blackmailed by some of them in turn. Now Sidonie needed to form a plan. A freshly pressed midshipman's uniform hung in her wardrobe, and it was time to put it to good use. Lord Bodley, she vowed, was going to rue his next little stroll through the park.

Sidonie slipped in through the mews and headed toward her back door a little nervously. She was returning home far earlier than usual, and it would not do for the voluble Meg to see her dressed as a newsboy. Sidonie considered lingering in the shadows until the lights belowstairs went out. But at that very moment, through the adjacent window, she saw Julia's silhouette. She was waiting. She must have fresh gossip, or some word of warning. Sidonie went up the rear steps, and scratched lightly at the window. Julia threw open the door and dragged her inside.

"Quiet!" she whispered, urging Sidonie up the stairs. "Meg's not yet abed. Come, I've something to show you."

With Julia on her heels, Sidonie slipped into her room, half-hoping Devellyn had called again, then mentally kicking herself for being such a fool. She tossed her empty news bag on the bed, tore off her hat, and went at once to the bottle of sherry. After getting a good look at Lord Bodley in action, she needed a bit of fortification. But Julia made an eager sound in the back of her throat. Her excitement was palpable. As soon as Sidonie pressed the wine into her companion's hand, Julia pulled something from her pocket and held it up triumphantly.

"What's this?" asked Sidonie, dropping into a chair.

Julia sat down, too. "This, my dear, is an invitation to one of the season's grandest events," she answered. "Lord Walrafen's annual charity ball! Forgive me, but I recognized the seal, and just had to open it."

Sidonie took the invitation from Julia's outstretched hand. *Lord Walrafen?* "But I do not know him," she protested. "I mean, I know *of* him—who does not?— but why would he invite me to his ball?"

Julia withdrew yet another slip of paper and fanned it back and forth. "I daresay it has something to do with this urgent missive which preceded it," she answered. "Mrs. Arbuckle wrote to say that they have been invited, and she asks that you escort Miss Arbuckle, who very much wishes to attend."

The Arbuckles? Suddenly, something inside Sidonie's brain clicked. "Yes, Lord Walrafen is a patron of the Nazareth Society, is he not?" she murmured to herself. "Just like Lady Kirton."

"Perhaps, but what of it?"

Sidonie considered it. "After Lady Kirton's musicale, I remember Miss Arbuckle saying she meant to ask her father to make a sizable donation to the Nazareth Society."

"Well, it must have been enormous," said Julia. "This is the event to which all of society aspires. Will you go?"

Sidonie considered it. "Yes, why not?" she said, lifting her chin. "It is a wonderful opportunity for Miss Arbuckle. And Lord Walrafen is something of a reformist. Indeed, George says he is a very fine man."

Julia's eyes widened. "George *knows* Lord Walrafen?"

"Oh, you would be surprised whom George knows," said Sidonie. "Do you remember the trips he made to Somerset and Scotland last year? It was some sort of mysterious errand for Walrafen."

"Ooh," said Julia. "George has a lot of mysterious errands, doesn't he? Shall he be invited to the ball?"

"It is possible," she answered. "Walrafen is said to be quite liberal in his choice of friends. But George would never go."

Julia's face fell. "No, he wouldn't, would he?"

Sidonie set aside her wine and gave a long, languid stretch. "So," she said on a yawn, "when is this ball, Julia?"

Julia looked at the invitation. "Just a week hence," she answered. "Oh, my dear girl, we must get you something to wear! I can remake, perhaps, the wine-colored silk that was your mother's. Or the green satin, perhaps? Do you have shoes to match? Yes, I'm sure you do. Then we'll need to poke through your mother's jewelry, to find just the right thing . . ."

As Julia rattled on about stockings and necklaces and hair, Sidonie's thoughts turned inward. She would escort Miss Arbuckle to Lord Walrafen's great ball, yes. But she was not quite ready to think of it or plan for it. She had not yet erased from her mind the expression she had seen on the face of Bodley's young naval officer tonight. That, she feared, might haunt her sleep.

On Friday morning, Lord Devellyn shocked himself—and stunned his staff—by arising at nine and going downstairs to breakfast.

"*B-R-E-A-K-F-A-S-T,*" he grumbled at the brace of

footmen whose brows flew aloft at the sight of him coming down the stairs fully dressed *and* fully upright. "A morning repast of eggs, bacon, and toast. You have heard of it, I daresay?"

The first footman bolted toward the kitchen stairs. "I'll tell Cook."

Lord Devellyn took a seat in the breakfast parlor, which gave onto Bedford Place. The day looked sunny, even a little warm, and the drapes in his bow window had been drawn to take full advantage of its glory. The first footman's steps had scarce faded from earshot, however, when the door opened across the street at Number Fourteen, and Madame Saint-Godard and Mrs. Crosby came out. The former was looking especially fetching in a gown of daffodil yellow muslin, which contrasted beautifully with her inky hair and faintly olive skin.

Devellyn turned around in his chair. "You, there!" he said to the footman by the door. "Henry Polk, is it?"

Polk darted into the room. "Sir?"

Devellyn pointed toward the street. The two ladies were almost past the front window now. "Any idea where they're off to at such an hour?"

Polk seemed stunned by the question. "I've no notion, sir."

"None?" barked the marquess.

Polk recovered quickly. "Shopping, I daresay, my lord. Ladies do love to shop of a morning."

The marquess grunted. "What about that girl, Meg. Does she never mention their plans?"

"Only if I ask, sir."

"Well, ask, damn it," he grumbled. "And ask often. Do you follow me?"

Devellyn leaned deeper into the window. He was bloody tired of not knowing the comings and goings of Sidonie Saint-Godard, though why, or why it was any of his business, escaped him. He had no sooner cast off his foolish obsession with the Black Angel—well, to an extent—than he'd found himself caught up in a new one. He had called at Number Fourteen twice this week, never to find Sidonie in, and he had a sneaking suspicion he could have called every day of the week, and still have been sent away disappointed.

Devellyn couldn't decide if he was just getting a cold shoulder, or if Sidonie Saint-Godard was suddenly the most popular woman in town this season. What in God's name did she do with her evenings?

The ladies were disappearing around the corner now. Polk cleared his throat loudly. "Perhaps it would help, sir, if I had an extra half day."

"Hmph!" said Devellyn. "Quite the negotiator, aren't you?"

"I try, sir," Polk admitted.

"When is Meg's half day?" snapped Devellyn.

"Oh, she has Wednesday *and* Saturday afternoon, sir."

"Fine, take 'em," he grumbled. "But I'm warning you, Polk, I shall want something in return."

"I comprehend, my lord," he murmured. "You may count on me."

"Well, tomorrow is Saturday," returned the marquess. "Make hay while the sun shines."

Unfortunately, the sun did not shine again for several days. April came to London in a terrible torrent and to Sidonie's undying frustration, it rained for three days solid. She knew it would do her no good to attempt to track Lord Bodley; neither man nor beast would venture through the park in such a torrent, and she already sensed that Bodley was a man who cherished nothing so much as his own comfort. And so Sidonie watched the incessant spatter run down her windows and busied herself with hemming and darning and needlepoint until she thought she might well go mad.

Lord Devellyn had stopped dropping by; whatever he'd wanted—if anything—he seemed not to want it any longer. Sidonie tried not to feel any sense of disappointment. Her objective, she reminded herself, was to avoid the man, after all—and to forget about that little interlude on his bedroom carpet, too. Especially late at night, in those strange, heated moments when a rush of emotion would draw her inexorably to her window. There, she would look out across the distance at Lord Devellyn's house and wonder. Was he at home? With another woman? Did he ever think of *her*, of Ruby Black? It was a little pathetic, really. Sidonie, often impulsive but rarely stupid, was turning into a mooncalf.

Julia busied herself during the bad weather by preparing Sidonie's wardrobe for Lord Walrafen's ball. After standing Sidonie half-naked on a chair for what felt like an entire morning, Julia set to work pinning and stitching and occasionally ripping something viciously apart. But Sidonie had no doubt that on the evening of the ball, she would be one of the best-dressed ladies in attendance. Julia had come up through the theater from the bottom, starting as a wardrobe girl. But as a result, Julia possessed many skills in addition to her acting talent, and she had forgotten none of them. She also had ideas of her own. Like how the bodice of Sidonie's gown should be cut.

"Julia, no!" said Sidonie during one particularly arduous fitting. "I'm to be the duenna, not the debutante."

Julia just laughed. "No deb could keep this bodice up, dearie," she returned. "And it's all in good taste—not to mention the height of fashion."

A debate ensued, which resulted in the bodice creeping up half an inch. Sidonie was about to argue further when Meg came into the room, her face glum, her eyes downcast.

"What is it, Meg?" asked Sidonie.

"Cook's sniffle's turning to quinsy, she says," reported the girl morosely. "It's all this damp, she says. She's going to bed with a hot mustard poultice, she says, and I'm to tell you there's naught for dinner, and the marketing's yet to be done."

Julia and Sidonie exchanged glances. Most likely, Mrs. Tuttle had been at the sherry again. Julia turned back to Meg and sighed as if deeply put upon. "Can you take care of it?"

"Yes, ma'am." The girl stared at the floor.

Sidonie hopped down off the chair. "Oh, bother!" she said. "I can do it. The morning's half-gone, and Wednesday is Meg's half day."

The girl's face brightened. Julia was still holding her pins aloft. "But what of this ball gown?"

"Tomorrow," said Sidonie, already sliding out of the dress. "Meg, fetch me the list and the basket, then finish your chores and go. I can fix an omelet for dinner."

The excursion was one she was soon to regret. With the basket swinging from her elbow and her lightest cloak tossed over her shoulders, Sidonie went down the steps and onto the pavement, only to have her arm seized roughly from behind.

She whirled about to see a pair of narrow, ugly eyes burning through her. "You!" said her assailant. "By God, I'll have a word with you, I will!"

Sidonie tried to draw back. "Mr. Hannaday!" she said archly. "Kindly take your hand off my arm."

But the man gripped her more fiercely instead. "You put my Amy up to this!" he hissed. "You! You and your *laissez-faire* French foolishness! Now look at the trouble you've caused me."

"Mr. Hannaday, I beg your pardon." Sidonie stepped away, but he followed. "I wish you to unhand me, sir. Then we may talk about your trouble like well-reasoned human beings."

"So you admit that you knew!" he growled. "Interfering bitch."

"Sir, I admit to nothing save the fact that your fingers are now cutting off my circulation."

Suddenly, a huge fist thrust between them, seized Mr. Hannaday's wrist, and squeezed it so hard his bones cracked. "I believe," said the Marquess of Devellyn, "that the lady just asked you to remove your hand, sir. Now, you may do it. Or I shall do it. Permanently."

Hannaday drew back, rubbing his wrist. "Who the devil are you?"

"Who indeed," murmured Devellyn. "Let us just say that I am a concerned neighbor."

"Well, your *neighbor* here is concerning herself in the management of my family," he said shrilly. "She has put brazen, disobedient notions into my daughter's head. But it is no business of yours, I'm sure."

Lord Devellyn was looking deep into Sidonie's eyes, as if to reassure himself she was all right. "It would appear I've just made it my business," he said, returning his attention to Hannaday. "And you, sir, are no gentleman, to accost a lady thus on the street."

Hannaday drew back as if he'd been struck. It was the worst sort of insult, apparently, that one could level at a middle-class social climber. "By God, sir, I ought to call you out for that," he swore. "This woman is a liar, and a meddler, and none of your concern."

"I can now save you the trouble of calling me out," said Lord Devellyn, stripping off one glove. Unhesitatingly, he struck the man through the face with it.

Hannaday's hand flew to his cheek, his expression one of utter shock. His fingers came away from his face, and he stared at them as if expecting blood.

Devellyn stared down at him in disgust. "Sir, I must ask your name."

His gaze lifted from his hand. "Thomas Hannaday," he answered a little hollowly. "Who are you?"

The marquess bowed stiffly. "The Marquess of Devellyn," he answered. "But those I meet on the dueling field usually call me the Devil of Duke Street. I've a reputation for shooting to wound, but on this occasion, I suggest you not rely upon that small mercy."

Hannaday obviously recognized Devellyn's name. "You! You're insane!"

"So they say," said Devellyn. "Now, your second will be?"

"But—but—*my second*—?"

"Sir, you have attacked a lady in public, and verbally impugned her good name," Devellyn reminded him.

"You're lucky I haven't stripped the hide off you here and now."

"But—but—my business is with Madame Saint-Godard!" cried the man. "She encouraged my daughter to run away! An elopement, no less! Off to Gretna Green with a nobody bookkeeper, she is—and never would have done it had *someone* not put the notion in her head."

Devellyn was unmoved. "Name your second, sir, or make your apology."

"But my Amy was to wed the Marquess of Bodley!" whined Hannaday.

"Good God, man!" Devellyn's face twisted with disgust. "I'm not sure an apology will suffice for that."

Hannaday suddenly decided to cut his losses. He snapped his mouth shut and sketched a perfunctory bow in Sidonie's general direction. "Your pardon, Madame Saint-Godard," he managed. "I spoke rashly."

He turned to go, but Devellyn seized him by the arm and led him a little down the sidewalk. "A word of warning to you, Hannaday," he whispered, so quietly Sidonie could barely hear. "Let that lady's name so much as pass your lips in public, and I'll kill you where you stand. Do you comprehend me, sir?"

Hannaday's eyes narrowed farther, an amazing feat.

Devellyn's lip curled. "You believe me, don't you?"

Finally, Hannaday gave a terse nod. "Oh, I know all about you."

Devellyn released his arm and bowed. "Good day to you, then, Mr. Hannaday."

He returned to Sidonie's side. She still stood near her bottom step, one hand still clutching the iron railing. He touched her gently on the shoulder. "Are you all right?"

Sidonie let go of the railing. "Thank you, yes," she said. "What a horrid, horrid man."

Devellyn looked at her appraisingly. "Did he really mean to marry his chit to old Bodley?"

"Yes." Sidonie spat out the word.

"Christ," said the marquess. "And I thought *my* father disliked *me*."

"It is too vile to contemplate, is it not?"

"You know what he is then?"

Wordlessly, she nodded, her eyes still fixed on the back of Hannaday's coat. Her blood ran cold. Hannaday, she realized, had caught her off guard, a very bad thing indeed. And he'd nearly ruined her good name. A few words in the right ears, and he could have ensured she never took on another pupil, never attended another society event, no matter how small. But thanks to Lord Devellyn, he would not dare do so now. She was sure of that much. And she was grateful.

"Come on, Sidonie." Devellyn surprised her then by offering her his arm. "Let's go."

Jerked back to the present, she looked at him uncertainly. "Go?" she echoed. "Go where?"

He smiled. "Wherever it was you were going before that scurrilous dog laid his hand on you," he said. "Covent Garden Market, I'm guessing, since you've a basket on your arm."

It was indeed her destination. She only hoped there was something left to buy. But suddenly, the notion of going to do the marketing with the Marquess of Devellyn struck her as wildly incongruous. She looked at him curiously. "You do not ordinarily shop in Covent Garden, do you?"

"Well," he said sheepishly. "Not in the daylight."

Sidonie just shook her head and took the proffered arm. Mr. Hannaday almost forgotten, they set off. Devellyn's long legs ate up the ground, and from time to time he would check himself and slow his pace with an apologetic smile.

Sidonie smiled back. Oh, Lord, what a fool she was! She shouldn't be with him. It was dangerous—and disturbing. Just clinging to his arm, she could smell that same erotically masculine scent his room had held that night. For a moment, she forgot where she was, almost clipping a newsboy who was taking a corner too quickly.

Devellyn hauled her against him, and stopped. "You are all right?"

Embarrassed, she dropped her gaze. It landed, regrettably, on the fall of his trousers. Color heated her cheeks anew as the memory of what they had done flooded back, and, suddenly, Sidonie could not quite catch her breath.

"That bastard upset you." Devellyn's voice was a low growl. "Perhaps I'll shoot him yet."

"I am fine," she insisted. "Come on. Let's go."

The streets leading out of Bloomsbury were quiet. Lord Devellyn kept her hand tucked over his arm, and kept her tucked a little closer than was perhaps prudent. But Sidonie was still grateful for his help. And glad for his size, and his almost overwhelming personality. She had forgotten entirely her vow to avoid him.

Suddenly, Devellyn leaned very near. "Now forgive my suspicious nature, my dear," he said, his breath warm on her ear. "But *did* you facilitate Miss Hannaday's untimely disappearance?"

She looked at him askance. "Just what are you suggesting, my lord?"

Devellyn gave an odd half smile. "I'm not entirely sure," he admitted. "All I know is that when we're together, I find myself suspecting you have hidden depths."

Sidonie was quiet for a moment. "If I helped her— *if*—then I have no regrets," she finally answered. "He was going to marry her off to a sick, cruel man just so his grandchildren could bear a title. But Amy loved another, and while he is neither wealthy nor titled, he is a good man."

Devellyn lifted one huge shoulder pragmatically. "Then she may starve for love, my dear."

"It might be worth it."

Devellyn looked skeptical, then relented. "Yes, perhaps it is better than Bodley."

Sidonie cut a swift, sideways glance at him. "Tell me, my lord, have you ever been in love?" she asked lightly. "No, do not look daggers at me! You once asked me that very same question."

He opened his mouth, then closed it again. "No, not . . . in *love*," he finally said. "Something worse, perhaps."

"What an odd turn of phrase."

"It was a dashed odd situation," he muttered.

She listened to the sound of his boot heels on the pavement, and said nothing, hoping he would continue.

"Have you ever wanted something, Sidonie, so badly that it almost maddened you?" he finally said. "Something that made you itch from the inside out, that kept you sitting on the edge of your bed every night with your head in your hands and your heart in your throat? Something you almost, *almost* had—and then you lost it so suddenly it made you ache with . . . with what, I don't know. Frustration? Thwarted desire? No. I have no word for it."

Sidonie shook her head. "I never have."

"Well, pray you never do," he said.

"We are talking about a woman?"

"A vixen," he corrected. "A witch. A strange, flame-haired enchantress."

"Heavens! Who was she?"

For a moment, he was quiet. "I don't know, exactly."

"But how can you—" Sidonie's words broke on a sudden realization.

"How can I not know?" he finished, oblivious to her discomfort. "That, perhaps, is a story for another day."

Sidonie halted abruptly. "This woman, my lord," she said, looking at him. "Are you . . . over her?"

The muscles of his face seemed to tighten. "I am—" His words faltered, his eyes filling with sorrow. "No, Sidonie. I have to say that I am not. And yet, I am done with her. That much, I promise you."

Well. Sidonie had the answer to at least one of her questions, didn't she? Unless she missed her guess, Devellyn did occasionally think of Ruby Black. Indeed, it sounded as if he were obsessed. But why? Ruby Black was just a dockside prostitute, or so he thought.

They resumed their walking, both silent, and she realized again what a fool she was to remain in his proximity. What would she do if he were to suddenly wheel about and accuse her? She cut him a sidelong glance and felt that strange, warm, melting sensation in the pit of her stomach again. Good Lord, she was *melting*. Turning into a soft, gooey, emotional mess. Over a scoundrel.

Still, there was no denying Devellyn's physical magnificence, if one preferred men who were a little more rugged than refined, more masculine than graceful. He was striking with his dark, tousled hair and hard cheekbones. The broken nose and sparkling eyes lent him a dashing sort of charm, and he paid just enough attention to his wardrobe to look refined, but not so much so that one would ever accuse him of foppishness.

And those lips! Oh, they were wickedly, sensuously full. The memory of his mouth on hers, hot and demanding, kept returning to Sidonie in a breathtaking rush. He was a man's man, too, possessing every archaic quality that the term implied—and surprisingly, Sidonie no longer thought that that was necessarily a bad thing. Perhaps it had something to do with the way he'd crushed Mr. Hannaday's carpal bones in his fist.

Moreover, she was beginning to think that not only was Devellyn more clever than she'd given him credit for, he was also far more profound. While he gave every appearance of being a dissolute wastrel, on closer acquaintance, one could begin to see he was nothing quite so simple.

"Lord Devellyn—" she began abruptly.

"I do have a first name, Sidonie," he interjected, smiling down at her. "It is Aleric, if you wish to use it."

Aleric. An unusual name. She felt something flicker deep in her memory, then it was gone. "Before we left Bedford Place," she continued, "you made a jest about your father disliking you."

There was a long pause. "It was not precisely a jest," he

answered. "As I once said, my father and I are estranged."

"Yes, I recall it," she said musingly. "Would it be terribly forward of me to ask why?"

They had walked as far as the wide, steep steps leading up to St. George's. Devellyn stopped on the pavement and squinted his eyes against the midday sun. Then, as if making some sort of decision, he reached around and opened the gate which gave onto the narrow swath of churchyard. He led her in, and Sidonie went with a willingness that surprised her.

Just a few yards along sat a stone bench. He brushed it off with his handkerchief before offering it to her with a sweep of his hand. Surprisingly, he did not join her. Instead, he paced back and forth along the tender spring grass.

"You have been in London but a short while," he finally said. "A year, I believe?"

"About that," she said.

Lord Devellyn laughed a little bitterly. "So I've become the stuff of old gossip by now, perhaps," he said. "Father and I fell out when I was young. No—not young. That implies I did not know what I was doing. I did. I was two-and-twenty, and very experienced."

"*Very* experienced?" she echoed doubtfully. "I remember being twenty-two."

Devellyn gave a mirthless smile. "I don't," he answered. "I spent that year—and the three or four which preceded it—in a stupor of drinking, gaming, and whoring. My brother and I—" Here, he stopped, rummaged in his pocket, and withdrew the all-too-familiar miniature. "This is my brother," he said, snapping it open easily. "His name was Gregory."

Sidonie reached out, and touched the gold frame. "You . . . you found it," she said. "I am glad."

For a moment, he simply stared at it. "I found it," he said, gently closing the case. "I swear, Sidonie, I don't know which of us was worse, Greg or me. We were utter hellions. And inseparable, too. Yet we were forever trying to get the better of one another. But it was just a good-natured rivalry, I swear. That's all it ever was."

"My brother was far older than I," said Sidonie. "But I think I understand."

Devellyn smiled sourly and shook his head. "I wish I did," he said. "I wish I could understand what happened that spring. In hindsight, I suppose Greg fell in love. Not with a woman of experience, either, but a girl making her come-out. I swear, I did not believe him serious. I thought he was just courting her a little to appease Father."

"He wished your brother to settle down?"

"Desperately," said Devellyn. "And I suppose Greg had actually begun to consider it. But then someone in our crowd of well-bred wastrels wagered ten guineas I could not persuade the chit into a dark library and steal a kiss."

"Did you?"

"I was cocksure enough to try," he said. "And she seemed willing. But Greg followed us and burst into the room. He was livid. He accused me of trying to ruin the girl, and took a swing at me. I hit him back. It was not the first time we'd come to fisticuffs over something foolish. But this time, my first blow felled him. He fractured his skull on the corner of a desk."

Sidonie drew in her breath sharply. "Good God," she whispered. "Did he . . . die?"

"Not quickly." Devellyn would no longer even look at her. "My parents took him upstairs—it was a ball, you see, at our house in Grosvenor Square—and he lingered there unconscious for . . . I cannot recall. A fortnight? A month? God, I don't know! They called doctors and surgeons—soothsayers and faith healers, too, I don't doubt. Father was frantic. They bled him. They cupped him—good God, have you ever seen that done?—and then they trepanned his skull, all in some hopeless effort to wake him. But he didn't. And then he died."

"Oh," she said weakly. "Oh, my lord, I am so sorry."

His mocking sneer was back. "It almost killed my father," he said. "His despair was immeasurable. Unremitting. And he made it all too clear he wished I had died instead. He said it was a travesty that I was to take Greg's place as heir, when I had killed him with my own hands."

"Oh, my lord, I am sure that is not true."

He turned on her suddenly, his eyes aflame. "I'm sure it is," he gritted. "He said it. He said it over and over. And that isn't all he said, either. He said—and he was quite right, too—that only his good name had kept me from the gallows. Men have been hanged for less. And sometimes I would to God they *had* hanged me."

He was holding the gold pocket case clenched in his fist now, the leather of his gloves drawn so taut she began to fear he might break it. She thought of the glass plate inside, and reached out. Devellyn did not even look down as she peeled his fingers away from the case and returned it to his pocket.

"It was an accident," she said, holding out her hand. "A tragic one, yes, but an accident nonetheless."

"I don't know," he muttered. Then he seemed to realize he was holding tightly to her hand. "Come on, let's go, before God strikes me dead with a lightning bolt for standing on consecrated ground."

Sidonie had not the heart to question him further. Indeed, she wished she had not brought up the subject at all. She squeezed his hand reassuringly, and rose. As they walked together in silence, she thought of what Jean-Claude had told her that night in the alley. *The Marquess of Devellyn had killed his own brother.*

Sidonie had not believed it true. Now, however, the truth seemed to make no difference in her opinion of the man. It only made her more thankful that she had run the risk of restoring to him his miniature.

They did not speak another word until they were turning from Drury Lane. Devellyn drew to a halt, covered her hand with his, and gave it a reassuring squeeze. "I should leave you here."

Sidonie could see the bustle of the market stalls in the distance. The flower sellers were few, but the barrows of vegetables still rolled to and fro. A weary costermonger trudged past them, returning from his rounds, still calling his wares in a halfhearted voice. "Cabbage! Carrots! Endive!"

"Thank you for seeing me this far," she said. "I realize marketing cannot possibly be your idea of a pleasant afternoon."

Some strange emotion passed over his face. "Sidonie, it is not that."

"What, then?" she asked. "Devellyn, what is wrong?"

Abruptly, he took her by the hand and pulled her into the shadows of an alley. He set her back to the cool brick and looked down into her eyes with a startling intensity. "Sidonie, I'm not the sort of man a woman like you should consort with in public," he said. "Not if you wish to keep your reputation."

Sidonie forgot her vow to avoid him. "I value friendship above all things, my lord," she said. "If we were to be friends, I would not care what conclusion others drew."

"Friends?" he echoed, setting his big, warm hands on her forearms. "I hope we are already that much, Sidonie."

She thought of how quickly he'd leapt to her aid today. "Yes," she admitted. "Yes, of course we are."

His grip tightened and, still holding her gaze, he dipped his head. "I'm just not sure it's enough," he whispered.

The kiss was inevitable. Sidonie felt her arms go slack. Heard her basket clatter to the cobblestones. And in the next moment, Lord Devellyn brushed his lips over hers. It was a kiss neither urgent nor wild, but instead, a caress of exquisite tenderness. A question. A plea. And she answered him, though she'd sworn she would not. Instead, Sidonie tipped back her head, closed her eyes, and offered herself to him.

His mouth moved on hers, his lips slanting back and forth as if she were something fragile and precious. His hands left her arms and came up so that his warm, wide palms might cup her face. His thumbs brushed along her cheekbones, delicate as a bird's wing.

Sidonie exhaled on a sigh and let her hands skate up the powerful span of his back. Foolishly, she urged the warmth of his body against hers, urged him to deepen the kiss. Instead, he tore his mouth from hers. His words were clear and controlled.

"Oh, Sidonie, this has to stop." He bowed his head until his forehead rested against hers. "Look at what I'm doing to you! In an alleyway, for Christ's sake. I am so sorry."

He was sorry. He wanted her, yes. But not, apparently, in the way he had wanted Ruby Black. There was no heated madness in him. Sidonie forced away the sting of disappointment and cupped his cheek in her hand. "Devellyn, it's all right," she whispered. "No one is here. No one can see."

"I want you, Sidonie," he responded. "Damn it, don't you see that? You should probably backhand me for the audacity. But I want you, as—as a *lover.* Not some light-skirt to flash about in public, but . . . but something else. I don't know. Something private, just between us."

"A secret lover?" she whispered. The notion did not strike her nearly as incongruously as it should have. But somehow, she set her hands on his chest and forced the notion away. She could never give herself to the Marquess of Devellyn. Sidonie bit her lip and mentally cursed the day she'd gotten that damned foolish tattoo.

Devellyn misunderstood her hesitance. He dropped his hands and looked past her, into the depths of the alley. "Good girl," he said quietly. "Don't do it. Don't waste yourself."

It was the second time he'd given her such a warning. She set her hand against his cheek and turned his face back into hers. "It would not be a waste, Devellyn," she said. "Trust me to choose my friends, and choose them well. But to be your lover? I am sorry. I cannot."

His eyes were very solemn. "It would be futile for me to hope, then?"

Sidonie swallowed hard. "For anything beyond friendship?" she asked. "Yes."

He bent down and picked up her empty basket. "I understand."

"No, you don't." She shook her head, and hooked the basket over her arm. "And I cannot explain it."

"A lady need not explain such things," he said, smiling. But it was a forced smile, and they both knew it.

"Come to the market with me," she said impulsively. "I shall need help carrying my purchases."

"What a liar you are, Sidonie Saint-Godard," he said.

But he took the basket and followed like a dutiful spaniel as Sidonie picked over the merchandise displayed in the stalls along the marketplace. But her mind, strangely, was still on Ruby Black, the woman Devellyn desired with a passion he had called maddening. A passion which left him aching and sleepless. Powerful words, indeed. What would it be like, she wondered, to be the object of such a man's obsession?

And then it struck her that she was. *She* was Ruby. Why did she keep feeling those little stabs of envy? Good Lord! This was becoming ridiculous. She felt like a love-struck schoolgirl again—over an unrepentant rake! She shut the thought away and forced her mind to her marketing.

This time of year, there was an abundance of root crops and a dearth of the green vegetables Sidonie loved. She made her way deep into the market, methodically picking over the produce and dropping the best into her basket. Suddenly, from the corner of one eye, she spied one last bunch of hothouse broccoli lying in a shallow basket just an arm's length away. She reached for it just as a thin, long-fingered hand scooped it up.

Sidonie did not believe in surrendering gracefully. "I'm afraid that was mine!" she insisted, just before looking up into the wide, golden eyes of her brother.

"I cower before such steely resolve, my dear." George Kemble let his gaze sweep down Lord Devellyn, then dropped the broccoli into their basket. "Pray introduce me to your escort."

Lord Devellyn liked neither the looks nor the tone of the slender, perfectly dressed man who stood opposite them. He was strikingly handsome, but in a dangerous way, like a serpent slithering through sunlit water. He was neither young nor old, and his gaze drifted haughtily—and quite fearlessly—down Devellyn's length.

Sidonie slipped her arm awkwardly from Devellyn's. "Hello, George," she managed. "What a surprise."

"I gather," said the man. "Now, my love, about that introduction?"

Sidonie recovered herself. "Lord Devellyn, this is my brother, George Bau—I mean, George Kemble."

Fleetingly, Devellyn wondered what she had been about to say, but the concern was short-lived.

"A pleasure, I'm sure," said Kemble, his glittering eyes belying his words. Then he returned his attention to Sidonie. "My dear, I wish you to dine with me tonight. At seven. I shall send a carriage."

Sidonie's brow furrowed. "I cannot," she said. "I promised to prepare dinner for Julia."

George Kemble did not take the refusal well. "What rubbish!" he snapped. "The woman is your companion. Surely you need not act as her cook?"

"George!" Sidonie's voice was chiding. "Tuttle is ill, and Meg is off. I cannot be away." She leaned forward and gave a little tug on the man's cravat, though it was already flawlessly arranged. "There, you are perfect now. I shall see you on Friday as usual, George."

Her brother bowed stiffly to them. "Then I bid you both good day."

A very black mood came over Lord Devellyn as he watched the man stalk away. And he already knew Sidonie would be seeing her brother long before Friday arrived—whether she wished to or not.

Beside him, Sidonie cleared her throat. "Onions," she said, moving as if to lead him in the direction opposite her brother. "I need onions. And eggs."

Out of sheer irritation, Devellyn took her hand and laid it back on his arm. "Well, my dear," he murmured. "Shall I still trust you to choose your own friends?"

Sidonie's eyes widened. "Whatever do you mean?"

Devellyn smiled tightly. "Well, perhaps I misinterpreted," he managed to say. "But it certainly looked to me as if your brother means to choose them for you. Perhaps it's best I go."

Sidonie's faint smile faded. "Don't. Please."

"I am sorry," he said quietly.

Sidonie's mouth tightened. She nodded stiffly, then turned away. When next he looked back, she had vanished around the corner and into the next row. Frustrated and disheartened, Devellyn wound his way between the rows and stalls, back in the direction they'd come, mentally berating himself for putting Sidonie in such an awkward position, even as he damned George Kemble to hell.

Unfortunately, Kemble had not gone to hell. Instead, he stood at the last stall, almost blocking the way as he picked over a selection of bundled herbs. He shot Devellyn a venomous look as he passed and stepped boldly backward, right into Devellyn's path.

"A word of advice, old chap," he murmured, lifting one dark brow. "Trifle with my sister, and you'll rue the day."

Devellyn jerked to a halt and glowered down at the smaller man. But Kemble did not back away. Instead, he leaned ever so slightly into Devellyn, which was disconcerting to a man accustomed to intimidating people with his size.

"Just what the hell is your problem, Kemble?" he finally asked.

A mocking smile curved the man's lips. "I don't have problems," he said, returning to the job of picking over his herbs. "Not for long, at any rate. Instead, I have a vast array of solutions. Stay away from my sister, or I shall find one for you."

Devellyn felt a red-hot rage rush through him. "By God, that sounds like a threat."

"Then you're not as dumb as you look." Kemble dropped a bundle of greenish gray sprigs into his basket. "Still, it wouldn't trouble me one whit to put a bullet through your brain—if you've still got one."

"Why, you dandified little upstart!" Devellyn grabbed him by the elbow, but Kemble threw it off in disgust.

They had begun to draw a small crowd, and the girl tending the herb cart had backed judiciously away. Kemble's smile had turned caustic. "You've no notion who we are, have you?" he hissed. "You are ignorant about what is going on here. You are a fool, Devellyn. A bigger fool, even, than I expected."

For the second time that day, Devellyn found himself tearing his glove off. But Kemble just laughed and waved the back of his hand dismissively. "Oh, keep it on, Devellyn," he said. "I'm not a gentleman. I don't have to accept your challenge. I can just shoot you in the back if I wish. Now, take yourself off and go find a card game to sharp, or some wench to tumble. Something—*any-thing*—to distract yourself from my sister."

Devellyn just stood there, stunned, with his glove half-off. George Kemble dropped some coins on the edge of the herb cart and calmly walked away.

Chapter Ten

In which Ilsa and Inga are Justly rewarded

Mother Lucy's was a particularly disreputable bordello perched on a particularly disreputable corner of Soho. There, the wine was tolerable, the women willing, and Lucy so ugly it made her girls appear as swans by contrast. And so Lord Devellyn had little difficulty in saying *yes* that night when Alasdair and Quin Hewitt turned up to drag him there for what they termed "a good bucking-up." After all, what reason had he to say no? He was a free, rich, and perpetually unattached male.

They arrived at ten, surveyed the merchandise, and by half past, Quin had chosen himself a particularly hard-looking blonde and taken her upstairs for what he described as a quick poke. It was near midnight now, and Quin hadn't been seen since.

Alasdair leaned an inch nearer. "Dev, d'you reckon she ate him alive?"

"Depends on what he paid her." Devellyn took a languid sip of his wine, which did not seem at all tolerable tonight. He was still stewing over his altercation with George Kemble.

They were lounging on a pair of overstuffed divans covered in some freakish purplish fabric and watching Ilsa and Inga Karlsson entertain a small crowd of especially dissipated-looking gentlemen with what passed for their famous song-and-dance routine, but which consisted of a vast deal of bouncing, squealing, and bending over. And they were naked—or so bloody near it as made no difference. Everything the good Lord had given them back in Gothenburg was poking out through a slit or a crack or a little wisp of something. It was cheap, vulgar, and—well, a jolly good show. A man would have to be dead not to get a rise out of Ilsa's bare bottom, and at the moment, Devellyn had a stellar view.

Ilsa and Inga, who aspired to a career in theater, were such a rarity that Mother Lucy served them up as more of an appetizer than a main course. Or perhaps it was more of a bait-and-switch routine. Only the wealthiest of gentlemen could afford the outrageous sum Lucy asked for the pleasure of the twins' company, so she set them up on a little dais in the drawing room, as a more egalitarian entertainment offering which brought customers through the door in droves. However, after a chap watched long enough, or got desperate enough, he either paid the price, or hired something cheaper. Mother Lucy had cheaper.

"You know, tonight I just don't fancy something cheaper," said Alasdair, who was fiddling with his cuffs or his coat sleeves or some damned thing, in a calculated effort to avoid looking Devellyn in the eye. Alasdair was nothing if not predictable. "Let's hire Ilsa and Inga," he went on. "No one else has, and Lord knows we can afford it."

Devellyn was too tired—or too *something*—to argue. "Fine," he said, getting up off his divan. "I'll go pay the piper."

"Why, I wouldn't hear of it!" said Alasdair, leaping to his feet. "Allow me, old boy."

Devellyn knew that when a Scot insisted on paying for anything, a wise man got suspicious, but he was too distracted to remember it just then. Alasdair wandered off for what, in hindsight, seemed an overlong chat with Mother Lucy, who looked as if she'd forgotten to shave that morning. Twenty minutes later, he wandered off again, leaving Devellyn alone with the twins in a dark, overheated room upstairs—his way of apologizing, perhaps, for the Vespasian coin fiasco. And Inga—at least he thought it was Inga—was kneeling between his boots and pushing his knees wide. She eased one hand up his crotch and made a sound of pleasure which needed no translation.

Devellyn was only human; he felt his groin grow warmer and heavier. The girls were breathtakingly beautiful. Ilsa giggled and circled behind his chair. He could feel her bare breasts, warm and heavy, brush his body as she leaned over to suck his earlobe between her teeth.

"Sucking is very good, ya?" said Inga, looking up at him through a sweep of pale lashes. "We like to do it to you. Already we cheer you up, see?"

Damn Alasdair for painting him a charity case! But Inga's clever fingers had already slipped half his buttons free. Devellyn's erection sprang from the folds of linen and wool as Inga pushed them away. Yes, very cheerful, indeed.

"Ooh, so big," purred Inga, her expression coquettish

as she rolled his stiff cock between her palms. "Too big for little Inga, I am thinking."

Devellyn laughed. "Oh, I very much doubt that, my dear."

And he did doubt it. The girls at Mother Lucy's were as well-worn as yesterday's stockings. While Ilsa reached around to untie his cravat, Inga bent forward until he could see her heart-shaped buttocks. Deftly, she ran the tip of her tongue along his length.

"Take it, Inga," encouraged her sister. "You can do it."

But that well-worn stocking image was abruptly and indelibly fixed in Devellyn's mind. He looked down at what Inga was doing, and suddenly, it sickened him. Not, precisely, *what* she was doing. Or that it was being done to him. But it was just . . . just the place. The atmosphere. The fact that he had to pay for his pleasure; that no one ever had or ever would just offer it up to him gratis because they wanted *him*. In fact, until today in Covent Garden, he'd never even asked anyone to take him on without having one hand already on his purse. But Sidonie was not the sort of woman one offered money to.

Inga had her mouth on him now. "She is good cheering up, ya?' whispered Ilsa, rubbing her bare breast against his cheek in invitation. But it was not especially good. Certainly, it was not cheering—well, save for that one perky little part of his anatomy.

God, this is not what I want, he thought.

What he wanted, he wasn't going to get. He reached down and threaded his fingers through Inga's cornsilk hair. "I'm sorry, my dear," he said gently. "This just isn't working for me."

Ilsa stopped rubbing her breast against him, and

leaned over his shoulder to glare at his crotch. "What you meaning, is not working?" she asked indignantly. "*Stenhård,* like a big brick, that thing is!"

"Ya, thick like one, too," muttered Inga, sitting back on her heels.

And for the first time in his life, Devellyn had grasped the fact that his body could want one thing and his mind quite another. And that his mind, once he actually allowed it to function, was going to win. Always. Which probably explained why copious amounts of alcohol had so often come in handy.

This truth came to him so suddenly and so clearly, he was already up and stuffing in his shirttails in when Inga stood, looking a little grateful. Ilsa, however, was less than pleased. She circled around Devellyn's chair and began to jerk on the little wisps of frothy fabric she'd just divested.

"Dashing bloody hell," she said, clearly struggling with her frustration and her English. "Come on, Inga. He is no good. We go to dance."

"*Nej då!* No more dancing!" said her sister wearily. "My feet hurt. I want work only on my back now."

Devellyn hitched up his last button. "Never mind the dancing," he said, artfully arranging the fall of his trousers around his difficulties. "I'll slip out through the alley. You two just squeak the bedsprings a bit, make a good show of it, then lock the door and . . . well, have a nap or something."

"Ya?" said Ilsa disbelievingly.

"Ya," said Inga. "Nap sounding good to me."

"Then I insist, my dear," said Devellyn, tossing Inga an extra ten-pound note.

The girls widened their eyes at one another as if they couldn't fathom their good fortune. Or perhaps they were just questioning Devellyn's sanity. Certainly, his still-erect cock was. But in any case, by the time he had his cravat retied, Ilsa was bouncing up and down on the bed for all she was worth, while Inga sat in the chair moaning, panting, and screaming, "Yes! Oh, oh! Yes, yes, *YES!*"

Devellyn watched in admiration. Perhaps Ilsa and Inga had a future in the theater after all? He just shook his head, and, somewhere between an *oh! oh!* and a *yes, yes!* he seized his moment and slipped quietly out the door.

The following afternoon, the rain returned to London, this time followed by a fog which settled over the city like a blanket smelling of coal smoke and old fish. And the fog was not the worst of it. Belowstairs at Number Fourteen, household matters were not running smoothly. At the crack of dawn, Mrs. Tuttle had dragged herself out of bed to prepare breakfast, but her incessant cough had rattled the rafters all day. Sidonie felt a little guilty. It had not, apparently, been the sherry which had sent the poor woman to her bed after all.

Because of the damp, Meg had been dispatched to do all the cook's outdoor errands, which ensured they would take twice as long, since she always dawdled in front of Devellyn's house in the frequently fruitful hope that Henry Polk would come out and make sheep's eyes at her. Thus it should have come as no surprise that afternoon when Mrs. Tuttle sent the girl off to the bakeshop in Great Russell Street, and Meg did not promptly return.

All of an hour passed, and Sidonie had almost decided to throw open the door and just shout across the street through the fog when she heard the basement door slam below. Meg was back, then. Just in time to hear Tuttle's latest spasm of barking and hacking.

Concerned, Sidonie found Julia in the parlor. "Can you bear another omelet for dinner?"

Julia looked up from her hemming. "Tuttle really does not sound well, does she?" she mused, drawing her stitch taut. "I wonder if we oughtn't send for Dr. Ketwell?"

Sidonie gave her a wintry smile. "I shall go break the bad news."

But their cook was well enough, it seemed, to engage in a little light gossip. Sidonie was but halfway down the kitchen stairs when she overheard the two servants speaking in hushed tones interspersed with giggles.

"And one time, says Henry, they peeked into the study, and what did they see but that Sir Alasdair fellow passed out on the divan!" she heard Meg continue. "With Lord Devellyn laid out neat as a corpse, right in the middle of floor! Still in their coats and boots, they were, and staggered round like drunken sailors when the housemaid woke 'em up a'sweeping out the grates."

"Oo, that Lord Devellyn," said Mrs. Tuttle darkly. "He's a wicked one, I do hear."

"Oh, you hear right, ma'am," said Meg in an undertone. "Last evening, they went down to Soho and stayed out half the night. Afterward, they forgot poor Wittle, and walked all the way home with his lordship singing hymns, and Sir Alasdair keeping time with his walking stick a'thumping the bottom of the beer barrel. Been to a very rough sort of whorehouse, they had, Henry says."

"Watch that tongue, girl!" warned Mrs. Tuttle.

"Well, what am I to call it?" asked Meg. "A nunnery? Anyways, it's named Mother Lucy's, Henry says, and they're forever going. Once they stayed three whole days. Says it's a proper den of iniquity, whatever that is. Sounds rackety, though, don't it?"

Tuttle responded with another paroxysm of coughing, which allowed Sidonie to clatter loudly down the stairs. Both servants looked up innocently. "It's back to bed for you," she ordered Tuttle, who was peeling potatoes and onions. "I shall finish those vegetables whilst Meg fetches Dr. Ketwell."

When both servants began to protest, Sidonie cut them off, her tone uncharacteristically sharp. "Just this once, could the two of you simply do as I say?"

They did. Meg all but leapt back into her cloak, while Tuttle bustled off into her room, leaving Sidonie with a sharp knife and half a peck of peeled potatoes which she promptly hacked into untidy chunks while mentally naming off all the best parts of Lord Devellyn's anatomy.

So he'd been off to Mother Lucy's last night, had he? *Thwack! Thwack! Thunk!* Why was she surprised? *Thunk! Thwack!* Was it not just the tawdry sort of place she would have expected a man like Devellyn to frequent? And calling Lucy's "a proper den of iniquity" was like calling the Royal Pavilion a bastion of quiet elegance.

At least she could take comfort in one small thing, she decided, turning her knife on the onions. At least Lord Devellyn had not suffered overmuch from her refusal of her affections. At least he had found something pleasurable to do with his evening. Surely she had not imagined he'd keep some quiet, lonely vigil by the fire? No, of course not. The Devil of Duke Street had a reputation to maintain. Sidonie looked down and realized she had hacked the onions to shreds.

"Well?" said the Marquess of Devellyn when Henry Polk came back through the front door. "I hope you did not hang about my front doorstep in the fog for forty-five minutes to no good effect."

Polk looked flummoxed. "I'm not exactly sure, sir."

"Not sure?" boomed Devellyn. "Well, what did she say, man? What did she know?"

His words came out harsher than he'd intended. He did not like being put in the humiliating position of having to quiz his servants about the goings-on in his own house, let alone someone else's. Already the staff was wondering why their ordinarily oblivious employer was paying so much attention to the people who lived across the street.

Polk opened his hands expressively. "It's a queer situation, my lord," he admitted. "I don't think those ladies tell Meg much."

Perhaps her employers had noticed Meg's propensity for idle gossip, Devellyn almost remarked. Then he thought better of it and instead returned to the drawing room. "What do you mean, they don't tell her much?" he asked, sitting back down to the coffee service he'd abandoned moments earlier. "The girl lives in, doesn't she? She must know their comings and goings."

"You'd think so, sir," Polk agreed. "But when I tried to find out where Madame Saint-Godard had been all those evenings last week, Meg seemed uncertain whether she'd been from home at all."

"The devil! How can that be?"

Polk shrugged. "Meg says she hears *madame* coming and going at odd hours," the footman answered. "Says she has no maid, though Mrs. Crosby sometimes dresses her hair of an evening. Otherwise, she does for herself and keeps to herself. Says she has a suite of rooms upstairs, and stays shut up in 'em with that big black mouser she carried over from France. Talks to it, Meg says."

Better the cat than Meg, Devellyn supposed. At least Sidonie was not a fool. She was hiding something, he thought, and doing a bloody good job of it. "Well, what of this brother?" he asked. "This George Kemble?"

Polk was actually scratching his head now. "Well, we've a bit o' confusion there," said the footman. "Meg allowed as how *madame* might have two or three brothers, for all she knew, but she's still never seen one come round the house."

Devellyn wracked his brain. *My brother,* Sidonie had said, *fell in with a bad, dangerous crowd.*

Certainly the fellow had had a nasty edge to his personality. He did not look like a chap one would want as an enemy, either. So just how bad and dangerous was George Kemble? Or was he even her brother? Sidonie—or so he'd assumed—was French, though her accent was admittedly faint. The man Devellyn had met in Covent Garden had spoken with an unmistakable English accent—and a very upper-crust accent at that.

"Begging your pardon, sir," interjected Polk. "But did you say Kemble? Like the acting family?"

"No, definitely not," said Devellyn irritably. "He was a good deal more well bred than that."

"But you never said his name before, sir," Polk pressed. "Is it spelt the same?"

Devellyn considered it. "I daresay. Why?"

My brother Ben——the one who works for the River Police?——he knows a chap in the Strand by that name," said Polk. "A very toplofty sort of fellow who deals in fancy things."

"Fancy things?"

"Fine folderol, it says on his door," Polk explained. "Just round from St. Martin's Church. He trades in art, jewelry, and very expensive old things——what do they call 'em?—— *antiquities.* Like sculptures from Egypt, and old carvings made by Chinamen that's been dead a thousand years."

"You don't say?" mused Devellyn.

Polk nodded effusively. "Lots o' rich nobs do business there," he said. "Ben took me once to buy a hatpin for Mum's birthday, and the prime minister himself was there. Buying an ormolu clock, he was."

"Wellington, eh?" said Devellyn. "I daresay this Kemble could be the same man."

Polk shot him a warning glance. "Well, this Kemble chap I'm talking of is well-known to the police," he said. "That's how Ben knows him——or knows *of* him."

"He is of questionable character?"

Polk shrugged. "Well, he certainly knows a lot of 'em," he admitted. "Smugglers and fences, for starts. And Ben says the police inspectors do go in and out o' there on a reg'lar basis asking him certain things and showing him certain things. Kemble does help them out from time to time, but very quiet-like, if you know what I mean. And sometimes, Ben says, you don't know whether to trust him or not."

The marquess snorted. "That definitely sounds like the fellow."

"Well, it's not my place to offer advice, sir," said his servant, who was obviously getting ready to do so. "But I should have a care if I were you. Ben says this Kemble chap has friends in very high places. Knows Mr. Peel personally, he does, and has the ear of lots o' the beaks round the parishes."

"Beaks?" said Devellyn.

"Magistrates," Polk explained. "And folks over at the Home Office, too."

Devellyn set his coffee aside. "So, not just a simple shopkeeper, eh?"

"Oh, no, sir," said Polk. "That he definitely is not."

"Hmm," said Devellyn. "Very odd. Thank you, Polk. You are dismissed."

Polk turned to go, then suddenly turned back again. "My lord, there was one more thing."

"Yes?"

"You wished to know, you said, if the ladies had any engagements," he answered. "Meg says *madame* is to go to a ball in a few days' time. A very posh affair, she says, given by a friend of Mr. Peel's who is high up in the government. She knows, she said, because Mrs. Crosby is working on her ball gown."

"How odd," said Devellyn. "Who? When?"

"She did not know the *when,* sir," Polk admitted. "But the name she heard, for Mrs. Crosby was crowing about it. It was Walrafen, sir. Lord Walrafen."

That night, Sidonie dressed for her evening engagement with the utmost care. After twisting her hair up, she put on her midshipman's uniform; a white waistcoat, snug trousers, and an elegant coat of dark blue trimmed with gold buttons and deep cuffs. A touch of makeup to harden her facial bones and suggest the merest shadow of a beard, then she was ready for the hat. Thus attired in perfect naval splendor, Sidonie began to practice her rolling sailor's gait. She had seen enough of it in her travels, so it was not such a great challenge.

Thomas looked up, surveying the sight with feline indifference. "What do you think, old boy?" she asked him, studying herself in the mirror.

Thomas unsheathed his claws and began to dig into her carpet.

"An excellent notion!" murmured Sidonie. She rummaged through her dressing table until she found her sheath and blade. Carefully, she tucked it away and bent to pet the cat.

Thomas rose up onto his hind feet and rubbed his cheek over her knee. Inexplicably, a strange chill ran through her. Thomas was not normally so affectionate; not unless food was involved. She shook off the odd feeling, picked him up for a kiss, then settled him in the center of the bed.

"Keep it warm, Tommy," she said, giving him one last scratch beneath the chin. "I'll not be long."

She looked again at the mirror, studying the hat. It could be her undoing, she thought ruefully. Bodley had arranged to meet his last lover at an inn. A gentleman would be expected to remove his hat under such circumstances. Reluctantly, she let her hair down again, and took up her scissors.

Just then, Julia came in and shut the door quietly behind. "Meg's abed now, and Tuttle's sleeping off Dr. Ketwell's laudanum." She jerked to a halt, and looked with horror at the scissors Sidonie held aloft. "Oh, Lord, Sidonie, this is madness!"

Sidonie smiled. "Come, Julia, do I not look the part of a sailor? My makeup is well-done, is it not?"

But there was no pleasing Julia any longer. Sidonie's schemes, she swore, had gotten out of hand. Sidonie accused her of having grown fainthearted. Julia threatened to tell George. Sidonie dared her to do so. As usual, they got nowhere.

"Well, at the very least," said Julia heatedly, "do not ruin your lovely hair for this."

"Then you must disguise it for me," Sidonie challenged. "I have not your skill."

With obvious reluctance, Julia stalked from the room and returned with a wig from one of her trunks. Wordlessly jamming in hairpins, she twisted Sidonie's hair into painfully tight curls, then pulled the wig snugly over them. The result was remarkable. Sidonie kissed her friend's cheek, thanked her, then slipped out into the gloom of London.

She made her way west, thinking and moving as a young man might, with her chin up, shoulders back, and eyes roaming freely. No one spared her a second look, save for two sloe-eyed strumpets loitering in the murk beside the Golden Cross. Sidonie thought of how Bodley had lured his last young man inside, shivered, and quickened her step on past the front door.

The fringes of St. James's Park were softened by gaslight. It spilt in cottony, mustard-colored auras around the lampposts, unable to permeate far into the gloom. There was no rain, thank God, nor was it cold, but here, nearer the river, the fog had not begun to lift.

Fleetingly, Sidonie considered turning back. On the other hand, one could die of old age waiting for a clear night in London. And how many innocents might Bodley take advantage of while she waited?

She took the footpath which rimmed the park's easterly edge, just as Bodley had done. To her right, a fine unmarked carriage was parked at the corner of New Street, a groom holding the horses' heads, a coachman hunched under his many-caped coat, asleep by the look of his posture. Not Bodley's servants, though. Sidonie moved on through the gloom.

To her left, a courting couple strolled toward the water, their heads bent in conversation. A footman and a housemaid, by the look of them. It made her think of Meg and her growing infatuation with Devellyn's servant. She hoped the young man was sincere. And she hoped, too, that Meg was watching her tongue. Lost in such thoughts, Sidonie was well along the path before she realized it. She jerked her head up to get her bearings, and instead walked squarely into a young dandy, literally bouncing off him in the gloom.

"I say!" murmured the man, hastily catching her by the shoulder as she stumbled. "Steady on, lad!" He gave her a resounding thump on the back.

The gesture, so masculine in its execution, threw her off guard. Sidonie opened her mouth, and somehow found her midshipman's voice. "Beg your pardon, sir," she said. "Wasn't watching my step, was I?"

But the dandy's eyes were running down her with a calculated interest now. Swiftly, Sidonie took in the placement of his handkerchief, and the thumb which hung so casually from his waistcoat. "Going toward the

Admiralty?" he asked, as if to strike up a conversation.

Sidonie shook her head. "No," she said. "I mean, yes. In that general direction." She nodded by way of dismissal. "My apologies again, sir. Good night."

The dandy lifted his very elegant hat and watched her back away a little regretfully. She left him on the graveled path, still staring after her. Just a little farther along, she should see the spot where Lord Bodley had left his footman. Yes, just by that tree. She exhaled and relaxed a little. Despite the gloom, she began to see little groups of well-dressed gentlemen strolling about the trees and bushes, smoking and making idle conversation. More than a few of the gentlemen had women of a certain class hanging off their arms, all of them gay and laughing. Cynically, Sidonie wondered how many of them were truly happy, and how much of the gaiety was simply an act calculated to earn them a decent meal and a warm bed for the night.

A few yards along, she came out on the side near the parade ground. At the foot of Great George Street, a coach had drawn up at the curb, and as she passed downwind of it, she caught the unmistakable scent of opium clinging to the damp air. *Opium?* In St. James's? After nightfall, the park did indeed seem to become the place one went when in search of a little vice.

Sidonie strolled back and forth along the easterly edge of the park for a good hour but saw no sign of Bodley or his servant. On three occasions, however, other gentlemen began to approach her, their gazes assessing, yet guarded. She turned them away with her eyes. It was understood. They moved on, or let their attention drift elsewhere. But eventually, even these handsome, idle men began to fall away, some alone or with women, others in pairs, taking their cheroots and laughter with them. In the distance, a clock was striking midnight, the sound muffled and forlorn in the damp.

It was no use, she realized. Bodley would not come this night. Even the sound of traffic outside the park was beginning to wane. Sidonie shook off the disappointment. The evening had made for a good trial run. She set a swift pace toward the busy, well-lit Strand. She would go along the back of it, she decided. Off the beaten path, just in case George was out for a stroll, but near enough to be safe. Suddenly, she heard gravel crunch behind her.

She jerked at once to a halt, a stupid thing to do. She looked about. Nothing. But an awful chill ran up her spine. *Good Lord.* It was just her imagination. She was alone in the gloom, but not far from civilization. She could hear a carriage clattering toward Charing Cross, barely a two-minute walk away. She set off, feeling marginally safer, but she rechecked the blade in her coat pocket just the same.

Within moments, however, she again heard something—or perhaps sensed something. Or perhaps she was just losing her nerve. Admittedly, her life of crime had gone somewhat awry ever since she'd run into the Marquess of Devellyn. Sidonie was beginning to believe that the man had put some sort of curse on her.

Cautious now, she turned to take a shortcut toward Whitehall. She hastened across the street, which was devoid of traffic, and lost herself in the rabbit warrens approaching Scotland Yard. It was, perhaps, an unwise choice. The government buildings along the river lay quiet this time of night, while the pubs and coffeehouses of the Strand were tantalizingly beyond her reach.

She felt a whisper of motion an instant before he grabbed for her.

Sidonie spun around, whipping one leg into a high, vicious kick, a trick she'd learned from a Cantonese sailor. She caught her assailant hard in the ribs. He staggered back. She caught her balance, rolled onto the ball of one foot, and spun around again. Her boot caught him in the throat as he started up. The whole thing lasted but two seconds. Sidonie was outnumbered. Another man caught her from behind, and hauled her up hard against him.

"Well, look'ee what we got here, Budley," he rasped over her shoulder. "Seems peg-boy knows him a trick or two."

"Sod off!" growled Sidonie, struggling to throw him off. "The both of you." But fear gripped her throat. She fought it. *They're hoodlums,* she told herself. *Cutpurses, at worst.*

The one called Budley was approaching her now, still rubbing his ribs. He was young. Unshaven. His hands were grubby and his clothing rough. "Sod off, eh?" he said. "High talk for a sailor boy with 'is back to the wall."

He grabbed her roughly, and together the two men pinned her shoulders against the dank stone.

"Looks like a pretty madge-cull to me, Budley," said the second, forcing his face into hers. "Wonder what's in his pockets, eh? Coming from the park, he was. P'raps peg-boy made him a bit o' blunt tonight with that nancy little arse of his."

Budley leaned in and thrust one hand into her pocket—the empty one. Sidonie had to jerk her face away. She could smell him now. Sour breath. Unwashed skin, rank with old sweat. And both were foxed, or near enough it to hamper their judgment and timing.

She jerked hard, and almost caught him with her elbow again. "I said *sod off!*" she growled.

Budley leered at her, and extracted his hand. "You little Mary-Anns do like to troll through St. James's of a night," he said. "Hey, Pug, you ever had one?"

"Not me." Pug sounded suddenly horrified.

Budley shoved at her shoulder. "Well, what say we get them navy togs down round his ankles, and bugger him good?"

"Christ Jesus! *Here?*"

Budley grinned. "Why not?" he said. "I like the looks of 'im, I do."

"Gawd, Budley, you want your cock ter rot off?" said his cohort. "Let's just nick what's in 'is pockets and pike off."

Sidonie seized the moment of uncertainty. She threw back an elbow for all she was worth. Air exploded from Budley's lungs, and he bent forward on a loud, gagging sound. She whipped around and caught Pug across the throat with the edge of her hand. It connected. Budley lunged, but Sidonie danced away, whipping out her knife.

"Back off," she snarled, "or I swear to God, I'll trim both your sails."

Budley blanched and dropped his hands. The hooligan called Pug still clutched his throat. Sidonie took three steps backward, then turned and plunged into the darkness, sprinting in the direction of the Strand.

But they did not, apparently, mean to give up. She could hear the pounding of footfalls in the darkness behind. Sidonie rushed headlong into an alley, splashing through puddles and worse, bursting out near the Scotland Yard coal wharf, gasping for breath. The wharf lay steeped in darkness. Nothing human stirred.

"In here." Budley's voice echoed ominously down the alley. "I seen 'im go in."

Sidonie ran blindly then, twisting and turning through the maze of yards, one leading into another, and then along the river. *Northumberland,* she thought. *Northumberland Street led to the Strand.* Desperately, she looked about. A little light leached in. A candle in an upstairs window. A lantern swinging from a passing boat. She could hear someone following relentlessly. She turned again. The river vanished. Her breathing seemed loud in the dark.

Suddenly, a face floated from the gloom. "Yer purse!" Pug growled. "Now give it over!" The glint of metal came at her.

Sidonie screamed, and drove at him with her own blade, catching him across the hand. He grunted, cursed, and fell back. Sidonie ran, flying past the Hungerford Market, its stalls dark and empty. She turned the next corner. The glow of a streetlamp burst into view. *Northumberland.* Thank God. She could see the odd angle where it met Craven Street, and bolted for it.

It was only then that she felt the pain. Still running, she clasped her upper arm with her empty hand. Warm. Wet. Lamplight swam before her. Sidonie faltered and dropped her knife. It clattered onto the cobblestones.

*   *   *

George Kemble was savoring a glass of twelve-year-old vintage port, and rereading his favorite passage from *The Age of Reason* when a decidedly unreasonable pounding commenced on his door downstairs. Kemble was a night owl, yes. But he did not approve of anyone disturbing Thomas Paine and a bottle of Quinta do Noval '18 without an appointment.

The pounding came again. Across the room, Maurice stopped snoring and lifted his head from the back of his club chair. "We've got drunks again, George," he grumbled. "In the alley."

With a withering sigh, Kemble laid aside his book, withdrew a pocket pistol from the sideboard, and took up his candlestick. Thus reinforced, he went down the stairs leading to the rear of his shop.

The pounding was actually slowing, more of an ir-regular, halfhearted thump now. Kemble turned the three massive bolts which secured his back door, then lifted his candle as he cracked it. In the gloom, a young naval officer slumped drunkenly on his doorstep, one shoulder braced on the brickwork, one hand clasping his opposite arm.

"*Please . . .*" he managed thickly. "*Please . . . Cut . . .*"

Kemble wasn't about to put down his pistol—he'd learnt the tricks of his trade in a hard school—but he set aside his candle to slip a hand under the lad's elbow. Alas, too late. The midshipman's eyes rolled back into his head, his knees buckled, and he fainted dead across the threshold. It was then that Kemble noticed the blood. It stained the blue fabric, which was torn where the lad's hand had been, and it was worse in back.

Kemble let his hand drop. "Well!" he muttered.

"There goes my evening." Then, louder, up the stairs, "Maurice! Maurice, you'd best come down! Some clodpate middy managed to get himself frog-gigged out in the alley."

"Again?" Maurice was already thundering down the stairs.

They were halfway back up the stairway, the boy slung over Kemble's shoulder, and Maurice bringing up the rear, when the latter spoke. "Hold up, George," he said, lifting the candle higher. "The lad's losing his bicorn." Maurice caught the hat just as it fell. "Well, well!" he went on. "What have we here?"

Kemble looked back over his shoulder, trying not to buckle under at least nine stone of deadweight. "I don't know about *we*, Maurice," he said. "But *me* has a bad knee. Move on."

Maurice tilted the candle. "But George, this boy is wearing a wig," he said, hooking a finger under its back edge.

"The devil!" said Kemble.

Maurice was silent for a moment. "More accurately . . . it isn't even a boy."

"The devil!" said Kemble again.

"No, it's worse than that," muttered Maurice, holding the wig between two fingers like a louse-ridden rat.

"Worse?" Kemble's back was about to give now. "What could be worse than a bleeding bluejacket on your doorstep?"

Maurice straightened up, lifted his candle, and shrugged. "Well, old thing, I do hope I'm wrong," he said. "But it looks like *this* bleeding bluejacket is your sister."

* * *

Five minutes later, they had the erstwhile midshipman laid out in an empty bedchamber. Kemble had quit wondering aloud what manner of harebrained, half-cocked scandal broth his sister had gone and gotten herself involved in, while Maurice had dashed off to roust the kitchen maid.

"Good God, I cannot believe you!" He ripped the buttons from Sidonie's waistcoat as he tore it open. "Wasn't sailing around the world whilst hanging off the rigging with a knife in your teeth dangerous enough? You had to go and join the bloody frigging navy?"

On the bed, his sister began to stir. *"Oooh,"* she murmured.

Snip! Snip! went Kemble's scissors, chopping open the waistcoat's shoulder seams. "I mean, I could have bought you another ship, Sid," he went on. "If that's what you wanted. Was it? *Was* it?"

"Ow," she murmured. *"Stop."*

He couldn't stop. His heart was in his throat. *Was there just the one wound? Was it shallow? Not a stab wound, please, God.* Already, he'd hacked the bloody coat from her body and tossed it to the floor. He yanked the blood-spattered waistcoat from beneath her, shocked to see that his hands shook. Good Lord, his hands *never* shook.

Blood had soaked like thick claret through her shirt. Bright white. Brighter red. Kemble felt a moment of panic, an emotion now all but unknown to him. He snatched up his scissors and slit the sleeve from wrist to shoulder. The first cut slashed across her upper arm, ugly and gaping. Still, the neckcloth he'd wrapped round it downstairs had stanched the bleeding.

Maurice brought in a shallow pan and hastened away again. A white face flannel floated like a small, ghostly presence in the steam. Kemble slit through Sidonie's other sleeve, saw nothing, then hacked through thicker fabric which covered her chest. Too late, he realized she'd bound her breasts with a strip of bleached linen. He tore away the scraps and tossed them to the floor. Sidonie would probably be embarrassed when she realized he'd seen her half-naked. Too bloody bad. It was punishment enough for scaring him so.

On that thought, Kemble laid aside the scissors, looked down at his sister's naked torso, and had the breath abruptly crushed from his chest.

Good Lord. Oh, good Lord . . .

"George?" she murmured weakly, her lashes fluttering. "Oh, George. So . . . stupid."

Stupid. Yes, that was one word for it. Kemble shut his eyes, then opened them again, but nothing had changed. The appalling thing—that *vile stain*—was still there, black as a scorpion on her breast.

Sidonie's hand crept down the coverlet and felt blindly for his fingers. "George," she whispered. "George . . . am I . . . going to bleed to death?"

"No," said her brother grimly. "Oh, no, my dear. Because I am going to strangle you first."

Chapter Eleven

The Interrogation Commences

In the end, Kemble forced a strong dose of black drop down his sister's throat, then stitched her up himself. Oh, she squalled and flailed and threatened to maim his private parts, using words no lady should know, let alone use with fluency. But eventually, the drug dragged her under. Kem finished his job, snipped off the last little bit of silk, then swallowed half a pint of brandy.

Certainly, it wasn't the first time he'd stitched someone up—and it was far better than the hangman's noose she'd likely get if the wrong person saw that bloody tattoo on her breast. So he sponged her face and paced her floor until, sometime that afternoon, Sidonie began to stir. Then, his wrath and his horror and his awful, gut-wrenching fear knew no bounds.

"So you are the infamous Black Angel!" he said that evening, as she sat up with a mug of weak broth. "That patron saint of fallen women! That Robin Hoodesque

crusader! *L'ange noire!*—which is, of course, French for
goddamned bleeding idiot!"

"George!" she said, as he whirled around and stalked
back to her bed. "You never curse in front of ladies!"

"But *you* aren't a lady!" he countered. "*You* are a sui-
cidal lunatic with a tattoo on your breast!"

Sidonie glared at him over the rim of her mug of
broth. "I cannot believe you cut my clothes off!"

"What would you have preferred me do?" he countered. "Leave you to turn septic from some gut wound
I'd missed?"

Sidonie sighed and set away the mug. "I begin to wish
you had done," she said. "I never dreamt, George, that
you would cut up so."

"Oh, what a bounder!" said Kemble. "You never
meant me to know—because you *knew* what I'd do."

"What?" she challenged. "What would you do?
You're not my husband, George. Certainly you are not
my father. You cannot stop me."

Kemble leaned across the bed and gave her his nastiest
sneer. "Can I not, my dear?" he growled. "Just try me. I'll
have you hogtied on your arse in the hold of a Boston-
bound freighter so fast you can't say 'Shiver me timbers!'"

Sidonie could not believe her ears. She'd never heard
George speak so coldly. Well, not to her. She tried to
draw a deep breath, so that she might haul him over the
coals properly, but something went wrong, her breath
hitched, and she burst into tears instead.

Her brother was beside her on the bed and dragging
her against him before she knew what he was about.
"Oh, Sid, don't cry!" he begged. "Oh, Christ, I'm sorry.
I'm sorry. I'm sorry."

"Ouch!" she said, hiccupping the word on a sob. "My stitches, George."

Gingerly, he set her away. "Oh, Sidonie," he said. "What in heaven's name have you been doing?"

She couldn't catch her breath. "Oh, It—it—it's so hard to explain!" she wailed.

"You must try," he said, extracting a handkerchief and holding it as if she were a child so that she might blow her nose.

And so she tried; tried to tell him everything, but it came out in a blithering, tear-choked ramble. How she'd begun to feel so world-weary and useless. So pained by the void in her heart that Pierre's faithlessness—and eventually, his death—had left. London had brought back too many memories of their mother; of the sadness of it all, and she was beginning to wonder if coming home had been a mistake when, somehow, all of it seemed to conspire and catch up with her one afternoon.

She had been window-shopping in Bond Street, in some vain hope that a new hat might change her life—or at least cheer her—when a lordly gentleman had strolled out of a millinery shop with a delicate, well-bred lady on his arm. Sidonie had watched as a servant girl hastened toward him, her expression fearful, her belly swollen with child. In response, the gentleman simply shoved her from his path and lifted the lady into his phaeton.

The servant began to beg. "How can you let your child starve?" Sidonie heard her whisper.

The man had laughed and whipped up his fine matched grays. *"Whores!"* he had muttered, looking disdainfully down from his perch. *"They have so many customers, they can't tell one from another."*

The girl looked as if she'd been struck, then burst into tears. The pretty lady had simply stared over her shoulder as they drove away, her expression a strange mix of pity and contempt.

Something in Sidonie had snapped. Her ennui was gone, and in its place burned a righteous indignation. She discovered the gentleman's name, and the Black Angel was born. His scullery maid now had four hundred pounds in the three-percents, and a cottage near the fens.

George surveyed her coolly and began to pace the floor again. "Please, my dear, continue."

Somehow, Sidonie blithered on with the rest of it. Everything, that was, save for Jean-Claude's involvement. She told her brother of the individual women she had helped and of the money she often delivered to the Nazareth Society, always in her widow's weeds and heavy veil.

"Ah, the Nazareth Society," said her brother warningly. "Have a care, my dear. The good ladies who volunteer there are not fools."

Sidonie thought again of Lady Kirton's shrewd gaze. No, hardly a fool. Sidonie shrugged it off and finished by telling George of Amy Hannaday's bruised face and of how she'd stalked Lord Bodley in St. James's Park.

George had suddenly lost all his color. "Good God!" he cried, sitting down on the bed and seizing both her hands in his. "Bodley! Listen to me, Sidonie—you have no idea the risks you are running!"

Sidonie narrowed her eyes. "I can handle men like Bodley."

"No, you fool, you cannot!" her brother whispered.

"Bodley is not one of your spoilt, indolent noblemen. He lives a life you know nothing of—a life I pray God you never know! You cannot fathom the workings of his world; that sphere of bawds and bullyboys and child prostitution. Sidonie, they will kill, even children, without so much as a backward glance. You have no comprehension of the danger."

"Oh?" Sidonie lifted her brows. "And you do?"

George's expression darkened. "I know far more of it than I should wish," he said. "You forget that I have lived by my wits since I was barely fourteen."

"In that sphere of bawds, bullyboys, and so on?" she pressed.

"The fringes of it, yes," he snapped, his eyes glittering with anger now.

She looked at him accusingly. "But you did not have to live by your wits, George," she said. "You could have come home. To Mother, and to me. Surely a life with us was better than a life on your own?"

George was silent; so silent, she feared she'd just rent an irreparable tear in their relationship. "I daresay it was," he finally answered. "I should have come home, Sid. But I was young and prideful. And I hated Father. I hated his visits. I hated his lies, and what he'd done to us. All of us, Mother included. Good God, she was so wheedling. So manipulative."

"So desperate," Sidonie softly interjected.

"Yes," he said. "That, too."

"George," said Sidonie softly. "Did you . . . did you know men like Bodley?"

His eyes were grim. "I learned how to avoid them,"

he said. "And I learned to be ruthless doing it. That, Sidonie, is the only way you survive on the streets."

Sidonie looked away. George would not let go of her hands. She drew a deep breath and pulled them from his grasp. "Mamma once said"—her voice fell to a whisper—"she said you sold yourself, George. To rich men. And she said you did it deliberately. To shame Father."

The anger glinted again. "Whatever I did, I did what I had to do," he gritted. "And by God, I changed my name—took up the first one that came to mind. I have not been George Bauchet in decades. And I have done what neither Mother nor Father ever did, Sidonie. I have made something of myself, by my wits, and by my relentlessness, and by the sweat of my brow."

"Oh, George!" Sidonie whispered, reaching out to him. "I have never been ashamed of you."

But her brother seemed no longer to hear her. "Yes, perhaps I was a thief and a sharp, or very near it," he rasped. "But I worked my way up, dear girl. Was I a gigolo, too? Some might say so. I don't give a damn. I learnt class and style, and I learnt it from the best-dressed men in town—a kind of class that always eluded Mother, for all her delicate ways."

She reached out to touch him. "George, I think I understand."

But George wasn't finished. "And when I became a valet, Sidonie, I was the best in London. And when I became a shopkeeper, I made myself rich in three years' time. I did all this because I never forgot what I learnt on the streets—what men like Bodley taught me. *Be ruthless.* No, Sid, I'll never be what Father was. I'll never be the Duke of Gravenel. But whatever I am, I made. I did not wait for my blue blood to bestow it on me. And whilst people may call me names behind my back, they bloody well don't do it to my face."

Sidonie felt her eyes well with tears. "No one calls you names, George," she whispered. "No one would dare. But no one would wish to."

George laughed a little bitterly, took her fingers again, and bowed his head until it rested on their joined hands. "Devellyn does," he said, addressing the counterpane. "I saw it in his eyes in Covent Garden."

"You goaded him, George."

Kemble sighed, and lifted his head. "Whatever it is you are doing to him, Sidonie, you must stop it now. He's a worthless scoundrel, I know, but we should wish him no ill."

"What do you mean?" she challenged. "What do you think I'm *doing* to him?"

Her brother shrugged. "Whatever it is, it is madness," he gently insisted. "Just stop it—*all* of it. You aren't changing the world, my love. You aren't reforming these men. It's futile."

His tone cut her to the quick. "How dare you say my work is futile!" she demanded. "I am helping these exploited women. I know I am! Perhaps I shall do it until they hang me."

Her brother seized her roughly by her good arm. "Sidonie, you fool, they *will* hang you!" he said. "There are safer, better ways to help the oppressed. And in case you are deceiving yourself, robbing a few selfish noblemen won't make us any less illegitimate. It won't elevate me and bring Devellyn down. It won't change what Father did to Mother—and it damned sure won't make what she became any more respectable."

Sidonie looked at him incredulously. "Why, I never thought it would!"

"Yes. You did. You are trying to avenge Father's sins as much as you are trying to avenge the sins of those foolish gentlemen you humiliate. Do not deceive yourself."

"What nonsense!" she said. "I shan't listen, George, do you hear?"

He shook her again. "Sidonie, I won't sit idly by whilst you get yourself killed trying to avenge a wrong that cannot be fixed. And that is what you're trying to do. Even I can see it."

Suddenly, Sidonie wanted to cry. Her head hurt, her arm hurt, and everything in her life seemed turned upside down. Was George right? Was she living out some sort of silly childhood fairy tale, where the wicked got what they deserved, and the good lived happily ever after?

"Oh, God!" she finally said. "Is there no justice, George? Mother had none. And no hope, either. Father did that to her. He took her hope away, but he never paid for it."

"And you can't make him pay, love," he returned, his voice gentler now. "Oh, perhaps you can make some of the others pay, some of the time. But only if you catch them. And only for a little while. It isn't worth your neck."

Sidonie sniffled. "So innocent women will continue to be deceived, used, and made miserable?" she said. "And no one can avenge it?"

"It's time to grow up, Sidonie." Her brother's voice

was tender. "Mother was never miserable—oh, perhaps at first, but it did not last. She liked high drama. She liked fine things. And she most assuredly liked being the center of attention. That's why *you* got sent away to school, my dear, remember? Your youth and beauty became too great a contrast."

Sidonie's head was beginning to throb now. "Perhaps you're right," she whispered, pressing her fingertips to her temples. "Oh, God, George! I just don't know anymore!"

Her brother kissed her lightly on the forehead, then rose from the bed. "I wish to show you something," he said. He left the room and returned with a newspaper, folded open. He pointed at a small notice of some sort.

"This is why I want you to stay away from Devellyn," he said. "He is looking for you, my dear. Asking questions. Poking. Prodding. And sooner or later, someone may talk."

"There is only Julia, and she would sooner die." But Sidonie took the paper. The type was tiny, but the words were clear.

If Miss Ruby Black, late of Southwark, will report to Mssrs. Brown and Pennington in Gracechurch Street and prove her true identity, she will come to no ill, and will receive a financial offer which will be very much to her advantage.

"Good Lord!" she whispered. "Is this today's paper?"

"Several days old," he admitted. "But you are running a grave risk, Sid, by even allowing Devellyn to see you stroll down the street. And whether you're the

Black Angel or not, you've certainly got no business going about town on his arm."

George was right. She knew he was. She bought herself time by reading the message again. "George," she said curiously. "How do you know this?"

"Know what, my dear?"

"That Devellyn placed this notice," she answered. "The name *Ruby Black* has doubtless been bandied about in half of London's clubs. Obviously, you have heard it. Perhaps someone else placed it?"

George shook his head. "Not likely," he said. "Brown and Pennington are, after all, his solicitors."

"But how do you know?"

George gave a slow shrug. "Well, I merely assume it," he admitted. "But they have been the solicitors to the Duke of Gravenel and his heirs since time immemorial. That's why the ad caught my eye."

"The Duke of Gravenel?" she echoed hollowly.

"Father's solicitors, Sidonie," he reminded her. "God knows I've seen the name on enough documents. That little annuity Mother received? It came via Brown and Pennington. Every quarter-day, like clockwork."

"George!" she whispered, her hand going out to grasp her brother's arm. "Oh, God, George, what are you saying?"

Her brother's expression gentled. "You do not know?"

Sidonie set the heel of her hand to her forehead. "*Aleric*," she murmured. "His name . . . is Aleric. And his family name, why, it is Hilliard, is it not? I am guessing now, you see. I do not know. I never asked. Oh, God. How stupid I have been!"

"Hilliard, yes," said George quietly. "He became Gravenel's heir after his brother died."

A strange, sick feeling clutched at her throat. "That was an accident, George," she protested. "Just an accident. Still, to think that we are . . . are related! How *closely?* Good Lord, George, tell me!"

"Distantly," he said, shrugging. "A second cousin once removed, perhaps? When Father died without a son—"

"A *legitimate* son," she interjected.

"Yes, whatever," he murmured. "Anyway, then the title passed so far down the family tree, I lost count. The present duke is a very staunch, upright sort of chap. Nothing like Father. Certainly nothing like his own son."

But Sidonie's head was pounding now. "Cousins!" she groaned. "George, why didn't you warn me when I first mentioned him?"

"Because I loathe revisiting the past," he retorted. "And I detest talking about Devellyn, who has had every advantage in the world and is squandering it. Besides, my dear, I hardly thought it mattered. How was I to know what you were up to?"

Sidonie nodded weakly. "Yes. Yes, of course. I understand."

But George was watching her warily now. "My dear, was I wrong?"

"Wrong? About what?"

"Does it matter?"

Sidonie was silent for a long moment. "No," she finally whispered. "No, George. I suppose it does not."

"Good," said George, patting her on the hand. "For a

moment, you had me concerned. Now sleep, Sidonie. Another few days' rest will set you to rights."

She set aside the mug, and shook her head. "I must go home," she said. "Walrafen's charity ball is Thursday. I am to take Miss Arbuckle."

"You must rest," said her brother more sternly. "We will see how you go on when Thursday arrives."

Sidonie watched him withdraw, glowering at him from the bed. But on the threshold, George spun about. "One more thing, old girl," he murmured. "Those chaps who cut you, did they have names?"

Sidonie closed her eyes. "Pug," she said. "One was called Pug. And the other, he was called Budley. Why? Do you know them?"

George smiled faintly. "Regrettably, I have not the honor," he said. "An oversight which I shall shortly rectify."

Chapter Twelve

When Lightning Strikes

"A man's nature," Francis Bacon said, "is often hidden, sometimes overcome, but seldom extinguished." It was the Marquess of Devellyn's nature to be wicked and self-indulgent. But contrary to Mr. Bacon's fine theory, his nature seemed to have become unreliable of late, and some of his most entrenched watchwords—apathy, indolence, and intemperance, to name but a few—were failing him. He'd worn his nerves nigh to a frazzle lusting after—no, *obsessing* over—two different women, neither of whom he could now locate.

Sidonie had seemingly vanished. He watched her door incessantly when he was home. When he was out, he watched for Ruby Black on every street corner, his eyes running over the crowd, feverishly searching for a glimpse of red. He had told Alasdair that he'd no further interest in finding her. But that had been a lie. He couldn't get the feel of her, the taste of her, out of his mind.

He had begun to feel as if a mischievous fiend lurked in the back of his mind, yanking his strings in spastic fits and starts like some sadistic puppeteer, and making him do things which were decidedly un-Devellynish. And it had to have been that same fiend who, with his curst pitchfork of fate, prodded Devellyn from the gloom of Alasdair's carriage the following Thursday evening, and onto the plush red carpet which ran into Lord Walrafen's ballroom.

There he stood like some lamb to the slaughter whilst his name was shouted out for half the *ton* to hear. All turned to gape. Then, pretending they'd done neither, they averted their eyes and began whispering. Alas, the fiend was not done with Devellyn. It sent him straight down the length of the room to the corner where Sidonie Saint-Godard lingered with all the dowagers and duennas. Some might have thought it a bold move. But it was more reflexive than that; an unthinking bolt toward the familiar and the comforting. Somehow, Sidonie had become that and more.

She, too, was staring at him. He took her firmly by the elbow. "Dance," he gritted.

It wasn't an invitation. Sidonie closed her mouth and thrust her glass of orgeat at someone standing next to her. It was then that Devellyn grasped the true depths of fate's cruelty. Lady Kirton——one of his mother's bosom beaus——turned to take the glass.

"Good Lord!" she said. *"Aleric——?"*

Devellyn stopped dead. He'd thumbed his nose at society for two decades, but even he dared not cut Isabel, Dowager Countess of Kirton and Professional Paragon of Virtue. "Good evening, ma'am." He gave a curt bow. "You are well?"

"Well enough to survive the shock of seeing you." She stared at the hand grasping Sidonie's elbow. "Madame Saint-Godard, do you require an introduction to this rapscallion?"

Sidonie blushed. "I—no, thank you," she said. "We are well acquainted."

"I can't believe you would admit that," he said, pulling her to him.

Sidonie set her hand in his. "Had I a choice?" she retorted. "By the way, Devellyn, if you wish to play Attila the Hun, Julia has one of those pointy helmets in her theater trunk."

Devellyn was trying to think of a pithy retort when he noticed the music. Oh, God. *A waltz?* But just as well. He wasn't especially good at the more intricate dances, and by God, he had something to say.

Sidonie looked bemused, but swept gracefully into the first turn. "I never saw a man look more miserably out of place," she said. "Why on earth are you here?"

"Where on earth have you been?" he demanded.

She drew back, almost missing a step. "I beg your pardon?" she said stiffly. "I did not know I was accountable to you, my lord."

"You said we were friends, Sidonie," he said gruffly. "Friends do not vanish for three days with no word. If you're avoiding me, I'd rather you just say so."

"Devellyn, half the House of Lords is watching me waltz with you," she reminded him. "What, precisely, do you think I'm avoiding?"

Just then, the music trickled to a halt. "Blast!" he said. "Is it over?"

Sidonie's expression softened. "It was over when we

started, Devellyn," she said. "The ball, too, or much of it. That was the supper dance."

Devellyn looked around the room, the need to escape surging stronger. Dancers were trickling from the floor, but he had not released Sidonie's hand. She tugged on him impatiently. "Devellyn, I must go."

His gaze snapped to hers. "No, please," he whispered. "Sidonie, I need to talk to you."

"I cannot." Sidonie looked about in frustration. "I am chaperoning Miss Arbuckle."

"Just five minutes," he pleaded. "Everyone is going in to supper. Surely she will be safe enough?"

Sidonie scanned the crowd. "Probably," she agreed. "I shall just see who she is dining with. Where will you be?"

"Upstairs," he said. "Waiting."

Miss Arbuckle, as it happened, was clinging to the arm of a baby-faced baronet just up from the country. They were surrounded by half a dozen equally innocent-looking young people, with a maiden aunt thrown in for good measure. Sidonie nodded her approval and slipped away. Lord Devellyn was pacing the upstairs corridor by the ladies' retiring room and garnering all manner of horrified looks in the process. He seemed oblivious.

"In here," he said, when the passageway cleared. He pushed open a door and dragged her into a small, dimly lit parlor. A low fire burned in the grate, but the room was unoccupied. Without another word, he turned and kissed her.

His last kiss had been surprisingly tenuous. This one

was not. This time, he claimed her, opening his mouth over hers at once and tasting her deeply. His hands slid up her back, holding her gently but firmly to him. Sidonie could not help herself. Somewhere inside her, a spark burst to flame. She melted against him, her arms going round his waist. Devellyn's breathing roughened, his nostrils flaring wide as he slanted his mouth over hers again, thoroughly tasting her.

His hand fisted in her skirts and began inching them up. She had to crush the urge to encourage him. She felt wanton, almost foolishly desperate. And then she remembered just where she was. *Who she was with.*

"Stop," she whispered, as his open mouth slid down her neck.

"Oh, Sidonie," he rasped. "Must I?"

She closed her eyes and let her head fall back against the wall. She wanted nothing so much as to give herself up to his skilled touch. But she would be starting something she dared not finish.

"Yes, stop," she said. "We cannot."

He pulled back incrementally. In the firelight, his gaze held hers as his hands came up to cradle her face. "I know it's wrong, Sidonie, to want you," he said. "But I do. Enough to make a damned fool of myself. Enough to put your reputation at risk. And for all my blunt ways and bad temper, you are not indifferent to me. Are you? Tell me, Sidonie. I need to know."

Sidonie tore her eyes from his and stared blindly into the depths of the room. "You know I am not," she said. "I wish I were. It might be easier."

"They say nothing worth having is easy," he said. "By God, I'm beginning to believe it."

"Is that why you came tonight, Devellyn?" she asked. "To try to seduce me?"

"I shouldn't have come at all," he said. "We'll be the talk of all Mayfair tomorrow. And your brother will likely try to kill me. But Sidonie, I need you."

"You *need* me?" Her voice was incredulous.

"Need, yes." He shook his head and closed his eyes. "I can't explain it, Sidonie, not even to myself," he went on. "Let me come to you tonight. Let me make love to you. Please."

His touch was sinfully tempting, his words almost persuasive, and Sidonie was beginning to suspect just how he'd earned his nickname. "Why me, Devellyn?" she answered. "There are a thousand other women you could have."

He laughed mockingly. "Sidonie, I've had a thousand other women."

"But I have taken no lover since Pierre," she returned. "I know nothing of how such things are done."

"With discretion," he answered, setting his lips to her temple. "Tonight, when you arrive home, light a candle in your parlor window if all is quiet. I shall come to your door. Will you let me in?"

Sidonie swallowed hard. "Yes," she answered. "But because we need to talk."

"Talk!" he groaned. "Christ Jesus, Sidonie! Why do women always want to talk? I'm no bloody good at it. Let me take you to bed, love, and show you what I feel."

Sidonie licked her lips. "I hate to admit how much you tempt me, Devellyn," she whispered. "There, are you satisfied?"

He rested his forehead on hers, and Sidonie felt his

body sag with relief. "Satisfied?" he echoed. "Nothing has satisfied me since I laid eyes on you, Sidonie. But I am a little reassured."

"Reassured? Why?"

"Two days ago, I thought never to see you again," he whispered. "Every time I called, you were out, and Mrs. Crosby has been avoiding me."

Sidonie cleared her throat. It was time to be honest with Devellyn, so far as she could. "The truth is," she began, "I had a slight accident. Julia knew little about it."

"An accident?" His eyes searched her face in the candlelight. "Of what sort?"

She hesitated. "I was walking alone near the river one evening when—"

"Alone?" he interjected. "At *night?*"

"Yes, that would have been Julia's reaction, too," murmured Sidonie. "And yes, I have learnt my lesson, thank you. Two footpads wished to rob me. I did *not* wish it. And in the midst of a rather heated debate, someone drew a knife."

"A knife!" His eyes ran over her desperately. "Good God, are you all right?"

Sidonie dropped her gaze. "Quite all right," she said. "I got away, and went to George's with nothing but a slight cut. He stitched it up and made me stay put until I was mended."

"Cut—!" Devellyn's voice was hollow. "My God! Where?"

Sidonie touched her right shoulder.

His hands were on her at once, pushing away her shawl. "Show me," he ordered, tugging at her sleeve. "Take this down, Sidonie. I wish to see it. *Now.*"

His motions were oddly desperate. Her shawl slithered to the floor. Already designed to bare her shoulders, the low-cut sleeve slipped down easily to reveal the top of the bandaging around her upper arm.

"Dear God," he whispered, running an unsteady finger along the top of the dressing. "I'll kill the man who did this. How bad? How many stitches? Christ Jesus, Sidonie, your brother's got no business sewing up wounds! What if it should turn septic? What? Take off that bandage. I wish to see it."

"This is not necessary," she said tightly. They had begun to tussle over the sleeve, Sidonie tugging up, and Devellyn tugging down. "It is healing. It is fine."

"Damn it, don't argue!" he growled.

Just then the door beside them flew open. "Oh, dear, this isn't Walrafen's office!" chirped a female voice. "Did we take a wrong turn, Cole?"

Sidonie and Devellyn froze. One hand still clutching the doorknob, a tall, handsome gentleman stood on the threshold, staring straight at them—or more specifically, at the very naked shoulder Devellyn was intent on baring.

"I do beg your pardon!" he said, horrified. Then, over his shoulder, "The room is engaged, Isabel," he murmured. "Let us go elsewhere."

But the lady—Lady Kirton, to be exact—had already swept past him. "Madame Saint-Godard!" she murmured, her face bursting into color. "Oh, dear!"

Sidonie could only imagine the impression she made with her hair and clothing in disarray and her lips swollen from Devellyn's kisses. Clumsily, the marquess tugged up Sidonie's sleeve, then shot her a questioning look, his eyes aggrieved. "Out!" she mouthed.

With a curt nod, the marquess started toward the door. "I daresay I waste my time saying so," he gritted in Lady Kirton's direction. "But this isn't what it appears."

Lady Kirton pursed her lips.

Devellyn bowed stiffly. "I beg your pardon. I must go."

On that, the tall gentleman hastened out, too, his expression still stricken. "Isabel, we shall look over those papers later," he said before slamming the door.

Lady Kirton looked at Sidonie and smiled faintly. "I do apologize, *madame,*" she said moving nearer. "Are you perfectly all right?"

"Quite, thank you," said Sidonie coolly. "But in defense of Lord Devellyn, my lady, I should say that he—"

"Oh, you needn't defend him to me, my dear!" Lady Kirton interjected, but her cheeks were still pink. "I knew that scamp before he was breeched."

"I think it my duty," said Sidonie tightly, folding down her sleeve so that the bandage showed. "You see, I suffered an accident last week. I was set upon by cutpurses."

Lady Kirton blanched. "How dreadful!"

"Indeed," Sidonie agreed. "When he heard of my injury, Devellyn simply wished to—to reassure . . ." Words failed, for how was she to explain what she barely understood? "We are neighbors, you see. Friends. I fear he was seized by concern."

Her eyes warmed. "Yes, well, that bandage would concern anyone, my dear."

Sidonie tried to adjust the sleeve, but the fabric caught on the bandage. "Allow me," murmured her ladyship. She laid aside a sheaf of papers she'd carried in, and moved to help Sidonie. "Have you sutures underneath?"

"A half dozen, I collect," she said. "I was not quite awake when they were put in."

Lady Kirton smoothed the sleeve over Sidonie's shoulder. "There, now," she clucked. "All is in order. Goodness, footpads! What an exciting life you do lead!"

"Exciting?" Sidonie turned to face her. "I hardly think so."

Her ladyship blinked innocently. "But I'm given to understand you sailed the world with your late husband," she answered. "And you have—well, you have your students. And your tutoring. And everything else that you, well, *do*. Now you have been set upon by footpads. Nothing exciting ever happens to me."

Lady Kirton sounded dithery, but she was getting at something, Sidonie feared. "I was unaware, ma'am, that teaching was thought particularly exciting."

Lady Kirton lifted her brows, and reached for Sidonie's fingers. "I also noticed *this* at my musicale," she said, lifting Sidonie's gloved hand in her own. "When you were turning pages for Miss Arbuckle at the piano. Meddlesome, am I not?"

"I beg your pardon?"

Before Sidonie realized it, Lady Kirton had slipped Sidonie's glove down. She ran her forefinger lightly around Sidonie's bare wrist. "This is an unusual scar," she murmured, staring at it. "A rope burn, I collect?"

"An accident aboard ship," she admitted.

"Yes, the deck of a ship can be a dangerous place," said her ladyship. "But I daresay an intrepid girl could soon learn to tie seamen's knots, rig sails, climb masts, and do all manner of skillful things."

Sidonie smiled weakly. "It is sometimes necessary,"

she agreed. "In this case, I was helping furl a sail, but I grew careless."

"Ah, one must never do that!" said her ladyship, patting Sidonie's hand. "All manner of dangerous things can happen when one grows careless. Do you know, my dear, I've seen but one other scar like this in all my life."

Sidonie faltered. "A-Another?"

Lady Kirton's eyes held hers quite steadily. "These sorts of scars are quite rare, are they not?"

"I—why, I should have said they were quite common."

"On men, perhaps," her ladyship agreed, releasing Sidonie's hand. "But I've known only one other woman so marked. So be watchful, my dear, if you wish no one to notice it. Have a care when you—oh, let me think of an example!—yes, when you reach across a wide counter to hand something to someone. Money, for instance? A short glove, you see, will gape just a little when you tilt your hand."

Sidonie felt suddenly sick. She reached out, and seized the back of an armchair to steady herself. George's warning about her visits to the Nazareth Society echoed in her ears. *"Have a care, my dear,"* he had said. *"The good ladies who volunteer there are not fools."*

But Lady Kirton was still rattling on about ships and balls and violins, as if nothing earth-shattering had happened. "I beg your pardon?" Sidonie finally managed.

"A quadrille, my dear," Lady Kirton repeated, smiling blandly up at her. "I hear the violins striking up a quadrille. Supper must be ending. Shall we return to the ballroom and find Miss Arbuckle?"

*　　*　　*

Sidonie wasted no time in lighting her candle upon arriving home. She was anxious. Anxious over Lady Kirton's veiled suggestions and anxious to tell Devellyn what she had learned from her brother. The lies were beginning to suffocate her. A part of her believed Devellyn would laugh and say he didn't care. But Sidonie cared. She had hidden enough from him. She would not hide this.

Carefully, she opened the velvet drapery and set the candlestick on the window ledge. The glass was fogging, and it had begun to rain again. Across the street, Devellyn's house was dark. Still, he must have been nearby, for it was but seconds before she heard a faint knock at the door. She moved the candle to the table and closed the drapery again.

He was drenched when she opened the door. "Good heavens, come inside!" she said, helping him from his greatcoat. She shook the rain from it and carried it into the parlor to dry over a chair.

He moved at once to kiss her, but she pushed him gently away. "Please sit down," she said. "I have something I wish to say."

He scowled. "I am not going to like it, am I?"

But he sat down, and did not interrupt while Sidonie repeated what George had told her.

"Incredible!" he said when she was done. "Claire Bauchet, eh?"

"You knew her?"

His gaze was distant. "I have heard her spoken of," he murmured. "Her relationship with the previous duke was hardly a secret."

Sidonie got up and began to pace the room. "I know,"

she said. "But I have been away for a dozen years, Devellyn. No one remembers me now. And I did not wish to claim kinship to Gravenel—or to my mother, if you wish the truth."

A certain knowledge came over his face. "George *Bauchet*," he said slowly. "That is what you almost called your brother in Covent Garden. Why does he call himself Kemble?"

"George became estranged from our parents when he was young," she whispered, still pacing. "I collect he changed his name to avoid the association. He . . . he also chose a way of life which our parents strongly disapproved of. You know, perhaps, what I mean?"

Devellyn shrugged. "I daresay," he answered. "It matters little to me. But what does this mean to us? Why does your brother loathe me so?"

She looked at him with sorrow in her eyes. "I think my brother is only human, Devellyn," she said softly. "Someday you will bear the title that would have been his had life been fair. Can you understand the resentment he probably harbors and yet cannot recognize, even in himself?"

"Yes, of course, how could he not?" Devellyn held out his hands to her. "I am sorry, Sidonie," he said, taking her fingers in his. "You and George got a bad bargain, but you both made the best of it. I got better than I deserved and buggered it up pretty thoroughly. I wish the title would pass to him—he'd do it more credit than I ever would—but it's a fate we can neither of us change."

"I know." Sidonie tightened her grip on him, and he squeezed her fingers reassuringly.

He held her gaze. "Well, we can't fix our family troubles tonight, can we?" he said, slowly pulling her to him. "Come, Sidonie, give your new cousin a kiss."

She went to him, knowing full well she should not allow the embrace. Knowing that if she ever gave in to him, if she ever went to his bed, he would see the truth and hate her. Why was it so hard to say *no* to this man? She was not sure. She knew only that something in him seemed to draw her, complete her. They were wandering souls, she and Devellyn, both of them touched with a darkness of the heart. Outwardly, they were different. But inwardly, she feared, too similar. She felt now—had felt from the very first—a bone-deep hunger for him. It was something which transcended sensuality, though they were both, she thought, very sensual creatures.

He pulled her another inch, and they came together. His mouth came down on hers, gentle but insistent. She opened beneath him, and let him have his way. *Just a kiss,* she told herself. But it was a lie. She did not want to stop at a kiss.

One of his heavy hands slid down her back, and cupped her buttocks, drawing her fully against him. He felt as he had felt that night at the Anchor, his erection already hard and demanding beneath the fabric of his formal trousers. His mouth slid down her neck. "God, I still want you, Sidonie," he said. "I want to f—no, blister it, that's not right!" He swallowed hard. "Sidonie, I want to make—"

"I know what you want," she whispered, her lips pressed to his ear.

"Do you?" he rasped. "That's good, since I've so little experience in asking for it prettily."

"But prettiness is rather like charm, is it not?" she

murmured, looking up at him through her lashes. "Superficial. Fleeting. Sometimes . . . a little dull."

He kissed her again. "Let me," he whispered, one hand going to her breast. "Let me have you. Let me get just a taste of you, Sidonie. God, it's been an age since I wanted anything so desperately."

But it had not been an age, thought Sidonie. It had been but a few days. He had wanted Ruby Black very desperately indeed. But she could not bear to think of that now. Devellyn was massaging her breast in his warm, wide palm, and all rational thought was leaving her.

"Devellyn," she whispered. "I can't do this."

"You can," he insisted, tugging down the fabric to bare her right breast. Her nipple hardened at once to his touch, and Devellyn stroked it with his thumb as if it were a rare jewel. "Sidonie," he whispered, his voice soft but commanding. "I've tried to resist, but I cannot. I have to have you."

"Here?"

"Here is perfect," he said. With that, he pushed her left sleeve down her shoulder, fully exposing her breast. Her breath came fast and sharp. Urgent. She had to stop. She *had* to. But Devellyn's mouth was on her now, sucking the hard tip of her breast into the swirling heat of his mouth. She looked down at his full, sensual mouth, watching as his tongue teased her so wickedly, and her mind swam with desire. She wanted him. God, she was going to have him, too, and damn the result.

"The candle," she choked. "Put it out."

"Put it out?" His voice was soft with disappointment.

She let her hands skim down his back. "Yes, please," she whispered. "Do you mind terribly?"

"Not at all." He turned without releasing her, and blew it out. Darkness washed the room, which was cool and still. He buried his face against her neck. "You're freezing," he whispered, the words warm on her skin. "I'll build up the fire."

"No," she said hastily. "You will warm me."

He ran his hands down her sides in a long, smooth caress. Then he returned his mouth to hers. One hand kept weighing and caressing her breast while the other went to the buttons at the back of her dress, expertly slipping them free as if he'd done it a thousand times. He probably had. She should have said no. But instead, she pressed herself urgently against him and lost herself in his next kiss. She felt her dress slither down her hips and pool around her ankles.

It was not just a yearning of the body she felt for him now. It was a yearning of the heart and soul. She had tumbled off the edge of reason. She had fallen hopelessly in love, and no one would have been more surprised than she. Devellyn deepened the kiss, and her last sliver of doubt melted away. *At least this once,* she told herself. At least this once, she would give herself to him, and hope the memory of it would sustain her.

Outside, the rain was growing stronger, the wind whipping it into sheets which lashed at the windows and brickwork. In the slender gap between the draperies, she could see it running down the window, the trickles catching the feeble gaslight. But inside the darkened parlor, a sense of quiet intimacy was building, as if they were two lovers alone in a secret world. Sidonie let her hands roam at will. It was the ultimate luxury. Devellyn was all masculine strength and physical beauty, his limbs long and thick, his muscles taut with power. Though she had seen him naked only fleetingly, the memory of it was burnt into her brain.

In the darkness, they undressed one another, neither asking, neither speaking. Words seemed so unnecessary, so disturbing to the natural rhythm. His coat fell away, her chemise followed. Waistcoat, trousers, stockings, and drawers sailed to the floor, until they stood naked together in the darkness. He let his hands run over her, as if blindly memorizing her curves and turns. He shaped her face and shoulders, her hips and her waist, then weighed her breasts in his hands again. Sidonie's nipples felt afire as his palms brushed up. Something warm and delicious went twisting through her, all the way to her belly, until her knees sagged with longing.

She reached out to steady herself, and in response, Devellyn swept her up in his arms, a graceful, shockingly romantic gesture. A thick wool carpet lay in front of the hearth, and he knelt there. "Do you wish my coat for cover?" he asked as he gently laid her down.

Sidonie's hands reached eagerly for him. "Just you."

He spread his body over hers, shielding her from the night's chill and taking his weight on his elbows. He covered her completely, his long, muscular legs pressing hers down into the softness of the wool. For long moments, he just kissed her, his lips opening over hers, his tongue plumbing the depths of her mouth, then curving sinuously around hers. His patience and tenderness shocked her. As always, he smelled of lime and of something woodsy—chestnut, she thought—and of warm, aroused male. She breathed him in, and felt a bone-deep ache. His mouth was at her breast now, sucking and teasing as his other hand caressed her nipple. Desire surged, making her hips rise against him.

"Are you eager, love?" he murmured. "What do you want?"

Sidonie's head went back against the carpet as she writhed involuntarily beneath him. *"You,* Devellyn." She whispered the truth into the darkness. "Always you."

"Aleric," he said softly.

"Aleric."

His mouth returned to hers, and she took him hungrily, drawing his tongue into her mouth, sliding hers along it. She kissed him deep, and her need seemed to drive him. With a deep groan of pleasure, he stroked his hand down her belly, making her skin shiver as he touched it. Then he slid his hands between her thighs, touching her intimately.

Sidonie writhed again. "Mmm," she said. "I want you *now."*

He chuckled softly in the darkness and moved until she sensed he was kneeling between her legs. Firmly, he set his hands on her inner thighs, and pushed them wide, but did not mount her as she yearned for him to do. "Come back," she pleaded, the words soft and thready. "On top of me. Please, Aleric. Please."

Instead, he lifted her ankles over his broad shoulders, and slid his hands beneath her hips. It was the most decadent position imaginable, her hips tilted up by his powerful hands and arms. Still on his knees, he bent his head, and touched her lightly with his tongue, right at her most sensitive place.

Sidonie made an inarticulate sound, all she was capable of.

"Do you like that, love?" he rasped. Then he slid his tongue deep into her folds, stroking her deep, all the way through. Raw lust shuddered through her like nothing she'd ever known.

She wanted to wait, to draw it out, and savor the decadence. But when he stroked again and again, touching his tongue to her sweet, secret center, she began to shake. She dug her fingers into the carpet, trying to hold off the waves threatening to pound her. Her effort was useless. His every stroke was a sweet, hot flame which sent the warm, delicious swirling sensation into the pit of her belly again, and lower still, until she was writhing and sobbing and coming undone.

She returned to earth, and reached out for him, heard her voice softly pleading for him. She yearned for his weight and his warmth.

"Eager girl," he said, easing her back onto the carpet. He moved on top, and spread her legs wide with his knee. For a time, his fingers worked her, sliding deep inside, deep into the wetness she could feel and hear. "So pretty," he whispered. "So needy, Sidonie. You flatter me."

"I want you," she said. "Please, Aleric, now?"

And she did want him, with surprising desperation. She wanted the weight of his body to bear her down into the softness of the carpet, wanted his jutting hardness to fill her. She reached out, and took him into her hands. He groaned, a deep, raw sound and leaned back to expose himself fully to her touch. His obvious pleasure emboldened her. Again and again, she stroked the thick length of his erection, marveling in the silky, warm weight of him, in the sense of barely suppressed power inside him.

He groaned again and bent forward to brace himself on one arm, his head bowed low over hers. Then with deliberate, excruciatingly slow movements, he sheathed himself inside her. Eager, Sidonie lifted herself to take him deeper, but he forced her hips back to the carpet with his powerful arms. "Oh, slow, love!" he warned. "Go slow. I don't think you realize what you do to me."

Deliberately, she tightened her flesh around his heated length, and Devellyn made a sound of pure pain. "Oh, minx!" he rasped. "Be still, or I'll be of no more use to you tonight."

She settled greedily onto the carpet. Inch by heated inch he buried himself inside her, then began to stroke hard and deep in earnest. Somewhere in the distance, thunder rolled through the sky, and the lashing rain heightened. Two lovers, hidden from the world. Sheltered by the night. On and on he stroked her, pulling at her flesh, then sheathing himself deeply and sweetly, caressing her body with every stroke.

Devellyn's rhythm was perfect. Soon, the rough sound of his breath sawing in and out of his chest filled the darkness. "Sidonie! Oh, love!"

Beneath him, she felt her body quicken and begin to shake. The thunder came again, louder and closer. Devellyn buried himself deep on a guttural cry, and then, quite unexpectedly, Sidonie was torn from every earthly thing. Light and joy surrounded her. And then she was dragged under by the rolling waves of pleasure.

Eons later, Sidonie came half-awake to the feeling of Devellyn sliding a sofa pillow beneath her head. Then he curled himself around her, and drew her back into the curve of his body. She relaxed against the firm wall of his chest, blissfully oblivious to the storm, and drifted away again.

Though he could barely make out the shape of her face, Devellyn watched Sidonie drowse for what might have been hours. He could not sleep. The stormy weather was nothing to the turbulence in his mind and in his heart. *His heart.* Until now, he'd not been sure he had one. Sweet heaven, he was in deep. That gut-wrenching need he had felt for her was real, he realized. And it was barely—just *barely*—sated. His heart and mind wanted her again. But his body needed rest.

Lightning splintered the sky and lit the room, casting a sliver of light over Sidonie's face. But he needed no light to remember her every feature. Her delicate nose. Her fine, oval eyes which were set at just a bit of an angle. The inky, finely arched brows which accented them. How odd that she should be half-English—half-*Hilliard*—when she looked so very French. How had he not known? Not guessed? There was so much he yearned to know about her. So much he wished to ask. She was still a mystery to him, and he found it tantalizing. He was surprised it should be so. He had known many women in the carnal sense, but his curiosity had never gone much further.

Distant thunder rolled again, and Devellyn wondered at the time. Servants might be stirring soon. He should wake her, perhaps, and take his leave? She would take him to her bed again, and soon, he hoped. He had pleased her well. And never had he taken such pleasure in doing so. That, too, was disconcerting. He slid reluctantly away from the warmth of her body. By the occasional flicker of light, he could see she lay on her right side in perfect repose, her face half-turned into the pillow he'd slipped beneath her head. He found it hard to leave her.

Perhaps he need not go just yet? He dug through the pile of clothing, extracted his pocket watch, and went to the window, pulling back one of the drapes. But the wind had blown out half the streetlamps, and in the feeble yellow light, he could not make out the numbers. Frustrated, he turned from the window, but in that instant, the room exploded with light, flashing once, twice, three times, before the crash of thunder swept it from the sky. Devellyn froze, his arm still holding the drapery, his eyes still fixed on her beautiful body. On her warm ivory skin. On her full, perfect breasts . . .

Something like panic seized him. Devellyn jerked the drape fully open and strode across the room. He dropped to his knees, staring at the small spot the lightning had illuminated. For a moment, he could not breathe. He felt his fingers clawing into the carpet she lay upon, and yet his hands were numb.

He had *seen* it. He dragged his arm across his brow, and felt the cold sheen of sweat on his face. Good God Almighty. That could not be! Fate could not be so cold and cruel. No, not even to him. In the yellow gloom, he could almost pretend it was a bruise. But it wasn't. *That* was not something a man imagined after having the most sensual, most earth-shattering experience of his life. Good God, he had to think!

But an inhuman sound was already clawing its way up through his chest; something heavy and choking, like a sob too long suppressed. He wanted to howl with beastly pain. He wanted to make her cower, naked, while he demanded his answers. He felt his throat constrict, and felt the hot, urgent press of tears behind his eyes.

This was not just trickery. This was betrayal. He was not at all sure he could survive another. As if beyond his control, his hand encircled her slender throat. In the gloom, she looked so tender, so innocent, but in that moment, he wished mightily to strangle her.

Sidonie must have felt his fingers tightening, for she woke with a start and went stiff. "Devellyn—?"

He grabbed her by both shoulders, and jerked her half up. "Get up, damn you!" he growled. "Who are you? Tell me!"

Sidonie tried to push him away. "Stop," she whispered. "You're hurting me."

He gave her a good shake. "You deceitful bitch!" he said. "How could you do this?"

He sensed her come fully awake, sensed the moment she suspected her ruse was over. "Devellyn, stop!" she said, scrabbling onto her knees. "You're having a nightmare."

"You're damned right, I am." She moved to flee, but he grabbed her and dragged her down again. "I saw it, Sidonie. I *know* who you are."

"S-Saw . . . what?"

He shook her again. "By God, don't pretend! The oh-so-proper Madame Saint-Godard! You've fooled them all, haven't you?"

He sensed her body sag with resignation. "It is not what you think," she whispered, trying to jerk from his grasp. "It's *not.*"

He tightened his grip ruthlessly. "And where have I

heard that before?" he retorted, gripping her arm. "What are you up to, Sidonie? What's your game?"

Sidonie was sobbing softly now. "Leave me alone," she whispered, collapsing. "Get out, Devellyn. I did not ask you to come here. And I am not *up to* anything, except making a fool of myself over you."

He shoved her away, and she fell back onto the rug. In the gloom, he saw her reach for her chemise, as if she wished to cover her nakedness. He looked at her in disgust. "The Black Angel!" he said, getting to his feet. "You really thought to make a fool of me, didn't you? Well, it won't happen twice, you scheming little witch."

He was jerking on his clothes now. Sidonie still cowered on the rug. "I didn't think anything," she whispered. "I didn't plan this!"

Devellyn gave a bitter laugh. "People like you are always planning, Sidonie," he answered. "Always on the dodge, always looking for a scam. You think you can just part your thighs for me, drag me in deep, then dupe me again? What were you after this time? More money? Or just your own amusement?"

Sidonie pressed the back of her hand to her mouth, stifling a sob. "I gave back your money, Aleric," she whimpered. "I gave you everything. Damn you, I gave you my heart."

Devellyn felt his own tears welling more urgently against the backs of his eyes. To quell them, he stabbed in his shirttails violently, and turned to find his waistcoat. "Filthy lies and crocodile tears," he gritted. "Give up the theatrics, Sidonie. You betrayed me."

"What do you mean? Where are you going?"

"Home," he said. "Home to get drunk. And I mean

to remain drunk for a good long while, so stay the hell away from me, or I won't be responsible for what I do, do you hear me?"

Both hands had gone to her mouth, and she was crying softly. "Are you . . . are you going to the police?"

Devellyn bent down, snatched up his coat, and sneered in her face. "Over *you?*" he asked incredulously. "Why would I bother? You are dead to me, Sidonie. As dead as if I'd driven a stake through your faithless little heart."

He left her and slammed the door behind. He could hear the sobs that wracked her body now, echoing through the house. He did not give a damn if every servant in the place heard. He strode through the darkened passageway and let himself out into Bedford Place, slamming that door so hard the windows rattled. The rain was still pouring. Christ Jesus! He felt suddenly sick, reeling from loss and disbelief.

He turned on the doorstep, the rain spattering off him, and stared at the window which had glowed with her candle just a few hours earlier. He felt frozen in time, uncertain what to do. Rage still coursed through him. He wanted to break something, burn something. Oh, God help him! He thought of how he'd waited in the rain, praying she would light that candle, and of the hope which had surged in his heart when the little flame sputtered to life. What a cruel emotion that was. Hope was not for him. He'd long known that. And now, Sidonie's betrayal was as bitter as blood in his mouth. He had seen it. The Black Angel.

Worse, he had *known* it. Devellyn forced himself to remember. Had he not felt—yes, the very first!—that she reminded him of Ruby Black? Had he not wondered how he could burn for two women at the same time—two such seemingly dissimilar women—and feel himself going mad with thwarted lust for both? They had looked nothing alike, it was true. Yet in his heart, he had *known*. But what the heart had known, his logic had hurled aside as impossible.

Last night, he had behaved scandalously, singling Sidonie out for unwanted attention, then allowing them both to be caught out at something far worse. He had been heartsick afterward. Yet again, he believed, he had compromised a lady; this time, one he cared for deeply. This time, his life and his heart, and yes, even his hope, weak and nascent though it had been. But she was no lady. And he had no future. He should have remembered that. But somehow, he'd lost himself in Sidonie's smoldering eyes and let himself be doubly deceived.

He reached out and set his palm against the window where the little flame had burned. Cold. Cold as death. The tears came again, and this time, he simply forced himself away from her door and let them fall. He stood in the middle of Bedford Place, and let the deluge rain down, until water soaked his hair, and his coat, and even his clothing beneath. He thought of Sidonie, and feared that this time, the aching sense of loss might kill him.

Alasdair turned up in Bedford Place shortly after midday. The previous evening, he and Devellyn had parted ways upon entering Walrafen's town house, and that had been the last they'd seen of one another. Alasdair was shown into Devellyn's study by Honeywell, who mercifully carried in a tray of coffee. Alasdair must have sensed something was wrong, but he paced the room quietly until Honeywell had gone out again.

He watched from the windows as Devellyn poured coffee with an unsteady hand. "Are you all right, old chap?" he asked. "You look to be coming off a three-day drunk."

Devellyn opened his mouth, but no words came out. "I wish I were," he finally admitted. "But I confess, I've been unable to stomach so much as a sip of sherry."

His friend studied his face for a moment. "Dev, are you ill?"

Devellyn looked at him despondently. "Alasdair, something dreadful has happened," he whispered. "Unless I'm going mad. I begin to wonder if I am."

Alasdair set a heavy hand on his shoulder. "You look your usual sane self to me, old boy," he said. "Except you're pale as death. Lord, you lost less color when Porterfield pinked you in the shoulder for sleeping with his wife."

Devellyn motioned toward a chair. "Sit, for God's sake."

Alasdair sat. "Done. Now talk."

"Your silence, Alasdair," Devellyn rasped. "On your honor—no, on your *life*—I must have your silence."

Alasdair leaned forward intently. "If you ask it, you have it, Dev," he said. "You know that."

Devellyn stared into the depths of the room for a long, silent moment. "I have found my nemesis, Alasdair," he said. "I have found my Ruby Black."

"Have you?" said Alasdair, his brow furrowing. "That's good news, isn't it? But I did not think you were looking."

"Nonetheless, I have found her, and quite by accident." Devellyn's voice was hollow. "Ruby Black, you see, is . . . she is . . . Jesus, Alasdair. She is *Sidonie.*"

Alasdair was quiet for a moment. "You mean to say Madame Saint-Godard and . . . and that tart from the Anchor . . . ?"

"Yes."

"Balderdash, Dev! How can you even think it?"

"I *know* it," he said hollowly. "You must trust that I have seen proof."

Alasdair lifted one brow. "Even sotted, Dev, you don't have much of an imagination," he agreed. "And at the moment, you do look frightfully sober."

"Frightfully, yes," he echoed. "I almost fear dulling my senses, afraid of what next I might learn."

"I think you've been misled, Dev," said Alasdair. "Madame Saint-Godard is so refined. Are you utterly certain?"

Was he certain? Damn it, *was* he?

Yes. The light had been fleeting, but he had seen it. And because of it, he had left her in a blind rage. Good God, he'd made a fool of himself at Walrafen's ball last night. Then he had left the ball with every intention of doing something even more foolish. He'd even gone round to the house in Grosvenor Square, desperate to find his mother, who had not, thank God, been at home. And he'd been stone sober through all of it. Including what had happened next.

He let his head fall forward into his hands. "Christ, Alasdair, I don't know!" he said. "No, that's not right. I am *certain*. But she neither denies nor admits it. I think she has driven me mad."

Alasdair was silent for a moment. "Well, if the two women were one and the same," he said grudgingly, "it would help explain a few things. Like why some swear the Black Angel is French or Italian. And why Sidonie is so often from home."

"But how can it be?" asked Devellyn, now wishing he could counter his own argument. "Polk watches her door constantly. He's never seen her go out dressed as a prostitute or chambermaid or any of those guises the Angel has used."

"Oh, she's far too clever for that," said his friend. "She's likely slipping out through the mews, or a back window. We already know the Black Angel can climb, and Sidonie spent a lot of time at sea, where one learns all manner of useful things. As to the tattoo, well, that's not something easily had in London. But on some of the tropical islands . . ." Alasdair lifted his shoulders and let his words fall away, as if to give Devellyn time to absorb them.

"Good God, I should have throttled her when I had the chance!" he gritted, pounding one fist on the arm of his chair. "I might yet do it, too!"

"Crivvens, Dev!" Alasdair's hand came out to stay the fist. "Why such rage? Even if we are right, what bone have you to pick with the Black Angel?"

Devellyn looked at him in stark amazement. "Good God, man! She robbed and humiliated me!"

Alasdair set his head to one side and studied him. "Yes, and if I remember correctly, she made full restitution," he said quietly. "As to the humiliation, Dev, you and I did a bloody good job of that. You kicked up that ugly ruckus at the Anchor, then I spread the tale all over town. But so far as you or I know, not one word of it ever passed the Angel's lips."

Devellyn had not thought of it in quite that light. The Black Angel had returned all his possessions, it was true. And she'd gone to a vast deal of trouble to do it. But that made him recollect how he'd treated her. Good God! He had *struck* her. He had rutted with her as if she were a common whore. A man had no right to treat anyone like that. He felt a new wave of nausea. How could she even look him in the face now? How could she not hate him?

Well, perhaps she did. Perhaps this was all about vengeance.

No, no, that wasn't right. He shook his head as if to clear it. That wasn't how Sidonie had behaved at all. She had behaved as if she desired him beyond reason. She said she had given him her heart. Lord, could this nightmare get any worse?

At that moment, Henry Polk came into the room. "Your pardon, my lord," he said, hesitating. "I did not realize you were engaged."

"Never mind," said Devellyn. "What is it?"

The footman shot an uneasy glance at Alasdair.

"What? What?" said the marquess. "Never mind him."

Polk came reluctantly into the room, and handed Devellyn a note which had been badly scorched on one corner. "Meg saw *madame* fling this into the fireplace this morning," he said. "And another odd thing, my lord. She says that *madame* has been crying all day."

Alasdair shot Devellyn a suspicious glance.

"Meg says Mrs. Crosby is in a terrible state, too," Polk went on. "Something happened late last night, a commotion of some sort in the front parlor. Meg didn't know what."

Devellyn took the note. "How did Meg get the note if Madame Saint-Godard threw it into the fire?"

"*Madame* was distraught, and careless," said Polk. "It didn't catch, so when Meg went in to clear breakfast, she got it out again. She thought it might have something to do with all the upset."

The note had been secured with black wax bearing the seal of a griffin couchant, now slightly melted. But there was no address, not even so much as a name. Devellyn flicked it open and skimmed the masculine script, which would have been elegant, had the writer not been in a rush.

> *Tonight at the Cross Keys.*
> *Taproom. Urgent. Nine o'clock.*
> *Bonne chance, J-C*

"Who delivered this?" barked Devellyn.

Polk shook his head. "Meg says she's no notion how *madame* got hold of it, nor who it's from. Worded a bit queer, though."

"And damned sparsely," muttered Devellyn. "*Bonne chance.* French, isn't it?"

"Aye, it means 'good luck,'" said Alasdair.

Polk shifted his weight uneasily. "I daresay they'll sack Meg now, sir, won't they, sir? If they find out she gave it to me?"

"Quite likely," the marquess murmured, flipping the note over again.

Alasdair held out his hand. "Let me have a look, Dev."

But Polk was still hovering. "My lord?" said the footman. "If they dismiss her without a character, why, I'll have to do the honorable thing, won't I? I shall have to marry her."

"My felicitations," grunted Devellyn, passing the note to Alasdair.

Alasdair skimmed the note. "Christ, Dev, what are you going to do?"

Devellyn shook his head. "Why would she do such dangerous things, Alasdair? Why? Damn it, I need to know."

"Sir?" said Polk, looking pointedly at his master. "What do you think?"

"What?" Devellyn finally looked up at him. "What is it, Polk?"

The footman exhaled wearily. "If Meg gets sacked by *madame*," he said, "and I have to marry her, I'll be needing larger quarters, won't I, sir? And a little privacy?"

Devellyn crooked one brow. "What, no extra salary?"

Polk seemed to consider it. "That's generous of you, sir," he said. "But I'm not one to take advantage. Perhaps you could just give Meg a place until the children come?"

Devellyn sighed, and tucked the note into his coat pocket. "Why is it, Polk, that I've a feeling I'll be caring for you, Meg, and your imaginary offspring until *Kingdom* Come?" he asked. "Go on, then. Marry the chit. Someone around here might as well be happy."

Just then, someone dropped the knocker on the front door, the sound echoing through the house.

"I'll have to get that, sir," said Polk, dashing from the room.

Alasdair looked at him uneasily. "Expecting anyone, Dev?"

Devellyn consulted his watch. "Oh, I fear so, Alasdair," he muttered grimly. "That will almost certainly be my mother."

Alasdair was out of his chair in a flash. "I'd best be off out the back, old boy," he said. "And I think you ought to go down to the Cross Keys tonight, and settle this business with Sidonie once and for all."

"Why the hell should I?"

From the door, Alasdair looked at him a little sorrowfully. "Anyone can see, Dev, that you are in love with the woman," he said. "You've quit whoring, gambling, and drinking. It would be a shame if Sidonie managed to get herself killed after such an extraordinary show of contrition."

Get herself killed? A chill settled over him as he withdrew the note again. Alasdair had a point. He had assumed Sidonie would put an end to her tricks now that he'd learned who she was. But this note suggested she meant to play the Black Angel again. Its words smacked of cloak-and-dagger ambiguity. And it had been delivered by some anonymous street urchin, or slipped under a doormat, on that Devellyn would have bet his last shilling. It was her signal to do something. But what?

Then it struck him. The note did not say "meet *me* at the Cross Keys." It was entirely possible the Angel was to meet *someone else*. Someone, perhaps, that the writer had chosen? Or targeted? Indeed, the more he thought on it, the more Devellyn believed the author was some sort of coconspirator. Many prostitutes had bawds and fancy-men. The comparison left a bad taste in Devellyn's mouth, but it was quite likely the Black Angel, too, had someone's help.

Devellyn had no time to consider it further. Suddenly, his mother was sweeping into the room, looking utterly regal in a dress of ice-blue silk, and a feathery confection of a hat which perfectly matched her eyes. She looked radiant, too. And a little . . . *triumphant*. Oh, that was not good.

"Aleric, dear boy!" she said, taking both his hands into hers when he approached. "How pale you look today."

"I'm well enough, Mamma," he answered, turning his cheeks for her kisses. "You look to be in a fine fettle."

Honeywell, who had spent twenty years in the duchess's service, dutifully followed her with a fresh tea tray. He swept away the old coffee, leaving Her Grace to strip off her gloves and pour. "Well!" she began, passing Devellyn a cup. "I'm told you called in Grosvenor Square last night."

Devellyn wished very sincerely he had not. Too late. "Yes, ma'am. But it was rather a spur-of-the-moment thing."

"And I'm told, too, that you were seen last night at Walrafen's little charity gala," she gently prodded. "Quite a stir that has raised, my dear. However did you get invited?"

Devellyn shrugged. "Alasdair arranged it," he muttered. "Apparently, Walrafen will invite anyone who might possibly vote Tory anytime this century or the next."

The duchess blinked. "Goodness! I did not know you had political leanings."

"Neither did I," he said dryly. "But you know Alasdair."

"I certainly do." His mother smiled tightly, as if that circumstance pained her. "In any case, I was at Greataunt Admeta's playing piquet with Horatio last night when Cousin George burst in and said—"

"Wait!" Devellyn threw up a staying hand. "You were playing *piquet*? With a *terrier*?"

His mother colored. "Oh, it's hard to explain," she said, waving dismissively. "Anyway, as I was saying, Cousin George swore he'd seen you at Walrafen's, which was shocking enough. Then, when our footman said you'd called in Grosvenor Square, I was quite beyond words."

"Yes, well, you've got over that, haven't you?" said Devellyn.

His mother refused to be baited. "Indeed, my love, had I known I might expect you, I'd not have waited so many years to open the house back up."

Absently, Devellyn began to stir sugar into his tea. "As I said, it was a spur-of-the-moment thing."

He looked up to see his mother watching his hand in horror. "My God, Aleric! You do not take sugar. Certainly not three heaping spoons of it."

"Ma'am?" He looked down, not having realized until that moment what he'd done. "Oh, I must have picked up the habit somewhere."

"Well, shed it at once!" she advised. "It is not at all the thing for one's waistline."

Devellyn sipped at the tea. "I'll keep that in mind, Mamma."

His mother looked at him oddly. "Goodness, you are docile today! Are you ill? Have you a fever?"

He put the cup down and sat silently for a moment. He had gone to his mother last night because he'd been worried about Sidonie's reputation and did not know where else to turn for help. Now he was tempted to just let Sidonie hang, socially speaking. But in her case, that was just one step from being truly hanged.

The truth was, Sidonie was only safe from harm whilst her reputation was above reproach. He would not have her caught on his account, no matter what she'd done to him.

"No, I haven't a fever," he said, venturing onto thin ice. "Actually, Mamma, I have a problem. Or rather, I may have created a problem for someone else."

His mother's pale brows flew aloft at that. "Dear me," she murmured. "What has happened?"

Devellyn did not mince words. "Oh, the usual thing," he said. "I lured an innocent young woman into a dark room and attempted to compromise her virtue. At least, that is how it appeared to the people who walked in on us in Lord Walrafen's parlor."

His mother paled. "Oh, God," she said. "How bad?"

The marquess shrugged. "I had been kissing her pretty thoroughly, and she looked it," he admitted. "Worse, I had one of her sleeves down, almost to the elbow."

His mother closed her eyes. "Oh, Aleric!"

Her soft words piqued his temper. "Oh, for God's sake, I was examining a cut on the lady's arm!" he said defensively. "She had been recently set upon by cut-purses."

The eyes flew open. "How horrid!"

"Well, she was wayward enough and foolish enough

to go out after dark alone," he said snappishly. "And I'm not at all sure she means to stop."

"Heavens!" said his mother dryly. "Wayward *and* foolish? She'll be rather a handful."

"Spare me the sarcasm, Mamma," he grumbled. "I'm trying to explain how I came to be wrestling with the lady's clothing."

Her grace suppressed a smile. "By all means, do continue."

Devellyn scowled. "I wished to see the wound," he reiterated. "I needed to see how bad it was. She did not wish me to. We were struggling with the sleeve when we were discovered. And it looked, I am sure, like an entirely different sort of struggle."

"And now you are asking my advice?"

"Yes, because I know how scandal can taint an innocent woman," he said, quite forgetting that Sidonie might be far from innocent. "I'll not have another female suffer for my crude behavior."

Her face fell. "Ah, you are thinking of Jane," she murmured. "But Jane is now Lady Helmshot, Aleric, as she has been for nearly a dozen years. Indeed, I cannot see as she has suffered overmuch."

"She was forced to marry a man twice her age."

"Forced?" said his mother archly. "The only thing you forced was Lord Helmshot's hand."

"I don't know what you mean."

"Well, you proposed to Jane, did you not?"

"The following day, as Father ordered," he snapped. "And she refused me in her next breath."

"Yes, but at the time, your brother still lived," murmured his mother. "And we all, Jane included, had every hope he would awaken and resume a normal life."

"Yes, well, he didn't, did he? And that, too, is my fault."

The duchess set down her teacup and pressed her fingertips into her temples. "Aleric, I have not the heart to fight that battle just now," she said wearily. "Moreover, I am making an altogether different point."

"Then for God's sake, Mother, just make it."

"I shall give you a question instead," she returned. "Why do you think Jane went into that dark library with you? *You* had no expectation of a title."

"She went to make Greg jealous," he admitted.

"Yes, and it worked, too," said his mother. "Gregory came storming in, ready to guard his little conquest from his brother's ravening hands. How very romantic!"

"Well, I guess I'll know what to say next time I'm accused of being cynical, Mamma," said Devellyn. "I'll say I got it honest."

His mother laughed. "A cynic, am I?" she answered. "Well, I have every idea that had the two of you not quarreled, and had Greg not fallen—"

Devellyn cut her off. "Good God, Mother, he did not fall," he interjected. "I hit him, and damned deliberately, too."

But his mother spoke over him, saying, "As I said, had Greg not fallen, I have every idea Jane would be Lady Devellyn now," she went on calmly. "But instead, Lord Helmshot offered for her two days later, and Jane—how do they say it at White's?—yes, she hedged her bet and set a long engagement."

Devellyn smiled bitterly. "You never did like Jane, did you?"

His mother shrugged her narrow shoulders. "She knew what Greg would think when she went into that room alone with you," she said. "She was an opportunist. And eventually, Greg would have seen it, but he might well have married her by then."

"I am not sure how we came to be discussing Jane and Greg, Mother," said Devellyn.

"Yes, forgive me, you wished my advice, did you not?"

Devellyn smiled sarcastically. "And I'm paying dearly for it, aren't I?"

His mother began to rearrange the pleats of her blue dress. "It would help me vastly to know the lady's name, Aleric."

"Oh, no you don't," he answered. "The lady's name makes no difference." *Lord, what gammon!* It would make a vast deal of difference if it got out.

His mother sniffed. "Well, is she respectable? Virtuous?"

"Blister it, if she were some lightskirt, would I be here now, having myself dragged through your briar patch?"

"Point taken, Aleric," she said. "So the lady is virtuous. Is she virginal?"

"A widow," he said stiffly. "But young, and not well connected."

"Ah, I see," said his mother, then she paused for a long moment. "Of course, if you sincerely wish to protect her good name, the best alternative would be marriage."

Devellyn looked at his mother as if he'd not thought of it. "Marriage?" he said. "Marriage to *me*? You're as mad as Great-aunt Admeta if you think my name would offer her reputation one shred of protection. And frankly, Mamma, I don't want the woman."

His mother seemed to concede the point. "Very well," she murmured. "No wedding bells, then. How many people witnessed this compromising situation?"

"Just two," grumbled Devellyn. "It was your crony Isabel, and that friend of hers. The tall, blond Adonis of a fellow who married Lady Kildermore."

"Ah, the Reverend Mr. Amherst!"

"Damn! A parson? Worse and worse!"

"Do mind your foul mouth, Aleric," said his mother perfunctorily. "And you've little to worry about with Amherst. One could not pry gossip out of that man with a crowbar."

Devellyn relaxed a little.

His mother leaned across the table and set a hand on his arm. "Perhaps I should just pop round to Berkeley Square and drop a card on Isabel," said his mother. "We are old friends, you know."

She moved as if to rise, but on impulse, he seized her hand. "Mamma, wait," he rasped. "Perhaps you oughtn't go yet."

Her color faded, and she settled back down with a worried expression. "What is it, my dear?"

He chewed at his lip for a moment, a habit he thought he'd conquered in boyhood. "I lied," he finally said. "The lady's name might matter."

She patted his hand. "I was just going to ask Isabel anyway."

"Isabel does not know all," he said. "You see, the lady was wed young, to a French sea captain. After his death, she came over from France, and took a house opposite mine in Bedford Place. I thought until recently she was French."

His mother raised one brow. "And she is not?"

Devellyn shook his head. "Her name is Madame Saint-Godard," he said. "But before her marriage she was Sidonie Bauchet. Do you know her?"

His mother frowned and shook her head.

"She has a brother, who calls himself Kemble," Devellyn went on. "He is a businessman in the Strand, and very wealthy. And I've discovered he has influential friends, Walrafen amongst them. But the family otherwise moves on the fringes of society. They are not well placed, and she values her good name."

His mother clucked sympathetically. "Isabel will not talk, my love."

"Mamma, are you sure?" he asked stridently. "I feel doubly responsible here. The lady, you see, is a distant relation to us. She is the daughter of the previous duke."

His mother looked confused. "No, dear, she died in India."

Devellyn reached across to squeeze her hand. "His *illegitimate* daughter," he said. "She is the child of Claire Bauchet. Gravenel's courtesan, Mamma."

"Oh, dear!" His mother's gaze softened. "Was there a daughter? The little boy, now, that I recall all too well. Your father was outraged, of course, but he had no recourse."

"He knew Claire Bauchet?"

His mother shook her head. "Aunt Admeta did, I collect," she said. "Poor, poor girl. He ruined her, you know."

"Ruined her——?"

His mother's eyes came back into focus. "The previous duke," she said softly. "Mademoiselle Bauchet was his daughter's governess at Stoneleigh. She was young, and very beautiful. When she would not return his flirtations, he forced himself on her. Our senior servants still whisper about it."

"Good God! Sidonie never mentioned that."

"Then don't bring it up," cautioned his mother. "The duke was her father. She may feel affection for him."

Or she might feel outrage, thought Devellyn. She might even want revenge. But her father was dead. "And this poor Claire Bauchet," he murmured, "she stayed with that contemptible dog? All those years?"

His mother's eyes widened. "What choice had she?" she asked, lifting her elegant shoulders. "She was carrying his child."

Devellyn was enraged and hardly knew why. "By God, I would have killed him!"

"Oh, Aleric, you fool." Irritation flared in his mother's eyes. "You'd have done nothing of the sort."

"I would," he insisted. "And gone to the gallows gladly."

"Spoken like a man!" she snapped. "The poor girl was *ruined,* Aleric, and she was with child. She could not afford the satisfaction of killing him. I declare, you men know nothing of motherhood. Even before birth, a mother will tolerate anything, and sacrifice anything, just to protect her child. You cannot begin to comprehend what that kind of devotion is like."

Devellyn fell quiet and considered it. Perhaps his mother's anger was justified. He thought of her, of how slender and fragile his mother had always seemed. And yet she had defended him nearly to the death during those last dark, hellish days of Greg's life. He remembered the quarrels, the ugly accusations she had flung back in his father's face. Her defense of him had all but torn asunder her marriage. And when his father had remained embittered, she had gone to her own father, a very wealthy man, and begged him to support Devellyn.

His grandfather had done that, and more. He had made Devellyn his heir, enabling him to continue his life as a gentleman. And while Devellyn had been deeply grateful, he had still proceeded to throw much of it away out of rage and bitterness. How could he have failed to appreciate her sacrifice?

He stared at the coffee, and dragged both hands through his hair. "I am sorry, Mamma," he whispered. "I am not thinking clearly today."

His mother relaxed into her chair. "This woman," she said. "Sidonie. Is she a good sort of person, do you think?"

He nodded. "Yes," he said. "Yes, she is wonderful."

And in that moment, he meant it. His wrath toward her was forgotten, and he felt that Sidonie was the best sort of person he'd ever met. She possessed every womanly virtue one could imagine. Indeed, she reminded him very much of the woman who sat opposite him. Delicate. Elegant. Pragmatic. With the heart and the spirit of a lioness.

He looked up to see his mother standing before him. "Aleric, I must visit Isabel now," she said, kissing him again. "Please trust me, my dear, to take care of this. I hate to see you so worried."

Devellyn felt the last vestige of fear drain away. He

did trust his mother. She would not promise what she could not deliver. Sidonie's reputation would remain untarnished—at least by his hand.

His mother was already halfway out the door. "By the way, congratulations," she said, halting. "Honeywell tells me the Duke Street house is finished, and you'll be returning next week."

"Does he?" muttered Devellyn. "I daresay we shall, then."

"Aleric! You don't sound pleased."

Devellyn shrugged. "Oh, I don't know, Mother. I'm a little tired of living in Duke Street, if you know what I mean."

His mother wrinkled her nose. "Well, Bloomsbury is not very fashionable nowadays."

Devellyn laughed richly. "Nor am I, Mamma," he said, rising and offering his arm. "Nor am I."

The Duchess of Gravenel wasted not a moment in racing across town to Mayfair. By this hour, the streets were choked with fine carriages and footmen, as the *haute ton* rushed back and forth between one another's houses, dropping cards, delivering flowers, and making a general frenzy of the social season. Nonetheless, the duchess was quite certain she would find her girlhood friend at home in Berkeley Square. Lady Kirton was little enamored of society.

Lady Kirton was not, however, at her desk. In fact, she must have been peeking out her parlor window, for she threw open the door herself. "Elizabeth, at last!" she said. "Go into the library at once. We've not a moment to waste."

The duchess was taken aback. "You know why I've come?"

Lady Kirton nodded sagely. "About Madame Saint-Godard, yes?" she whispered, pulling the duchess down the passageway. "About what happened last night in Walrafen's parlor? You should have seen Aleric's face, my dear."

"Oh, I think he is done in by this one, Isabel," said the duchess. "I think he is head over heels."

"I agree," said her friend. "Never have I seen Aleric lose his composure so thoroughly—and all of it over a cut!"

The duchess lifted her brows. "Do you believe that silly story, then?"

"The story that Madame Saint-Godard had a run-in with some common criminals?" asked Isabel. "Oh, indeed! But I do not think it silly. I find it quite chilling. You see, my dear, I know a little something about our dear Madame Saint-Godard and her penchant for trouble. More, perhaps, than does Aleric."

"Do you indeed?"

"Oh, I fear so," said Lady Kirton, quietly shutting the door. "And believe me, Elizabeth, when I say that we have not a moment to lose in getting this pair to the altar!"

Chapter Thirteen

An evening at the Cross Keys

By half past eight, Devellyn was strategically positioned in a room overlooking the entryway of the Cross Keys Inn. He'd taken the precaution of sending Polk down to Cheapside to engage the bedchamber some six hours earlier. Then he had paced the floor of his study until the footman returned with the key, along with some ludicrous tale about having bribed the innkeeper for the best view using the change from Devellyn's ten-pound note.

Devellyn had taken the key and waved away the explanation. He had clutched it tight as he paced, the metal digging into his flesh. He had told himself there was no need to arrive much before nine. Nonetheless, he'd been standing—or stooping, rather—by the window for better than an hour now, staring down at the traffic in Wood Street. He'd sent down for a piece of beefsteak, but tonight, it tasted like boiled boot leather.

The room was little better. Tucked up under the eaves like an architectural afterthought, it was small and drab. Devellyn had to hunch in order to stand near the window or go through the door, and the place was furnished with nothing but a narrow bedstead, a washstand, and a stout deal table with two chairs. Thwarted and impatient, Devellyn was beginning to feel like a caged lion in the room's tight confines.

Still, it was the view he'd wanted, not the ambiance. He had the strangest feeling that if he could just see Sidonie in the role of the Black Angel, he would be able to come to terms with the truth. Accept it, perhaps, and move on. And yet, his every nerve seemed on edge. *Would she come? And would he see her?* Yes, by God, he would. And he was determined to put an end to this, once and for all.

Despite the hour, the Cross Keys was full of activity. In the lamplit yard below, pedestrians and ostlers dashed madly about. Carriages rattled in and out constantly, a few of them sleek blue mail coaches, returning from their rounds. People of all classes hastened through the front door, some seeking accommodation, others just a pint of porter in the taproom.

The taproom. The note had mentioned it specifically. A respectable lady would not wish to be seen meeting a man in a common taproom, would she? The Black Angel would be dressed, then, as someone with less propriety. Perhaps he was watching for Ruby Black?

Ruby. Yes. It might be Ruby.

Good Lord. There was no Ruby. He needed to get a grip. Devellyn dragged a hand through his hair and tried to focus through the gloom beyond his window. And in that instant, he saw her. She crossed through a pool of lamplight, her stride bold, her hips swaying.

Ruby Black. Though she wore a dark cloak tossed casually over her shoulders, her red velvet dress and garishly clashing hair were unmistakable. From above, she looked and moved so little like Sidonie, Devellyn marveled at the alteration.

He hastened down the two flights of stairs, then made his way through the inn's public areas until he reached a side entrance to the taproom. This chamber was slightly better lit than the Anchor had been, and it was easy enough for Devellyn to take up a position just outside the door. He drew back into the shadow of a large cupboard and watched her saunter between the tables.

She was looking for someone. Without success, it seemed, for she finally sat down at a narrow trestle table in the rear and turned her face to the main entrance of the room. Still, at least a dozen pairs of hungry eyes were watching her, taking in her mouth and her breasts and the enticing curve of her hips, which were snugly—*too* snugly—encased in red velvet. They looked at her boldly, as if she were for sale. Which was, after all, the impression she sought to give. Devellyn felt his temper ratchet dangerously upward. He bloody well hoped Sidonie was enjoying her little ruse. It was the last one he meant her to have.

Just then, a newcomer entered the room, a striking young man with quick black eyes. He was thin, slightly built, and dressed with Bond Street elegance. In the lamplight, he cast his eyes unhurriedly over the room. Eventually, however, he caught Sidonie's eye and approached. After exchanging a few words, he sat down with a measured grace.

Ruby—*Sidonie*—leaned across the table eagerly. Her skin was darker, her face less drawn, and her mole, he noticed, had moved from her mouth to the corner of her eye. Careless of her. Still, it taunted him. After some five minutes, the conversation grew more intense. The young man's expression became fervent. Which meant it was likely just a matter of time before Ruby enticed him into doing something foolish.

That moment, a serving girl bearing a tray full of tankards passed by, fleetingly obscuring Devellyn's view. Devellyn tried to look around her, uncertain what his next move ought to be. Perhaps he should simply walk over and warn the young man, who was quite obviously in over his head. Yes, apparently he was naive enough to be lured into the Black Angel's trap. He reached across the table, and seized her hand. She drew back, nodded, then relaxed again, as if some sort of bargain had been struck.

The taproom was growing crowded, the conversation and the smoke thickening. The tension was thickening, too. And then came the ugly moment. The man reached into his coat pocket and pulled out his purse. Still, only an experienced gamester would have noticed the money he so cleverly palmed, then passed across the table.

Sidonie took it, slipped it into her shabby reticule, and moved as if to rise. The gentleman did the same. Devellyn was halfway across the room before he knew what he was about.

Ruby—no, *Sidonie*—saw him coming. She panicked and dropped the reticule. The young man remained unaware until Devellyn grabbed Sidonie by the arm and jerked her from the table.

The man whipped around, his gaze glittering furiously. "See here, *monsieur!*" he said, his accent heavy. "Unhand her at once!"

Devellyn stuck his face into the young man's. "See *here,* you naive little coxcomb," he growled in a low undertone. "This is no twopenny whore you're dealing with. Now get out, and count your blessings before she strips you of everything but your knackers."

For Sidonie, the game was obviously up. She seemed to turn from Ruby into Sidonie before his very eyes. "Go!" she ordered the young man as Devellyn dragged her away. "Go, now!"

The young man shot her one last reluctant glance and headed for the door. Devellyn snatched up the reticule, and flung it after him. "And take your bloody money!" he bellowed. "She is not for sale."

Sputtering indignantly, Sidonie tried to wriggle from his grasp. "Let go, you brute!" she said. "Stop! You're hurting my wrist."

One or two patrons started from their chairs as if to intercede. Then, taking in Devellyn's size, they sat back down again. Sidonie was trying to wrench herself from his grasp, but Devellyn was ruthless. He dragged her through the taproom to the stairs and started up, ignoring the pair of serving girls who were gaping at them.

"Let me go, you swine!" Deliberately, Sidonie snared one toe on the lip of the stair and dragged at him until she was worse than a deadweight. Devellyn just bent down, grabbed her round the waist, and tossed her over one shoulder. She landed with a loud *oomph!* and was momentarily winded.

Devellyn dashed up the stairs, then turned to start up

the next flight. But Sidonie kept squirming and flailing. He smacked her soundly across her arse with the flat of his hand. "Hold still, you little hellcat!"

"Put me down!" she screeched, pounding on his back with both fists. "Devellyn, damn you, put me *down*." Then she altered her tactic. "Help! Help! I'm being abducted!"

Devellyn kicked open his door, tossed Sidonie onto the bed, and slammed it shut again. "They can't hear you, *Ruby*," he snarled.

Sidonie scrabbled up awkwardly, her breasts nearly spilling from the tight velvet. "What do you want from me?" she snapped. "What?"

He jerked his head in the direction of the taproom. "Perhaps I'll just take what your pretty Frenchman paid for," he suggested, his hands going to the fall of his trousers. "It would be a bloody shame to let a fancy piece like you go to waste."

"Look here, Devellyn, that wasn't what it appeared." Her eyes darted about the room as if looking for an escape route. "Jean-Claude is a friend. He was trying to warn me. Someone—a fence—was just arrested."

Still glowering, Devellyn folded his arms across his chest and leaned back against the door.

"Oh, I don't have to put up with this!" Sidonie bolted for the window and shoved at it impotently.

"Sweeting, you'll never make it," he warned. "And you'd likely break a leg if you did."

She looked over her shoulder contemptuously. "Don't be a fool, Devellyn," she hissed. "I wouldn't so much as chip a nail."

Devellyn held up one hand. "Why, I'd forgotten!" he

said. "The Black Angel can practically fly out windows, can she not?"

"Why should you give a damn?" she challenged. "I thought I was dead to you. I thought you wished—now, let me get this straight—yes, to drive a stake through my heart. Do I remember correctly?"

Her tone made him inexplicably angrier. He crossed the room in two strides. He gripped her arm again, dragged her bodily to the washstand, and slopped a quart of water into the basin. "Wash that filth off your face," he growled. "Before I take my hand to your arse again."

Sidonie whirled around, and cracked him through the face with her palm. "Just try it." Her tone was like ice, her eyes glittered with fire, and suddenly, she looked not like Ruby, nor even Sidonie. Instead, she was George Kemble made over, the resemblance startling.

Devellyn let her go and touched at his stinging cheek with two fingers. "Just wash it off, Sidonie," he said again. *"Please."*

She held his gaze defiantly. "Wot's wrong, gov'nor?" she said. "Yer liked it well enough last time, aye?"

Devellyn gave her a little shake, then backed away, his gaze locked with hers. "Stop it!" he demanded. "Damn you, stop using that voice. Those clothes—take them off. Stop this! All of it, do you hear?"

But the devil, it seemed, was in her now. She backed him across the floor. "What's wrong, Devellyn?" she whispered, her own voice now. "Is that naughty Ruby too much woman for you? Don't you just wish you could rip her clothes off yourself? Isn't that what's driving you mad?"

"Shut up, Sidonie!" he shouted. "You aren't—you aren't *her.*"

It was her turn to force him up against a wall, though he could have stopped at any moment. Instead, he came up short by the foot of the bed, his head bent against the low ceiling. For a moment, she simply stared at him. "Do you know what your problem is, Devellyn?"

"My problems," he gritted, "are legion. And none of your damned business."

Sidonie shocked him then by setting the flat of her hand against his belly, and sliding it down until he closed his eyes and trembled. And she kept going, too, down the close of his trousers, all the way down, until she found his cock, already rock-hard and throbbing, damn it. Easing her hand up and down his length, Sidonie made a sound of pleasure and bent her head until her lips almost touched his throat.

"Your problem, Devellyn," she whispered, her breath warm on his skin, "is that you *want* women like Ruby. You want the predictability. The simplicity. The luxury of walking away. And you don't want any questions when you're done—because you're half-afraid of what the answers might be."

He closed his eyes, and listened to the breath saw in and out of his lungs. "Stop it, Sidonie."

But she didn't. She just kept easing her hand up and down his cock, making him strain at the wool of his trousers. "Yes, I'm the Black Angel, Devellyn," she whispered. "I'm Ruby Black, that bad, bad girl you still burn for, and I've got my fingers wrapped round the proof. But you can turn your back on Sidonie without so much as a fare-thee-well, just because she turned out to be something less than your virtuous little widow next door."

"Shut up, Sidonie." His voice seemed disembodied now. "Just shut up. It is *not* like that."

She set her lips to his skin. "Are you sure?" she whispered silkily. "Perhaps you think women like Ruby are all you deserve. Or perhaps you're just too afraid to take on anything more complicated."

He seized her wrist and tore it from his body. "That might have been true once," he gritted. "But now, I— hell and damnation, I don't know! I left you, Sidonie, because you're a liar. I saw the truth. The *tattoo*. How could you hide that from me, damn you? How could you let me go on yearning for you, making love to you, and never tell me? How?"

Some of the fight left her then. "I . . . I made a mistake," she whispered, her gaze softening.

"What mistake?" he demanded, jerking her body against his. "Lying to me? Giving yourself to me?"

She closed her eyes, and shook her head. "No," she whispered. "Making love with you might have been reckless. But it didn't . . . it didn't feel like a mistake. Not until you left me."

Devellyn drew in a deep, rough breath. "Good God, I thought I was in love with you," he managed. "Now I just think I'm insane. So explain *that,* Sidonie, if you're so bloody damned clever. Because that's what tortures me at night nowadays. I worry about your getting your throat slit in some alley, or caught in the hangman's noose. Not some fuck-fantasy about a dockside tart who never really existed."

Her sweep of black lashes came down, and she

looked up at him with a strange mix of fascination and wariness. "Oh, the Black Angel exists," she whispered. "And she isn't finished."

Devellyn snapped. And then his mouth was on hers, hot and hard. His hands, too, took her. His head swam with the scent of her, and he couldn't think straight. Despite her bold talk, Sidonie tried to squirm away, but he held her to him with a powerful desperation. Finally, he felt her surrender, felt her lean into his body, giving herself over to his ravening mouth and urgent touch.

For long moments, he kissed her, holding her still to his onslaught. She kissed him back, her tremulous hands moving over him, her breathing softly audible in the stillness of the room. He filled his hands with her breasts, and plumbed her mouth with his tongue, deeply and sinuously. She sighed, and whispered his name into the darkness of the shabby little room.

Aleric. Aleric.

And something about the sound of it on her lips made him want to cry. It was so near, yet so distant, like an echo from his past. A call. A pleading, to what he had once been. He needed her. Needed to spend the hurt and anger and frustration, and to feel again what he'd felt last night. Raw emotion swept over him, and with it came a bone-deep ache. For her. Always her. Whoever she was.

He could feel his own heartbeat throbbing through him. His eyes raked the room. The rickety bed had not a prayer, not for what he was about to do. Instead, he pushed her back two steps to the table, and unthinkingly shoved the pewter platter onto the floor. Metal clattered across the planked wood, but Devellyn didn't stop.

He laid her back on the sturdy oak and dragged up her skirts with one hand. With the other, he released his own clothing, then pulled her to the edge. He must have torn away her drawers—he had no recollection of it—then sheathed himself deep on one smooth stroke.

She cried out and reached up from the table for him. Still standing, Devellyn bent over her body and kissed her. She kissed him back, long and deep, then tried to catch her breath and couldn't. Need burned through him as if last night had never been. Apart, they were nothing. Wrong. Incomplete. Together, tonight, they were like the rush of a firestorm, fast and incendiary.

In the gloom, Sidonie sobbed out his name again, and it was sweeter still as she arched against him. He lost himself then, thrusting and thrusting, letting the white light flow over him until he lay over her body, tremulous and eviscerated.

Long moments later, he somehow found the strength to lift her from the table and carry her to the bed. He sat down gingerly and settled her across his lap. He set his lips to her forehead. "Did I hurt you?" His voice came out a rough whisper.

She made a sound, something between a sob and a laugh. "No."

Suddenly, he tore his mouth away. "I am sorry," he murmured. "I am so sorry, Sidonie. I did not mean to— you are not like—" He couldn't form the right words to explain what he barely comprehended. "Ah, Sidonie. I can't bear to be without you. May God help us both."

She shook her head in astonishment. "Why, Devellyn?" she whispered. "Why me?"

"I don't know," he whispered, his mouth pressed to the turn of her throat. "I don't know why, Sidonie. It's insanity. But I've fallen in love."

She captured his face in her hands, and brought his gaze to hers. "You know what I am, Devellyn."

"It doesn't matter," he said, realizing how true the words were. "I want you. *Need* you. And I'm not at all sure you deserve such a fate."

Her eyes filled with confusion. "You asked me if last night was a mistake," she whispered. "Well, you see what has come of it. I took a foolish risk to have something I desperately wanted. And now, I am discovered. But how can it have been a mistake, any of it? I keep asking myself that, you see. How can something that was . . . so *beautiful* be wrong?"

"It wasn't," he said.

She turned her face into his shirtfront. "Oh, God," she whispered against his disordered cravat. "Whatever happens, it was worth it."

Devellyn set his lips to the top of her head and breathed in her warm scent. Her words let the fear close in again. "Good God, the Black Angel!" he said. "Why, Sidonie? Why? Oh, my love, don't you know they could hang you? Why in God's name are you doing these dangerous things and living this strange, secret life?"

Sidonie watched the uncharacteristic emotions play over Devellyn's face. Fear and uncertainty. A measure of grief. He deserved an answer. Haltingly, she tried to give him one. But it made no more sense than when she'd told George. And Devellyn liked it even less.

His eyes darkened, but as if to temper his words, he

lifted one hand to stroke her cheek. "Sidonie, there are better, safer ways to help the less fortunate," he said. "What you are doing is so dangerous, it is madness."

"You sound like George."

His voice was firmer now. "This has to stop, Sidonie. No matter what happens between us. *Promise* me."

She sighed. "How can I?" she finally answered. "I won't, Devellyn. I can't. Don't you understand? I did not mean to fall in love with you. I tried so hard to stay away, but you wouldn't—you wouldn't . . ."

"Take no for an answer?" he supplied. "That's right, and I shan't take it now, either. Sidonie, the Black Angel is dead."

"No," she whispered. "Not to me."

"Stop before you get caught," he begged. "Can you swear to me that won't happen?"

She was silent for a long moment. "I don't think it will," she whispered. "But Lady Kirton—oh, God!—I think she knows, or suspects, at the very least. Still, I think she won't say anything."

"I shall deal with Lady Kirton," he said grimly. "But Sidonie, who else besides you and Julia might know? Who else might possibly figure this out?"

"That the Black Angel and I are one?" she whispered. "No one else knows enough to figure it out. Save you, Aleric. And yet . . . and yet, you did not."

"Strangely enough, I think I did," he countered. "But it was so incongruous, my mind could not make sense of it. I fear, however, someone else's mind will be more astute. I fear that eventually, someone, somewhere will say or remember something, Sidonie. And what will we do then?"

"It shan't happen," she vowed. "I have been exceedingly careful."

Devellyn wished he felt so confident. "The best protection, you know, would be to marry me," he said. "My reputation won't afford you much in the way of respectability, but at least no one would dare accuse you of a crime."

Sidonie lifted his hand, and kissed his knuckles. "You are more chivalrous, Devellyn, than you like to admit," she said. "It was one of the first things I noticed about you. You have no charm, it is true. And yet . . . you charm me as no man ever has."

He held his breath a moment. "Is that a *yes?*"

She shook her head. "It is a definite *no,*" she replied. "There are too many who need help. So many wrongs to right. Try to understand, Aleric. Besides, your family would be appalled."

His body seemed to stiffen. "My father is appalled by every breath I draw," he said. "But my mother would be so grateful, she'd likely fall at your feet."

"Aleric, they would see me as just a poor relation," Sidonie warned. "An *illegitimate* poor relation, whose mother was a——"

He touched a finger to her lips, cutting her off. "Don't say it, Sidonie," he whispered. "She was your mother. As to my mine, she would be grateful you'd have me."

Sidonie looked askance at him. "You must be mad."

"Probably," he admitted. "Still, I could not bear you to be hurt, or get yourself hanged. Sidonie, it still stuns me when I think of it, but I want you to marry me, and bear my children. I have lived in hell these past few hours, just considering what might happen to you. Oh, Sidonie, don't you care for me? Just a little?"

Sidonie closed her eyes. "Oh, I care," she whispered. "It frightens me a little, the depth of what I feel for you. I—I love you, Devellyn. There, I have said it. Will you turn it on me now and use it as a weapon?"

Instead, he kissed her feverishly. "Thank God," he rasped. "Marry me, Sidonie. Please."

She opened her eyes, and stared at him. "Oh, how you tempt me."

"Then just say *yes,* Sidonie!" he commanded. "Just say it. I will keep you safe."

She hesitated, and it gave him hope. "Oh, Devellyn! What would people say?"

"They would say you made a dreadful match," he said, taking both her hands in his and looking deep into her eyes. "Listen to me, Sidonie," he said. "In a few days' time, my mother will be giving a ball. A grand affair in honor of my father's birthday. Sidonie, I want you to come. My mother is going to invite you, and introduce you into society. And—and your brother, too. Already, I have told her—"

"About *us?*" Sidonie interjected, her eyes widening. "Oh, Devellyn, surely you did not!"

He smiled awkwardly. "About you, yes," he said. "And your brother. She was not displeased. Indeed, she went so far as to suggest that, given our unfortunate scene in Walrafen's parlor, I *ought* to marry you."

But she looked up at him with sorrow in her eyes. "Aleric, it would not work," she said. "I have a past. A past I am not sure I can give up. And even if your mother accepts me, your father never will."

"The devil!" he answered. "What does it matter?"

"Perhaps it does not," she agreed. "But I suspect it matters to you more than you will admit."

He started to protest again, and she set two fingertips against his lips. "Yes, all right, you overbearing bully," she said. "I will go to this ball. Yes, I will drag my family history from the closet and even air it in public. And whilst there, I will do my best to make a good impression. But you are asking me to give up the Black Angel. And that is the most meaningful thing I have ever done in my insignificant little life."

He held her hands tight. "Be my wife," he said. "That alone will be a monumental task, Sidonie. But at least I am rich. There is much good the Marchioness of Devellyn could do with her husband's money."

She looked at him suspiciously. "And if I made such a sacrifice—not that I am promising to do so—what, in turn, would you do?"

"What would I do? What the devil does that mean?"

"Your father is prideful, I'm sure," she said. "But if he extends the hand of reconciliation, no matter how tenuously, will you reach for it? For the sake of your mother?"

"I just want to marry you," he muttered. "And Father would sooner die than extend a hand."

"You might be surprised." She touched him lightly on the arm. "Or you might be quite right. All I am saying, Aleric, is this: Do not leave anything unsaid between you. I did it, and the wasted words have left a bitter taste in my mouth."

He cut her a skeptical glance. "What do you mean?"

Sidonie fell silent for a moment. "George says my

ruse as the Black Angel is all mixed up in my feelings about Mother," she finally said. "And I . . . well, I fear he might be right. When I was young, I did not understand how wretched her life was and how much shame my father forced her to bear. I was hurt, you know, when she sent me away. I felt unloved. So I ran away."

"Poor girl," he murmured, setting his lips to her forehead.

Sidonie pushed him back so that she might hold his gaze. "And I stayed away, Aleric," she went on. "Even in those later years, when Father was dead, and she began to plead with me to visit, I ignored her every overture. Indeed, I took a perverse sort of pleasure in doing so. I have thought about it a great deal these last few weeks, and I think that in the back of my mind, I always felt there would be time later to reconcile. I never dreamt she would die so young. And now, I don't even know, really, what kind of person she was. I know only that she was human, and filled with faults, as we all are. And I know that whatever it was she wished to say to me—if anything—cannot ever be said now."

Devellyn knew she was right. There was a terrible permanence to death. "But my father resides just a few miles away in Kent," he countered. "If he wished to reconcile, he could have long since done so. Our anger, Sidonie, is of a colder, more lethal, sort."

"Fine!" she said on a sigh. "But just remember, Aleric, that should I agree to what you ask, I shan't hesitate to express my opinions and concerns."

Devellyn cut her a dark glance. "By God, Alasdair warned me this would happen."

"That *what* would happen?"

"Meddling. Poking. Prodding." His lip twitched with humor, but somehow, he held the scowl. "All those things females commence doing as soon as a fellow thinks about settling down."

Sidonie drew back and looked at him. "You wish to withdraw your offer of marriage, then?" she said, suppressing a small smile. "Pray feel free. My brother will doubtless be thrilled."

Devellyn did not wish to withdraw his offer. Instead, he sat, fascinated, as Sidonie peeled little bits of rubber from behind her ears, washed off her makeup, then took down her real hair. A few simple twists, and the hair was once again restrained and elegant. She turned the cloak inside out, to a drab shade of gray and buttoned it snugly. It was time, thank God, to go home.

She kept her hand on his arm as they walked, and the warmth of it comforted him. He was still awash in a sense of relief. She was safe. She did love him. Perhaps he had not yet convinced her he was worthy of that love, and worthy of the sacrifice which must be made. But for the second time in his misbegotten, misspent life, Devellyn allowed hope to kindle in his heart.

The hope soon dimmed. He had avoided the inn's busy front entrance by leading Sidonie out the back and into an alley that cut across Gutter Lane. He wondered now if that had been a mistake. The lane was in some ways aptly named. Despite its proximity to the City's business district, several brothels dotted the area, becoming more apparent when the coffee shops and counting-houses closed.

Suddenly, at a house just ahead of them, a girl burst backward through the front door, cursing like a sailor as she tumbled down the steps. She landed on her arse in the street. A plump, gaudily dressed woman came out as far as the doorstep, and spat after her.

"And that's what you can do w' your fine, pretty ways, me dear," she said. "I've no work for the likes of you."

The girl was on her feet now, but her yellow hair was tumbling down, and her bright purple dress was streaked with filth. "Ow, buggar off, you wicked old witch," she shouted up the steps. "I ain't swiving no crusty goat wiv not a real tooth in his head. Give 'im ter Maryanne, and let 'er do 'im. Fuck anything, she will."

At that, the bawd came down the steps and soundly backhanded the girl. Sidonie, of course, had broken away from Devellyn and was rushing forward. "See here!" she cried, pulling the bawd away. "Leave her alone! What right have you to hit her?"

"What right?" asked the bawd incredulously. "Owes me rent, she does. What's it to you, anyways?" Then she eyed Devellyn suspiciously. "Get back up them steps and shut yer gob, Bess. We'll let these fine folk be on their way."

But Sidonie was having none of it. She went to the girl, who was wiping away a little smear of blood with the back of her hand. "My dear, you do not have to stay here," she said. "I have money. I can find you a place to sleep tonight."

The girl looked at her derisively. "Ternight?" she echoed incredulously. "And wot good'll that do me? I gots to work, don't I? And I ain't being clapped up in the bloody workhouse, if that's wot yer meaning."

Sidonie put a hand on her arm. "My dear, anything would be better than this."

The girl lifted one brow and yanked her arm away. "Would it, now?" she said softly. "Well, I'd rather rub me knees raw getting worked over by an old goat than scrubbin' floors whilst I starve." And with that, the girl flounced back up the steps and into the house.

"Wait!" cried Sidonie. "I'm not talking about the workhouse. Please! Hear me out."

But the girl was gone. The bawd gave them a patronizing smile, and slammed the door shut.

Sidonie looked as if she might burst into tears. Devellyn circled an arm around her shoulders and drew her to him. "You tried, love," he said quietly. "She's set her course."

"And there are a thousand more just like her," she said sorrowfully. "She knows no other way. It's that or the workhouse! That's what she thinks. And it isn't right, Devellyn! It isn't fair."

"That girl isn't like your mother, Sidonie," he gently reminded her. "In fact, they have almost nothing in common."

"They both felt trapped, didn't they?" Sidonie snapped. "That is something they have in common. Lord, I wish I'd never told you about George and his blasted theory!"

Gently, Devellyn urged her down the street. "You cannot save them all, Sidonie," he answered. "Even the Black Angel doesn't have enough tricks up her sleeve."

Sidonie's shoulders had fallen. "But the Black Angel could do *something*, Devellyn," she whispered. "And surely even a little something is better than nothing."

They walked in silence for a time. "That, I believe, is your problem, Sidonie," he finally said. *"A little some-*

thing. That is what you keep trying to do. Work the edges. Play the margins. But perhaps, my dear, you ought think on a grander scale?"

Sidonie sighed wearily. "And just what is that supposed to mean?"

Devellyn rubbed his day-old beard pensively. "I am not perfectly sure," he said. "Let me give it some thought. Perhaps I might just surprise you by having an original thought in my rusty old brain."

Devellyn awaited his father's seventieth birthday like a man going to the gallows. He dreaded another foray into society, and half feared that his father might simply give him the cut direct. Following his strange interlude at the Cross Keys, Devellyn had met with his mother and pitched his devil's bargain: Sidonie and her brother were to be embraced like long-lost kin in exchange for Devellyn's presence at the ball. His mother had leapt at it almost too quickly, and there had been an odd little gleam in her eye.

There was a strange sense of expectancy in the air, like the feeling a fellow got just before his luck took a turn at the card tables. It was as if he were being dealt a new hand at life. So would it come up kings and knaves? Or just the usual disaster of deuces and treys?

Waiting for Sidonie's answer was utter torture. When they were together now, it was hard to restrain his urge to press her. Still, all hope was not lost. Her kisses had grown more heated than ever, even as her protests grew noticeably weaker. He laid siege, romantically speaking, to her doorstep, sending flowers every morning, chocolates every evening, and jewelry as often as he dared. The latter she always returned, but at least he was getting her attention.

At last, the appointed evening arrived. Sir Alasdair MacLachlan turned up early, of course, to badger him, and to give all manner of unsolicited, crack-brained advice about life, love, and the dangers of the female mind. Alasdair sipped brandy in a chair by the dressing table as Fenton trussed Devellyn up in his evening dress. It was not long before the conversation turned to the Duchess of Gravenel.

"And you will tell her, then, that I forced you to come?" asked Alasdair, holding his glass to the lamplight and peering at the golden liquid within.

"I shall tell her nothing of the sort," Devellyn returned. "In fact, I think I'll tell her I've come to announce my engagement."

"The deuce!" said Alasdair, lowering the glass. "I'll never get that Vespasian denarius now. Look, Dev, does Sidonie know what you're up to?"

"Not exactly." Devellyn lifted his chin so that Fenton might pull his collar snug. "I just might surprise her and announce it anyway. And once it's done, she'd have to marry me, wouldn't she?"

Alasdair looked doubtful. "Well, old boy, you know what they say," he warned. "A cracked bell will never mend. She mightn't forgive you."

"Spare me your Scottish platitudes, Alasdair," muttered Devellyn. "Someone has to keep that woman safe, and I'm at my wit's end."

"So this romance is a purely humanitarian gesture, eh?"

"Chin up, my lord," grumbled Fenton, wrestling with his cravat now.

Devellyn fell silent as his valet finished dressing him. "Thank you, Fenton," he murmured when the job was done. "You've wrought another miracle."

"Indeed," said Alasdair coolly. "He looks almost civilized."

"What a flatterer you are, Alasdair," said Devellyn, setting a hand on his friend's shoulder. "Come on, then. I've business in the Strand, and I fear it won't be pleasant."

As it happened, George Kemble was not the only resident of London destined to receive an unexpected caller that evening. Shortly before dusk, the bell rang at Number Fourteen. With Julia making a last-minute tuck in Sidonie's ball gown, and Meg off on another lark, Sidonie rushed to answer it herself. Her breath left her lungs sharply when she opened the door to see the Countess of Kirton standing on her doorstep, and her ladyship's crested carriage pulled to the curb.

Her ladyship smiled warmly. "Good evening, Madame Saint-Godard," she said. "I thought you might wish to accompany me to Gravenel's ball."

"Accompany you?" Sidonie looked at her stupidly.

A pair of purple feathers bounced cheerfully on her hat as her ladyship nodded. "Elizabeth and I decided it was not quite the thing, your arriving alone," she murmured. "And I understand your brother has declined the invitation. May I come in?"

Sidonie regained her manners. "Yes, please do," she managed. "Who is Elizabeth?"

"Why, the Duchess of Gravenel," said Lady Kirton, as if it were obvious. "We are girlhood chums, you know. Did Aleric not mention it?"

Sidonie motioned her ladyship into the parlor. "No, not in those words," she answered. "And you wish me to go with you? To the ball?"

Lady Kirton opened her hands. "Unless you've other plans?"

Suddenly, Sidonie understood. "She has told you, then?" she managed. "The duchess, I mean. She has told you that I was once—or that I am—distantly related?"

Lady Kirton stepped forward, and patted Sidonie rather firmly on the cheek. "A dear cousin recently home from abroad," she corrected. "Not long out of mourning. That, you see, is why you've been so little in society. Now, buck up, dear child. And for pity's sake, get the story straight!"

It was almost dusk by the time Devellyn's carriage drew up at Kemble's shop in the Strand. All along the street, the storefronts were falling dark, while the coffeehouses were rapidly filling. Devellyn threw open the door and leapt down, dreading the task before him.

"Coming in?" he asked Alasdair from the pavement.

Alasdair waved his hand lazily. "Three is such a crowd, old boy," he said. "And the sight of blood makes me woozy."

Devellyn turned and went into the shop, pausing to read the brass plaque on the door. His entrance set off a little bell overhead. At first glance, he was amazed. Fine folderol indeed! Cachepots and clocks, vases and vinaigrettes, tea services, chandeliers, shields and swords—all of it jostled for space. And all of it looked frightfully old and expensive. Then there was the half mile swath of antique jewelry, which shimmered like liquid fire in the showcases.

But Devellyn did not have time to study it. A young man—a very familiar-looking young man—emerged from behind a set of green velvet draperies. Fleetingly, alarm lit his face, but he masked it and stared at Devellyn disdainfully. "We are closing, *monsieur*," he announced. "You must come another day."

"By God, I know you!" said Devellyn, striding up to the counter. "And I'll deal with you later. Right now, I wish to see Kemble."

The young Frenchman's brows went up. "But I cannot recommend eet, sir. He eez consulting weeth the chef about dinner."

Devellyn planted his big hands on the glass counter and leaned across. "I don't give a tinker's damn if he's trimming his toenails stark naked in his bathwater!" Then he relaxed again. "Oh, bother! There must be a door here someplace!" he muttered, then strode behind the counter and through the draperies.

"*Non, non!*" shouted the Frenchman plunging through the velvet after him. "Stop!"

But Devellyn had already found the back stairs and started up. "Thanks," he said over his shoulder. "I'll just surprise him."

He reached the door at the top, and gave a perfunctory knock. But George Kemble, it seemed, had finished with his chef. Devellyn found him in a small but luxurious drawing room, pouring what looked like sherry for a second chap, who seemed vaguely familiar. They

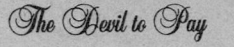

turned their gazes to him at once, the second laying aside a newspaper and rising from his chair.

Kemble's gaze swept down him. "Well, if it isn't dear Cousin Aleric!" he said contemptuously. "What a surprise."

"Sorry to barge in," said Devellyn, propping one shoulder against the doorway as if he meant to stay awhile. "But I knew you'd refuse to see me."

"You have an amazing grasp of the obvious, Devellyn."

Devellyn lifted his chin. "Look here, Kemble," he said. "You and I must set aside our differences. I need you to come with me tonight."

"Come with *you?*" Kemble sat down his wine decanter.

Devellyn felt suddenly awkward. He needed this man's help, much as it galled him to admit it. "To my father's ball," he pressed. "I know you received an invitation."

"And mightily amused I was, too," said Kemble, with an acid smile.

The second man had approached. "George, pray introduce us."

"Forgive me, Maurice," he said, then obliged him.

Devellyn offered his hand. "You look dashed familiar," he said, his brow furrowing. "Wait! *Giroux.* You're my new tailor, aren't you?"

"One of my assistants made you a pair of waistcoats," said Giroux with a sniff. "But I did not care for the colors your man chose."

Devellyn narrowed one eye. "Horse piss yellow? And a sort of moldy shade of gray?"

"I fear so." Giroux's gaze slid critically down Devellyn's evening attire.

Devellyn shrugged. "Well, let's go, then," he said. "The both of you."

Giroux drew back a pace, horrified. "To Gravenel's ball?"

Devellyn looked back and forth between them. "You two ought to think of Sidonie," he said. "Tonight is important. She needs her family with her."

"Sidonie means to go through with this?" asked Kemble.

"She promised me again, just last night," said Devellyn confidently. "She will go, and I think you owe it to her to go as well."

Giroux had returned to his chair. "You must be mad," he answered, giving his newspaper an energetic snap. "I've probably fitted half the gentlemen there."

"Good," said Devellyn. "Then you won't need to be introduced."

"Let me explain it more thoroughly, my lord," said Giroux waspishly. "Men do not wish to *know* men who have enjoyed such intimacies as measuring their waistlines and rearranging their testicles in order to achieve a flawless drape. And I, frankly, do not wish to *know* them. It would be very bad for business. I am in trade, and should like to remain so, if you please. And I've no wish, believe it or not, to see your family made to look like fools for inviting me."

He was right, of course.

"I've no more business going than he does," interjected Kemble. "And even less interest."

Devellyn snapped under the strain. "But you are my

long-lost, much-loved cousin, damn it! Mother wishes to publicly embrace you and return you to the bosom of the family."

"Oh, come!" said Kemble. "You cannot imagine I'd swallow that?"

"The *ton* will swallow it," growled Devellyn. "Think of your sister's future. I hate to break it so bluntly, Kem, but Sidonie and I are marrying by special license next week."

Kemble looked horrified. "You must be joking."

Devellyn smiled tightly. "I am afraid I have compromised her virtue just a tad."

Kemble's visage tightened. "You scoundrel!" he snapped. "I ought to take a horsewhip to your hide."

"I thought you were going to shoot me in a dark alley," Devellyn reminded him.

Kemble was pacing the floor now. "My God! Surely she did not agree to this! No, she did, didn't she? Blister it! I *knew* that girl would land in trouble! But *marriage*? To *you*?"

Devellyn forced himself to be calm. "I realize, of course, that I don't deserve her," he said. "Indeed, I would not even consider saddling her with me, but there is another, even more dire reason Sidonie needs a husband. My wealth and title will shield her from any sort of vile rumor which might spring up and cause questions. Consider, old chap, and I think you'll grasp my meaning."

Kemble eyed him nastily. "You manipulative blackguard."

Devellyn stared down his broken nose at the smaller man. "Nonetheless, we are already betrothed," he boldly lied. "The announcement is tonight. My mother means to ensure that Sidonie is embraced by all of society. You may call me out later if you wish. But for now, you owe your sister a duty."

Maurice rattled his newspaper. "Afraid he's got you there, George," he said almost cheerfully. "Wear the cream silk waistcoat. It makes your eyes look a little more honest."

"I still like the horsewhip option," muttered Kemble to the carafe of sherry. "That, and a fast ferry to France will solve most of Sidonie's problems."

"Perhaps she likes it here?" suggested Devellyn evenly. "I hate to say it, Kem, but your sister is not altogether indifferent to me."

Kem was still glowering, but he was obviously giving in. "I shall likely be ruined by this, you know," he snarled. "Christ, I'll be publicly acknowledged as a member of the Hilliard family! My anonymity will be gone. My underworld contacts won't wish to know me. How is a man to do business under such circumstances?"

Devellyn eyed him for a moment. "Speaking of anonymity," he said, "I'd best ask you about that name. Kemble. Where the devil did you get it?"

"Off a theater marquee when I was fourteen," snapped Kemble. "You'll pardon me if I'd no wish to go on being a Bauchet, or worse, a Hilliard."

Devellyn thumped him companionably between the shoulder blades. "I know just what you mean, old chap," he muttered. "The bloody name's been like a dead-weight round my neck."

Kemble shot him a sour, sidelong glance, then swilled

down the last of his wine, as if dressing for a ball required fortification.

"Good God!" Devellyn stared at the hand which grasped the glass stem. "Caught those knuckles in a vise, did you?"

Kemble stared down at his bruised joints, gingerly fisting his hand. "No, not a vise," he said coolly. "I just made some new acquaintances last night in St. James's."

"Yes, good old Pud and Bud," said Maurice Giroux with another disdainful sniff. "Charming young men. We'll be having them to dine any day now."

Kemble sneered. "Pug and Budley," he corrected. "And the only thing they'll be dining on is beef tea and mashed turnips. Now, I suppose I must go dress and prepare to throw away life as I know it. But you, Devellyn, are going to pay for this."

"Well, think of it as a sort of compromise, old chap," said Devellyn, following him from the room. "You will recall that there is a dukedom floating round in this family. One which should have been yours, and one which I don't particularly want."

"Yes, well, it hasn't exactly been keeping me up at night," said Kemble, striding down the passageway.

"Still, it would be best if we could keep the title safely hanging from our branch of the family tree, would it not?"

Kemble whirled around to face him. "My branch of this tree snapped off long ago," he said coldly. "And I assure you, Devellyn, that there is nothing we need compromise about."

"I think there is," he said. "After Sidonie marries me, we'll all be blended together rather indelibly, won't we? And eventually, all will be set to rights in a manner of speaking, since the dukedom will eventually pass to your nephew."

"I don't *have* a nephew," said Kemble stiffly.

Devellyn threw an arm around his shoulders. "A dreadful oversight on your part, Cuz," he said. "But one which I am working hard to correct."

A long, heavy silence held sway over the passageway. "Be glad, Devellyn, that my right fist is bruised," Kemble finally answered. "Be very, very glad."

Sidonie was already dreading her promise to Devellyn when she found herself queued up in the crowd at the Duke of Gravenel's door. With its solid marble steps and the elegant fanlight spanning its width, it was an entrance she recognized all too well. As a child, she'd stared at it every time they had driven through Grosvenor Square and wondered why she and George weren't good enough to live there.

She and Lady Kirton passed beneath the fanlight, and a haughty footman lifted Sidonie's cloak from her shoulders. A thin, black-garbed butler bowed and smiled superciliously as she passed. Then Lady Kirton laid a hand upon her arm and gave it a supportive squeeze. Sidonie plastered a smile on her face and kept moving into the crush. And then she saw them. The Duke and Duchess of Gravenel.

Aleric's mother was a pale, fine-boned creature dressed in a froth of pink lace, which should have looked silly on a woman of her years. Instead, it looked exquisite. She saw Sidonie standing with Lady Kirton, and her eyes widened. "Oh, my dear girl!" she exclaimed, reaching for her as if they were the best of friends. "Look, my love! Here is Cousin Sidonie."

No one watching would have guessed it was their first meeting. The duchess pulled Sidonie close and kissed both her cheeks, an action which did not go unheeded by the elderly tabbies who waited behind Lady Kirton. And then Sidonie was standing before the Duke of Gravenel, a tall, angular man who little resembled his son. There was no warmth in his eyes, but merely an odd smile playing at one corner of his mouth.

"Dear Cousin Sidonie!" he murmured, lifting her knuckles almost to his lips. "What a surprise."

"I daresay," she managed.

He gave her a dry smile. Somehow, Sidonie curtseyed and moved on without falling flat on her face. But she could feel the duke's eyes burning into her as she plunged into the crowd. Clearly, he was humoring his wife's wishes.

Inside the ballroom, there was no one she knew well and only a few who looked familiar. She had mingled with London's upper crust before, yes. But this was an altogether different stratum of society. This was the highest of the *haute*. The bluest of England's blood. She was grateful Lady Kirton had insisted they arrive together.

Just then, a dark, broad-shouldered gentleman brushed by, catching the countess's elbow. He turned as if to beg her pardon. "Why, Isabel!" he exclaimed. "How lovely to see you! Two balls in one season? A record for you, isn't it?"

Lady Kirton exchanged pleasantries, then smoothly turned the topic. "Oh, I have neglected to introduce my friend!" she chirped. "Madame Saint-Godard is Gravenel's cousin, recently returned from abroad, and a generous patron of the Nazareth Society. Sidonie, this is Sir James Seese, who sits on our board of governors."

A patron of the Nazareth Society? Well, that was one way to put it.

But the handsome man was bowing and asking her to dance. Lady Kirton tilted her head in the direction of the ballroom floor and widened her eyes. Sidonie smiled and took the proffered hand.

As they danced, Sidonie looked about for Devellyn. He was late. When the music ended, Sir James returned her to Lady Kirton, who promptly clipped another gentleman with her elbow. This one was introduced and sent to fetch champagne. Young gentlemen, tall gentlemen, fat, bald, and handsome gentlemen. Lady Kirton knew them all. Some she attracted with a wave or a crooked finger. And all of them seemed happy to do her ladyship's bidding.

"That elbow will be black-and-blue by tomorrow if you keep it up," Sidonie muttered to the countess as another handsome gentleman drifted away.

"Oh, I shan't need to!" said Lady Kirton, her sharp eyes running over the crowd. "Look at the glances being tossed our way. Soon *they* will come to us. Followed by their wives, their mistresses, and their mammas. Society cannot abide a mystery, and my dear, you are an enigma of the first water."

Sidonie's heart sank. "I feel like an imposter," she confessed. "The duke's cousin, indeed! People are already wondering why they never heard of me."

The countess shrugged. "Gravenel has been out of society for many years, and you have been abroad," she countered. "And you are, in point of fact, his cousin."

"Yet His Grace just met me tonight," Sidonie murmured. "I feel as if I've been foisted upon him."

But Lady Kirton was still on her tiptoes, studying the

throng. "He will do as his wife wishes," she murmured. "Gravenel's pride has got him nowhere. Look, is that not your brother with him now? Just there, through the corridor by the card room?"

Stunned, Sidonie turned. Relief flooded through her. George had come after all! He stood with both hands behind his back, looking vaguely uncomfortable as he conversed with Gravenel. He was dressed exquisitely, as always. Tonight he wore a severely cut formal coat of darkest black, and an ivory silk waistcoat which looked to have cost a fortune. The duke was speaking to him in hushed tones, but neither looked angry or even particularly unfriendly.

But George's gaze remained distant. He seemed to be answering a number of questions. Poor George. He was a deeply private person. It would have been his last wish to turn up at an event of this nature. He had come for her, of course. Gravenel could hardly embrace one of them but not the other.

Still, there would be the inevitable whispers about their background, about their illegitimacy, and their mother's lifestyle. They would say that Sidonie was little more than a glorified governess and that her brother was worse. He was *in trade*. And all of this, for what? So that she could make an entrée into Gravenel's world?

No. So that she could be with the man she loved. Suddenly, Gravenel set a hand on George's shoulder as if saying a warm good night, then headed into the ballroom. He waded through the crowd, pausing to accept the good wishes of several who hailed him. Eventually, he reached Sidonie and bowed.

"I would ask you to dance, Cousin," he said. "But my

doctor tells me I may not. Will you stroll through the gardens instead?"

A hundred pairs of eyes burnt into her as she left the ballroom on the duke's arm. By now, her identity would be on everyone's lips. Soon they were beyond the view of the ballroom. Gravenel carried himself with an air of authority, and yet she had the sense that he was much diminished. His color was not good, and he walked very slowly. At the end of the portico, Gravenel paused for breath. "They have told you, I suppose, that I am not very well?"

Sidonie was shocked. "No, Your Grace," she answered. "I am sorry."

He lifted one shoulder. "Ah, well," he said. "Only the good die young. I am seventy today, by the way."

Apparently, he shared his son's self-deprecating sense of humor. "Your doctors can do nothing?"

He shook his head, his eyes still surveying the lamplit garden. "Oh, I shall cling to the wreckage for another few months—perhaps even a year or two," he said, his tone oddly detached. "But eventually, everyone dies."

"I am sorry," she said again. "Aleric had not informed me."

The duke's gaze turned inward. "But she must have told him," he mused. "My wife, I mean. She must have. Else he'd never have come."

"Aleric has arrived?" Sidonie felt a rush of happiness. "I had not seen him."

"His mother is forcing him to squire her around the ballroom, I collect," said Gravenel. "He is champing at the bit, of course, and wishing to rush to your side, but his mother has reminded him of decorum."

She could sense neither approval nor censure in his tone. Behind them, the sounds of gaiety drifted on the night air. The tinkle of laughter and of glassware. The strains of a violin being tuned. "So they say I am dying," he said, crooking one gray eyebrow. "And my wife asks but one last thing of me. That Aleric and I reconcile. When I am gone, she shall have no one else to lean on, she claims. She wishes peace between us all."

"It sounds as if she cares deeply for you both," said Sidonie.

"My son and I are but strangers to one another now," he said flatly. "It is how we have preferred it."

Sidonie was not at all sure that was how Aleric preferred it, but she bit back the retort.

His breathing had steadied now. He offered his arm again, and together, they went down the three steps into the gardens. "Has my son asked your hand in marriage, Madame Saint-Godard?" he asked bluntly. "My wife believes so."

She saw no point in denying it. "Yes. He has."

"I see," said the duke. "Then he has, at the very least, treated you honorably."

Sidonie felt a spike of anger. "I have never known Aleric to act dishonorably."

"Some might disagree," said the duke matter-of-factly. "Will you say yes?"

For a moment, there was no sound but the soft crunch of gravel beneath their feet. "I am not sure," she finally answered.

He looked at her oddly. "You think him poor marriage material?"

"To the contrary," she murmured.

"Well, they do say a rake reformed makes the best husband," the duke mused. "You do not love him?"

Sidonie was on the verge of telling him none of it was his business. "I love him very much," she answered. "But I am a widow, and used to having my way. I am also mindful of what society might say."

He stopped and looked at her in some surprise. "The circumstances of your birth are, of course, unfortunate," he answered rather coldly. "But the shame is your father's. If you and Aleric wed, it will doubtless provide a fortnight of fodder for the scandalmongers. But we Hilliards are beyond being destroyed by scandal."

Sidonie did not like his tone. "Old gossip hardly matters," she answered. "Perhaps you ought to continue this conversation with Aleric. Give him your blessing, or if you cannot, then give him your advice. Your duty is to him."

Sidonie intended to walk away, but the duke caught her by the shoulder. She saw sorrow in his eyes. "I did not mean to fail my son, *madame,* if that is what you suggest," he answered. "Did I do so? Perhaps. But we have gone on this way for so many years. One wonders if there is any point trying to turn back."

"There is always a point," Sidonie responded. "As long as one draws the breath of life, there is a point. You have your son, sir. You have but to go to him and say your piece, whatever it is. Some parents do not have that choice."

Sidonie wanted to feel sorry for him, but it was difficult. She had seen in Aleric's eyes what this man's pride had done to him, and a part of her wanted to scream the truth at him. But in the end, she had not the heart. In the end, she simply turned and walked away.

Chapter Fourteen

In which Horatio has his Say

Lady Kirton, of course, was waiting just inside the French doors which opened onto the ballroom. Sir James had returned to her side. When she saw Sidonie and the duke, she came toward them with a smile, but her face fell instantly. "Your Grace, you look most unwell," she murmured.

"I am unwell," he returned. "As my doctor delights in reminding me every day."

"This walking has been too much." She scolded him with her eyes. "You must go into your study and rest. You know, Frederick, what the doctor says! Ten minutes with your feet up, every hour, on the hour."

Gravenel obliged her by pulling out his pocket watch. "Very well," he grumbled. "But I'd promised Elizabeth I'd spend a few minutes with my dotty old aunt."

"Oh, is Admeta here?"

"I fear so," he said. "Brought that blasted dog, too. Wearing a red velvet waistcoat."

"Admeta?" echoed Lady Kirton. "In a waistcoat?"

"The dog, Isabel. The dog."

Lady Kirton tapped the pocket watch the duke still held open. "Dispense with Aunt Admeta. Then into the study immediately!"

The duke departed, and almost instantaneously, Lady Kirton said, "Heavens, the social scene is quite wearing, is it not? I believe I shall go and rest my feet, too. Sir James, will you give Sidonie your arm until I return?"

"It would be an honor," he answered. But Lady Kirton was already leaving.

With his mother's hand lying lightly on his arm, Devellyn strolled through the ballroom without really seeing the faces in the crowd. He greeted people perfunctorily. Answered questions mechanically. He felt trapped again, a stranger in his own skin.

It had been a long time since he had been inside the house on Grosvenor Square. Not since Greg's death, and the dark, fearful days which had preceded it, when his father had remained constantly at Greg's bedside. To comfort herself, his mother had begun to pray, often for hours at a stretch. Devellyn had sought comfort, too, but his had come from a bottle. Both of them, however, had ended up on their knees, and to no avail. They had lived like shadowy wraiths, all three, waiting on this side of eternity for what looked more inevitable with each passing day.

And then inevitability became reality, and Greg was gone. His brother. His best friend. And left behind was only his mother, softly weeping, and his father, eyes burning with blame. His father's rage had been uncontrollable, his accusations ugly. And all too true. He had held Aleric solely accountable, and he still did.

Tonight, Gravenel had greeted George Kemble—a distant, illegitimate cousin whom he'd never met—with more warmth than he had his heir. Aleric had warranted nothing but the severest of bows. In response, his mother had welcomed him with too much enthusiasm and begun to fluff at his neckcloth and prattle on banally, as if doing so might keep others from noticing that Gravenel had all but cut his own son. Again.

Aleric smiled and shook the hand of the man to whom his mother was speaking. He exchanged another mechanical greeting. Suddenly, someone grasped his other arm with a grip that was very firm.

"I beg your pardon, Elizabeth," said Lady Kirton. "May I borrow your son a moment? I need a bit of air."

His mother's smile froze. "Isabel, are you unwell?"

Lady Kirton was fanning herself dramatically. "Nothing a few moments' rest won't cure."

Aleric was suspicious, but so grateful to be leaving the crowd behind, he little cared where Lady Kirton took him. She led him in the direction of his father's study, walking rather briskly for a plump, elderly woman on the verge of asphyxiation.

Inside, the room was little changed from his boyhood. He was still absorbing the memories when Lady Kirton went to a leather settee by the windows, and settled down as if she meant to be a while. Recalled to his duty, Aleric went at once to open a window, but she waved him away. "A ruse, young man! Just a ruse."

He narrowed his eyes. "I thought as much."

"Aleric," she said peremptorily, "I wish to speak with you."

Devellyn folded his hands behind his back, and

gripped them very tightly. "I'm not much given to chitchat, ma'am."

The countess waved a hand dismissively. "I shall do the talking," she assured him. "You need do nothing more than grunt a few answers at me."

He looked at her askance. "I make no promises, ma'am."

Lady Kirton was undeterred. "I like your Madame Saint-Godard," she said. "Your mother thinks you quite taken with her. It is true, is it not?"

Devellyn considered refusing to answer on principle. But what was the point? "It is true," he said.

She looked at him a little slyly. "Do you mean to marry the girl, Aleric?"

He was silent for a moment. He had already thought better of his rash notion to simply announce their betrothal, and wished ardently that he'd never mentioned it to Alasdair. "I think we can all agree I'm not much of a catch, ma'am," he finally said. "But yes, I have asked her."

Lady Kirton relaxed a little. "And she has said . . . ?"

Devellyn gave a slight, stiff bow. "The lady is considering my offer," he answered. "I cannot say what will happen."

Lady Kirton seemed to carefully consider her next words. "How well, Aleric, do you know Madame Saint-Godard?"

Devellyn stiffened. "Well enough, ma'am. Let us leave it at that."

"But do you know her . . . her habits and pursuits?" the countess pressed. "Her leanings on, er, social issues? The things she cares deeply about?"

What the devil was the old tabby getting at? Then he remembered Sidonie's words. *"Lady Kirton—I think she knows, or suspects."*

Devellyn looked at the countess very directly. "I know everything, ma'am," he said. "Everything a husband has a right to know. There is no chance I might come to learn of something in her past which would alter my feelings for her. They are immutable."

Lady Kirton waved her hand again. "Oh, I do not doubt the depth of your affection, Aleric. You have always been a most devoted sort of young man to those you love. I am speaking more of . . . of her volunteer work."

"Her *volunteer* work?"

Lady Kirton widened her eyes innocently. "Yes, she—er, she has some, does she not?"

Devellyn could no longer repress a grin. "Like a church guild, or a ladies' aid society?" he suggested. "Come to think of it, she did once mention she liked sewing for the poor. Or perhaps it was knitting. She seemed uncertain."

Lady Kirton looked at him chidingly. "Aleric, Madame Saint-Godard has been playing a dangerous game. I think you may have guessed what."

"Ah, that!" he said. "I wondered if you might get round to it. Rest assured that Sidonie's 'volunteer work' will soon come to an end."

"Did she agree to that?" asked the countess sharply.

Devellyn hesitated. "Not in so many words," he admitted. "But she will."

Lady Kirton looked somewhat relieved. "Ah, you will see to it, then!" she said. "Thank God. Aleric, I think you must marry her at once. I have told your mother so, and Elizabeth says—"

Good Lord! "My *mother says*—?"

"Aleric," said the countess. "We none of us have any time to lose. If you truly love her, I think you must marry by special license as soon as possible. Your mother agrees."

Aleric grunted. "Thinks no one else will have me, eh?"

Lady Kirton shook her head. "No, no, it is not that at all," she assured him. Then she dropped her voice dramatically. "Aleric, a man came to the Nazareth Society some ten days ago. A police sergeant."

Devellyn's heart leapt into his throat.

"He was asking questions, my dear," she went on. "Questions about a woman in black who had been seen at the society. A lucky bit of happenstance, perhaps, but . . . ?"

"Good God!" he whispered. "Sergeant Sisk?"

"You know him?" asked Lady Kirton. "I met him once myself—one meets all kinds in my sort of work— and he is well-known to certain friends of mine. Aleric, he is tenacious."

An awful chill had settled over Devellyn. "Good God," he said again.

Lady Kirton reached for his hand. "Aleric," she said, squeezing it. "How well do you know Sidonie's brother?"

"Well enough to be disliked," he answered. "But he tolerates me."

"This police sergeant, he is an acquaintance of Mr. Kemble's," she said, her voice a whisper now. "I know this from past experience. Perhaps you ought to tell him about Sisk? *Could* you? Kemble, you see, is a man who can get things taken care of. Make problems go away. If you know what I mean."

Judging from the bruised knuckles George Kemble was sporting, Devellyn knew precisely what she meant. Kemble was not a large man, but he was lean and quick, with eyes which were just a little vicious. And the marks on his knuckles had been distinctly patterned, a pattern that but one man in fifty would have recognized. Devellyn did, and he'd have laid odds Kemble had been wearing a bit of brass around his knuckles when he'd pummeled Sidonie's attackers halfway into the hereafter. And that wasn't the sort of thing most chaps carried around in their coat pockets.

In the stillness of the study, Devellyn nodded. "I shall talk to him," he agreed. "And if—"

His words were forestalled by the sound of the study door swinging open. Devellyn looked up to see his father silhouetted in the doorway. He jerked at once to his feet, all rational thought leaving him.

Lady Kirton, too, had risen. "Your Grace!" she said pleasantly. "Well! I was just on my way out." And with that, the countess headed straight for the door, forcing Gravenel to either step fully in or fully out.

He stepped fully in.

Devellyn started to follow Lady Kirton, but his father held up a hand. "Stay, please."

Devellyn halted.

His father closed the door, then began to drift deeper into the room. "A frightful crush, is it not?" he said almost absently. "I believe society has missed your mother."

"She is an excellent hostess," said Devellyn.

His father went to his desk and slid open a drawer. "Cheroot?" he offered, withdrawing two.

Devellyn eyed them skeptically. "Are you allowed to smoke, sir?"

His father laughed. "By whom? The doctor? Your mother?"

Devellyn did not answer.

After a long, expectant moment, his father sighed, re-opened the drawer, and tossed them back in again. He moved from behind the desk and stood silently for a moment, his gaze distant. He was not the man he used to be, Devellyn saw. Not physically, at any rate. His skin was ashen, and the flesh had thinned from his face.

"Did I fail you, Aleric?" he asked out of nowhere. "Tell me. Have I failed as both a father and a husband?"

A dreadful silence held sway. "I beg your pardon?"

His father shook his head, and sat down on the sofa, propping his elbows on his knees and hunching forward as if exhausted. "I see it, you know, in her face," he said. "Every bloody day. Elizabeth blames me for all this. Even for Greg's death."

Mystified, Devellyn started to the sofa. "Father, I—"

"Oh, yes," he said, as if countering an argument. "For *Greg*. If I had been more strict. If I had forced you both into university. If I had cut off your allowances when you first began to run wild. *If, if, if!* If I'd been a better father, perhaps all this grief—or some of it—could have been avoided. That is what she thinks."

"I cannot say that you have failed me," said Devellyn. "Perhaps, Father, I have failed myself."

His father sat silently for many moments, but Devellyn could hear the breath wheezing in and out of his lungs. "The longer you stayed away," he finally whispered, "the easier it was to blame you."

Devellyn hesitated before answering. "You are speaking of Greg's death, are you not?" he said softly. "With all respect, sir, you blamed me from the beginning."

"Did I?" he muttered. "Yes, yes, I know I did. Elizabeth tells me so. But I cannot now remember those terrible days. Neither before nor after. It is the unconscious mind's way, you know, of shielding us. But I am not sure if I am being shielded from the tragedy of Greg's death, or . . . or something else altogether."

"What else is there?" asked Devellyn quietly.

For a time, the silence was filled with nothing but the sound of his father's labored breathing. "My appalling behavior afterward," he finally whispered. "My—my insanity, I daresay, for that's what it now seems. Blind insanity. My God, Aleric, you cannot know how I have suffered."

Devellyn's jaw was set so firmly, he feared it might crack. "I think I do, sir," he said tightly. "I have lost my brother and my best friend. I have had most of my family torn from me. But I've borne the blame as best I could. I was left with no choice."

"Ah, you were so young!" The duke shook his head. "So inexperienced in the ways of the world."

Devellyn shook his head. "Not so very young, sir. And not as inexperienced as you would like to think."

His father made a strange sound, something between a sob and a cough. "But you were my child," he said between gritted teeth. *"My child.* Elizabeth kept reminding me of that, you know. But I could bring myself to do nothing. Nothing."

"What do you mean, sir? What was there—or *is* there—to do? Greg is gone. The awful deed is done."

His father opened his hands expansively. "I do not know," he wheezed. "Apologize to you? Take a swing at you? Grieve with you? Pray? Scream? Tear out my hair by the roots?" His breath was sawing in and out of his chest now.

"Sir, I think you ought not overset yourself," Devellyn whispered. "It cannot be good for you."

His father did not seem to hear him. "You say that you have lost, too, Aleric," he rasped. "And that is so. God help me, it is so. You lost a brother. And a father, too, I daresay. *But I lost two children.* And I did not know how to find that which was lost. I still . . . do not know."

Devellyn's voice was almost fragile in the silence. "What, Father, do you want me to do? What do you want me to say?"

The answer came with more strength than he would have expected. "I want you to come home, Aleric," said his father. "To Stoneleigh. At least for a little while."

"To come home?" Devellyn's voice was laced with doubt. "Father, I . . . I do not know. Are you sure, sir, that this is what you want?"

His father tried to smile. "Does it matter what I want?" he asked. "A dying man has not the luxury of time, Aleric. I have a wrong to right and a wife to appease. An injury to heal—one which I thoughtlessly inflicted on my family."

Devellyn did not know what to say. For so long, he had prayed for his father to extend even the thinnest of olive branches. But this was not just a branch. It was at least half the tree. Still, he hesitated. The timing could not have been worse. He had Sidonie to think about. He wasn't about to leave her alone and unprotected with this chap Sisk on her heels. Besides, matters had to be settled between them, and soon, or he was going to go mad.

But his father spoke again, and this time, his voice was almost dreamy. "There is, you know, that old stone cottage by the lake," he said pensively. "I do not know about such things, but your mother tells me it is very romantic. Last year, she even redecorated it."

Devellyn was not following. "The cottage near the boathouse, sir?" he answered. "Yes, it's charming."

His father's eyes slowly met his. "It is the perfect spot, your mother says, for a honeymoon." He stopped, and cleared his throat roughly. "We thought—or your mother suggested—that you and your Sidonie might wish to spend a part of your wedding trip there."

Devellyn was reeling now. "Thank you, sir," he said. "But Sidonie has not said yes."

"She will," he said. "I've driven her to it, I think."

"I beg your pardon?"

His father stood, but with considerable effort. "Sidonie will say yes, Aleric. And then she will say that I want what I do not deserve," he whispered. "And it might be true. I want what I have told Elizabeth over and over that I did not want. Because my pride would not let me say otherwise."

"What, Father?"

"I want my family back before I die," he whispered. "And perhaps, if God is very forgiving, a grandchild."

Devellyn pondered it for a moment. *Did* his father deserve it? Well, had Greg deserved to die? Had Devellyn deserved to be punished for it? Tonight, a chap in St. James might get plowed down by an eastbound mail coach, whilst one street over, another would be pocketing a few hundred pounds of ill-got gain at Crockford's hazard table. And neither of them would deserve their fate. The truth was, people rarely got what was coming to them in this life. That was for the next life, one which Devellyn held no sway over. But he held at least a little sway over this one.

He opened his arms. And his father stepped into them.

Still, it did not yet feel right to embrace one another. Perhaps it would, eventually. Or perhaps not. They would simply have to muddle through and see what came of it all. Devellyn thumped his father soundly on the back. "I think you ought to sit back down, sir," he said. "And put your feet up."

"I must look at death's door," he grumbled, sounding suddenly like the father Devellyn remembered. "Half the people in the ballroom have told me that tonight." But he was stretching out on the sofa even as he grumbled, and propping his shoes up on the arm.

Devellyn had seized a pillow from a nearby chair, and was trying to slide it under his father's heels when the duke spoke again. "As to the ballroom," he said, his voice pensive. "Elizabeth wishes us to make a pretty speech during supper, thanking everyone for their good wishes, and so forth."

"An excellent notion," said Devellyn, sitting down in the chair.

"And there is something else, Aleric, which I think ought to be said," he continued. "If, that is, you will agree?"

Devellyn was taken aback. "Why, I don't know, sir," he said. "I can't think it's any business of mine what is said."

"Ah, then you would think wrongly," said the duke, folding his hands over his belly. "Be so good, Aleric, as to ring the bell."

"Yes, of course," said Devellyn, coming at once to his feet. "What is it, sir, that you require?"

"Dear old Cousin George," said His Grace. "Tell the footman who answers to fetch him."

Sidonie was relieved when Aleric came to claim her for the supper dance. He was a welcome sight, wading through the throng, a whole head higher than the rest of the crowd. After the stressful evening she'd suffered, Sidonie had to resist the impulse to throw her arms around his neck and rest her head against the wide, strong wall of his chest. Still, the girlish, giddy smile on her face did not go unnoticed, she was sure.

After the dance, they were joined by Sir Alasdair MacLachlan, who had not partnered anyone, and was at loose ends for supper. He graciously offered Lady Kirton his arm, and together, the four of them went in. The gentlemen left, returning with plates overflowing with crimped salmon, prawns in cream sauce, and chilled asparagus. Sir Alasdair proceeded to entertain them quite charmingly throughout the meal. Devellyn sat quietly, but once or twice, his hand crept beneath the table and into Sidonie's lap to give her own fingers a reassuring squeeze. Strangely, however, he scarcely ate a bite.

"Are you all right?" she whispered, when Lady Kirton and Sir Alasdair left to investigate the sweets on a table across the room.

"Well enough," he said, looking pale. "Come outside. Let's get some air."

He drew her away from the table and back through the empty ballroom. The portico doors were still open, and he continued on until he reached the very edge, as if he wished to get as far from the house as possible, without actually leaving it. He drew her gently to him, and circled his arms around her shoulders.

Sidonie rubbed her cheek against his lapel. "Did you see him?" she asked. "Was he . . . polite?"

She sighed with relief when she felt him nod. "He is sorry, Sidonie," he whispered, pausing to swallow hard. "I believe that he is. And we talked. A bit, anyway. And I don't know what will come of it, or how we will go on, but at least it is a start."

She smiled up at him, and his lips settled over hers, soft as the brush of a butterfly's wing. "I love you, Sidonie," he said certainly. "I love you so much." Suddenly, he pulled away from her, and shoved his hand in his pocket. "Look here, I have something for you. A wedding gift, of sorts."

She frowned a little as he extracted a thick fold of paper. He opened it, and gave it to her. Sidonie skimmed it, then stared at him dumbly. "A deed?" she murmured. "To a *house*? But I have a house. Aleric, I—I don't understand."

Devellyn beamed at her boyishly. "Not just any house, Sidonie," he said, proudly pointing at the address. "A whorehouse."

"You bought—" She paused to swallow hard. "You bought me a—a house of prostitution as a wedding gift—?"

His eyes widened with alarm. "Just look at the address, Sidonie," he protested. "See? It's the one by Gutter Lane. The house near the Cross Keys Inn."

She looked at him, dumbfounded. "Oh, my God."

His grin returned. "I told you, Sid, to think big," he said. "Now the house is yours. If you don't like what it is, then you may make it into something else."

"Why, I hardly know what to make of any of this!" she murmured, returning her gaze to the deed.

"Sidonie, don't you see?" he answered impatiently. "If you will just marry me, you will have the means and influence to change things on a grander scale. Perhaps—well, I am no good judge of such things, but perhaps the house ought to be—oh, I don't know—I was thinking of a tea shop?"

She looked at him incredulously. "A *tea* shop?"

"With some rooms to let above?" he suggested eagerly. "It is, after all, quite a large house. A tea shop, a coffeehouse, or an inn. Whatever. Any of those things would provide honest work for those women. They would no longer be trapped, and they would not need the Black Angel to avenge them. Ask Lady Kirton to help. She has vast experience in such charitable endeavors."

Sidonie stood on her toes, and kissed the corner of his mouth. "Oh, Aleric, I love you," she said. "I love you with my whole heart. Not the fluttery, silly sort of love the poets speak of, either. It is something deeper and more all-encompassing than that."

He cupped her face in his broad palm. "Sidonie," he whispered. "You will marry me, will you not? Give up this dangerous life and have a very long and dull one with me instead. I know I do not deserve you, but I swear I'll try to be worthy if you'll have me. Indeed, it seems my mother is already planning the honeymoon."

"You must be jesting."

He smiled, and shook his head. "I am afraid not," he answered. "Now, you will do it, won't you? Please say *yes,* my love."

Sidonie returned her gaze to his and gave him a glowing smile. "Yes," she whispered. "Yes, my love, I would be honored to marry you. Not because you bought me a house, but because I have realized I cannot live without you."

Just then, a strange scrabbling sound came from the direction of the gardens. Sidonie turned around to see a small, gold-brown dog hurtling up the pathway to the portico, his claws digging into the gravel. The creature wore a little red waistcoat, and his tongue was hanging out like a short wool scarf blown back in the wind. He bounded exuberantly up to Aleric and began to hop about on his hind legs, front paws waving.

"Oh, there you are, Horatio!" said a creaking voice from the gardens. A wizened old lady in a matching red dress stepped into the lamplight and made her way across the wide lawn onto the portico. "Why, Aleric, you scamp! Horatio has been looking for you all evening."

Aleric had released Sidonie and stepped aside. "Has he, indeed?" he asked, squatting down to pet the dog. Amidst the dog's exuberant hopping and panting, Aleric introduced Sidonie to his aunt Admeta.

Sidonie extended her hand. "A pleasure, ma'am, I'm sure."

Admeta's smile faded, and she turned back to her

dog. "What is that, my love?" she said. "You wish what?"

Aleric looked up from the portico. "I did not say a word, aunt."

Admeta shook her head impatiently. "Horatio," she said. "I'm talking to Horatio. Come here, my love, into my arms."

The dog spun around, and bounded to her. She scooped him up, and stood with remarkable grace for one so frail. "Yes, yes," she encouraged as the dog wiggled and licked at her face. "Do you think so? Yes, I will. I shall ask."

She turned to Aleric with a beaming smile. "Horatio says I must congratulate you!" she said. "He says, Aleric, that you two have just become betrothed! Is it true?"

Aleric and Sidonie exchanged sidling glances. "It is true," he admitted. "But not yet public."

Admeta laughed gleefully. "But Horatio knows!" she said. "He sees things, you know, from up there!" With her free hand, she pointed skyward. The dog began to wiggle again. "Yes, yes, my love, I am sure you may." She handed the dog to Sidonie.

Eyes wide, Sidonie took him.

"Horatio wishes to kiss the bride," said Admeta slyly.

And so he did, licking Sidonie from chin to ear. "Thank you," she murmured, gingerly passing the dog back.

"Well," said Admeta, "we are late to supper. Our heartiest congratulations!"

Sidonie could only stare after them. "What on earth?"

"One wonders," said Aleric dryly. "She thinks that dog

is her dead husband. Or that he is some sort of psychic medium. I'm not entirely sure what silly notion she has."

Sidonie turned to look at him. "Aleric, that woman is ninety if she's a day," she said grimly. "She could not possibly have overheard us from across the lawn. Perhaps it's not so silly?"

Aleric just shook his head and took her hand. Arm in arm, they returned through the ballroom to join the other guests, who were by then finishing supper. They entered just as a little bell rang sharply through the air. Quickly, they slipped back into their chairs, but Sidonie did not miss the odd gesture Aleric shot his mother.

Sidonie looked up to see that Aleric's parents had stood. Her Grace was delicately tapping her fork against her wineglass. "Dear friends!" she began in a clear, carrying voice. "Thank you all so much for coming out tonight to celebrate the happy occasion of Gravenel's seventieth birthday. And to celebrate with us the reopening of this lovely house, which we—"

Gravenel cleared his throat impatiently.

Her Grace glanced at him, then hastened forward. "Here, Frederick, I leave it to you."

The duke cleared his throat again. "It is not just my birthday we've come together to announce tonight," he said. "But rather, a far more important occasion—one which, frankly, I often thought I might never live to see. So I would like to ask my cousin George to stand up. George? George, where are you? Ah—yes, there he is in the back."

"Aleric—?" whispered Sidonie, her hand squeezing his sharply. "What is going on?" She turned to glance at her brother, who was standing deep in the room.

Aleric had gone slightly pale. The duke raised his glass. "Some of you know my cousin, Mr. George Kemble," he went on. "Others of you may not. But both of us ask you to raise a glass now, and to join us in celebrating the betrothal of my beloved son and heir, Aleric, Lord Dev—"

The entire room cut him off with a collective gasp.

The duke laughed. "Yes, you see now why I thought I might die first," he said, to which the entire crowd roared with laughter. "And so Elizabeth, George, and I ask you to congratulate Aleric and his intended bride, my cousin Sidonie Saint-Godard, George's sister."

From the back of the room, George's voice rang out clearly and calmly. "To Aleric and Sidonie," he said, lifting his glass.

"To Aleric and Sidonie," the confused crowd responded. But they were already looking around one another's wineglasses in bewilderment and trying to pin their gazes on the happy couple. In response, Aleric dragged Sidonie to her feet, and bowed, still clutching her hand. Somehow, Sidonie managed to curtsey without fainting dead away. Across the room, the duke held Sidonie's gaze.

"Cousin Sidonie," he said. "Welcome to the—well, it is a bit redundant, I daresay—but welcome, my dear, to the family."

The duke sat back down. George promptly vanished. In a matter of seconds, all the guests had returned to their plates or their gossip, or whatever it was they had been doing.

Sir Alasdair and Lady Kirton were beaming; she with pleasure, he with amusement. Sidonie looked at Aleric.

"Did you know he was going to do that?" she demanded.

Aleric grinned sheepishly. "I did not realize he would make it quite so public."

"Saved you the trouble, then, didn't he?" remarked Sir Alasdair. "Now you won't have to make an ass of yourself."

Sidonie turned to him. "What is that supposed to mean?"

Alasdair looked back and forth between them. "Dev, did I misunderstand? Didn't you say something just before the ball about seizing the bull by the horns, and surprising Sidonie with a betrothal announcement so that she would have no choice but to—"

"Alasdair," Devellyn coldly interjected, "for once could you just shut up?"

Alasdair shrugged cheerfully. "I do tend to babble on dreadfully, do I not?" he agreed. "One never knows what next I might say. By the way, Dev, your mother and I were chatting earlier about that Vespasian denarius. Wasn't there something you wanted to tell her? Something about your reason for coming here tonight?"

Devellyn shoved back his chair. "Yes," he gritted. "Yes, by God, there was. I'm going to tell her, Alasdair, to give you that bloody Roman coin once and for all. And then to strike you *permanently* off our guest list."

Epilogue

In which the Good die Young

Sidonie came awake to sensation of light and shadow shifting above her eyes. She opened them and sat up in some surprise. Lifting one hand to shield her eyes from the sun, she pushed away her book and sat halfway up to see that their rowboat had drifted far from the cottage again, leaving Thomas behind to lounge lazily on the distant shore. They were floating now in the rushes on the opposite bank. The willow trees along the water were stirring in the breeze, casting fluttering sunlight across the boat's length.

Sidonie sat up, marked her page, and set aside the book. Well, not a book, really, but instead, one of her mother's many diaries. Somehow, they were less painful to read now, and bit by bit, Sidonie was at last beginning to understand Claire Bauchet: a woman who had been neither good nor bad, but simply human. She was very glad now that Julia had not thrown the books away.

Relaxing in the bow opposite Sidonie, her husband

reclined against a rolled blanket. He wore nothing but his trousers and shirt, with his sleeves rolled up to reveal a fine pair of forearms. The sun dappled his dark hair attractively, but Aleric did not notice her besotted gaze, for he was thoroughly absorbed in his reading.

With an inward smile, Sidonie moved to the center seat, grasped an oar, and gave a little push against the soft mud of the lakebed. Startled into awareness, Aleric looked up, his dark hair tossing lightly in the wind. "Oh," he said. "Drifted out again, have we?"

"Some captain you are," she grumbled good-naturedly. "Now I must push us into the sun again."

"Yes, well, that's the first mate's job," muttered her husband. "And your nose is going to sunburn."

Sidonie stroked both oars deep and watched her husband read as the boat slid back into the lake's languid current. He smiled up at her again, and her heart soared with sudden joy. It was an overwhelming rush of emotion, and it came upon her more and more frequently now.

They had been here at Stoneleigh for all of six weeks, ever since their return from a month's honeymoon in Italy. Here, in the blissful peace of Kent, they had loved, laughed, and begun to build the foundation of a perfect marriage. The cottage Aleric's parents had offered them was charming and private. Private enough for passionate midnight swims and romantic picnics along the shore.

Aleric's mother was ecstatic to have them so near. Gravenel was trying hard to be a father again, and Aleric, she realized, was almost at peace with the world. But one dark shadow yet lingered, and it troubled him, she knew, though he rarely spoke of it. The shadow of the Black Angel. Oh, nothing could be proven now. And Aleric could almost certainly protect her. Still, with so much in their lives finally going right, he worried that something might go wrong.

This afternoon, however, he was being strangely silent. She ceased her rowing and settled back onto her pile of pillows to study him. The boat rocked soothingly on the water, almost lulling her back to sleep.

"What are you reading, love?" she asked, stretching drowsily in the sun. "Is that the letter which arrived from Alasdair this morning?"

Aleric looked up and winked at her. "Yes, and chock-full of town gossip, too."

Something mischievous in his tone made her sit upright again. "Such as?"

Aleric consulted his letter. "Such as the fact that your old friend Lord Bodley has fled to the Continent with what few valuables he could lay hands on," he answered. "It seems he'd become totally insolvent, and his debtors were pressing him into court."

"A life of penury on the Continent is still better than he deserves."

"Patience, my love," he murmured, unfolding something from the letter. "In time, men like Bodley always do themselves in."

Sidonie looked at him curiously. "What's that you're unfolding?"

Aleric had begun to laugh. "Alasdair has sent the front page of Wednesday's *Times*," he answered. "There was something in it, he said, which he wished me to see."

"What?" Sidonie moved toward the bow, causing the boat to rock precariously.

Aleric looked at her with humor in his eyes. "Some sailor you are, Sid," he said. "Sit down before you drown us."

Forcing herself to be patient, Sidonie sat and folded her skirts around her knees. She watched, mesmerized, as her husband's expression began to shift from one of mild amusement to something which looked like apoplexy. Or agony. Or outright spleen-splitting hilarity. Sidonie was not sure.

"My love," she finally said, rising onto her knees, "what is it? What is wrong?"

"Prepare yourself, my dear," said her husband solemnly. "I fear I have bad news."

"What? What sort of bad news?"

"The Black Angel," he said. "I fear she has met an untimely end."

"Aleric, you are speaking nonsense," said Sidonie.

A spurt of something like laughter escaped him. "Nonetheless, my dear, she is dead," he managed. "Caught in the act, and shot dead as four o'clock."

Sidonie looked at him in some astonishment. "That cannot be! Who has perpetrated such a hoax?"

"Spoken by an expert," interjected her husband dryly. "You know all there is to know of hoaxes, do you not, my love?"

Sidonie tried to snatch the newspaper, but Devellyn lifted it high above his head. "What were the circumstances?" she demanded as the boat rocked perilously. "Who claimed to be the victim?"

He consulted his newspaper again. "That infamous rakehell, Sir Alasdair MacLachlan was the Angel's mark," he said. "And it happened at—yes, let me see here—in a box at the Drury Lane Theatre, according to the police sergeant, one Mr. Mortimer Sisk. Isn't he a friend of your brother's?"

"Sisk!" Sidonie said indignantly. "That dog! I shall throttle him with his ugliest cravat!"

Devellyn looked at her in mock sympathy. "It seems the Black Angel had lured the lust-lorn Sir Alasdair into an empty box for a tête-à-tête after the play," he went on. "Alas, when she tried to strip him of his possessions, she discovered Alasdair was armed—with something more than his usual wit and charm. It must have been frightfully exciting. The Black Angel tried to wrestle the gun from his hand and accidentally shot herself."

"That's—why, that's utter nonsense!"

"There were witnesses," warned her husband.

"Witnesses?"

"Indeed, several," answered Aleric. "Two fledging actresses, Ilsa and Inga Karlsson, were still hanging about backstage. And that paragon of virtue, Lady Kirton, had dozed off in her adjoining box. The ruckus roused her, and she saw the whole thing."

"Lady Kirton?" said Sidonie. "But—but this is incomprehensible!"

"Not to me, my dear!" said her husband. "Indeed, it looks to me as if the Angel has had the curtain dropped on her existence in order to avoid any suspicions—or encores—upon our return to London."

"Julia!" Sidonie's eyes flew wide. "She was a part of this!"

"Indeed," murmured her husband, returning his gaze to the letter. "Alasdair says she made a lovely corpse."

"Ooh, I shall throttle her."

"Hmm," said her husband. "With one of Sisk's ugly cravats?"

Sidonie fell back into the boat and burst into laughter. "Ah, well, my career as a criminal was over, wasn't it, Devellyn? At least the Black Angel went down in dramatic fashion."

She stared up at the cerulean sky and listened as her husband cast his papers aside. He came creeping over the seats on hands and knees, and dragged himself on top of her. "Sidonie, my love," he said, then he kissed her long and deep. "Sidonie, the only role I need you to play now is that of my lover, and my friend."

"Oh, that sounds a little dull, Devellyn," she said, making a pout with her lips. "Still, those *are* my personal favorites."

He shrugged, and a grin broke out across his face. "Well, if ever I get out of hand, Sid, I suppose you could put on your red wig, tie me up, and play Ruby Black for a night or two?"

"*If ever—?*" Sidonie laughed. "Oh, I fear Ruby is going to be a busy girl."

His expression turned serious, and he brushed his lips over her forehead. "Now, have I told you, my love, how proud I am of you?" he asked. "You are braver and truer than anyone I have ever known. You can't save everyone, it is true. But you have, most assuredly, saved me."

She kissed him back, and stared into his eyes. "Aleric," she said. "Row us ashore, my dear."

He drew back, and looked at her with curiosity in his gaze. "Methinks she has another nefarious plan," he murmured.

She pushed him up, rocking the boat again. "Yes, for

I have one role yet to play, my love," she murmured. "One which you failed to list. Now, up with you, sluggard! You, too, have a duty here."

He grinned at her across the distance. "Have I indeed?" he said. "I wonder what!"

"I think you can guess," she said, setting a bare hand on his thigh, and easing it slowly upward.

"I am not sure," he said, eyes fixed on her fingers. "I think my brain just disengaged."

Sidonie looked up at him through her fan of dark lashes. "You have promised your father that there is one more thing you'll accomplish before he dies," she murmured. "I am just suggesting, my love, that it's time to set to work in earnest."

With that, her husband seized the oars. "Well, heave ho, Sid!" he said, drawing them back with a mighty force. "Let it never be said that the Devil of Duke Street is the sort of man who shirks his duty!"

POCKET BOOKS
PROUDLY PRESENTS

One Little Sin

LIZ CARLYLE

Coming soon in paperback from Pocket Star Books

Turn the page for a preview of
One Little Sin. . . .

Chapter One

In which a thunderstorm breaks.

Upon returning home, Alasdair waved away his butler's questions about dinner, tossed his coat and cravat on a chair, and flung himself across the worn leather sofa in his billiards room. Then he promptly slipped back into the alcohol-induced stupor which had served him so well on the carriage ride from Surrey. A copious amount of brandy had proven necessary in order to endure the company of his traveling companions.

For a time, he just dozed, too indolent to rise and go up to bed. But shortly before midnight, he was roused by a racket at his windows. He cracked one eye to see that the unseasonable heat had given way to a thunderstorm. Snug and dry on his sofa, Alasdair yawned, scratched, then rolled over and went back to sleep, secure in life as he knew it.

But his lassitude was soon disturbed again when he was jolted from a dream by a relentless pounding at his front door. He tried mightily to ignore it, and to cling to the remnants of his fantasy—something to do with Bliss, the beautiful Gypsy, and a bottle of good champagne. But the pounding came again, just as the Gypsy was trailing her fingertips seductively along his backside. Damn. Surely Wellings would answer it? But he did not, and the knocking did not abate.

Out of annoyance rather than concern, Alasdair crawled off the sofa, scratched again, and headed out into the passageway which overlooked the stairs. In the foyer below, Wellings had finally flung open the door. Alasdair looked down to see that someone—a female servant, he supposed—stood in the rain on his doorstep carrying, strangely enough, a basket of damp laundry.

Wellings's nose was elevated an inch, a clear indication of his disdain. "As I have twice explained, madam," he was saying, "Sir Alasdair does not receive unescorted young females. Get back in your hackney, please, before you fall dead on the doorstep of pneumonia."

He moved as if to shut the door, but the woman gracelessly shoved first her foot, and then her entire leg, inside. "Now you'll whisht your blether and listen, sir!" said the woman in a brogue as tart as Granny McGregor's. "You'll be fetching your master down here, and making haste about it, for I'll not be taking *no* for an answer, if I have to knock on this door 'til God himself and all his angels come down those steps!"

Alasdair knew, of course, that he was making a grievous error. But drawn by something he could not name—temporary insanity, perhaps—he began slowly to descend the stairs. His caller, he realized, was not a woman, but a girl. And the laundry was . . . well, not laundry. More than that, he could not say. Halfway down the stairs, he cleared his throat.

At once, Wellings turned, and the girl looked up. It was then that Alasdair felt a disembodied blow to the gut. Her eyes were the clearest, purest shade of green he'd ever seen. Like the churning rush of an Alpine stream, the cool, clean gaze washed over him, leaving Alasdair breathless, as if he'd just been dashed with ice water.

"You wished to see me, miss?" he managed.

Her gaze ran back up and settled on his eyes. "Aye, if your name is MacLachlan, I do," she said. "And you look about as I expected."

Alasdair did not think the remark was meant to be a compliment. He wished to hell he was fully sober. He had the most dreadful feeling he ought to be on guard against this person, slight, pale, and damp though she might be. Somehow, beneath her bundle, she extended a hand. Alasdair took it, realizing as he did so that even her glove was soaked.

"Miss Esmée Hamilton," she said crisply.

Alasdair managed a cordial smile. "A pleasure, Miss Hamilton," he lied. "Do I know you?"

"You do not," she said. "Nonetheless, I'll need a moment of your time." She cut a strange glance at Wellings. "A *private* moment, if you please."

Alasdair looked pointedly down at her. "It is rather an odd hour, Miss Hamilton."

"Aye, well, I was given to understand you kept odd hours."

Alasdair's misgiving deepened, but curiosity overcame it. With a slight bow, and a flourish of his hand, he directed the girl into the parlor, then sent Wellings away for tea and dry towels. The girl bent over the sofa nearest the fire and fussed over her bundle a moment.

Who the devil was she? A Scot, to be sure, for she made no pretense of glossing over her faint burr as so many of his countrymen did. And despite her damp, somewhat dowdy attire, she looked to be of genteel birth. Which meant the sooner he got her the hell out of his house, the safer it was for both of them. On that thought, he returned to the parlor door, and threw it open again.

She looked up from the sofa with a disapproving frown.

"I fear my butler may have mistaken your circumstances, Miss Hamilton," said Alasdair. "I think it unwise for a young lady of your tender years to be left alone with me."

Just then, the bundle twitched. Alasdair leapt out of his skin. "Good Lord!" he said, striding across the room to stare at it.

A little leg had poked from beneath the smothering heap of blankets. Miss Hamilton threw back the damp top layer, and, at once, Alasdair's vision began to swim, but not before he noticed a tiny hand, two drowsy, long-lashed eyes, and a perfect little rosebud of a mouth.

"She is called Sorcha," whispered Miss Hamilton. "Unless, of course, you wish to change her name."

Alasdair leaped back as if the thing might explode. "Unless I wish—wish—to *what?*"

"To change her name," Miss Hamilton repeated, her cool gaze

running over him again. "As much as it pains me, I must give her up. I cannot care for her as she deserves."

Alasdair gave a cynical laugh. "Oh, no," he said, his tone implacable. "That horse won't trot, Miss Hamilton. If ever I had bedded you, I would most assuredly remember it."

Miss Hamilton drew herself up an inch. "Good God! What a revolting notion!"

"I beg your pardon," he said stiffly. "Perhaps I am confused. Pray tell me why you are here. And be warned, Miss Hamilton, that I'm nobody's fool."

The girl's mouth twitched at one corner. "Aye, well, I'm pleased to hear it, MacLachlan," she answered, her gaze sweeping down him again. "I'd begun to fear otherwise."

Alasdair was disinclined to tolerate an insult from a girl who resembled nothing so much as a wet house wren. Then he considered how he must look. He'd been sleeping in his clothes—the same clothes he'd put on at dawn to wear to the boxing match. He'd had rampant sex in a pile of straw, been shot at and chased by a madman, then drunk himself into a stupor during a three-hour carriage drive. He had not shaved in about twenty hours, he was sporting a purple goose-egg between his eyes, and his hair was doubtless standing on end. Self-consciously, he dragged a hand through it.

She was looking at him with some strange mix of disdain and dread, and, inexplicably, he wished he had put on his coat and cravat. "Now, see here, Miss Hamilton," he finally managed. "I really have no interest in being flayed by your tongue, particularly when—"

"Och, you'd be right, I know!" The disdain, if not the dread, disappeared. "But I've been on the road above a sen'night, and another two days trying to find you in this hellish, filthy city."

"Alone—?"

"Save for Sorcha, aye," she admitted. "My apologies."

Alasdair reined in his temper. "Sit down, please, and take off your wet coat and gloves," he commanded. "Now, tell me, Miss Hamilton. Who is the mother of this child, if you are not?"

At last, some color sprang to her cheeks. "My mother," she said quietly. "Lady Achanalt."

"Lady Acha-*who?*"

"Rosamund, wife of Lord Achanalt." The girl frowned. "You—you do not recall the name?"

To his consternation, he did not, and admitted as much.

"Oh, dear." Her color deepened. "Poor Mamma! She fancied, I think, that you would take her memory to the grave, or some such romantic nonsense."

"To the grave?" he echoed, fighting down a sick feeling in the pit of his stomach. "Where the devil is she?"

"Gone to hers, I'm sorry to say." Her hand went to the dainty but expensive-looking strand of pearls at her neck, and she began to fiddle with them nervously. "She passed just last month. My stepfather is not precisely grief-stricken."

"My sympathies, Miss Hamilton."

Miss Hamilton paled. "Save your sympathies for your daughter," she said. "Her full name, by the way, is Lady Sorcha Guthrie. She was conceived at Hogmanay, two years past. Does that jag your brain a wee bit?"

Alasdair felt slightly disoriented. "Well . . . no."

"But you must recall it," Miss Hamilton pressed. "There was a ball—a masquerade—in Edinburgh. A bacchanalian rout, I collect. You met her there. *Didn't* you?"

His blank face must have shaken her.

"Good Lord, she said you told her it was love at first sight!" Her voice was a little desperate now. "She said it was a grand passion!"

Alasdair searched his mind and felt sicker still. He *had* been in Edinburgh some two years ago, because his Uncle Angus had returned from abroad for a brief visit. They had spent Hogmanay together. In Edinburgh. And there *had* been a ball. A raucous one, if memory served. Angus had dragged him to it, and more or less carried him home afterward. Alasdair remembered little, save for the roaring headache he'd suffered the following day.

"Oh, well!" Miss Hamilton's voice was resigned. "Mamma was ever a fool for a pretty face."